PRAISE FOR DARYNDA JONES

"Magically delicious! Darynda Jones knocks it out of the park with Betwixt. If you love Charley, you're going to be be obsessed with Defiance. Hilarious, heartwarming and oh so positive."

ROBYN PETERMAN ~ NYT AND USA TODAY BESTSELLING AUTHOR

"Darynda Jones brings her original style to paranormal women's fiction, and I for one couldn't be happier. Also, maybe be wary of inheriting from strangers...or not. Go get this book!"

MICHELLE M. PILLOW, NEW YORK TIMES AND USA TODAY BESTSELLING AUTHOR OF THE WARLOCKS MACGREGOR SERIES

"This series takes readers on a heartwarming, spellbinding journey packed full of intrigue. Ms. Jones has outdone herself with this gem."

MANDY M. ROTH, NY TIMES & USA TODAY BESTSELLING AUTHOR

BEGUILED

BETWIXT & BETWEEN BOOK THREE

DARYNDA JONES

This is a work of fiction. All of the characters, organizations, and events portrayed in this novel are either products of the author's imagination or are used fictitiously.

BEGUILED: A PARANORMAL WOMEN'S FICTION NOVEL

(BETWIXT & BETWEEN BOOK 3)

Cover design by TheCoverCollection

EBook

ISBN 10: 1-7343852-3-5

ISBN 13: 978-1-7343852-3-6

Print

ISBN 10: 1-7343852-6-X

ISBN 13: 978-1-7343852-6-7

"I'M NOT THAT TYPO GIRL"

Sadly, all books have typos. Including this one. If you see any and would like to let us know, please email us at writerlyd-books@yahoo.com. No pressure! THANKS SO MUCH!

www.DaryndaJones.com

Available in ebook, print, and audio editions

 Created with Vellum

For Dana
For putting up with me.
:)

BEGUILED

Newly indoctrinated witch, Defiance Dayne discovers there's more to life after forty than she'd ever imagined possible. Especially if one is a charmling, one of only three in the world, with enough magics to make her a target for every power-hungry warlock out there. When one of them sends a hunter to town, she knows it's time to take her talents seriously before the hunter takes her life.

She decides she has three things to do before she can die. Find out who killed her beloved grandmother, teach her BFF the finer points of spellcasting before she blows up the world, and figure out how serious her relationship with the Adonis living in her basement really is. If it's heading in the direction she's hoping for, she can die happy. Though, admittedly, she'd rather not. Die. Happy or otherwise.

None of that will matter, however, if she can't figure out how to foil the supernatural assassin who's been sent for her. Until then, it's business—and hopefully romance—as usual. Now if she can only figure out how to tame a lacuna wolf.

ONE

Anticipation—or possibly terror—washed over me in unre-
lenting waves. Whatever the emotion, it caused my stomach
to clench. My pulse to quicken. My lungs to seize. The man
walking up the stairs toward my bedroom was the sexiest
thing I'd seen since first discovering boys in kindergarten. I
was an early bloomer. The fact that this particular boy lived
in my basement was a definite plus. But at the moment, the
heavy footsteps treading purposefully toward my door
caused a flush of warmth to spread throughout my chest.
And my nether regions.

Mostly my nether regions.

Wearing only a T-shirt that proclaimed *Witches do it on
the fly*, I curled my fingers into the sheets on either side of
me and held my breath.

He knocked softly before easing the door open, and the man standing at the threshold took my breath away. He crossed his arms over a wide chest—thankfully it was his—and leaned against the frame. Auburn hair streaked with gold brushed the tops of his shoulders. Olive irises canopied with thick lashes shimmered in the low light as they studied me. A full, sculpted mouth held steady even as his strong jaw flexed.

And the kilt.

He wore a dark leather kilt, a khaki T-shirt, and heavy work boots. With his hair, his build, and the tattoo ink lacing over his forearms and up one side of his neck, he defined that rare quality known as panty-melting sex appeal.

"Ms. Dayne," he said, his voice smooth, deep, and intoxicating.

"You heard me?" I asked, both surprised and impressed. I'd barely whispered the words that summoned him here. And he'd been downstairs, probably in his basement-level apartment.

"I heard," he confirmed. "And the answer is very."

I blinked, trying to get past the fact that he literally dripped sensuality. "Very?"

"You asked how well I hear."

My fingers twisted further into the sheets beneath me. "Yes, but I barely whispered it."

"Thus the *very*."

I untangled my fingers and scooted up until I sat against my headboard, my legs stretched out before me, my T-shirt suddenly way shorter than I remembered. I tugged at the hem self-consciously.

He dropped his gaze to watch me tug and my hands froze. The question now became: Could I get off the bed without exposing the jay-jay? Not that he hadn't already seen all that I had to offer. We'd had an amazing encounter where I'd reached a level of euphoria I hadn't known existed, but we had yet to seal the deal. And it was a deal I most definitely wanted to seal.

I couldn't stop thinking about his mouth when he kissed me. His tongue when he brushed it over the most sensitive parts of my body. His long fingers when they slid inside. Yet he stayed glued to the spot.

Fine. If he wouldn't come to me, I had no problem going to him. I swung my legs over the side of the bed and stood.

He pushed off the doorframe and walked closer, only to walk past me and head toward the bottle of Patrón I had on my nightstand. The one I'd bought on a whim since I didn't drink tequila. He took it to a small side table between the two floor-to-ceiling windows the massive room boasted, now black with the darkness of a moonless night, and poured us both a drink.

Okay. This could work. I was a little wound up with all the happenings of late. I could use a drink after the most eventful times I'd ever had in my life.

The last six months had turned my world upside down. First, I'd been bequeathed a house by a total stranger. A stranger who turned out to be a powerful witch. And my biological grandmother. And no longer dead.

Long story.

And the house turned out to be inhabited by my biological grandfather, who'd died at the hands of said grandmother—at his behest. Then I learned I was also a witch. But not just any witch. A charmling. One of only three in the entire world. So there was that. Then I accidentally brought my grandmother out of the veil, fell into a state of suspended animation for six months, and turned my best friend into a bird.

It had been a strange few days. For me anyway. While I'd taken possession of the house—aka Percival—six months ago, I'd only been conscious for a few days during those six months. The months of respite and the new powers I'd acquired had discombobulated me. On one hand, I felt like I'd only been in Salem for about a week. On the other, I felt like I'd been here my entire life. Like I belonged here, in this very cool town famous for its witch trials and in this very cool house covered in vines and black roses.

Roane handed me a drink, then waited. But I wasn't born yesterday. When he didn't drink from his own tumbler, I narrowed my eyes and sloshed the clear liquid in my tumbler in front of his face. "Is this poisoned?"

"Not that I know of."

"Are you trying to kill me?"

"Not at the moment."

"Would you tell me if it were?"

"I'd like to think so." One corner of his exquisite mouth tilted up, and I had to give praise to whoever invented the lopsided grin. They deserved a Nobel Prize in chemistry for creating more covalent bonds than all the oceans combined.

Despite his affirmations, I still wasn't totally convinced, so I traded glasses with him.

He laughed softly and took a sip, leaving me to wonder if he hadn't poisoned his own glass in anticipation of my figuring out his devious plan with my keen intellect and expected me to switch glasses all along. If only I'd spent the last few years building up an immunity to iocane powder. Then I might have a chance.

"My grandmother was poisoned right under two perfect noses, yours and Percy's." I leaned closer and poked him in his chest. "Mighty convenient if you ask me. Not that anyone ever does." I lifted the glass to my lips and said "No idea why" into the tumbler before downing the entire contents in one huge gulp.

My chest exploded. The combustible liquid scorched my throat, set my esophagus on fire, and doubled me over. Coughs wracked my body for a good five minutes along with a couple of gags and an occasional horrifying sound similar to someone trying to start a chainsaw. Humiliation surged through me as I tried not to barf on my grandmother's Persian rug.

After an eternity of hacking while trying to retain a matching set of lungs, I took several deep breaths, straightened, held out my tumbler, and said, "That was good. Can I have another?" My voice was a little strained, but I thought I pulled the whole thing off rather well.

He stood there, a humor-filled grin on his face, and took my glass before granting me an unequivocal "no."

"Really?" I feigned disappointment. "It's so... smooth." Clearly, I needed to drink more.

After setting the glass on the table, he turned back to me. "I thought you drank Patrón."

"No, I bought it in celebration of my divorce being finalized about a year ago because that was my ex's favorite. I'm not a big drinker."

That lopsided grin reemerged. "I would never have guessed."

"I like wine," I said in my defense. "And champagne. And mudslides because chocolate."

He nodded and went to sit in one of two chairs covered in clothes, one chair holding the freshly washed selection and the other displaying the only-worn-a-day options.

"Let me get that," I said, rushing around him to gather them up.

"It's okay." He leaned back.

I tugged. "No, really, I can move them."

He leaned back harder. "No."

"But these aren't clean."

"They're better," he said. "They smell like you."

I stopped and stood back, horrified. "Like, in a bad way?"

"There is nothing bad about the way you smell."

A rush of excitement laced through me. I walked over to the chair opposite him, scooted the clothes over, and sat on the edge of the seat. My throat still burned, but I think it was more from the coughing and gagging than the tequila.

"So you can smell as well as you can hear?"

He kept his glittering gaze locked onto mine. "Wolf."

"Right." And he was a wolf because of me. Because I'd used one of the noble beasts to bring him out of the veil. He'd been killed—by his sadistic father, no less—when he was five. I was three. At his traumatized mother's behest, I'd used my magics to find him, but I was too late. His father had already taken his life.

I brought him back, but to do so, I had to use something living near him. And that happened to be a wolf pup his father had captured.

Thus, a wolf shifter was born. Something that, until a few days ago—or months, depending on how much sleep one got—I would never have dreamed was possible.

An actual shifter. A werewolf... in a non-horror-movie kind of way.

"So," I said, suddenly at a loss for words, possibly because I wanted nothing more than to crawl onto his lap and plant my mouth on his. "How have you been?"

His gaze slid over me as though out for a leisurely stroll. "Better after the coughing fit you just had."

My face warmed. "Sorry about that." I gave him two thumbs up. "All better now."

"You misunderstand." He took another sip, smiling wickedly from behind the tumbler before continuing. "I knew you had a nice ass, but damn."

"Oh." The warmth on my face turned into an inferno. I tugged at the hem of my T-shirt again. "Thank you. Would you like it?" The words left my mouth before I could stop them.

"Yes." His expression turned appreciative, but he kept the tumbler in his hand. Made no move toward me or any move to suggest he wanted me to come to him.

If I were brave, I would walk over and straddle him on the chair. Sadly, I'd never been known for my bravado. Broccoli salad, yes. Bravado? Not so much. I bit my lower lip and said instead, "Then it's yours."

"Always."

I glanced back. "Always?"

"That's why I'm here." He set the tumbler aside at last, leaned forward onto his elbows, and steepled his fingers. "I think we need to be honest with each other."

My stomach clenched again, painfully this time. I was so bad with honesty, and this conversation was not going in the direction I'd hoped.

"I've never been good at sharing," he continued.

"Oh... okay." Again, not the direction I was expecting, but...

"I want you all to myself."

My lungs stopped working.

He tilted his head and studied me before adding, "Forever."

That sounded ominous. "Say, you've never been a serial killer, have you?"

"Wolves mate for life."

Ah. Of course they did. And I was up for mating. So very up for mating.

He lowered his voice, and said, "I want to know everything about you."

That was just asking for trouble. "Okay, what do you want to know?"

"Everything."

This could take some time. "Could we maybe narrow that down a bit?"

He pierced me with a stare so glitteringly intent, it took my breath away. "Everything."

I swallowed hard. "You already know me better than most."

"I want more."

"More Patrón?" I guessed.

"More of you."

I held out my hands, acquiescing. "I'm all yours."

He leaned closer and softly tapped an index finger on my temple. "I want in."

"I don't understand."

"I want to be let past the gates. You can keep the wall up." He leaned back again. "I'm fine with that. I understand it better than most. I just want to be on the other side of it. With you."

Frustration grated along my nerve endings. "Look, I want you. And you want me, right?" When he gave me the barest hint of a nod, I said, "Then I don't get the problem."

"I'm selfish. I want all of you. Not just your body." He dropped his gaze to my chest. "I want that."

"My boobs?" I looked down at them, then back. "Hon, they are all yours."

"I want your heart."

"Trust me, my heart is nothing to write home about."

"I've done my homework."

I sank back into my chair and covered my face with my hands. "There was homework? No one told me."

"A charmling and her mate have an unbreakable bond. Whoever she chooses is hers for life."

I peeked from between my fingers as he spoke.

"I want to be the one you choose."

"Then we don't have a problem. Done. I choose you." I held out my hand to seal the deal.

He smiled. "Not hardly. Marry me."

My jaw hit the floor. I was certain of it. He could've thumped me on the head with a paper towel tube and I would've been less surprised. Shock ricocheted from nerve ending to nerve ending like electricity arcing over my skin. "I... I don't understand."

The subtle grin that softened his features sent a pang of longing straight to my core. "It's this ceremony where two people who really like each other stand in front of an officiate and make a promise—"

"I know what marriage is." I stood and paced along the floor in front of the windows. "Trust me, Roane. I've been through two and... and you do not know what you're asking."

"I think I do."

I stopped and gave him my best warning glare. "No. Really. You don't."

"I've had six months to think about it."

"Yes, and I was unconscious for most of those six months." Unfortunately, those six months had not been a vacation. They'd been filled with a malevolent darkness. A nightmarish ogre stalking me to the farthest reaches of my mind. If Percy hadn't kept me safe, I didn't know what would've become of me. "Technically, we've only known each other for a few days."

"Do you really believe that?"

I hesitated but only for a moment. "I do."

He leaned back against a barely worn Arizona Coyotes jersey. "You know as well as I do, we've known each other for years. Decades, actually."

Was he talking about when we were kids? When I'd turned the wolf into the boy? Or... or did he remember at last? Not just the fact that he would steal into my dreams as the wolf when we were kids, when he would show affection by licking my fingers. We'd clearly bonded psychically when I brought him out of the veil. But I'd come to realize there was more to it.

I started pacing again. I'd been dreaming about him since I was three, and I was now convinced I was somehow seeing the real Roane. I literally watched him grow up in my dreams. I watched him blow out birthday candles and take his first driving lesson and get his first tattoo. And those visions, while fleeting, were crystal clear. I knew the boy. I knew the man. But I was confused. If he was the same boy I'd watched grow up, why didn't I recognize him the instant we first met in my grandmother's kitchen?

I chewed a nail as I paced, turning the questions over and over in my mind before an answer came to me: because I'd only seen parts of him. His strong hands when he tied his shoelaces. His sculpted jaw when he shaved. His sparkling eyes when he looked into the rearview. As though I was seeing him through his eyes. Watching his life unfold through his vision. His hearing. His sense of smell and taste and touch.

Especially touch.

From the time I was seventeen, I'd had dreams of a delicious lover. The epitome of a schoolgirl's fantasy. As I got older, I just thought I was having very vivid, very wet dreams. I'd climaxed more in my sleep over the last twenty-seven years than I had with both of my exes combined. Not to mention the handful of boyfriends I'd collected throughout my life.

But lately, I began to wonder if the dreams were not all connected somehow. Were they him? This boy who grew up in my dreams? This lover who stole into them?

I sank on the edge of the chair, my head bent in thought. Even if it was him, even if he'd dreamed about me as much as I'd dreamed about him, did we really know each other well enough to consider the M-word?

"Roane, you don't know what you're asking."

"I'm certain I do."

"No, I mean, with me." I turned to him and pleaded. "I... I have horrible luck when it comes to marriage. Can't we just table the M-word and have sex for the next few years? We can always revisit the idea in the future." I let my gaze slide past him as my marriages, both of them, flashed before my eyes. "In the very, very distant future."

His expression gave nothing away as he took a long moment to consider my offer, but his piercing gaze never wavered. "You're more like your grandmother than I thought."

I gasped. "I am nothing like... wait, really?" I asked, realizing that was a huge compliment. My grandmother was amazing.

"Am I going to be like Houston? Hanging around for forty years until you decide to accept my hand?"

Police Chief Houston Metcalf had apparently been proposing to my effervescent grandmother for decades before she finally accepted his hand a few hours ago.

In all honesty, I had no idea why they didn't get hitched sooner, other than the fact that, like my two, her first marriage went horribly, horribly south. Like deep south considering she and her coven had to kill her estranged husband with some kind of witch fire when the black magics he'd been using consumed him. The fact that he'd asked her to kill him made the mental image a little easier to bear. And Percival had stuck around and had essentially become the house we were in now.

Whatever the reason, I was certain my grandmother had her reasons. I set my jaw. "I think their relationship is complicated."

"I think every relationship is complicated."

He had me there. "You do know I've been married twice, right?"

"Third time's a charm."

"It's just..." I stood and started pacing yet again. "Both times were absolute disasters."

"You told me about that asshat who took everything from you."

"Yes. Everything besides the Bug, my vintage mint-green Volkswagen Beetle."

One corner of his mouth tilted up. "Everything besides the Bug. But you never told me about your first marriage."

"That's my point! We've only known each other for a few days. We haven't had time to talk about all of the things men and women talk about."

"I'm not discussing china patterns no matter how long we're together."

I stopped in front of him and crossed my arms. "I just meant there is so much we don't know about each other. The fact that you didn't know about my first marriage proves that."

He stretched out a leg and braced an elbow on the arm of the chair to lean his head against a thumb and two fingers. "I said you didn't tell me about your first marriage. Not that I didn't know about it."

"Fine, you googled me."

"No. Well, yes, but you know damned well we've been in each other's lives a lot longer than a few days. Do you think I wasn't there for your wedding night? Swimming in your memories of it while you slept? In your... disappointment?"

I sat again and asked hesitantly, "Do you remember me in your dreams like I remember you in mine?"

The penetrating gaze that traveled over me spoke volumes, and I found myself tugging at my hem again. "I do."

Holy crap. "What..." My voice broke, and I cleared my throat before continuing. "What did you see?"

"What did *you* see?"

I picked invisible lint off my tee. "I asked first."

He thought a moment, then said, "I saw your first bite of chocolate."

"Heaven," I said, thinking back.

"Your first day of school."

"Scared out of my wits."

"Your first kiss."

"Oh my God." I scrubbed my face in embarrassment. "Wait. Are you counting the time Harold Pesci kissed me on the playground after throwing dirt in my face? Because—"

"No. Your first real kiss."

"Ah. Gibby Saldana behind the gym."

"Was that his name?"

Even the kiss had been a disaster. I'd had braces. He'd had very chapped lips. As brief as it was, it did not end well.

Still, did he remember more? Did he remember stealing into my dreams and giving me impossible expectations? Because no man had ever measured up to the apparition who seduced me in the darkest corners of my imaginings.

"I remember everything," he said, as though reading my thoughts.

Heat pooled in my abdomen, and I pressed my knees together. "I have to admit, I feel like part of the reason my marriages failed was because I was cheating on them with you every night."

"Right. It had nothing to do with the fact that both of your husbands were assholes."

"My first one wasn't," I said in Martin's defense. "He was just—"

"Malicious."

"Misguided."

"Self-absorbed."

"Lost."

"Narcissistic."

I gave up. "We married too young."

My dads had tried to tell me. Naturally, I didn't listen. I'd wanted more. I'd wanted to hold the man making love to me. To get to know him. To laugh and cherish and savor the little moments. While my nights were filled with unimaginable pleasures, my days were empty in comparison. A shell of what I'd come to crave. But I quickly discovered my dream lover had tainted my ideals of what most men were capable of.

I decided to keep that little chicken nugget to myself and changed the subject. "You didn't recognize me when we first met?"

"Though I knew who you were, I did not recognize you."

"And I didn't recognize you. How? I saw so much of your life. We shared everything."

"Through our dreams. How often do you look at yourself in a dream? How often do you see your own image?"

"True. It's just all so surreal. And you're insisting we've known each other for decades. I disagree."

"How so?"

"I only know what you dreamed about. I only saw the snippets of your life that filtered into your unconscious mind. I never got to know the real you. Your hopes or interest or aspirations."

"Right now I only aspire to you."

As delicious as that sentiment was, he was missing the point. Clearly on purpose.

I couldn't believe any of this was real. And I had questions. Many questions. I decided to start with one that had haunted me for years. "When you were in middle school, a bully took you down and punched you over and over." The memory caused a sharp ache in my chest. "He just kept hitting you. Bloodied your nose. Almost broke your jaw. But you didn't fight back. You could easily have taken him even though he was twice your size. By that point, I'd seen what you were capable of. You could've killed him, but you just let him hit you. Why?"

He dropped his gaze to the tumbler in his hand. "I take it that's a no?"

"What? No. Not... I just think we should wait." I pulled a thread on my hem and started unraveling the shirt. "I think we should get to know each other a little better. We could... we could keep this purely physical while we think about it."

"It's okay." He set the tumbler on the table and stood to leave.

My heart jumped into my chest. Had I hurt his feelings? Was he mad? I couldn't decipher anything from this impossible man. He was the hardest person I'd ever tried to read.

I stood and spoke to his back. "Roane, you don't understand. My marriages were unmitigated disasters. I promised myself—"

He turned, and the uncompromising expression he leveled on me silenced me instantly. He wasn't angry. He wasn't hurt or irritated or bitter. He was determined. "Marry me or lose me forever," he said softly, his smooth voice evoking spasms of desire from somewhere deep in my core. They were the same words Houston had said to my grandmother that very night.

"That's blackmail."

"Coercion, but yes."

"And by *lose you forever*, you mean..."

"I'll leave. You'll never have to see me again." His gaze darted to the massive windows behind me as though he could see into the blackness beyond. Then again, he was a wolf. Maybe he could.

"You're going to force my hand?"

"Yes," he said without a hint of hesitation. Or guilt. His eyes held little warmth when he looked back at me. "You've left me no choice."

How did this get so serious so fast? Wasn't it just

yesterday we were playing doctor on the kitchen counter? Quite admirably, I might add. And now he wanted to get married?

I'd been so betrayed in the past. By men I thought loved me. There were few things more disappointing than finding out you were nothing more than a means to an end. My first marriage lasted all of two months. We were both nineteen. I'd had a small apartment and a decent job while I went to school and he'd needed a place to live. But he knew my fathers had money and began manipulating me to get *his fair share*. On our wedding night, no less. Unfortunately, I saw his true nature only after the ink had dried.

My second husband was much cleverer. He took his time. Planned meticulously. Stole everything out from under me when I wasn't looking. Clearly, I could not be trusted when it came to men with a penchant for saying exactly what a girl wanted to hear.

"Your marriages didn't work because they weren't with me."

I shook out of my musings and stared at him. "That's a bold statement."

"And true." He stepped closer and bent his head until his mouth was at my ear. His warm breath fanned across my cheek when he said, "You chose me. I have no choice in this. Do you think I want to beg for your attention?"

I leaned back to look at him. "I would never ask that of anyone."

The half-smile that flickered across his face was anything but joyful. It held a deep sadness that left me winded. "And yet here we are."

"That's not true."

"It is." He locked his hands behind his back. "I've

waited for you for years. From the moment you changed me, I've been yours."

"Roane." I started to step closer, but he tensed as though he would step back if I did. Or maybe he wanted me closer. I had no idea. I simply could not read him.

He studied me another moment, weighing his options, then said softly, "Every breath I take is for you."

My response, if I'd had one other than the gawk I'd fixed on him, would've been drowned out by the explosion that shook the windows and rocked the house.

TWO

An explosion ripped through the house, the concussive sound causing an instant ringing in my ears. Roane tackled me to the ground and covered my body with his as dust and particles of sheetrock rained down from the ceiling.

Once the rattling stopped, we exchanged horrified glances, then scrambled to our feet. Roane darted out of the room before I found my balance. As I ran toward the balcony overlooking the foyer, he sailed over the balustrade. I skidded to a halt and watched in awe. He landed on the first floor unfazed, bending at the knees to soften the impact, then sprinted into the kitchen while I took the stairs.

Thick black smoke billowed out of the back of the

house, the kitchen drowning in the stuff. Then I heard the coughing.

"Annette!" I flung myself into the smoke-filled room.

Roane flung me back. Sort of. He picked me up with one arm and rushed me out of the house along with a short, curly-haired vixen named Annette Osmund. After planting both of us on the front porch, he went back in to open windows and... what? Put out the fire? Was there a fire? Was Percival in real danger?

I glanced at Annette and did a double take. She didn't have an ounce of soot on her face. She had several pounds, and she was wearing them like a bear wears its coat. Either she'd been in the middle of her nightly skincare routine or her face had been at the epicenter of the explosion. Her curls sprang out in wiry coils on top of her head, and a trail of smoke wafted up off of them.

I wiped the lenses of her turquoise cat-eye glasses, making the situation worse, then hugged her to me. She didn't protest, which proved how stunned she was.

Then it hit me again how loud that explosion had been. Smoke alarms screamed all over the house, and my thoughts turned to my grandmother. She'd been staying in a second basement apartment with an entrance right off the kitchen. Panic shot through me. I was just about to go back in when Roane emerged carrying another passenger: Ruthie Goode, my grandmother and the latest love of my life.

He lowered her to her feet and tried to steady her, but I threw my arms around her shoulders before he could accomplish his goal.

"Gigi!" I said, holding her tight.

Her face and blonde hair had a light dusting of soot, making her bright eyes look even bigger as she glanced around in wonder. She coughed softly and huffed out a puff of smoke.

"Are you okay? Oh my God, what happened?"

"I... I don't know."

I hugged her tighter. "You could've been killed."

She patted my shoulder reassuringly, then coughed again as I led her and Annette farther out. Then another thought hit me. I'd brought home a stray. Minerva, a skittish twenty-something member of Gigi's coven whose uncle almost killed us both that very day. And I'd left her to burn alive.

I sprinted toward the front door again only to be tackled once again. Roane carried me out of the house in one arm and Minerva in the other. He deposited us both on the lawn, gave me a warning growl, then went back in.

Minerva hadn't quite gained her balance. I steadied her, then gave her a thorough once-over.

"What... what happened?" She looked back at the house. She'd been in one of the upstairs rooms, and she'd been sound asleep when the explosion went off by the looks of her. The poor girl had been through so much in the last few days, and now this.

"I know it was loud," I told her, worried about PTSD, "but we're all okay." I leaned closer. "You're okay."

Her lashes fluttered as she tried to gain her bearings. "What was loud?"

"The explosion."

Her lashes formed a circle around her pretty brown eyes. "There was an explosion?"

I almost laughed and pulled her into my arms. "One that you slept through, apparently." And I thought I was a deep sleeper.

She hugged me back, suddenly on high alert.

I glanced around at everyone. "Is everyone breathing okay? Gigi?" The smoke had seared my already raw throat as well, and I'd barely gotten a couple of lungfuls.

Gigi nodded but kept a hand at her throat as she watched smoke billow out of Percy's front door.

I looked over at Annette. Her ash-covered face was now streaked with tears, her eyes swollen and red-rimmed. She'd clearly been the closest to the explosion. "Annette, what happened?"

She coughed. There was a lot of that going around. "I don't know. The oven exploded."

"The oven?" The graveness of the situation began to sink in. "Do you mean the Wolf double convection oven with gourmet mode, dual fuel range, six burners, signature red handles, and a French top that costs more than my car?" Admittedly, that wasn't saying much.

"Yes. I was making a cake."

"You were making a cake in the middle of the night?"

"Yes."

"Why?"

She blinked up at me and tried to focus through the soot on her lenses. "What?"

Keeping a hand on Ruthie's shoulder, I stepped closer to Annette. "Why were you making a cake in the middle of the night?"

She shook her head and looked back at Percy. "It doesn't matter. I just... How did this happen?"

Realization dawned like a sledgehammer to my chest. "Oh my God, Annette. Today's Austin's birthday."

She lifted a noncommittal shoulder. Her brother had disappeared when they were kids, never to be seen again. She always celebrated his birthday, wishing on his candles that he would find his way home. "I can't believe I forgot."

"I'm so sorry, hon." I wrapped my arms around her again. I truly was the worst friend ever. The day had been filled with one horrifying event after another, but to completely forget her brother Austin's birthday...

She patted my arm. "Still not a hugger."

I hugged anyway.

When she could take no more of the torture I was subjecting her to, she squeaked a protest and wiggled out of my embrace.

I finally gave up and stepped back, but she kept her hand locked in mine. I'd take it. "We've had a lot going on," I said.

"I know, but I didn't call my mom. You know how she gets." Her smudged glasses sat lopsided on her nose. She pushed them up, then said, "She texted me. That's how I remembered."

"Did you tell her why you forgot?"

"Kidnapped," she said, pointing to herself. "Turned into a bird. How am I supposed to explain that to her? She'll never forgive me."

That was true. She'd been kidnapped by Minerva's uncle, who'd been trying to force me to bring his dead wife back to life so he could get her inheritance. As leverage, he'd placed my bestie in a building about to be demolished, and the charges went off before anyone could get to her, so I had to turn her into a bird so she could escape.

It really had been a busy day.

Despite my best efforts, I hugged her again. The thought of her being crushed by a building, buried under its debris, almost ended me.

She didn't fight as hard this time.

When I finished, Gigi hugged her, too. "I'm sorry about your brother."

"Thank you," Annette said, hugging her back.

Hugging. Her. Back.

What in the sphincter hell? She'd only hugged me back, like, twice our whole lives. She was probably still upset that I'd turned her into a bird, but she'd bounced back. She's all womanly again, girly bits and all. Though I was dying to ask her more, I figured now was not the time. Especially since we were about to lose our home.

Speaking of my grandfather... I turned toward the vines that covered the house and held out my hand. A vine curled around my wrist and laced into my fingers. "Are you okay, Percy?"

A black rose, almost impossible to see in the starless night, blossomed, its crimson underbelly barely visible.

"I'm glad," I whispered to him.

He squeezed my wrist then unlaced himself as a dark figure walked out of the house toward us, his gait like a predator, quiet and smooth. The last remnants of smoke billowed around him, curled, then sank back toward him as though reluctant to leave his side. I knew the feeling.

"Should I call the firefighters?" I asked.

"No," Roane said. He stepped out onto the porch. The smoke that wafted around his shoulders gave him an even more surreal quality. A supernatural mystique. He gave me a quick inspection from over a bandana he'd wrapped around his nose and mouth before tugging it down and turning to check on Gigi. "The fire is out." He stepped closer to her. "Are you okay, love?"

She nodded and put a hand on his forearm for support. "Yes. Thank you, sweetheart. Was it a gas leak?"

He covered her hand with his, and my heart melted. "No, but I turned it off just in case. I'll have to disconnect the stove before I can turn the gas back on. I'll do that tonight, but first we need to let Percy air out for a bit."

"What happened?" she asked, clearly shaken.

We turned in unison to Annette.

She stepped back, her face still a picture of shock. "I was just baking a cake."

"With nitroglycerin?" Roane asked, eyeing her suspiciously, though I doubted the suspicion was aimed directly at her. It was more of a general suspicion. A wariness.

A master of the deadpan, she speared him with one of her best. "No, that's a different recipe."

"Wait," I said, making a time-out with my hands. "What do you mean nitroglycerin?"

"There was nitroglycerin in the oven. It's all over the kitchen now."

"How do you know that?"

He turned back to me, let his gaze linger, and reiterated his earlier sentiment. "Wolf."

Of course.

He looked at Annette. "Was there anything in the oven when you put the pan in?"

"No." She lowered her head in thought. "And I preheated it. If there was anything in there, it would have exploded before I put in the pan, right?"

"Then how did it get there?" I asked, worry kneading my brows. I edged closer. "Is someone still trying to kill my grandmother?"

She'd died over six months ago from poisoning. Someone had snuck into the house, a house guarded by two supernatural entities: my departed grandfather, Percival, and the wolf shifter standing before us.

"No one knows she's alive," Roane said.

That wasn't entirely true. Her coven knew. And the fact

that she had been poisoned without either Percy or Roane knowing suggested the culprit possessed some powerful magics.

"Could whoever poisoned you, Gigi, have put nitroglycerine in something?"

"It's certainly possible, but why nitroglycerine?" she asked. "Even if I didn't smell it, I would've tasted it instantly. I doubt I would have ingested enough to do any damage."

"She's right," Roane said. "Nitroglycerine is strong. It has a distinct scent. I would've smelled it long before now."

"So it just showed up?" Annette asked. "Out of the blue? That doesn't even make sense."

She was right. None of this made any sense. The only person new to the house was Minerva, and I doubted she carried nitroglycerine in her backpack.

I looked over at her. She was back to biting her abused nails, worry lining her flawless face.

The chief pulled up, skidding his cruiser to a halt behind the Bug. I rather thought he would've stayed the night after Gigi had accepted his proposal earlier that evening. It was so romantic, especially since they'd been *dating* for more than forty years.

The fact that he was here meant someone called 911. Surely more first responders were on the way. We needed to get Ruthie inside, away from prying eyes since, having died six months ago, she was supposed to still be dead.

Also, the adrenaline was wearing off and I was in a T-shirt. In Massachusetts. In the middle of November. The cold was beginning to seep into my bones.

"Ruthie!" the chief said, sprinting toward us, spry for a sixty-something. He pulled her into his arms. "Are you okay? What happened?"

"Nannette blew up my house."

Nannette's jaw fell open. That happened when being thrown under a bus.

Roane walked over to me and pulled me into his arms, his embrace warm and inviting. He rubbed my back. "We should probably get you some clothes."

I nodded in agreement. Nannette was shivering, too, I thought to myself, giggling on the inside. I was totally getting her a Nannette bracelet. And a Nannette T-shirt. And maybe even a Nannette vanity plate for her car.

Roane looked at Gigi. "I think you guys should get a hotel for the night. Let me get this cleaned up."

"No," she said. "I'll just have my granddaughter clear out the smoke. It'll be fine." She turned to me, her gaze expectant.

"Oh. Is that one of my powers? I'm a smoke whisperer?"

"Defiance," she said, her tone admonishing, "you are a charmling. If you want to clear smoke, you'll clear smoke."

Great. No pressure. "Is there a spell for that?"

"I keep telling you, sweetheart, you're the charmling. I have only the vaguest idea of how you accomplish anything."

"Super helpful. Thanks, Gigi."

"Of course, dear."

"Are you guys okay?"

We turned to see Parris Hampton standing at the black cast-iron fence that separated our property from theirs. The chief wrapped his jacket around Ruthie's shoulders and pulled her closer, keeping her from Parris's view, as Minerva maneuvered herself to block the woman's line of sight. I knew I liked that girl.

"We're okay, Parris," I said, offering a wave. "The oven threw a tantrum. It's all good. Hey, Harris." I waved at her husband as he scurried off to his own house. He lived on Percy's other side. They maintained separate mansions yet still ended up in bed together several times a week, according to my grandmother.

"Defiance," he said with a sheepish wave.

"Thank goodness everyone is okay," Parris said. "It sounded pretty bad."

Of course it did. Her presence spurred me to get this over with. We needed to get Gigi inside.

I stepped onto the porch. Most of the smoke had cleared out, but what lingered still watered my eyes and scraped against my throat. Roane stayed beside me as I walked through the house to the kitchen. The oven door hung lopsided off its hinges. Black soot covered the floor, the island in front of it, and the ceiling. It was the only room in the house that had a white ceiling. Until now.

It made me realize just how dire the situation had been. Nannette could have been killed. If she'd been standing close to the oven, she likely would've been. And that infuriated me.

"Honestly," I said to Roane, "is someone just fucking with us?"

"I don't know, but we need to find out sooner rather than later."

He was right. They'd already killed Ruthie once. They could kill her again, I assumed. Or Nannette. Or Minerva. Or Roane. The thought seized the only heart I could lay claim to.

I was the finder of lost things. Couldn't a murderer be considered a lost thing? Someone who needed to be found just like a missing loved one would be? Or a missing pet?

Anger flared inside me. I stormed out of the house,

stopped short in front of Ruthie, crossed my fingers in hope, and asked, "Gigi, what are you searching for?"

She'd blocked me somehow. I'd never been able to penetrate her magics. To see what she most wanted in life. What she was searching for. But she'd been murdered. She wanted to know by whom. Surely she'd let me in now.

"Defiance," she said, suddenly confused, "what are you talking about?"

I doubled my efforts. Gazing into her cerulean eyes, I lowered my head and repeated, "Ruthie Ambrosia Goode, what are you searching for?"

A quivering hand rose to her throat as she said softly, "Defiance, don't do this." The veil began to part, just barely, centimeter by centimeter, when she said, "Please."

I felt a hand tug at my T-shirt. Minerva. But it was the chief's loud "Defiance!" his voice hard and stone cold, that jerked me back to the present.

I looked at him, then back to Ruthie. It hadn't been an hour earlier that I'd been contemplating just how fast my newfound magics could take hold to a devastating degree, and I'd almost used them on Ruthie. My own grandmother. The woman who'd given up everything to keep me safe. "Gigi," I said, stepping closer, "I am so sorry."

"It's okay." She put a trembling hand on my arm. "Sweetheart, it's okay."

No, it wasn't. I was about to force her to let me into her most private thoughts. Or try to, at least. To let me see through her and into the veil so that I, the finder of lost things, could see who killed her. But for some unfathomable reason, she didn't want me ransacking her memories. Tearing through her past. Upending her life. Go figure.

I'd always considered myself level-headed. I was beginning to question that consideration.

I backed away from her. "I'm so sorry." I looked at Annette, who was clearly none too pleased with me either.

"Daffodil," the chief said softly to let me know he wasn't mad, "we need to get your grandmother inside."

He was right. Ignoring Parris, who still stood at the fence trying desperately to see the tiny woman in the chief's arms, I turned back toward Percival. Of course, to do so, I had to look past an equally concerned Roane.

I gave him my best sheepish expression of apology and thought about what I wanted to accomplish so that I could get it done and hide in my room afterward. I found it quickly. The spell. It appeared in my mind with little effort. It wasn't so much a smoke-clearing spell as a house-cleansing spell, but it should work.

I lifted my hand and drew it on the air with two fingers.

In all reality, the spells pretty much drew themselves. The lines of this one burst to life in front of me. They cracked open, and a bright hot yellow seeped out, its glow almost blinding. The smoke in the house obeyed its command. It swirled, converging into one billowing mass like a tornado. Then it darted out the front door and into the night air, dispersing above us.

"Okay," I said softly to the chief. "It should be safe to go in. Let me distract Parris."

He nodded. I looked at Annette for backup, but she was standing there with her mouth parted, staring at... nothing. I followed her gaze to... Percy? The front door? The lantern-shaped bug zapper? Poor little things. I made a mental note not to let my vintage mint-green Volkswagen Beetle anywhere near it.

I waved a hand in front of her face. "Blink if you're still in there."

"I saw it," she said, raising her hand to point at... nothing. Again.

After a thorough examination of the area, I turned back to her, trying desperately not to giggle. She looked like a cartoon character who'd been struck by lightning. Her glasses were still lopsided on her button nose, the turquoise frames barely visible in the starless night. Her bow-shaped lips formed a pretty O as she stood motionless. Her recalcitrant curls a wiry mop on top of her head. She was, in a word, adorable.

"You saw what, honey?" I asked softly as I patted her back. Rubbed her shoulder. Smoothed her hair as though petting a cat. She hated that.

It worked. She snapped out of it and slapped my hands away. Then she gazed up at me, her expression full of awe. Or horror. Probably horror. "The light."

"The bug zapper? I know. Poor little guys."

"No. The spell. I saw it on the air."

"Shut the front door." I gaped at her, but she only nodded.

She'd never been able to see the light from my spells. Only other blood witches and a handful of people with various mental illnesses could see the spells. Annette had never been able to.

"Why now?" I asked. "What's changed?"

Coming out of her stupor, she crossed her arms over her chest. "Gee, I can't imagine."

"The bird thing?" I squeaked. "Surely not." I'd only turned her into a bird to save her life. I never imagined there would be other repercussions.

"I can see them," Roane said.

I scowled at him. He was not helping. "You don't count. You're a—"

"A shifter?" Annette asked, pursing her lips, her soot-covered glare accusing.

Minerva stood staring, too. Or, well, gaping. As a witch with some degree of magics, I wasn't surprised she'd seen. I was surprised she seemed just as shocked as Annette. I knew, as a charmling, my powers were different from most witches, but I didn't figure they'd be *that* different.

"Daffodil," the chief reminded us.

"Right," Annette said, coming to attention. "Sorry."

"Sorry," I said, reiterating. My eighty-something-year-old grandmother—though she didn't look a day over fifty-nine—was only freezing to death. "Sorry, Gigi."

Annette and I walked over to the fence.

Parris's lids had rounded to saucers.

"Sorry we woke you," I said to her.

"Oh, no. I was awake. I'm one of those people who only needs about four hours of sleep a night." Her hazelnut hair hung in tangles over her shoulders, and she wore a thick white robe and fluffy slippers that I would've given my left kidney for, as it was the more obstinate of the two.

"Wow," I said, blocking her line of sight when she tried to look over my shoulder. "I wish I only needed four hours of sleep." As opposed to six months.

"Me, too," Annette said. "If I don't get at least eight, I'm a monster."

I laughed softly, and my teeth chattered. Nette was about as monstrous as my left pinky toe which, although a little deformed, was hardly vicious.

"No, but really, what was that?" Parris asked, her eyes glued to the house.

Annette cringed inwardly. "The oven. There must've been a gas leak."

"No, not that." She pointed much like Annette had. "That bright light. Just now."

THREE

Question everything.
Except coffee.
—Meme

I stilled for a solid minute before Annette and I exchanged furtive glances. After looking over my shoulder to make sure the chief got Gigi and Minerva inside, I took Annette's hand in preparation to follow suit. "That was weird, right? That light? I have no idea what that was."

"My new 10,000-lumen flashlight," Roane said, walking up behind us. He draped a blanket over my shoulders and kept his hands there.

I sank into the warmth of him.

He pulled me back against him, and added, "Sorry about that, Parris. I accidentally turned it to strobe. I must've blinded you with it."

"Oh." Parris hardly seemed convinced, but the bones in my feet were screaming, the cold slicing into them mercilessly as cold was wont to do. "Who was that woman?" she asked, and my lids slammed shut.

How was I going to explain the presence of my departed grandmother? Since lifting her out of the veil, she had yet to leave Percival for this very reason.

"My aunt," I said without thinking it through. I had no idea how much Parris knew about my family. She'd been neighbors with Gigi for years, and I didn't know how close they'd become. But the woman defined busybody. She probably knew more than Gigi knew. Add to that the fact that her husband, Harris, lived on Percy's other side. Between the two of them, I could only imagine how much they'd gleaned from Gigi's comings and goings.

"Night, Parris," Roane said, leading us away.

"Oh... okay, night."

I kept hold of Annette's hand as Roane led us into the house. The door opened when we approached. "Thanks, Percy," I said.

He'd used the vines to open the massive wooden door and closed it softly behind us.

"Thank you, Percival," Annette said.

The vines shrank back, but not before they paused and bent slightly, as though tipping a hat to her. She eyed them adoringly. They stilled a long moment then slowly faded into the woodwork. Fascinating.

Before I could follow Roane into the kitchen to inspect the damage, a cat rushed over my feet, its claws adding to the needles prickling my frozen skin. He was followed by a tiny spectral of a boy, blond and dimpled and precious. But only the cat would've been affected by the smoke, and he looked to be on his last legs as it was.

He scurried under a hutch in the drawing room, trying

to hide from the boy, but it would take more than that to ditch a ghost.

"Ink," I said, kneeling down to look under the hutch. Though he looked as though he'd been at the epicenter of the explosion, his tattered charcoal fur and battle-scarred face were part of his everyday countenance. Then again, he was over forty years old. He had a right to look as though he were at death's door. Especially since he probably was. "Are you okay, buddy?"

The boy, still wearing the Puritan attire he'd died in, replete with a wide white collar, knee-length breeches, and buckled shoes, turned to look at me with his huge blue eyes. "He keeps running away." He crossed his arms and lowered his blond head to pout.

"I'm sorry, Samuel." I started to reach out to him before remembering my hand would go right through him.

Roane took a knee beside me and tapped on the floor. Ink shot out from under the hutch and flung himself into his arms. Samuel was clearly traumatizing the ragged thing. Roane wrapped him in his embrace, the hills and valleys of his biceps contracting with the movement, then beckoned Samuel over with a nod.

The boy beamed at him and stepped closer, his shoes silent on the hardwood floor. Ink let Samuel run his hand through him, mimicking a petting motion. The three-year-old cooed, and Ink purred, content to be in his owner's arms.

But it was the look on Roane's face that turned me into a soppy pile of mush. The warm smile he gave the boy. The patience he exhibited as he let Samuel pretend to pet him. An odd pressure tightened around my heart.

Roane would certainly understand the circumstances of how a child could die so young, having done so himself. We didn't know how Samuel died, but considering the time period, it probably had more to do with an illness than anything malicious. Unlike Roane's tragic passing.

The surrealness of my situation hit me again, as it had often over the last few weeks. Those in which I was conscious anyway. If I were to explain my current predicament out loud, no one would believe me. It would sound like the opening of a joke. A wolf, a cat, and a ghost walk into a drawing room...

I wrapped the blanket closer and rose to my feet to see Annette doing it again. Staring. I followed her line of sight to Samuel, looked back at her, then back at the boy.

"Annette?" I asked warily. She'd never been able to see the light from my spells, yet she did that very thing moments earlier. And now she was looking at Samuel, an entity she could not see yesterday, as though she was seeing a ghost. Literally.

But why now? Had my turning her into a bird really given her the ability to see into the veil? Had I somehow created a supernatural creature in all her curly-headed glory?

I stepped closer. She'd tried to clean her glasses, but she must've used her shirt, which was just as soot-covered as the rest of her. The lenses were still streaked with black and gray, and I wondered if she'd let me grab my phone to get a few shots. For posterity's sake. If I ever had children—not super-duper likely at forty-five—they'd need to see the trials and tribulations of what their auntie Annette went through. To appreciate her even more.

Her eyes began to well up behind the glasses.

I poked an arm out from under the blanket and wrapped it around her shoulders. "Annette, you're going to smudge your smudges." After laughing at my own joke, I looked closer. Her face was covered in soot, yes, but there were fine lines all over it like the silhouette of something she'd been behind when the blast hit her. In fact, they looked like vines. Had Percy tried to protect her? Was that how she came out of it unharmed?

While I marveled at this new discovery, Annette continued to stare. "He's beautiful," she said, her tone wistful.

I glanced over my shoulder and teased her by asking, "Which one?"

"He's so tiny." She covered her mouth with her fingers. "He's so..." She blinked, then turned to me slowly, her angelic face twisting into a scowl. "Why didn't you tell me?"

Taken aback by the sudden turn of events, not that it was unusual for the fiery vixen, I tucked my arm beneath the blanket again. "Tell you what?"

She pointed and then cast an accusing glare on me. "That."

After glancing between her and Samuel again, I glared back. "I seem to remember several conversations involving our newest guest."

"But he's so tiny and little and small."

"Have you been reading your thesaurus again?"

"He's just..." Clearly distressed, she covered her mouth again. "How did he die?"

"I'm still a little shell-shocked by the fact that you can see him."

"Right?" she said, snapping out of her stupor. "Ever since the bird thing."

I cringed. "I'm sorry."

"No, it's okay." She went to pat my arm but had refocused on Samuel and ended up patting my face. Oblivious, she knelt beside Roane and held a hand out to the little rascal. "I'm Annette."

He looked at her and giggled. "Your face is dirty."

"Really?" she asked, clearly in love, then his words sank in. "Wait, really?" She wiped at her cheeks. "Like how dirty?" She stood and whirled around to me. "My face is dirty? How's my hair?"

AFTER ANNETTE RAN UPSTAIRS, utterly mortified, I mourned the loss of my chance to snap a few shots for the children I would never have and followed her and Minerva upstairs to change. I ordered an exhausted Minerva to bed and hurried to my room.

Five minutes later, I came down in the same tee, but with an actual bra underneath and a pair of sweats below that. And just in case there was any broken glass, I donned my sneakers as well.

I stopped just outside the kitchen and girded my loins, metaphorically, before walking in. Roane was right. It'd been all but destroyed. The fact that no one was hurt was a miracle. I had to wonder again if Percy had anything to do with that.

Ruthie and the chief were wiping soot off the upended breakfast table and chairs.

"Gigi, I can get that," I said, hurrying forward to help.

She finished wiping down her chair and sat down in it to surveil the battleground. "I just needed a place to sit down."

Percy's massive kitchen was part industrial and part antique. A charming blend of several centuries. At least, it had been. Hopefully a good cleaning would fix most of it, but I feared the oven was a goner.

I sat beside her in shock. It was so much worse than I'd imagined. "I'm sorry, Gigi. We can fix it. It'll be good as new in no time."

"Oh, honey, I'm not worried about what happened. I'm worried about why it happened." She still had splotches of soot on her face, and a light coat covering her silvery-blonde shoulder-length hair. It almost looked black now, and it suited her in a strange way.

Then again, maybe I thought that because mine was so dark, an inky black so unlike Ruthie's or my mother's, according to pictures I'd seen of her. But we did have the same blue eyes. Apart from the fact that she was elegance and grace incarnate and I often resembled a headless chicken seeking out sustenance, we could've been twins.

The chief folded his large frame into the chair beside her and took her hand. His dark skin smooth against the graying stubble he now wore. "Don't worry, hon," he said, giving her hand a squeeze, "we'll find out who did this."

Roane had cleaned off the counter and sink, which was on the opposite side of the kitchen from the oven, and started a pot of coffee before beginning his quest. I watched as he opened cabinet doors and tested spices, tasted the sugar, and examined the canned foods.

Just now remembering no other emergency vehicles had showed up, I wondered how the chief had arrived so quickly. "How did you know there was an explosion?"

"I got a call on my cell."

"Parris?" I asked, surprised she would call him directly.

"Not exactly." Before he could finish his thought, someone knocked on the door. "And that would be him," he said, his face grave.

He started to stand, but I stopped him with a hand on his arm. "I'll get it. You guys rest." It seemed this day would never end.

I hurried to the door, not realizing Annette had come downstairs until I got to it. I glanced over my shoulder and grinned at her. She'd showered. And cleaned her glasses. And twisted her hair into matching mini-buns on the top of her head like bear ears. She looked even more adorable than usual. My heart could only take so much.

Realizing too late we needed a peephole, I opened the door to one Mr. Donald Shoemaker, a fifty-something who lived down the street and had been trying to get me out of the house since I got here. He'd even filed petitions with the city, claiming Percival was an eyesore.

Percival was magnificent. A moss-green brick, six-gabled three-story with more personality than a house had a right to. He only looked crumbling. He was strong and fierce, and I loved him.

Mr. Shoemaker, not so much. He stood on the other side of the threshold, a determined set to his jaw. Standing right behind him was one of the chief's patrolmen. Officer Pecs, to be exact. At least, that was the name Annette and I had come up with for him, mostly because he had pecs to die for. I turned on the porch light, hoping to catch a nametag, but he wore none.

"Oh, hi," Annette said, squeezing past me to hold out her hand to the towering officer. She smelled like citrus shampoo. "I'm Annette."

He took her hand reluctantly. "Ma'am. We've had a noise complaint."

"Of course you have," I said, eyeing Mr. Shoemaker.

"It was an explosion," he said to the officer, though he didn't take his eyes off me. "My windows shook."

I cringed at the thought.

"That was me," Annette said, a soft blush pinkening her cheeks. She hitched a thumb over her shoulder. "The oven and I went head-to-head. I lost."

"Your boss is just inside if you want to talk to him," I offered, my expression the picture of innocence.

"Yes, ma'am. I saw his car."

"He's looking at the damage now, but no one was hurt. Would you like to come in?"

"That's okay. As long as no one was hurt. I think the chief can handle it from here." He didn't seem as convinced as his words would suggest, and I wondered if he knew about all the strange happenings in this house on seemingly a daily basis. I wondered if all of Salem knew, actually.

Mr. Shoemaker bristled, his boyish face turning petulant. "You're not going to do anything?"

"What would you have me do?" he asked, honing his voice to a razor's edge. He probably had to be able to do things like that in his line of work.

Mr. Shoemaker had no answer. He turned back to me as the officer gave Percy's innards one last inspection, then walked away. "Ms. Dayne," the man said, his caramel hair showing more gray than I remembered, "I strongly suggest you go back to Arizona."

Annette folded her arms over her chest, probably reining in a sassy comeback.

"Right. You've suggested that several times, and I've ignored it. I feel we're at an impasse."

"Apparently." He tried to look past me into the house, but he was almost as vertically challenged as Annette.

"Maybe if you got another petition going," I offered. "Those are great."

Giving up, he bit down and pushed his black-framed

glasses up his nose, a nose reddened by the biting chill. His breath fogged on the air as he stood there, and I tried my best to get past his defenses. To see what he was searching for.

I was still learning why I could read some people from a block away and others evaded my probing, but I was beginning to believe it had more to do with intent than anything else. If someone was walking up my drive with the sole purpose of asking for my help to find something they'd lost, they were already open to my magics. They already knew what I could do whether they truly believed it yet or not. Mr. Shoemaker either didn't know or didn't want me probing him. Go figure.

But my own curiosity sometimes got the better of me, like with Gigi earlier. She'd acted as though I could get past her defenses whether she'd wanted me to or not. Maybe I could. Maybe all it would take for me to know what Mr. Shoemaker wanted was to insist.

I lowered my head, reached out with my mind, and asked him, "What are you searching for?"

He let out a long breath that misted in front of his face before leaning closer and saying, "A way to get you out of this house and out of this town."

"Then you'll have to get used to disappointment."

Something on the ground caught my, eye and I dropped my gaze to see Percy—well, Percy's vines—glide across the porch toward Mr. Shoemaker's sneakers. One of them curled around his shoelace and tugged it loose as another wound around and untied his other shoe.

Before Percy could do anything more, Mr. Shoemaker turned on his heel and walked away, pausing slightly when he noticed his untied shoes.

Annette hmphed as she watched him stalk off. "He's

like ninety-five percent dark chocolate. From the looks of it, you think it's going to be smooth and sweet. Instead, it's gritty. And bitter. And when you bite into it, it bites you back."

I crossed my arms and leaned against the doorjamb opposite her, eyeing the man suspiciously. "I don't know, Nette. I think there may be more going on here than simply a disgruntled neighbor."

"Like a disgruntled neighbor who has a thorn in his side and is determined to see you kicked out of Salem?"

I shrugged. She did have a point.

We walked back into the kitchen, and Roane carefully lifted a canister to Annette. "I don't know what you think you put in your cake, but it was not flour."

"What?" She hurried over, but he held up his other hand to stop her. "It says flour on the canister."

"What were you making, exactly?" I asked her.

"Pumpkin roll."

"And you blew it up?" Disappointment gripped me hard. I would've killed for a pumpkin roll. I'd killed for less. At least, I liked to tell myself I'd killed for less in those rare moments I tried to be a badass. A level of coolness I never quite achieved.

Roane put the canister on the counter and slowly opened the lid. After a quick sniff, he turned back to her and nodded. "Nitroglycerin."

What the actual fuck? I shot her an accusing glare. "Annette! We've talked about this. Friends don't kill friends with nitroglycerin."

She sank into a chair beside Gigi. The chief stood and walked over to him. "I need to get a team in here. There could be fingerprints."

"There aren't," Roane said. "None other than Annette's."

"And you know this because...?"

He gave him a sideways glance and said, "Wolf."

The chief nodded, accepting Roane's conclusion without further question, as though it explained everything. A fact I found more than a tad confounding. How could he, wolf or not, possibly know there were no other fingerprints on the canister?

I walked over to see what nitroglycerin smelled like. Roane pulled it away.

"Roane, what could I possibly do?"

"Do you know anything about your magics?"

"Yes," I said, my hackles rising. "Wait, why?" Clearly, he knew something I didn't.

Instead of explaining, he gave in and eased it closer, but just barely. "One sniff. Not too close," he added and slid his fingers into my hair to hold it back when I bent over the canister.

One sniff was all I needed. The acrid scent reminded me of burnt caramel. I rubbed my nose and turned to my grandmother. "Gigi, could this be what poisoned you?"

She'd hired us to ferret out who'd poisoned her. Breadcrumbs, Inc., the new venture Annette insisted we start so we could capitalize on my newfound ability as a finder of lost things, was off to a horrible start. Especially since Annette used part of the evidence in her cake and then blew up the kitchen with the rest of it. We'd have to up our game if we wanted to survive the rest of the week.

"No." Ruthie shook her head and thought back. "I distinctly remember the taste of belladonna and mushrooms, most likely death cap."

"I found those already," Roane said, gesturing toward

the pantry where Ruthie had died. Of course the wolf would sniff out any kind of discrepancies. "They were ground into a powder and tossed into a soup mix."

"Yes," Gigi said, nodding. "I'd made soup that day, but I'd had it not two days earlier as well."

"That narrows our window of opportunity." I sat beside her at the small oak breakfast table and took her hand into mine. "Then it's official. Someone definitely poisoned you." Not that we didn't already know that, but Roane's confirmation seemed to solidify it all. "I'm sorry, Gigi."

She lifted her delicate chin, as though refusing to let the incident hamper her life—her second life—any more than it already had. She patted my hand. "You two will find them. I'd bet my very existence on it."

I hated to state the obvious, but that was exactly what she was doing. Betting her existence on what she believed Annette and I were capable of. Because we'd led so many murder investigations throughout our careers, what with me being a washed-up restaurateur and Annette being an out-of-work office manager-slash-barista. Thank God we had the chief on our side.

The chief and Roane sat at the table.

"I'll have to dispose of that," Roane said, gesturing toward the canister, "but first you need to know it wasn't there earlier this evening."

"The canister?" I asked.

"The nitroglycerine."

I rested my elbows on the table. "What do you mean?"

He looked at Annette. "I found the belladonna and the mushrooms. But just in case, I checked out everything in the entire kitchen, including all of the canisters. Two hours ago, there was no nitroglycerin."

Annette straightened. "What are you saying?"

"There was no nitroglycerin in the flour," he repeated.

Was he accusing my BFF of something? "Roane, maybe you missed it. I mean, you were searching for—"

"Anything," he interrupted. "Anything out of the ordinary. I wouldn't have missed it. I have a lot of experience with nitroglycerin."

"Okay, then maybe... wait." I tossed him a wary frown. "Why do you have a lot of experience with nitroglycerin?"

"And no," he said, ignoring my question and glancing at Annette again, "I am not accusing you of anything. I'm just wondering if you saw anything out of the ordinary. Was the canister already out on the counter? Was the lid open? Anything unusual."

She shook her head. "Nothing. I found it in the cabinet between the canisters of sugar and coffee."

He nodded in thought, but I had questions. "Then how did it get there?" I asked him. When he didn't answer, I looked at the chief.

He was studying the table, deep in thought as well. "For now," he said, his voice grave, "everyone in this room eats only takeout. Nothing from the house until further notice."

"I agree," Roane said.

My heart sank in my chest. "But coffee."

"Not even coffee," he said, and the edges of my vision darkened.

The stark reality of the situation hit Annette then, too. "You can't mean it."

"How long will it take you?" the chief asked Roane.

"Tell me you don't mean it." She was beginning to hyperventilate.

Roane pressed his full mouth into a straight line. "Not long. I'll be back before morning."

"How are we going to survive?"

"Wait, what?" I asked as Roane stood. "You'll be back from where by morning?"

He winked at me, lifted his shirt over his head, and all seemed right with the world again. Gigi agreed. She perked up, and an adoring smile settled on her face. The chief covered her eyes, knowing what was coming next when Roane toed out of his boots. He walked to the mudroom off the kitchen and dropped the kilt to the floor, and I sat mesmerized. That ass.

Gigi tried to see past the chief's hand, but Roane stole out the back door before she got a good look if her disappointed expression was any indication. I scrambled to my feet, wanting nothing more than to see Roane shift into the red wolf, but by the time I reached the back door, all I saw was a patch of fur being swallowed by the darkness.

"God, I love when he does that," Ruthie said from behind me.

I stood there mourning the loss of witnessing Roane's shift and the majority of his assets—mostly the majority of his asscts—when Annette yelled, "There are laws against such cruelty!"

FOUR

A good night's rest can make you feel energized,
motivated, and ready to take on the world.
Oh, sorry, that's coffee.
Coffee does that.
—Meme

It took me a solid ten minutes to pry open my lids. When I slept, I slept hard, but this was ridiculous. For some reason, I'd dreamed of salt and ships, of wood cracking and bodies sinking as seawater swallowed men whole. They were helpless against the currents and the cold and the crashing waves, but when it came time for me to surface—out of the bone-chilling water and the soul-crushing dream—I couldn't quite manage it. I fought and fought to shake off the gremlins of sleep, but they kept pulling me back into the frigid oblivion of slumber, even with someone knocking on my door.

Then a knock registered in my unconscious mind. A

slow, persistent thing. One tap after another. Not meant to rouse me so much as make me aware of its presence. Its insistence that I take note.

After an eternity of fighting the lids that had somehow morphed into anvils as I slept, I managed to lift them just enough to reveal my surroundings. Darkness enveloped me, so it was still night, but that was hardly unusual. What was unusual was the wood beneath my feet.

Alarm shot through me, and my lids flew open, but I stayed motionless as my mind clawed desperately for my bearings. Salt and brine assaulted my nostrils, the scent so strong it made my eyes water. The floor was as cold as the seawater I'd dreamed about, and my bones ached from it as icy tendrils crept up my ankles and curled around my calves.

I stood there afraid to move. Mostly because, again, I was standing. I'd been sound asleep seconds earlier, and now I was standing in a frigid, suffocating darkness like a black ocean at night.

And the knocking continued. Not hard. Not soft. Just... there, barely two feet in front of my face, as though I were standing in front of a wall or a door.

After realizing my eyes would not adjust, the darkness was so complete, I lifted my hand and drew an illumination spell on the air. The room burst bright around me, light bathing every nook and cranny.

Blinking against the brilliance, I glanced around in surprise. I was in the attic, a hexagon-shaped room, completely empty save a few spiderwebs floating down from a single fixture on the ceiling. Six small doors surrounded me, like they'd been created for a child's play-house. Each door should have led to a small cathedral room, hence the six gables that formed Percy's circular roof. But when I first found the attic a few days ago, I'd sent my magics inside to find a vast, dark chasm that went on for what seemed like miles. I'd also found something that grabbed hold of my light. Sunk its teeth in. Wouldn't let go.

I stood in front of the door I'd tried to open earlier. The one in which I felt a presence, dark and angry, though admittedly, I hadn't tried the others. No one knew what the rooms held. No one knew why I'd created them when I was a child, including me. Ruthie had told me they'd just appeared one day, and when she asked me about them, I'd said they were for someone, or something, called Bead-uh.

I was three.

To this day, I had no idea how I did it, why I did it, or who Bead-uh was, though I couldn't help but wonder if it was Bead-uh knocking on the door now.

The knocking continued at the same pace, but it was slowly growing louder and louder. Last time, the entity inside almost broke down the door, it hit it so hard. This time it was being less aggressive but more persistent. I longed to know what was inside. Even more so now. Had it somehow summoned me here? In my sleep?

Even if it had, the doors could not be opened. Roane had told me they'd tried everything to open them over the years. They'd even bought some kind of explosive. One of the doors, scarred with black burn marks, held the evidence of their efforts. The fragile-looking things were simply impenetrable, so whatever lurked inside was SOL.

"Sorry," I said to the being, stepping away, and the knocking stopped.

I turned back, wondering again how I'd gotten here. The only way into the attic was via a secret passageway, one that even Percy couldn't infiltrate due to the salt-soaked shiplap the walls had been created from.

And here I stood. I hadn't sleepwalked in years. Decades, according to my dads. So why now?

When I gave up and started toward the stairs, the knocking started again. Harder this time. And much faster.

Whatever Bead-uh was would just have to deal. It had apparently been locked in that room for over forty years. It could take another forty to get it out. Then again, I'd obvs put it in there for a reason. I wasn't terribly keen on trying to get it out, and that fact seemed to upset it.

The knocking grew several decibels as I descended the narrow staircase. It was going to wake everyone in the house. Or demolish it trying.

I turned back and yelled, "Stop!"

The pounding ceased instantly.

I waited a moment, then continued down the stairs. The knocking started back up. Louder this time. Harder. Faster. A rapid succession so close together they made a continuous sound, like a boxer's punching bag.

I picked up the pace, almost falling down the stairs to get away from whatever lurked behind that door. Whatever I'd locked inside. It was clearly none too happy about its circumstances.

Once I hit the second floor and entered the passageway, the sound grew muffled, but apprehension prickled along my skin. Adrenaline rushed through me in tidal wave after tidal wave. I hurried to the secret entrance to my room and pushed on the shelves that opened into my bathroom, only then noticing the black ash along the threshold.

Concern quickened my pulse even more. Percy was waiting for me when I stepped inside. He'd filled my entire room with vines. I couldn't have walked from one end to another without getting a face full of razor wire, his thorns were so sharp.

Once across the threshold, he guided several vines around my back and urged me farther inside before closing the shelves behind me. Then he slid around me in what I could only perceive as a hug.

I crossed my arms over my chest and hugged the supple, thornless vines to me. "I'm sorry, Percy. I don't know what happened. I was asleep." I looked at the closed shelves and remembered what happened the last time I'd dragged part of him into the passageway. The vines had been turned to ash, just like the black powder on the floor. "Percy, did you try to stop me?"

I opened my palm. He curled into it and produced a black rose, meaning yes.

Dread filled my chest. "Did I... did I hurt you?"

He closed the rose and squeezed my hand, but I didn't believe him.

"I'm sorry," I said softly, hugging him to me again.

His hold tightened briefly, then he let go and shrank back into the walls. Guilt assailed me. Did it hurt when that happened? Did he feel pain?

I walked into my now vine-free room. Judging by the dim light, it was still early morning. The sun was just making an appearance, cresting over a sparkling ocean in the distance.

Three hours of sleep would just have to do. I hit the showers, pulled my hair into a ponytail, and went downstairs, ready to work. Working would at least take my mind off Roane for, like, five minutes. Seven if I was lucky.

The kitchen would need a thorough cleaning, possibly new paint as well, and then we'd have to see about getting a new oven. As a former restaurateur, I knew exactly how much an industrial oven cost. That knowledge caused an alarmingly sharp pain in my temporal lobe.

The citrus scent of cleaning supplies hit me when I stepped onto the first floor. I walked into the kitchen to find Minerva wrapped in a blanket and draped over the table, sound asleep, and Annette on her hands and knees in front of the oven in the same clothes she'd changed into the night before. Tufts of curly brown hair had fallen from her bear-eared buns, and she wore latex gloves, too big and bright yellow, with a sponge in one hand and a toothbrush in the other.

"Have you been up all night?" I asked, my voice rising an octave.

She looked up at me, the dark smudges on her cheek and above her right brow bringing out the gray in her eyes. They sparkled a deep, cool pewter, like a storm over a misty ocean. That, combined with her long, thick lashes, captivated anyone who happened to look her way. The effect was fascinating. "No." She rubbed her brow with the back of a yellow glove, smearing the smudge a bit further. "I slept a couple of hours."

"There's no need to clean the oven, hon. We'll have to get a new one either way."

"I'm not. I'm just trying to clean the floor." She sat back on her heels. The white tile did seem a little worse for wear. "Unless the insurance people need to see it all as is." Suddenly alarmed, she glanced around at all the work she'd put in.

I followed her panicked gaze.

She'd cleaned almost the entire kitchen. Even the white cabinets had a fresh glint to them. "Maybe I should have left it for the adjuster to see. Crap, I didn't think of that." She rubbed her brow again, creating two new smudges over her other brow.

"Do we even have insurance?" She'd been conscious a

lot longer than I had these last few months. She knew much more about the estate than I did.

She beamed at me. "As a matter of fact, we do."

"Do they cover mysterious explosions?"

"That, I don't know." She pointed to a small box of takeout coffee on the island. "Coffee and breakfast sandwiches."

"You went out?"

"I did."

"May the Goddess bless you with a dozen children," I said, reaching out a hand to her.

"Bite your tongue." She took it and struggled to her feet. "That used to be so much easier," she said with a groan, swiping at the knees of her gray yoga pants. She removed the bright-yellow gloves and threw them across the kitchen into the sink.

"A lot of things used to be so much easier," I agreed. "When did Minerva come down?"

"Shortly after I got up." We each grabbed a cup and a cheese croissant with egg and bacon and sat at the table. "She was asleep when I got back from my coffee run. Poor thing."

I sat beside her and tucked a lock of long black hair behind her ear before returning my attention to Nette the Jet. "Are you sure you're okay?" When she blinked over at me, confused, I elaborated. "Well, you were kidnapped, placed under a building being demolished, turned into a crow so you could escape—I still stand by that decision, by the way—then you shifted back into human form only to live through another explosion, and now you can suddenly see both my spells and the departed." When I thought about everything that had happened to her—to us —in the last few days, I shook my head, astonished we hadn't run from Salem screaming. "How are we still alive?"

"Right?" She scooted closer, the curls that had fallen loose bouncing around her face. "With everything that's happened over the last few days, we should be dead. And yet, here we are, alive and kicking. I think it's you."

Here we go again. I rolled my eyes and took a sip of my lukewarm coffee before getting up to reheat it. At least we still had a microwave. We wouldn't perish anytime soon.

"Hear me out." She rose to follow me the grueling ten feet it took to reach my destination. Because no way could I hear her from that great a distance. "You're a charmling. You must have some kind of protective"—she waved a hand in a circle to indicate my exterior—"mojo. Like a magical barrier that keeps you safe."

"Fine." I set the microwave and turned back to her. "What about you?"

"It must extend to those around you." She chewed on a nail in thought. "Like a shield. And you can push it out with your mind." She couldn't be more wrong if she'd proclaimed cheesecake a health food. Much to my undying chagrin.

"You've seen too many movies."

She pressed her mouth together. "Okay, then, Miss Debbie Doubter, how do you explain it?"

"I can't," I admitted before taking out my now-scalding coffee and hurrying to my seat, alternating the thick paper cup between my hands three times before I made it. "Holy crap, that microwave works well."

"I think you're like a superhero."

"You've said that before."

"Only, you know, way less cool." She sat across from me all nonchalant, like she hadn't just insulted my very being.

"What do you mean? I'm cool."

The unladylike snort she emitted would argue otherwise.

I wilted. "I used to be cool."

She shook her head. "You were never cool."

My lids narrowed to menacing, razor-sharp slits. "I'll have you know, I was totally cool in tenth grade."

"No, you weren't."

"I was so cool, they called me the ice queen."

"No one has ever called you the ice queen."

"I was so cool, I ate popsicles in January."

"I'm not sure that has anything to do with—"

"I was so cool, they once asked me to leave the swimming pool because I was turning the water to ice."

After a careful analysis that involved her staring at me for a semi-endless eternity, she reminded me, "They asked you to leave the pool because you swallowed half of it then coughed so hard you threw up before you could get out."

"Oh, yeah." The memory washed over me in disturbing waves of disappointment. "That was a horrible day."

"I know. I was still in the pool."

I tested my coffee, decided to give it another minute, lest I lose several layers off the roof of my mouth, and asked, "Can we talk about something else?"

She perked up. "Like... say... the business?"

Ah, yes. Our new startup. "How's that going?"

"Fantastic." She reached over Minerva and grabbed a notebook off the counter. Flipping through the pages, she said, "You have your first official office hours next week."

I'd been in the middle of testing my coffee again when I spit it onto her notebook.

She wiped it off with a sleeve and continued, unfazed. "And we have our first séance tomorrow night. Kind of like a kickoff, you know?"

I shot to my feet. "Annette!"

"What? We talked about this."

"*You* talked about this."

"There are at least two sides to every conversation."

She clearly had no idea how often I talked to myself. "As a possible draw for business in the future."

"No time like the present."

I realized I was freaking out over nothing and relaxed. "There's no way. How could you possibly set something like that up so fast?"

"That's just how I roll, I guess." She did a gang sign of some kind, probably inviting groups of bangers to shank us in the showers, then added, "*Bam*, bitch. I got this shit covered."

I sank into my seat and crossed my arms over my chest so I could glare at her. Due to my giving nature, I decided not to remind her that no forty-five-year-old white chick should be throwing gang signs, and asked instead, "Is this payback for the bird thing?"

"No. I set this up before the bird thing. Like three days ago." She pushed her coffee-stained notebook over to me. "I have some basic designs for our business cards you need to approve—"

"Oh, *now* you need my approval?"

"—and a couple for a promotional poster. We need a slogan." She looked up in thought. "Something like, *Bread-crumbs, Inc. Your loss is our gain.*" When I just stared, she added, "Get it? Because you find lost things?"

"Annette, how much coffee have you had?"

"How much coffee have *you* had?" she asked, deflecting.

"Annette Cheri Osmund."

She wilted in defeat. "Fine. If you must know, that box is the second one I bought this morning."

"You drank a whole takeout box?" I practically screeched the words, and Minerva stirred. Not much. Just enough to let out a moan of protest before falling back into oblivion. Sadly, she fell asleep on a waffle-patterned kitchen towel. She was going to have a wicked design on her face when she woke up.

"Yes," Annette said.

"And you're still alive?"

"'Parently." She leaned over and sketched a few lines on one of her designs. It was either a penguin holding a hockey stick or an angel holding a scythe. I couldn't see how either would represent us accurately.

"For the record," I said, watching her work, "twelve minutes of sleep between cups of java does not count." My only hope lay in the fact that she couldn't possibly have gotten the word out for a séance so quickly. Surely no one would show up. We weren't established, and there were plenty of other spiritual gurus offering their services in town. We were in Salem, after all. "Nette, I don't want you to get your hopes up about the séance. These events need to be planned months in advance. And promoted. If no one shows up—"

"Are you kidding?" She snorted. "It sold out in minutes."

"Minutes?" Disbelief hit me first, then panic. It rushed over me in pulsating, nauseating waves. I sat in stunned silence a long moment before replying. "You do realize I don't know how to perform a séance?"

"Pfft," she pffted. "Sure you do. We see it in movies all the time."

"Right, because that's exactly the same thing."

"And Percy can help. Right, Percy?"

Vines flourished around us, like a garden blooming in a fast-motion video, and I glared at him. "Traitor." I redoubled my efforts and marched onward. "I'll make you a deal. I'll agree to do the séance"—Goddess help us all—"if you'll try to shift."

"What?" She was appalled. I'd appalled her. I did that. "I will never try to shift. What if I get stuck? What then? I'll tell you what, since you're asking."

"I wasn't—"

"I'll have to live my whole life as an ugly feathered crow."

"Don't be ridiculous." I leaned over and took her hand. "You're an adorable crow."

She melted. "Really?"

"Or you would be if not for the beady eyes."

"I knew it." She pulled her hand out of my reach.

"Kidding. You were the most adorable crow I've ever seen. And practice makes perfect."

She almost gave in. I could see it in her eyes, but she changed her mind at the last minute and picked up her phone with a sassy "no."

"Please."

"Absolutely not."

"I'll do the séance."

"You'll do the séance either way."

"Yes, but I can either give the evening my all, really throw myself into the role, or I can confess to everyone that I have no idea what I'm doing and give them their money back."

She inhaled a sharp breath, the act so drawn out, I couldn't help but be impressed with her lung capacity. "You wouldn't dare," she said with a hiss I found almost as funny as the curl bouncing in front of her left eye.

"Would, too."

She set her jaw, too stubborn for her own good, and started tapping on her phone, ignoring me.

I bit my lower lip and waited. When I could stand it no longer, I asked, "Are you trying?"

"No."

"Are you trying now?"

"No."

"What about now?" Gawd, she was fun to pester.

"No. And I won't. Don't ask me again."

"Annette." I draped my body over the table, mimicking Minerva. "How are we going to know if you can do it at will, if you can control it, if you don't try?"

She sniffed, scrolling through her friends list. Probably to unfriend me. "It's... it's very personal."

"Wait a minute." I straightened and looked past her turquoise lenses and into her stormy gray eyes. The ones she was purposely averting. "You've already tried, haven't you?" When she didn't answer, my jaw fell open. "No way. You did it!"

Minerva groaned.

"You shifted," I added, only quieter.

She brushed a feather off her sleeve. A feather I should have seen the minute she sat down.

"Oh my God." I pressed my fists over my mouth in excitement. And I may have squeaked. "Please, show me."

"No." She put down her phone. "I already told you, it's very personal."

"This is the coolest thing ever. First Roane and now you. I just want to see it, you know? What I created. How it works. Like, do your feathers sprout from your skin? Do your bones crack? Does it hurt?"

"You're like an addict jonesing for a fix."

"Your point is?" When she didn't answer, I changed tactics. "I'll tell you a scary story."

She paused but didn't look at me. "I don't like scary stories."

"You love scary stories. And if it scares you, truly scares you, you have to show me."

"Is it a true story?"

So easy. "Yes."

She put down her phone with a huff. "Fine."

"Okay. I woke up in the attic this morning."

"That's weird. Not scary."

"I'm not finished."

"Okay, but for real? You woke up in the attic?"

I nodded. "Upright. I was standing up in my sleep."

"That's not creepy at all," she lied.

"Staring at one of the doors."

"*The* door?"

"And something on the other side was knocking."

She stilled. "Crap. That thing in the room with the claws?"

"Yes. The entity."

"With claws, right?"

"It was slow at first. The knocking. Not the entity."

"Have we figured out what kind of entity it is?"

"The knock was steady."

"Can we go back to the entity?"

"Knock... knock... knock." I added dimension and realism by knocking on the table.

She grabbed my hand. "I get it."

"Then it got all fast and loud and aggressive." I knocked faster with my other hand.

She grabbed it too, just as someone, in a moment that was both serendipitous and inspired, knocked on the front door. Annette almost jumped out of her skin. I did too, and if not for the fact that I almost toppled over my chair, no one would have known.

Ice queen.

"What are the odds the entity is at the front door?" she asked.

FIVE

You know you drink too much coffee if:
You haven't blinked since the last lunar eclipse.
—Meme

Minerva slept through it all, and I considered checking for a pulse the moment I got mine under control.

Annette pressed a hand to her chest to calm herself, then checked her watch just as Gigi came up from her hidey-hole in the basement. The chief followed her, his massive body dwarfing hers, his uniform starched and badge polished. Since he hadn't been wearing a uniform when he showed up last night, I could only assume he kept an extra here. Handy and scandalous. I'd have to rib Gigi about it later. Do my due diligence.

"You know you don't have to sleep in the basement," I said to her, guilt assaulting me again as I repositioned my chair.

She'd given up her room for me, but it wasn't like we

didn't have others. I would sleep in the pantry if it meant she would be more comfortable.

"And risk someone seeing me through the windows?" It was true. The bedroom windows, all thirteen of them, were massive floor-to-ceiling things, but that was what blinds were for. "And you know I love it down there," she added, referring to her room of herbs and dried flowers and all manner of magical concoctions.

She walked over to inspect the damage from the night before, and I couldn't help but be dazzled by her once again. Her elegance. Her grace. Gigi defined shabby chic. With her bob freshly coiffed, the blonde radiated youth and vitality. She wore a gauze dress, a cream bohemian with gold threads woven into the tattered handkerchief hem. A gilded vagabond. Of course, the fact that she could make a potato sack look chic did nothing to boost my self-esteem. I clearly got my assets from my father's side of the family, whoever that might be.

The chief joined her, wrapping a hand around her slender waist as someone knocked again.

"It's a little early for visitors," Annette said.

I eyed her with wary suspicion. "I swear, if my office hours start this early, you're fired."

Gigi shook her head. "Could you get that, dear? That'll be Serinda."

I hesitated a moment longer, hoping Roane would come up, too. We had a lot to talk about. When he didn't, I started the long journey to the front door, which was neither long nor much of a journey, when Annette shouted, "Would you really fire me?"

Sure enough, Serinda McClain, a member of Gigi's coven and one of her oldest friends, stood on the other side, her fiery red hair glistening in the early light.

"Defiance," she said, her breath fogging on the air. She seemed surprised I'd answered, and if I didn't know better, I would've sworn she bowed her head to me.

I decided to ignore it. "Hey, Serinda. Gigi's expecting you." I held the door wider for her to come in.

"Wonderful. Oh, hello, Houston."

The chief walked up behind me. "Hey, Serinda." He offered her a warm smile before looking at me. "I'm off to work, Daffodil. Don't hesitate to call if anything seems... off."

"I won't. Thanks, Chief."

He hurried past Serinda, tipping an invisible hat as he gestured her inside.

"Gigi's in the kitchen," I said.

"Actually, I'm here to see you."

"Me?" We'd only met a couple of days earlier when Gigi had set up a meet-n-greet with the upper echelon of the coven. "Well, come on back. It's a bit of a mess, but we have coffee and breakfast sandwiches."

"From Red's?"

"Yep."

"I'm in."

To Serinda's credit, she barely blinked an eye at the damage. The oven door hung off its hinges, and that part of the kitchen was still covered in black soot, but the tile was coming along nicely. Clearly, Gigi had told her what happened.

Serinda rushed over to her and pulled her into a warm embrace. "Are you okay?"

"I'm fine, sweetheart. I was downstairs."

She set her at arm's length. "Trapped?"

"No, there's an escape route I could've used had I needed it."

Appeased, Serinda poured herself a cup of coffee and chose a cheese croissant out of the box of sandwiches. We sat at the small table and worked around Minerva's prone body to doctor our respective elixirs. Minerva never moved. Ah, to be twenty again. Carefree. Resilient. Flexible. If I slept like that, my head would be stuck in the same position for a week.

Serinda swallowed a bite, took a sip of coffee, then focused her attention on me. "I wanted to thank you, Defiance. I don't know what you did, but my granddaughter is a different person."

Her granddaughter, Belinda, was the ultimate skeptic. So much so, she and her brother were seconds away from trying to have Serinda, one of the most lucid people I'd ever met, declared incompetent and put in a home. I'd shown Belinda what we witches were capable of, especially since her grandmother swore Belinda was one herself. Apparently, it worked.

"I don't even know how to describe it," Serinda continued. "Something about a crystal elephant?"

I nodded from behind my cup and took a quick sip before answering. "Yes. It was very special to her. Had been missing for decades. I simply told her where to find it."

Serinda pressed a hand to her chest. Her expression of awe would've been more appropriate had I parted the Red Sea. Finding a crystal elephant just didn't seem worthy of such reverence. "I can't thank you enough, Sarru. It's as if she's enjoying life again. Like all of the doubt and worry and skepticism drained out of her in one fell swoop. And"—she grinned at Gigi—"she's no longer denying her sensitivity to the spiritual realm. To the energies around us."

I decided not to ask about the word *sarru* and why she

would call me that, though it sounded oddly familiar. I'd heard it before.

Gigi's joy shined through her lovely face. "Serinda, I'm so happy for you. You know how much I love that girl."

"And she you, darling." She turned to me. "I don't know what you did, Sar—Defiance, but I am forever grateful."

"I'm just glad I could help."

"Ruthie," she said, her eyes glistening, "she wants to join the coven."

That must have been a big deal because Gigi stilled and placed a look of delight on her friend. "Oh, Serinda. Congratulations."

"I know we'll need the approval of the rest of the *cove*— the inner circle—and that she'll be in a probationary period for a year and a day while she studies, but I was hoping I'd have the doyenne's vote."

Gigi shook her head softly, her smile warm and genuine. "I'm so happy for you, Serinda. Of course you have my vote, but—"

"The doyenne?" I asked, unfamiliar with that word as well.

Annette straightened her shoulders like that student in class who always had the answer. She pointed at Gigi. "Ruthie. Your grandmother."

I fought a grin. "Yes, I know who Ruthie is."

"She's the doyenne. The senior member of our coven."

"*Your* coven?" I knew she'd gotten to know the members of Gigi's coven. I wasn't aware she'd become a full-fledged member.

"Well, you know, hopefully. Right now, I'm a novice. A neophyte. I'm a member, but I have to complete a year and a day of study, of which I've completed five months, but maybe someday I'll be invited into the cove." Her expression went from prudent apprentice to aspiration-filled dreamer as she imagined that day.

She'd been swearing she was psychic since we were kids. I'd always had my doubts, even when she accurately predicted the rise and fall of Nathan Blomquist's popularity in the seventh grade. Once the other kids found out he wasn't the real Prince of Genovia—he really liked *The Princess Diaries*—the attraction waned.

"So, you studied while I was in that whole state of suspended animation. You are way ahead of me, then."

"As usual." One corner of her mouth twitched.

"And the cove?" I asked, ignoring her.

Serinda nodded. "Our upper echelon, so to speak. The inner circle and senior members of the coven."

"So, like the board members?"

The woman's glistening smile bordered on starstruck when she answered me. "Something like that, Sarru."

"Serinda," Gigi said, her tone softly admonishing.

As though realizing what she'd said, she blushed prettily beneath the white powder on her face and dropped her gaze as though embarrassed. "I apologize."

"It's not your fault." Gigi patted her hand. "I apologize for not bringing it up sooner."

"Sarru?" I asked. "It's oddly familiar. What does it mean?" I looked at Annette, since she seemed to have all the answers, but she lifted a shoulder and fixed her inquisitive gaze on the two elder women.

"Familiar?" Gigi asked, seeming impressed. "The literal translation is *king*. It's Mesopotamian."

"Mesopotamian?" A charge ran along my spine. "That's the time period the charmlings were first created." I'd had a vision of that creation when I first came into my powers. Of the witches who'd banded together to create three powerful sisters to protect their fellow witches, though they weren't called that back then. They were sorceresses. Shamans with magical powers. But kings and paupers alike would abuse their powers. Use them for personal gain. So, they created the charmlings to protect both witches and humans alike.

Sadly, the practice didn't stop there. Unscrupulous witches and warlocks had learned centuries ago how to harness the powers of a charmling. Warlocks, no matter how powerful, can never absorb the power themselves, but they can control a witch who'd killed a blood heir and stolen her powers.

Still, any witch who did that risked almost certain death. Others would come. Others would do the same to them. Eventually, another witch would try to take from her what she took, the power that was never rightfully hers. Apparently, corrupt witches abound.

Those who did manage to hold on to the power were usually protected by a dark coven who used the magics for their own gain. The witches themselves were essentially chattel. Very well-guarded chattel with a startling lack of free will. Thus, either road led to tragedy.

It was all so new to me. Six months ago, I would've sworn magic wasn't real. Witches didn't exist. Warlocks were a myth. Admittedly, I still had a lot to learn, but I couldn't help but wonder about the term *king*. And why Serinda would be addressing me as such. And how I could get her to stop immediately.

"Defiance is fine," I told them both. "I'd rather not be addressed as royalty."

"Defiance," Gigi said, my turn to be admonished, "you cannot deny your heritage. Or your destiny."

"Destiny?"

"To do so would be suicide."

"Nobody said anything about a destiny."

"I doubt the sorceresses called their creations king—"

"Or suicide."

"But over time, they became known as such by those they protected. For the members of our coven, of any coven, to address you otherwise would be impudent."

"Gigi," I said, trying to keep the frustration from my voice, "I've only just come into my powers again."

"Which is why I didn't bring it up sooner."

"How about I get used to them before we start throwing titles around willy-nilly?"

She pursed her elegant mouth. "Fine. But there is something we must consider. The other two charmlings—"

"You mean the faux charmlings?" None of the current-day charmlings, save me, were from the bloodline. For decades, the other two charmlings had gained their powers by stealing them. One after the other. The stolen powers were passed from witch to witch. At least, that was my understanding. So, there were two other charmlings out there, but both were murderesses and servants.

"Be that as it may," Gigi said, "they are protected by very powerful covens and even more powerful warlocks." The sideways glance she directed toward her best friend contained more than a hint of worry. "You are now part of our coven whether you like it or not, and the other members need to know you are to be protected at all costs. They must be prepared."

I tugged on an ear, trying to wrap my head around it all. "I thought the whole reason for my creation was to protect you, my sister witches."

"It was," Serinda said, "thousands of years ago. The rules have changed."

Gigi agreed. "You are simply too powerful, Defiance."

"Then I should be able to protect myself."

"That power," Serinda explained, "is something witches and warlocks alike would do anything to get their hands on. The black arts are nothing to take lightly."

"Once the powers are stolen from a blood heir—"

"Exactly," I said, interrupting my grandmother. "Maybe that's been the problem the whole time. The witches who stole them aren't powerful enough to protect themselves, because the magics weren't theirs to begin with."

They exchanged perplexed glances before Gigi asked, "What do you mean, love?"

I straightened in my chair, trying to figure out how to make my point. "Maybe once the powers are stolen from a blood heir, they're even easier for another witch, one less powerful, to steal? Because that witch was not a true charmling. And the more they're stolen, the less powerful the witch has to be. Like, the magics become diluted. If the witch who stole the powers wasn't terribly powerful to begin with—"

"Oh, but she would've been," Serinda said. "In order to pull off something like that, she would've been very powerful."

"Probably more powerful than either of us are," Gigi agreed.

I had my doubts about that. My own mother had tried to steal my powers when I was three. She had to have gotten her powers from somewhere. Then again, I'd killed her. According to Gigi, I'd somehow known what she was doing, and I defended myself. In the process, I'd killed my own mother. That knowledge was still new. Raw. Abrasive. Thankfully, that was not a specific memory I had access to.

"In any case," Gigi said, lifting her chin majestically, "we are your coven and you, whether you want to be or not, are of royal blood. You are *sarru*, and we are prepared to lay down our lives to protect you."

I held up a hand to stop her. "I'm sorry, what?"

She drew in a deep breath. "Defiance—"

"No." I stood and walked to the island to look through the offerings for something to do. An excuse to buy a few moments to absorb what they were saying. After deciding two sandwiches had been plenty, I turned back to them. "That is not acceptable. I didn't sign up for anything like that."

"I can see why you didn't tell her," Serinda said. "Sarru—"

"Dee. Fy. Ance." Though I stressed each syllable, I said it softly. Lovingly. These amazing women were willing to give up their lives for me. As far as we knew, my grandmother may have done that very thing.

What if her death was all a ruse to find out my identity? Gigi had kept me hidden for over forty years. She'd somehow suppressed my powers to the point that even I didn't know about them. Didn't remember them. And no one else, witch or warlock, could use them to find me. The fact that she had the power to do something like that proved how strong she was. How powerful.

Serinda held her ground. "Sarru," she said, with a soft bow of her head, "you are a charmling. You simply must get used to the idea. And you, like all charmlings, are vulnerable to the most wretched of our kind."

I sat back down and only then realized Minerva had awakened. Her breathing wasn't deep anymore. I spared her a quick glance. Her eyes were barely open, watching me from behind a mass of long dark hair, her brows drawn in concern. As a member of the inner circle, she had to have at least a trace amount of power herself, and I wondered exactly what she was capable of.

I turned back to the two elder women. "Odd how those who are supposed to be the most powerful witches are the most vulnerable."

"The bigger the target," Gigi said.

But the words that Serinda said percolated inside my brain—*of royal blood*—and I remembered what the beauty in my Mesopotamian vision, her ebony skin decorated with bright, iridescent paints, had drawn on the air when we met. The symbol she'd christened me with: *of royal blood*.

What the actual hell?

Annette rifled through her notebook. "I don't think they always were. Targets. Then a warlock in the... oh... maybe the 1600s, figured out how to force another witch—a witch he controlled—to siphon a charmling's magics, subsequently killing her. There's a book..." She tore through her notebook faster as she got closer to her goal. She stopped and pointed. "Yes. An ancient text that talks about charmlings, only the author doesn't call them that specifically. The text was translated many times, however. It could be a bad interpretation. Add to that the fact that the author wrote in riddles for fear of being labeled a heretic, and you can see the conundrum."

Both Gigi and Serinda eased closer as Annette read from her notes.

"A book?" Gigi asked, struggling for a look at the notes. "What book?"

"Oh, let me find the title." She thumbed back through several pages as Minerva gave up the charade and craned her neck for a peek as well. "It's... here... somewhere. Oh, here. It's from one of several books called Centuries by Nostradamus."

"Nostradamus?" Serinda said, stunned.

All three women—Gigi, Serinda, and Minerva—dove in for a better look, almost knocking their heads together.

Annette frowned and eased the book closer to read. "Okay, according to this Nosferatu guy, who wrote in these really cryptic quatrains, *three daughters born on the sands of the Tigris will know great adversity and the victories of man.* No clue about the victories, but I figure he could be talking about the original charmlings." She glanced at me. "They were Mesopotamian in your vision, right, Deph?"

I nodded and couldn't help but lean in for a better look.

"The Tigris. It fits perfectly." She read some more. "Okay, next he says, *no true sorrow will touch their breasts, until the beasts descend and sup on spirit and flesh.* So, ew. But the beasts descending?"

"The warlocks," Gigi said.

"My thoughts exactly. From what I can tell, that refers to the original change of the power dynamics. But the second quatrain starts with the real clue: *For five thousand years, the daughters of the crescent will wait.*" She tapped the notebook. "Mesopotamian civilization was dominated very much by the Sumerians in the early Bronze Age. The first written history begins almost exactly five thousand years ago in Mesopotamia, which sat in what is called the Fertile Crescent."

I shook my head. "Annette, how did you find all of this?"

"Oh, but wait. There's more." She turned the page. "*The concealed queen rises first, seized by fire.*" She looked up at me. "It's you, Deph. Your powers were concealed, and then you caught fire—"

"I didn't actually catch—"

"Then Roane put you in the shower and, you know,

quenched it." Four women sighed dreamily. Five if one counted me.

Annette snapped out of it first. "But get this. *Her sisters of half-blood follow, of taint and of time.* Again, no idea what taint and time means. But it has to be metaphorical for your sister charmlings."

"Maybe," Serinda said. "But the other charmlings are not true blood heirs."

"Exactly," I agreed. "They're faux charmlings."

Annette waved a dismissive hand. "Again, this guy was super cryptic. There's just no telling. But the last line of these two quatrains states that *When eternal sands divide and all sisters unite, the final beast will fall.*" When she gazed at us expectantly and no one said anything, she added, "Don't you get it? The final beast. The last warlock. And it says when all sisters unite. Not just the three. I think all of the witches will have to unite to bring this guy down. The covens will play a part."

"This is all so fascinating," Gigi said. "How did you even find it?"

She lifted a shoulder. "Google. The next quatrain goes into kings and swords. He was super into that sort of thing. These were the only two quatrains I could find that I feel pertains to the charmlings."

"I'm astonished you found that much," Serinda said. "Who knew Nostradamus would prophesize about the charmlings? And I think this only reiterates the fact, Sarru, that we are your coven now. We are your protection, and we will be diligent in our endeavors."

"Calling me sarru, putting me on this pedestal, is still not acceptable."

Gigi flattened a hand on the table in front of me to emphasize her point. "Defiance, it is. It must be."

I took it into both of mine. "It's not, and it never will be."

Annette, ever the wordsmith, pushed her glasses up her nose and said, "Then I guess it sucks to be you. Can I call you Sarru?"

"No."

"Please?"

"No."

"If we may get back to the business at hand," Gigi said, getting back to the business at hand with a saucy toss of her silvery-blond hair, "Serinda, our coven must be strong. Now more than ever. It cannot have an absentee leader. Therefore, I am no longer the doyenne."

"Of course you are."

"I need to make that clear."

"There's nothing unclear about the situation."

"The coven needs to move on."

"No, it doesn't."

"Serinda," Gigi said, exasperated. "The position is yours."

"Teflon," Serinda blurted out, and I almost burst out laughing.

Both Gigi and Minerva looked confused, and Gigi proved that fact by asking, "What does that even mean?"

"It means I'm Teflon, and your words won't stick to me."

I couldn't help but see a little of Annette and me in their banter. In fact, when Serinda lifted her cup and took a long draw while batting her eyelashes at my grandmother, I had to hold back a giggle.

Annette coughed suspiciously as well.

Gigi looked away, refusing to fall for her friend's ploy at levity. "The position is yours now. And it's about time."

"Posh." Serinda set her cup down and waved a dismissive hand. "You were gone a few days. You are most certainly still the doyenne."

"Serinda, I died."

"I am very aware," Serinda said, her voice cracking. "But if you think that paltry excuse will be enough to shirk your duties, you're mistaken."

Wow. They had a really rigorous breach-of-contract clause.

"Paltry?"

"You are still very much the doyenne."

Serinda's chin quivered, the emotion almost too much for her, and she picked up her cup again to hide behind it, splintering my heart, spiderwebbing it with hairline fractures. Her best friend's death had surely devastated her. Had it been Annette, the vivacious and bubbly love of my life... I couldn't imagine what she went through.

Gigi took a moment to gather herself as well. It was a wonder they didn't have this conversation while I was out, and I was curious as to why. "But, Serinda," Gigi said, her tone exposing the fact that the words saddened her deeply, "even if I wanted to, I... I can't go back."

Serinda turned a curious brow on her.

"The inner circle knows what happened, yes. How I died. The fact that Defiance lifted me out of the veil, but the others. The novices. If word gets out about what Defiance is capable of... It's already almost cost Defiance her life. And Annette. And Roane. And I won't let it happen again."

Minerva winced at the reminder of recent days. "I'm so sorry," she said to Gigi before turning to me. "I am so, so sorry."

I wrapped an arm around her blanketed shoulders and

decided not to tell her about the waffle impression on the side of her face. "Minerva, that was not your fault."

"Yes, it was." She sloughed the blanket off and stood, her head bowed in shame. "I'm part of your coven, part of the inner circle even, and I let it slip that you brought Ruthie—the doyenne!—back to life." She looked at Serinda, wringing her hands like a child waiting for punishment. "I understand if I'm out."

Serinda dropped her gaze. "Minerva, that was partly my fault."

"What?" Minerva crossed her arms and eased back against the island. "Why would you even say that?"

"I knew what a horrible man your uncle was. I knew you could not be happy, but I had no idea he was so abusive. I wanted you to find your own way. To... to learn to come to me—to us, your sisters—for help when you needed it. I had no idea how much he'd beat you down."

She chewed the tip of an abused thumb. "You couldn't have."

"I could have, actually. I should have seen the signs, Minerva. The mistrust. The skittishness. They were all there. You had PTSD practically stamped on your forehead."

Minerva curled into herself, her shoulders concaving, and I saw it then. What she was searching for. Her heart's deepest desire. And, as happened so often, it was nowhere near what I expected. I may not be able to brew a love potion, but I could, at the very least, hook her up with the man she'd been pining after from afar for years.

I quirked an impish brow at Annette. She questioned me with a quirk of her own. I nodded toward Minerva, and her face brightened, knowing we were going to have some fun in the near future. To do some good. To help the girl get the thing she most wanted. Or, more specifically, the man she most wanted. Well, if he wanted her, too. I wasn't a monster. Or a pimp.

Admittedly, Annette could never have discerned all of that from my quirk, but she would find out soon enough.

"Please accept my apology, Minerva." Serinda rose and took the girl into her arms.

"It's okay. It's hard to separate the PTSD from genuine weirdness."

I laughed softly. I knew I liked her. "Then you are definitely in the right place."

"And," Gigi added, "in the right coven."

Minerva fought a wave of emotion by ducking her head and letting her long dark hair fall into her face. It was a tactic I'd used several times in my life, too.

"Still," Annette said, crinkling her nose in thought, "I think we need a name."

Gigi pursed her mouth to keep from grinning. "We don't need a name."

"All the cool covens have them."

"Which explains why we don't have one."

"I know you're dead set against calling it the Salem Arc of the Coven-ant, but what about Easy Bake Coven?"

Gigi looked at me, helpless.

"Or the Lovin' Coven? You know. Because of our policy on inclusivity."

People already suspected witch clans of having all-night orgies. That name would not help. I elbowed my bestie. "How about we table that for now, Nette."

"Okay, but I'm on it." She held up her pencil as though it were a sword and she was vowing her allegiance to the cause. "I'll come up with the perfect name. Don't you worry."

This was the same girl who came up with Breadcrumbs, Inc., so I had to remind myself she did have some aptitude for such things. "Okay, you think about it."

"For a long time," Gigi said. "Think on it long and hard."

Annette nodded. "Right. Like meditate on it. Really let it simmer. Gotcha."

Gawd, I loved that girl. But there was still something niggling in the back of my mind. We'd brought Serinda's granddaughter around, but what about her grandson? From what I'd gleaned when I delved into Belinda's thoughts, he would not give up the quest to have his grandmother committed just because Belinda had switched sides. Quite the opposite. He would possibly double his efforts.

He wanted the woman's money. He'd been the one campaigning to have Serinda put into a home in the first place. There was something horrible about a person willing to commit their own grandmother against her will to get at her savings.

I mulled over broaching the subject, concerned I'd over-step my bounds, then broached ahead regardless. When she sat back down, I attacked. "Serinda, I don't mean to pry, but I have to admit, I'm still worried about your grandson."

"Oh?" she asked, turning that starlit gaze on me.

"I doubt he'll give up his quest so easily."

She pressed a hand over her heart again, as though I'd just bequeathed her a live chicken for her dinner table. "Thank you, Sarru."

"Defiance," I insisted, hiding a grin behind my own cup.

"I'm honored, and humbled, but I can handle him." A mischievous twinkle in her eye accompanied the promise, and I was quite inclined to believe her.

Though not entirely appeased, I turned to the next problem at hand. "And you," I said to Gigi.

She raised an austere brow, her demeanor so opposite from Serinda's it was almost comical. "Me?"

"You," I confirmed, half surprised she didn't say *moi*. "You need to get back to your life, Gigi. You need to start living again. Meeting your friends for coffee and going to sabbath. The coven needs you."

"I wish I could, but—"

"I have a plan."

Annette looked up from her notebook. "A plan? I love plans. I make several a day."

Gigi nodded. "We know, dear."

"The way I see it, there's only one way to handle this. We have to introduce the world to Ruthie Goode's long-lost twin sister... Rachel. No, Rachelle. No..."

"Oh," Annette said, chiming in. "Romy."

"Rosalind," Minerva said, adding her two cents. And thankfully, the waffle impression was starting to fade. "She could be a Rosalind."

"Maybe." I narrowed my eyes on my grandmother, not quite convinced. "We're getting closer."

Annette clapped. "I love this. You'll have a secret identity."

Gigi started to argue, but stopped, seeming to turn the idea over in her head.

Then reality set in. "Wait." I sagged in my seat. "That won't work."

"Of course it will." Annette drew a hand across the air in front of her as though she were reading a headline. "*Long-lost Twin Comes Home at Last.* It's inspired. If she changes her hair a bit, throws on a little mascara, no one will be the wiser, and we can introduce her as Ruthie's twin immediately."

"Her estranged twin," Serinda offered, her telltale expression full of hope. "It's perfect, Sarru."

"Thank you. And, yes, that part works. It's the name. I was forced to live without Gigi for over forty years. I don't want to give her up just yet."

"She'll still be your great-aunt," Annette offered.

"Yes, but I want to be able to call her Gigi." I snapped my fingers. "I've got it." I leaned closer to her, inserted a dramatic pause, then said, "Georgiana. Yes. It can totally be shortened to Gigi." I looked up in thought. "Georgiana Rue Bishop."

Bishop was Ruthie's maiden name, so she'd have to go back to it for this to work. And Rue would be an homage to her eighty-plus years on the planet as Ruthie. But Georgiana was strictly for me, as no one would question my nickname for her. There were still a ton of logistics to work out, but...

My train of thought came to a screeching halt when I noticed the way Gigi was looking at me. Like I'd grown an extra head. I fluffed my hair to make sure I hadn't. "What is it? Do I have something in my teeth?"

"Georgiana Rue Bishop."

"You don't like it? We can work on it. I just wanted—"

She stopped me with a hand over mine. "Defiance, that was my grandmother's name. How did you know?"

I blinked, just as surprised. "I... I didn't. I must've read it somewhere."

"No." She shook her head. "You couldn't have."

"Okay," I said, more curious than ever. "Why?"

Serinda gasped softly as the truth hit her. She clearly

knew something I didn't. "Because Georgiana's father changed it the day after she was born."

Yep.

"Why would he do that?" Annette asked, touching pencil to paper, ready to take notes.

"Well, Nanette," Gigi said, "he'd been at sea when my grandmother was born, and they hadn't agreed on a name before he set sail. So when he got back the day after her birth and heard what my great-grandmother had named their daughter, he hated it and insisted they change it. They only recorded her new name: Ruthanne Ambrosia Bishop. My great-grandmother told no one of the name she'd first decided on and only told Ruthanne years later.

"So, you'll essentially be named after her twice."

Serinda did the starstruck thing again. "Sarru, how did you know?"

"I didn't." My gaze bounced between her and Gigi. "I'm not psychic. I promise."

"But you are," Gigi insisted. "You must be. To pluck a name so distinct out of thin air like that?"

I wasn't going to argue with her, though, admittedly, it was a tad suspicious. But the more important question was: "Why did your great-grandfather hate the name?"

Gigi pursed her lips to suppress a puckish grin. It didn't work. "Apparently, Georgiana was the name of my grandfather's first great love. The one who ran away with a solicitor. He didn't tell my great-grandmother until after Ruthanne's birth, and she insisted on knowing what he had against the name."

"Well, I love it," I said.

Annette nodded. "Me too."

"Me three," Minerva said as she nibbled a croissant.

"And you?" I asked Gigi, holding my breath.

"Not only do I love it, I'm terribly honored to have it."

"Oh, yay!" Annette clapped again.

A relieved smile spread across my face. "Now we just need a little hair dye."

Serinda held up a hand. "We've got this." She stood and herded Gigi toward the stairs, the ones that led to her basement apartment.

"You have hair dye in your basement?" Minerva asked.

Serinda glanced over her shoulder. "Not exactly."

"Serinda, for Goddess's sake." Gigi was not as convinced as Serinda was. "We haven't done anything like this in decades."

"Then it's high time."

"If you'll remember, the last time we tried it, the spell rendered me incapable of pronouncing the word cinnamon for six months. Everyone kept asking why I was talking about a thesaurus."

"The spell?" I asked, stunned. "You mean, you can do it with magic?"

Serinda beamed. "We can."

"We can try," Gigi corrected. "And if we succeed, it'll be more permanent than regular hair dye."

"That is so cool."

Annette stood and walked over to the toaster to look at her reflection, saying, "You totally have to do me, Deph. Maybe something in a..." She turned back to me, pointed to the smudges on her face, and asked, "Have I had these on my face the whole time?"

SIX

After Gigi and Serinda disappeared down the stairs, Annette wiped the smudges off her face with a kitchen towel, then turned to me. "You have to do me."

"Okay, but I've never been with a girl, so..."

"No." She rolled her eyes and sat across from me again, taking both of my hands into her own. This must be serious. "You have to do my hair."

"What? No. You're perfect." I tried to pull away. She wouldn't let go of my hands, her eyes pleading, so I slapped them away. Her hands, not her eyes. "Your hair is perfect," I said, slapping softly. We'd only been in a real fight once, and we were on the same side. Still, the girl had moves. She could probably take me.

"Defiance," she pleaded.

"No. Stop. I wouldn't even know where to begin. And are you forgetting the bird thing? You could end up with feathers for hair. Or Medusa hair. Or no hair at all."

"You had me at Medusa hair." She pressed her mouth together so hard, her dimples showed. Not in a good way. The disappointment was tangible when she turned to the only other witch in the room. "Minerva, you've got some mojo, right?"

"Um..."

"You have to do me."

"You have to stop putting it that way," I said with a giggle. Yes, I was twelve. "Besides, I need Minerva to go to the hospital and check on Leo."

The girl's eyes rounded to perfect, dark-lashed circles. "Leo?"

"Quinn. Why? Do you know him?" I asked, knowing full well she did.

"Leonard Quinn? I do. A little. He's in the hospital? Here?"

"I believe so, though they could've transferred him."

"What happened?"

Intrigued, Annette decided to explain. "Defiance got a message from him about male pattern baldness, but the message was glowing, and from that, she figured out he was in trouble. She could feel it across hundreds of miles."

"Ten miles," I corrected.

"A car engine fell on his leg while he was working on it. We got there just in time."

An audible gasp echoed around us. "Is... is he okay?" She started to bite her already horridly abused nails when she caught herself and started wringing her hands again.

Pride swelled in my chest. Not a lot. Not, like, a cup

size, but enough to increase my lung capacity a good half a liter.

"Would you mind checking on him for us?"

She bolted out of her chair. "Not at all. I'll go now."

"Well, it's still a bit early."

Annette grabbed her phone. "I'll check when visiting hours are."

"No worries," Minerva said, walking backward toward the front door. "If I'm too early, I'll just wait."

Annette winked at me from behind an impish grin.

I laughed and got up to walk Minerva to the entryway, where I raided a purse. Thankfully, it was my own. I tossed her my keys as she pulled on her coat. It hit her in the chest and fell to the floor. "Sorry. Here." I picked them up and handed them to her as she stuffed her hands into her gloves. "Take my car."

"Really? Thank you." She opened the door and said as she rushed out, "I'll text you with a status update, Sarru."

"Defiance. And thank you."

From what I could gather from Minerva's memories, he'd looked longingly at her almost as often as she'd looked longingly at him, so I didn't think I was setting him up for any kind of ambush. She was too shy to be a nuisance. That much I knew for certain.

The man's thinning hair must've made him look older than he was when we found him trapped under that engine. In contrast, his baby face would always make him look younger than his years. I scolded myself for not finding out his age sooner. Minerva was young and impressionable. And she'd almost died barely a day ago.

Then again, she was also a witch with at least some skill. Maybe I needed to trust her.

"Ah," Annette said when I walked back into the kitchen. "You read that off her, didn't you?"

"I did, but I have yet to figure out how I can read some people and not others."

"Okay, what about me?"

"What about you?"

She plopped her chin in a cupped hand. "What am I searching for?"

"Hmm," I hmmed as I refilled my cup, then sat down again. I narrowed my eyes. Looked into her soul.

"A first edition *Harry Potter and the Philosopher's Stone*."

"You already knew that. And I already know where to find one. I just can't afford it." She took off her glasses, then cupped her chin again, giving me access to her eyes. "What else?"

I drew in a deep breath, then gave in, concentrating. Nothing. "I have no idea. You've blocked me."

"I don't know how to block you."

"Then you aren't searching for anything." I took a sip and moaned aloud.

"Of course, I am. Everyone is. How did you do it with Ruthie?"

"Gigi. We'll all need to call her that if anyone is going to buy it as her nickname."

"That's your name for her. She's your grandmother. How about Georgi?"

"Oh. I like it."

"Great. Georgi, then. How'd you do it with her?"

I brushed a crumb off the table. "What do you mean?"

"Deph," she said, pursing her lips again in admonishment. "I saw what you did. You were getting into her mind even though she didn't want you to. It was like she had no choice."

I wrapped both hands around my cup and answered as honestly as I could. "I have no idea. I didn't mean to. It just sort of happened." When she didn't say anything, I added, "It was a huge violation, Nette. I will never do that again."

"Well, what if you need to? Like in an emergency?"

"Then maybe it'll just happen again. But for now..."

"Hey, girls," the chief said, walking in from the front door.

"Hey, Chief. Off work already?" He'd barely been gone an hour.

"I put out a few fires—metaphorically—and I called your insurance agent to come look at the damage. Place looks good, Annette."

"Thanks, Chief. Did you explain what happened to Officer Pecs?"

"You mean Officer Flynn?"

"Yes," she said, adding a snort. "I mean to say Officer... Paul Flynn?" When he only looked at her, she tried again. "John Flynn? George? Ringo?"

"Cory," he said, putting her out of her misery. And just in time, too. She'd run out of Beatles.

"Oh, right." She snapped her fingers. "I totally knew that. And how's his girlfriend?"

Gawd, she was good at interrogations. A born investigator.

When the chief crossed his arms and only stared at her, refusing to answer, she waved a hand. "Never mind. I'll ask her myself next time I see her."

"You do that."

When Serinda came up the stairs, we glanced in unison

toward her. She held out her arms with all the fanfare of a showman in the center ring, and said, "Ladies and gentleman, may I present to you, the lovely, the talented, the mysterious—"

"For Goddess's sake, Serinda," Gigi said, padding up the stairs.

Serinda giggled, then swept her arms toward the basement entrance, "Georgiana Rue Bishop."

A dark head popped up first, followed by the rest of Gigi. I hardly recognized her, and we gaped rather rudely for a solid minute.

Annette found her voice first. "Day-um!"

We rushed forward. Serinda stood back, her arms crossed, a satisfied smirk settling into place. She'd done it, and Gigi looked amazing.

"Gigi, Oh my God, you look incredible."

She wore the same cream gauze dress with golden threads, but the contrast of her now inky-black hair seemed to make it sparkle even more. That, combined with her cloudless blue eyes, was simply breathtaking. Gone was the elegant silvery-blonde bob. It had been replaced by sharp dramatic spikes and whimsical wisps around her beautiful face.

She glanced nervously at the chief. "Well, Houston? What do you think?" When he didn't answer, she assured him, "We can try something else. Serinda is much more adept at this than she used to be. Maybe something softer?"

"Ruthie," he said, breathless.

"Georgiana," Serinda said. "Or Gigi. Your choice."

"I don't know what happened here today, but I like it."

Relief washed over her, as evidenced by the minute release of tension in her shoulders. "Oh, thank the Goddess." She tugged self-consciously at the spiky locks behind her ear. "Because I love it. And I was worried..."

He stepped to her, his nearness emphasizing how many inches—or feet—he had on her. He took her into his arms, bent her back into a shallow dip, and pressed his mouth to hers.

"Chief!" I scolded, teasing them.

Annette cupped her chin and looked on dreamily.

When it became clear they were going to be a few minutes, I eased closer to Serinda. "May I ask you something?"

"Anything, Sarru."

I breathed a heavy sigh, and asked, "Is there a way I can interview the coven members about Gigi's passing?"

"Of course." She grabbed her phone. Perhaps to set something up?

"Bear in mind, I don't suspect anyone. Not at all. But perhaps someone let information slip about me to the wrong person, like Minerva did."

"You think the poisoning had something to do with you?"

"No. Maybe. I don't know. I'm just grasping at straws. But whoever killed her had to be able to get in and out unnoticed. A virtual impossibility with both Roane and Percival here."

She nodded, the lines of her face pulled in concern.

"Roane leaves the house, of course," I continued. "He has a life. But Percy is stuck here, and nothing gets past him." I was leaning against the kitchen counter, hands at my side, when a vine rose up and wrapped lovingly around my pinkie. I lifted it to my chest. It encircled my wrist and forearm, gave a soft squeeze, then shrank back to disappear into the wall.

"He feels guilty," Serinda said, watching the exchange.

"I think so, though he has no reason to." I looked up. "This was no one's fault but the person who did it."

The few vines that had bordered the room slid back into the walls. He disagreed.

Serinda tapped on her phone. "I'll set it up immediately."

The couple honeymooning in the middle of the kitchen broke apart at last. Gigi's grin fairly glistened when she gazed up at the chief. "If I'd known I would get that kind of response, I would've done this years ago."

The smile he gave her would've blinded a lesser witch. "You don't happen to have a nurse's uniform, do you?"

Gigi slapped him playfully on the arm. "Houston Dewayne, I think you've scandalized Defiance enough for one day."

He turned to us, his grin the very definition of mischief. "Sorry."

I laughed softly. "No, you're not."

The shrug he offered held no regrets. He handed me a file.

"What's this?"

"My investigation thus far."

Annette bounced up to get a look. "Into Ruthie's case?"

He nodded, his mischievous expression fading.

I opened the file and laid it on the island. It held his notes and little else. "This isn't a lot to go on."

He scrubbed his stubble with one hand in frustration. "Because I don't have a lot."

Gigi scooted in for a closer look, too, as the chief wrapped an arm around her. "Houston, it's not your fault. You can't possibly blame yourself."

"If anyone's to blame, it's me," Roane said, coming in from the back door. Fully clothed. And very wet. He smelled like pine and earth and rain. "I should've figured it out sooner."

"Nonsense. The only person to blame is the person who did it."

He lifted a shoulder, unconvinced, and nodded toward Gigi's guest. "Hi, Serinda."

"Mr. Wildes," she said, an appreciative slant to her mouth. It seemed everyone had a bit of a crush on the man.

I'd hoped for a different state of dress—or undress—when he came back from his commune with nature, but the fact that his wet shirt clung to every muscle he had sent my pulse into overdrive.

I filled my lungs and refocused on the issue at hand. "It had to be someone who knew Gigi well enough to be familiar with her habits. They had to know she ate that particular soup regularly."

"Maybe." He ran a hand through his wet hair, then shook it out, and I tried not to drool.

"Anything?" the chief asked him.

"Nothing." After hopping onto the counter, he lifted a booted foot into the sink to rinse off a thick layer of mud.

"Roane," Gigi said, appalled.

"Sorry, Ruthie." He started to get down. "I'll rinse off outside."

"What? No. Don't you dare." When he questioned her with a perfectly arched brow, she explained. "I don't care about the mud, sweetheart. I care about the fact that you've been out in this all night." She hurried to the laundry room and came back with a towel, which she wrapped around his shoulders. Then she rubbed those shoulders. The wide ones covered in muscles that flowed and ebbed with each movement.

Annette sighed aloud.

When the chief cleared his throat rather loudly, Gigi blushed and gestured me over. "Maybe you should do this part."

I stepped closer and took the towel to dry his hair. I squeezed a few of the shoulder-length locks, then found a dry corner and patted his face with it. He watched me from underneath lashes spiked and dark with wetness.

"Nothing?" I asked him.

"No one has entered or exited this house via the front or back doors besides us. And your dads, but I hardly think they put nitroglycerin in the flour canister."

"But it obviously rained last night," I said to him, gesturing toward his wet T-shirt and kilt. "Maybe it washed the scent away."

He shook his head. "I figured that out long before the rain."

"Then what were you doing all night?"

"Why? Were you worried about me, Ms. Dayne?"

It was the way he said my name that caused a ripple of desire to reverberate out from my core and lace along my skin. In my flustered state, I dropped the towel, and I gave him a half-hearted "oops" as I bent to retrieve it.

"Let me help you with that," Annette said, rushing over to help me with that.

We both picked it up and shamelessly tried for a peek under the kilt, since he had one foot in the sink and the other hanging over the edge of the counter. We rose slowly from the ground to give ourselves more time, but it was too dark. The goods were hidden by the shady physics of electromagnetic radiation and the visible spectrum of light disbursement. Damned shadows.

"So, nothing else of note?" the chief asked, and I could hear the humor in his voice.

"No." Roane finished with the first boot and tugged the towel out of our death grips to pat it dry. "Nothing directly connected to the explosion." He put his other foot in the sink and rinsed it off, too.

We immediately saw another opportunity but had nothing else to drop. Our gazes darted around the room, panic setting in. We only had so much time, but everything was either breakable or priceless, as Gigi had a few heirlooms here and there.

Annette pointed to the canister—the canister filled with nitroglycerin.

I gaped at her.

She winced, remembering the deadly substance inside, and offered me a sheepish grimace.

Before we could come up with a better plan, he finished and hopped off the counter, only in a very manly way, each movement somehow filled with sexual innuendo. Either that or I was projecting again.

"Wait," I said, when his words sank in. "Not directly connected to the explosion? So, then indirectly connected?"

He worked his jaw in thought as he strolled to the laundry room and tossed the towel into a basket. "I don't know. I'm still looking into it."

"Keep me in the loop," the chief said.

Roane nodded. "Back to Ruthie, what's the plan? How are we going to figure out who's doing this?"

Annette grabbed her notebook and found a list she'd made about all of the oddities of the case. "With everything that we know, it would have to be another witch, right?"

"Not necessarily," the chief said. "Had you been sick all day?"

"Not just that day. I'd been sick for a while. I didn't make the connection until... well, until that day. When I tasted the belladonna. But the more I think about it... it would take a pretty big dose to actually kill me, one that would be difficult to conceal. However, if I'd been receiving small doses for some time, it wouldn't take as much to kill me."

"And, of course, the mushrooms would've given it that extra kick," I said. "Serinda, no one was closer to her than the coven. Can you think of anyone who would've wanted to do her harm?"

"No." She crossed her arms in thought. "I can't imagine..."

"I should have picked up on the scent," Roane said. "Especially if it'd been going on for a while. I don't understand how I didn't."

"That's just it." I rubbed my temple. "How could someone—anyone—get past both you and Percy? It makes no sense."

"Unless..." Gigi looked up at the ceiling, aka her ex, and glared. "Unless it was Percy all along. He's been so bitter since that whole burning-him-alive thing."

Sometime in the sixties, Percy had gotten into dark magic the way addicts get into heroin. He couldn't stop and had begged Gigi to kill him. To put him out of his misery so he could do no more harm. She'd had to recruit her entire coven to perform the task. They'd burned him alive with a magical fire. But he'd never seemed bitter to me in the entire several days that I'd known him.

"Maybe you'll find something when you talk to the coven, Sarru."

"Defiance."

"You need to ask them what they're searching for. Compel them to open up."

"Wait, can I do that?"

"From what I understand," she said, giving Gigi a sideways glance, "you almost did last night."

"I'm sorry, Gigi."

"It's okay. I had no idea you could do that. I only told Serinda because it could work in our favor."

"Exactly," Serinda said. "Anyone who's just committed murder is going to be searching for something, right? They're going to want something. That's your in. Once you get in, you can get a read."

I decided to broach the subject again. "I hate to state the obvious, Gigi, but you're searching for something." When she didn't discourage me, I continued. "You're searching for your killer."

"Yes," she said, sinking into a chair and folding her hands in her lap.

The chief sat beside her. "Are you telling me Daffodil could see who killed you simply by looking?"

She lifted a shoulder. "It's possible."

"Then what's the hold-up, Ruthie? Let her inside."

"Because that's not my most sought-after desire, and there are simply some things my granddaughter does not need to know."

He sat back, astonished. "Ruthie Goode."

"Georgiana Bishop," I corrected. "And it's not a for-sure thing, Chief. Even if she let me in, it might not work. I'm still very new to this, and most people are searching for something known. A lost ring or a lost loved one. Something they once had. Gigi has no idea who did this, so it may not work either way."

He bit down, unconvinced, but he dropped it. I had a feeling Gigi would hear more on the subject later. She lifted her cup and took a sip of what had to be very cold coffee.

Then it hit me. The truth. The answer to everything. "It's Mr. Shoemaker! Why didn't I see it before?"

Gigi choked, her delicate cough so unlike my chainsaw imitation earlier. When she regained her composure, she dabbed a napkin at the corners of her mouth and insisted, "Mr. Shoemaker did not kill me."

"Okay, but who's to say he didn't try to blow us up?" I shook a fist in the direction of his house.

"Mr. Shoemaker did not try to blow us up."

She was not listening. "Gigi, he hates me."

Annette pointed and nodded. "He really does."

"He does not hate you, Defiance."

"The seventeen petitions he's filed with the city would argue otherwise."

"He's filed two petitions, and that does not mean he hates you."

"Seventeen. Two. Either way, he wants my head on a platter."

"He does not want your head on a platter."

I glared at his house. Metaphorically. It helped. "Thank the ghost of Marie Antionette beheadings are illegal."

Serinda's phone dinged. "Okay, it's all set. The coven will be here this afternoon, if that's good for you, Sarru."

"Defiance. And that's perfect."

"Oh!" Annette said, squirming in her chair. "I have a list of questions for the interviews."

I walked over, read a couple, then asked, "Annette, what does nail care have to do with my grandmother's murder?"

"They have amazing nails," she said, her defenses rising. "I just want to know who does them." She glanced at the oven. "And you need to call your dads. Tell them what happened. They'll never forgive you for not calling them immediately as it is."

She had a point. The fact that she was changing the subject didn't negate that.

I picked up my phone just as someone knocked on the front door.

"Parris and Harris," Roane said, heading toward the stairs that led to his apartment.

I understood. They were a lot, and I'd only known them a few days. I watched him descend the stairs, the view mouthwatering, then looked at Gigi. "Well?"

"Well what?"

"Let's introduce you."

"Now?" she asked, a flash of panic in her eyes.

"No time like the present," Serinda said.

Annette nodded. "That is how the saying goes. You can do it, Gigi," she said, trying the title out. "We're right here to back you up."

Gigi tucked a lock of black hair behind her ear. "All right, then."

Two things rushed over my skin at that moment—excitement and dread. What if it didn't work? What if they recognized her? What would Gigi do then? Hide in the basement for the rest of her life?

No. It would work. It had to.

I led the way to the front door. The fact that not one, not two, but four people were there to greet the Hamptons might have been overkill, but desperate times.

The minute I opened the door, Ink darted inside, followed by the adorable little blond.

Both Parris and Harris looked startled, but I couldn't tell if it was due to the cat or the kid. Parris had seen the light from my spell earlier. There were only a couple of explanations for that and, looking at her over-processed 'do and far too many dives under the scalpel, I was leaning toward a mental illness of some kind. But the odds of her being able to see the departed were still slim.

I beamed at them. "Hey, guys."

Harris spoke first. "Hi, Defiance. And... everyone." The rain was wreaking havoc on his short muddy curls.

Parris followed up with a hesitant, "We just wanted to check on you after what happened. Is everyone okay?"

"Please come in out of the cold." I opened the door wider. "We're fine, but there's someone I want you to meet."

"Oh?" They stepped inside.

I closed the door, then took Gigi's hand. "Georgiana, this is Parris and Harris Hampton. Our neighbors. On either side. It's a long story."

"It's nice to meet you," she said, holding out a hand.

They both stood blinking at her before Harris came to his senses. "Georgiana?" he asked, taking her hand.

"Bishop," she added with a nod. "Ruthie was my twin sister."

"Twin sister?" Parris said far too loudly. Her voice echoed off the walls. She cleared her throat and started over. "I'm sorry, did you say twin sister?"

"Yes," Serinda said, a challenge in her voice. The muscles on her face were drawn, and I got the distinct impression she didn't think much of the woman. "From Nantucket."

Parris snapped out of her stupor and took Gigi's hand. "Of course. The resemblance is uncanny. It's just, Ruthie never spoke about you."

"Yes, well, we grew apart." Very apart. "We weren't close for many years. Not until the end."

"I'm glad you two reunited." She held Gigi's hand in both of hers. "Ruthie was such an inspiration."

Gigi graced the woman with her best congenial smile and took back her hand. "In what way?"

"Well," she said, struggling for an answer, "in an inspirational way. The whole town loved her. Will you be living here, then? With Defiance?"

"Oh, goodness, no. Percy belongs to Defiance. Ruthie wanted her to have it. I'm just staying here until I find my own place."

I glanced at her in surprise. "Georgiana, you can stay here for as long as you want."

"Thank you, dear, but I think I should get my own place."

"Will you be keeping him, then?" Parris asked me. "Percival?"

Gigi was serious. I could tell. Would she really move out of her home?

"You are staying, right?" Parris asked. "I know you were entertaining the idea of returning to Arizona."

I refocused on her. "Yes, I'm staying for now."

"Oh, good," she said, seeming relieved. "More girls' nights."

"Exactly."

"We won't keep you," Harris said, backing toward the door. "It was very nice to meet you, Georgiana. Nice seeing you, girls. Chief." He gave a quick wave before heading out.

Parris couldn't seem to tear her gaze off Gigi and probably would've stood there gawking all day if Harris hadn't pulled her out the door.

"Bye, guys," she said, stumbling behind him. "Girls' night soon?"

"Absolutely," Annette said, closing the door. Once it clicked shut, she turned back to us, her turquoise glasses glistening in the low light. "Do you think they bought it?"

Serinda tapped an index finger over her lips in thought. "I wouldn't bet my life on it, but yeah. I think they bought it." She looked at Gigi askance.

Gigi, in turn, looked up at the chief. "You're more adept at these things with all of your training in interrogation. Did they buy it?"

"It's hard to say. Their nonverbals were all over the place."

Annette rolled her eyes. "I hate it when people can't keep their nonverbals in check."

SEVEN

You know you drink too much coffee if:
You run twenty miles on the treadmill
before you realize it's not plugged in.
—Meme

Serinda gave me access to the coven's private group pages before leaving, so I went upstairs to get to know the members a little better. To prepare for our meeting. And mostly to check out the more volatile members. There was one in every group. Sometimes more.

I propped up my pillows, sat on my bed, and opened my laptop, checking out the main group page first and fighting the urge to go to the attic. Why had I woken up there?

I recognized several members, having just met them a couple days prior. Thankfully, I would now be able to put names to the faces. Or at least try my best. The luncheon was all a blur at this point.

I read through about a year's worth of posts. It was an

active group, much like my other support group: My Ex is an Ass Anonymous. Most of the posts were about the daily life of a witch. Meditations and recipes and spells. Of the three male witches in the group, only one was super active online, a twenty-something named Theo. I remembered meeting him at the luncheon, so he was a member of the inner circle.

The Cove was for the thirteen members of the inner circle only, which was odd because counting me, there were sixteen people in the group. Maybe there were alternates? Admins?

After going back about a year and getting to know many of the more active members, I focused more on Gigi. Her posts were as elegant as she was. Even when she had to write something a little more admonishing, she did it with style. Gentle yet assertive. That was Gigi, all right.

Hearing footsteps, I looked up to see Roane headed my way. I straightened and waited, but he only nodded a greeting, propped up the other two pillows against the headboard, and sat on the bed next to me. He crossed his ankles, opened his laptop too, and went to work. Like we did this every day. Like we were a real couple just living our lives, apart but never far away from each other. It was comfortable with him. As much as I wanted to reach over and cuddle, just sitting there made me feel warm and safe and content.

I hid a smile and went back to my research, trying to suss out who might have a grudge against Gigi. Or who she may have inadvertently offended. But Gigi was too good. Even a couple of times when she could have come down hard on a member who broke this rule or that one, she handled it with diplomacy and graciousness, never belittling anyone. And she somehow managed to make the member feel edified and very much a valued member of the group. Heads of state could learn a lot from her.

As far as wanting what Gigi had, Serinda was next in line to the throne of doyenne, so that would not be an incentive for anyone to hurt my grandmother. But both women were treated with the utmost reverence. No one seemed poised to take over their positions. Nor did anyone want to. If anything, the group would be lost without them.

A little while after Roane came in, Annette joined us. She snuck in and took the chair with the only-worn-a-day selection, pushing the clothes aside so she could squeeze into the overstuffed chair to work. She alternated between her notebook and laptop, making notes and jotting down ideas, and creating any number of new lists.

I resisted the urge to lean over to see what Roane was working on, but I did seem to be gravitating toward him. First by easing closer. Then by touching knees.

Not long after Annette came in, Gigi joined us as well. She took the freshly washed chair, pulled up an ottoman, and started tapping on her laptop as well.

Roane got up and made a fire in my fireplace. The giant room warmed up in no time. When he climbed back onto the bed, he sat even closer to me. Our elbows brushed every so often, and I realized I was in a special kind of heaven. I wanted every day for the rest of my life to be like this. Working with my family in front of a fire. The Waltons had the right idea.

The past few days had been long. And trying. And eye-opening. But here we were. Stronger than ever. Doing our thing.

Annette left first, mentioning something about getting us some lunch. Gigi left to help her. Roane left soon after that, but before he did so, he took my hand and kissed the inside of my wrist.

I could still feel the warmth of his mouth when I made my way downstairs a little while later. Annette was back with lunch. I found the receipt. She'd used my credit card, thank goodness. We were still working out how she was going to get paid at the moment. She had no income to speak of. Hopefully, Breadcrumbs, Inc. would be successful. Otherwise, we could both be living on the streets. Houseless creatures searching for sustenance and shelter.

Well, she would be. I'd inherited a fortune, which was another thing. I'd soon be able to hire a housekeeper. And a gardener. And a chauffeur named Jeeves who could drive a stick, because the Bug was a standard.

"This smells amazing."

"Hopefully everyone's good with Italian."

"Who wouldn't be?" I asked, grabbing a bowl for the salad. "Minerva texted. Leo is doing great. They're saying it's a miracle he didn't lose his leg."

"Oh, thank goodness."

"She's going to grab some things for him from his house. She still can't go back to her own, what with it being a crime scene and all, so we might have to loan her a few things for now."

"Okay, but she can't have my Blue Oyster Cult T-shirt."

"I think it'll be safe. Anyway, I texted her back. A thumbs-up. Simple. Short. Almost elegant in its delivery." I shook salad out of a package and into a bowl, noting she'd also bought new salad dressings, just in case ours had been doctored with a deadly poison or a high explosive.

Annette lifted out a foil pan of spaghetti bolognaise. "I'm so proud of you, Deph."

"I know, right? Ever since I learned where to find the

emojis, I've been unstoppable. It's like a whole new world opened up."

She deadpanned me. Hard.

"We should take a plant when we go see him," I said, shrugging off her indifference. "Something in green."

"Deph, you did that. You saved that man's life."

I smiled. All over. Every cell in my body morphed into smiley face emojis. Trillions and trillions of smiley face emojis, coursing through my body. I was getting that good at them. In all honesty, these powers may take some getting used to, but they'd helped me save a life. Possibly more than one. Can't beat that with a hockey stick.

"Food!"

We turned to see my dads walk in. I hurried over to give them a hug. I'd just seen them the night before—they'd left before the big proposal and the even bigger explosion—but it seemed like days.

I leaned in, but the younger of the two, the one I called Papi despite his clear lack of Latino heritage, held up a hand to block me.

I stopped short and showed my palms in surrender.

"You're in trouble."

"When is she not?" Annette asked, not helping.

I was forty-five years old, and the thought of being in trouble with my dads still caused a prickling of dread along my spine. "What'd I do?"

They turned in unison, as though the movement were choreographed, and looked at the oven behind them.

"Really, *cariño*?" the older one asked. Dad was one of those Latinos who put the sigh in *le sigh*, with his silver-fox hair and well-maintained beard. Both of my adoptive fathers were hotties, but Dad was so striking. So debonair. So... angry.

Uh-oh. He'd said cariño rather than *Cariña*, his pet name for me. His usual cariña was a term of endearment born from our love of star gazing when I was a kid. He'd named me after one of the brightest stars in the Milky Way, Carina. Only, with his unique Spanish accent, he pronounced the name with a tilde over the *ñ*. But the fact that he used the real deal meant someone was in trouble. Probably me. Yeah. Definitely me.

Papi, part Viking, part peace maker, turned an admonishing frown on me. "Why didn't you call us?"

My dads were so rarely upset with me, it took me by surprise.

Roane walked in to witness my dressing down, and a warmth spread over my face. Only my dads could make me feel like a teenager getting caught sneaking into the house after curfew. Roane stopped at the top of the stairs and leaned back against the wall to watch, hiking one booted foot up on the wall. Gigi walked up behind him and took in the scene.

"Papi, what could you have done? I would've woken you up for nothing. We were fine."

"Someone tried to kill you and you're fine?"

"Not me, specifically. Just, you know, whoever decided to bake first. Annette drew the short straw."

She was busy opening containers and arranging a mini lunch buffet. She sprinkled parmesan on top of the spaghetti. "I was making a pumpkin roll. It ended up in my hair. Are you hungry, Georgi?"

Georgi. Hearing Annette call her Georgi reminded me we had a lot of explaining to do, but Papi noticed her first.

"Girl!" He walked over to her, his arms wide. "You're stunning."

She walked into his embrace, clearly enjoying the lurve.

"Actually, it's Georgiana now," I said. "Georgiana Bishop, Ruthie's long-lost twin sister."

"Oh, I like it." He set her at arm's length. "And it's genius."

"Gorgeous, *tesoro*," Dad said, and I was grateful for the distraction.

The chief walked in then, shook Dad's hand, and made a beeline for his fiancée. Papi stepped aside with a sweep of his arm. Always the gentleman.

Annette's dimple appeared. "How is it you always show up when we have food?" she asked the chief.

"Twenty-four-hour surveillance." When her eyes rounded, he laughed softly. "Or perfect timing. Take your pick."

"Well, come and get it."

"We'll finish this later," Dad said, his handsome face stern, and I wondered who'd ratted me out.

My shoulders sagged, and Roane laughed softly. The sadist.

We each made a plate and went into the formal dining room, gorgeously appointed with the same black walls and trim as most of the rest of the house. Yet it was bright. The large window on one wall offered enough light to give the room a fresh, airy feel.

"What are we doing about the explosion?" Papi asked the chief just as Ink jumped on the table.

He got a noodle from Annette's plate of spaghetti before she could stop him.

She laughed and shooed him away, jumping back when Samuel appeared beside her, looking on in curiosity. "H-hello there," she said, offering him a tentative smile. "You must be Samuel." He nodded, but he seemed much more interested in the food. "Good heavens, you're beautiful."

The blond-haired, blue-eyed toddler dressed in Puritan garb offered her a shy grin and then vanished.

She looked at me, and I knew her heart was lost. "He's adorable, Deph."

"I agree."

My dads looked at each other, and I realized we had more explaining to do. Mainly about how Annette could now see into the veil.

When they looked at me askance, I just nodded. "We think it's because I turned her into a bird."

"Then turn me," Papi said. "I want to see him, too."

I snorted and scooped up a bite of tortellini mantecati when a loud bang shook the table and reverberated off the walls.

Every set of eyes turned to the foot of the table where Roane sat.

He stood and held up a hand. "Stop. Don't eat anything."

I dropped my fork immediately, eyed my plate, then sighed aloud. "You've got to be kidding."

"Has anyone taken a bite?"

"I did," the chief said, easing away from the table. He stood and pulled Gigi back from it, and I could hardly blame him. For all we knew, it contained high explosives.

My dads just sat there, confused, but Annette and I eased back as well. I motioned for them to back up as Roane leaned over and sniffed his plate. He walked around the table, examining the plates, then strode into the kitchen.

We followed en masse, waiting as he checked out the food.

When he turned back to us holding the container of parmesan, his gaze landed on Annette. "Where did you get this?"

"I... I just bought it at Bella Verona. Everything here is either from the store or from Bella Verona. I didn't use anything from the house." She stepped closer. "Why, Roane? What's wrong?"

He exchanged a quick glance with the chief, shook the jar, then said, "Arsenic."

I practically shouted when I asked, "Arsenic?" I looked around at the shocked faces. What the hell was going on?

"That's... that's not possible." Annette was so flustered, I felt sorry for her. "I literally just bought it."

I walked over and draped an arm over her shoulders. "Annette, you have to stop trying to kill everyone."

"But... I..."

"I'm kidding. This is not your fault."

"First the flour, now the parm?" She blinked up at me. "I... I would never hurt anyone, Deph. You know that."

Guilt consumed me. I shouldn't have teased her. "We know that. No one thinks you did this."

The chief stepped closer. "I'm sorry, hon, but I'm going to have to place you under arrest for attempted murder." When the entire room gaped at him, he gave it a moment, then recanted. "Not really. I just wanted to see your reaction. That kind of shock is hard to fake."

"Because I'm not faking!" She hiked her glasses onto the top of her head and rubbed her eyes before returning them. "I swear, Chief, I would never hurt anyone. I don't even know where to get arsenic. Or nitroglycerine."

"Georgi?" Roane said, his expression askance.

She shook her head. "I have no idea, sweetheart."

He lifted the jar and looked at the clear bottom, giving it a shake, and his brows slid together.

"What?" I asked, easing closer.

"There's no powder at the bottom." He lifted out a sample and tasted it.

I stared at him, alarmed. "Should you do that?"

The chief took the bottle when he was finished and sniffed it, shaking his head. "It's definitely not cheese."

"Can you have it analyzed?" Roane asked him. "And the flour?"

"Of course."

Annette pressed a hand over her mouth. "Did someone spike it at the store before I bought it? How is that even possible? How would they know what I was going to buy?"

"You don't understand." Roane's mouth tightened across his face. "No one spiked it. It *is* arsenic. It looks like parmesan, but it's 100 percent ratsbane."

"Ratsbane?" I asked.

"Arsenic," he answered with a shrug.

Annette sank into a chair.

Dad walked closer to examine the contents as well. "So, you're saying this isn't parmesan-spiked arsenic. It's just arsenic."

"Exactly."

"How is that possible?"

When Roane looked at Annette, everyone else followed suit. Even me, but not to accuse her of anything. She would never.

She shook her head, her jaw hanging loose, her expression a thousand miles away. "I don't know."

"I do know one thing for certain," I said to the group. "There are far too many poisonings in this house. But Gigi was poisoned before we got here. Annette couldn't have had anything to do with that, and the events have to be connected. Right, Chief?"

The chief's expression turned grave. "I learned a long

time ago, Daffodil, not to jump to conclusions. We need to look at the evidence and go from there. I'll need to ask you a few questions, Annette."

"Of course." She turned to face us, but her gaze went far beyond the occupants of the room. She was in shock. She'd had little to no sleep. She'd been abducted and had a building dropped on her and had been turned into a bird. She'd had a hard couple of days.

I sat beside her and pulled her into a hug. The fact that she let me spoke volumes.

"Chief, can we do that later? I think Annette might need a break."

"Absolutely."

"No, I'm okay," she said, reaching over and patting my face. "I'd love to answer questions. I just don't think I have any."

"Questions?" I asked, teasing.

"Answers." Tears shimmered between her lashes, making her gray eyes appear even stormier. Even cloudier.

I squeezed tighter, totally taking advantage.

WE TOOK the party to Red's. Annette and I rode with my dads, the chief brought Gigi, and Roane followed in his truck. He was being very secretive, very protective, and I couldn't help but wonder if something else was going on.

We took a table near the window, but Roane trailed behind us and stayed outside, his jaw tense as he scanned the area. He wore a thin leather jacket despite the cold and dark sunglasses despite the clouds.

I texted him when we sat down. *You know you can join us.*

He stood against a building across the street, his ankles crossed, the picture of nonchalance. I watched as he took out his phone and couldn't help but notice his expression soften when he saw my text. A warmth spread throughout me.

He texted back. *I see more from here.*

What's going on?

What do you mean?

You're on high alert. Why?

You mean besides random explosions and near poisonings?

...yes

The wolves are restless.

Like metaphorically?

He started to text back, but something down the street caught his attention. He stopped and leveled his razor-sharp gaze on something—or someone—beyond my line of sight. After stuffing his phone back in his pocket, he lifted his collar and headed out.

So much for that conversation. Why would the wolves be restless? What did they have to do with any of this?

The server, a fresh-faced kid with floppy chestnut hair, handed out menus.

"Just coffee," Annette said to him, but the last thing she needed was more caffeine. The girl had to get some rest.

"How about decaf?" I asked her.

She blinked in confusion. "I don't understand."

"You're taking a nap when we get back."

"But decaf is the devil's juice."

"I know, but someone has to drink it." I looked up at the server. "Two decafs, please."

"Sure thing," he said with a chuckle.

Everyone else ordered their drinks as I perused the

menu, suddenly starving, but Annette sat staring into the abyss. Or into the kitchen. It was hard to say for certain.

I was about two seconds away from deciding on the chicken broccoli alfredo when the Cuban sandwich with sweet potato fries caught my eye. Damn it. I was so bad at making decisions. Either that or the man sitting two tables down was using up all of my brain cells.

I looked over. A man in a baseball cap and a tan tactical jacket with the collar turned up to cover his ears sat at a table alone. And he was desperately searching for something. I could feel the desperation on the air, hot and urgent, but I couldn't see what it was he wanted. The fact that he was in agony drew me closer to him. No, wait, my feet drew me closer. I'd stood and walked over to him.

"Cariña?" Dad said, but I kept walking.

Without asking permission, I sat across from him. I startled him. He looked up at me, his brown eyes red-rimmed, his dark skin streaked with salt from the tears that had dried on his cheeks.

"What are you searching for?" I asked him, praying he'd let me in. I didn't know a lot about my powers yet, but I did know they only led me to the direst situations. To people in the direst circumstances.

His expression morphed from shock to downright hatred. He wrapped a large hand around my wrist. "Did you send it?"

"Did I send what?"

He jerked me across the table, wrenching my shoulder. The edge dug into my rib cage, but I didn't try to move back. He could dislocate my shoulder at this point. Or break a couple of ribs. And he clearly missed the very large police chief sitting nearby and the two very protective dads.

Papi jumped up first, shouting a thunderous "Hey!" as he hurried over.

The room fell silent, and every set of eyes focused on us.

The man didn't move, his sneer implacable. The stuff of legend.

Dad stood, too, but the chief was actually the one I was worried about. I didn't want this guy arrested. He was searching for something and, based on recent experience, ignoring that could cost someone their life.

"Let her go," Papi said, literally getting in the man's face. "Now."

"What is this about?" the chief asked.

"It's okay, Papi. Chief." I held up a hand to halt the proceedings, wherever they may have led. This was my fault. I'd leaped before looking again. "It's okay," I said to him. I put my free hand over the one attached to my wrist. "I didn't send anything. Can you explain what you're looking for?"

The man finally noticed the chief standing there in full uniform and let me go. Tears shimmered in his eyes. Dad lifted me out of the chair like I weighed nothing and took my place to stare the man down.

"It's okay," I repeated. "There's been a misunder-standing."

Even surrounded by three rather large and very protec-tive males, the man didn't seem the least bit scared. He grabbed his ticket as he rose, shoved past Papi, and headed toward the register.

I realized Roane had been running to the scene. He barged into the restaurant and practically skidded to a halt when he saw me. Then he questioned me with a slight tilt of his head.

"I need that man's name," I said softly.

His gaze drifted to the man paying, and he nodded, his gaze wary, and stepped closer to the register.

The minute I sat down, Annette grabbed my arm. She must've missed the part where the man had nigh wrenched it out of its socket.

"What's going on?" she asked. "What happened?"

The chief and my dads took their seats.

"I need to know who that guy is."

"Why?" She leaned in and drunk-whispered, "Did you get something?"

"I don't know. He's searching for something. Something very valuable. I just don't know what."

"See? You are psychic."

"I'm not psychic."

"You'll do great at the séance tomorrow."

The reminder caused my stomach muscles to clench painfully. "No, I won't. You're the psychic, remember?"

"Oh, right." She put two fingers on her temples to concentrate. "Okay, I can't be 100 percent, but I think his name starts with an R. Or a T." Her lids flew open, and she whispered, "Or both. I think those are his initials."

If I weren't so worried for the man, I may have giggled at her theatrics. "Okay, thanks. Roane is going to find—"

"I'm on it." She stood and headed toward the register, and I could only pray she wouldn't mess up Roane's plan. At least she'd snapped out of her stupor. It was probably the decaf. Her system reported an error and had to reboot.

"What was that about?" the chief asked.

My dads were still glaring at the man's back, making sure Roane got a name for the guy.

Gigi came to my rescue before I could explain. "Her powers, Houston. She can't control where they take her any more than you can control the rising and setting of the sun." She patted my hand. "Are you okay, dear?"

"I am. Thank you, Gigi. But that man is not." I looked at the chief. "Do you know him?"

He shook his head. "He's not a local."

"I shouldn't have just sat down and started questioning him like that. His reaction was totally my fault."

Dad put down the spoon he'd been stirring his coffee with a little more forcefully than necessary. "That did not give him the right to accost you, Cariña. You understand that, right?"

I hopped up, walked around the table, and hugged him from behind. "I know, Dad." I did the same to the other man who raised me. "I love you guys so much."

He squeezed my arms, pulling me closer. "We love you more."

Laughing, I kissed his cheek, then looked over just in time to see Annette wedge her way between a pastry display and the man, conveniently as he was signing his credit card receipt. She practically shoved him aside to hand the cashier a dollar. "Here you go, Louise."

Though confused, the cashier took it and stuffed it into her apron. "My name's not Louise."

"Don't spend it all in one place."

When Annette jostled him again, her boobs the only obstacle in an otherwise expertly executed sting, the man stopped and glared at her. She couldn't have been more obvious if she'd been a bull sipping tea in a china shop, but she didn't break character. Goddess bless her.

Roane stood off to the side, pretending to wait his turn in line. When he lifted a hand to his forehead, I could only imagine it was to hide the grin he was fighting tooth and nail.

"Sorry," she said to the man before traipsing back to the table.

He watched her, then scowled at the lot of us, nigh setting us on fire, before leaving.

Louise, on the other hand, melted upon seeing Roane at her register. He nodded a greeting, then ordered a coffee to go. Louise was more than happy to accommodate.

"Were you right?" I asked Annette when she sat back down. "About R and T being his initials?"

Her satisfied smirk evaporated, and she suddenly needed to wipe invisible crumbs off her lap.

I took that as a *so close*.

Roane borrowed a chair from the next table and sat beside me, drinking his to-go coffee while we ordered lunch. Then the inevitable happened. The server got to me. Thus, I had a decision to make. I'd been waffling. It was a big decision. On the one hand, the pasta sounded delicious. On the other, the sandwich was calling to me like a siren in the sea.

Roane cut in. "We'll have the chicken broccoli alfredo and the Cuban."

"With sweet potato fries!" I added.

"With sweet potato fries." When I pinned him with a look of wonder, he lifted a shoulder. "We can share."

"How did you... can you read minds?"

He gave me a lingering once-over. "No, Ms. Dayne. I've told you. I cannot read your mind."

I wasn't entirely certain I believed him.

EIGHT

I don't think I get enough credit
for doing all of this unmedicated.
—Meme

The chief interviewed Annette as we ate, asking her things like: *Where did you get the food from? Did you see anything suspicious? Was anyone following you? Have you bought any arsenic lately?*

Annette hadn't been kidding. She had no answers. Nothing that would shed even an ounce of light onto the subject.

Gigi seemed to grow more introspective the longer the chief talked to Annette. Or worried, maybe. She kept eyeing Annette with suspicion, but she couldn't believe my BFF would try to harm anyone. Then her gaze would bounce to Roane, like they had a secret of some kind, and my curiosity rose to new, loftier heights.

Satisfied with Annette's innocence, the chief closed his

notebook, gave Gigi a kiss on the cheek, and rose to go back
to work.

My dads left to go antiquing. After all, those antiques
weren't going to buy themselves. They would soon have
enough to open their own museum.

And at last, I got the chance to confront Roane and
Annette. "Well? What was the guy's name?"

"Joaquin Ferebee," Roane said.

"Anything else?" Gigi asked.

"Only that his adrenaline was off the charts."

"You could tell?" Annette asked.

He ate another fry and nodded. "And his pulse was over
120."

"That's dangerously high," I said, biting my already
abused lip. I needed another nervous habit.

"Did you notice anything else unusual?" Gigi asked.

I glanced between both Roane and Annette. "Any clues
as to what he was searching for?"

"No. Nothing that—" Roane stopped suddenly and
looked out the window, so naturally the rest of us did as
well.

I was busy scanning the crowd outside—tourist season
was in full swing—when I heard a soft gasp from Gigi.
Annette and I turned to look at her, but Roane lowered his
head. Coiled his muscles. Dropped onto all fours, like he
was about to burst through the window and pounce.

Gigi's expression turned to one of pure fear, and she
eased back from the table.

"What is it?" When she slowly rose to her feet, I asked
again. "Gigi, what's wrong?"

"Roane," she said, her voice a scalpel in the dull hum of
the eatery's patrons, "Defiance first."

He continued to watch as my gaze darted from tourist to

tourist, searching for whatever—whomever—he was staring down. I followed his line of sight, and for the briefest of seconds, spotted a man in a black coat. Shoulder-length, solid white hair. Eyes so dark they were like inkwells.

Before I could register anything else about him, a tall woman crossed in front of the window and, for the briefest of seconds, I lost sight of him. When I looked at the same spot, he'd disappeared into the crowd. Literally vanished in front of my eyes.

Roane emitted an inhuman growl, giving away his supernatural status, and I weighed the pros and cons of putting a hand on his shoulder to calm him. I figured it could go one of two ways. He could snap out of it or he could snap at me. Either would be preferential to him jumping through the window, though surely he wouldn't.

"Roane," Gigi said with a hiss, and he finally stopped.

He stood and turned to her.

"Defiance," she ordered.

He nodded, tossed two hundred-dollar bills on the table, and ushered us all toward the back.

"Wait," I said, trying to grab the money. "My dads already paid."

But he took me by the arm and led us through the kitchen—much to the surprise of several employees—and out the back door. The crisp wind stole my breath. It cut instantly to the bone, and Gigi's sharp intake proved she wasn't immune either.

Roane tore off his jacket and wrapped it around her as he led us to his truck. He kept a close vigil on our path, checking over his shoulder every few seconds. When we got to the truck, he helped Gigi into the front seat as Annette and I slid into the back.

"Well, that explains it," Roane said when he climbed

into the cab.

"What?"

"The wolves." He took a moment to scan the area one more time, then started the truck. "Why they've been restless."

"Okay, then why? Who was that?"

His head whipped around to me. "You saw him?"

"The man with white hair and black eyes? He was hard to miss, though I only caught a glimpse."

Annette crossed her arms over her chest. "How did I miss him?" In all fairness, the top of her head barely reached my chin. It could've been a height thing.

Gigi turned back to me. "How did they find you?" Fear reverberated out of her, becoming palpable in the enclosed space. "The protection spell should have cloaked your powers. They should never have been able to lock on to you. I don't understand."

Roane pulled onto the busy street and headed home.

"Guys, seriously, who was that? Why is it such a big deal?"

"He's a hunter," Gigi said, her pallor ashen.

Roane took a sharp left onto Chestnut. "I need to get back."

"And do what?" I asked. "He's hunting me? Is that what you're saying?" When no one answered, I raised my voice. "Let's say he is. What of it? What is he going to do? And what are you going to do, Roane? Fight him to the death?"

The muscles in his jaw flexed as he pulled into Percy's drive.

Still no answers. His mind was racing a thousand miles an hour, his scowl distant, distraught, while Gigi seemed to be lost in the fantasies worrying her soft brow.

When he put the truck in park, the doors unlocked, and

Roane went for the door handle.

Without thought, I put my left hand on my door and drew a spell on the air with my right. The doors locked, trapping us inside.

Roane tried the door, then looked at me in the rearview.

"I want at least three answers before anyone leaves. I don't think that's too much to ask."

"We need to get you inside," he said, his voice a low warning.

"Then answer my questions."

"Defiance..."

"Roane..." I leaned closer. "I can do this all day."

He released a heavy sigh and laid back his head. "I need to get back."

"Why? Just answer that."

"Because he's a hunter, dear," Gigi said, as though that explained everything. She'd warned me about them before, when she first told me about my powers, but it had seemed like a fairy tale. All the talk of warlocks and hunters and black magic.

"And what do hunters do, exactly?"

Roane turned back to me, his expression almost sad when he said, "They hunt."

"I gathered that from the title. They hunt what?"

"All kinds of things, but in this case, they hunt you."

I'd gathered that as well, based on the urgency, but it didn't answer the most pertinent question. "And again, I ask why? Why would a hunter be after me?"

Gigi expelled a long breath. "We've been over this, Defiance. Because you're a charmling."

"Yes. I know. I get that, but why?" My frustration was growing by leaps and bounds. "A hunter hunts for a reason, right? What would he have to gain?"

Roane rubbed his brow, then condensed the problem into a nice, tidy nutshell. "Hunters work for warlocks. They're made by warlocks, actually. Warlocks control charmlings. They have for hundreds of years. Whenever a charmling comes into her powers naturally, when a blood heir inherits her magics, they're almost always woefully unprepared. The hunter grabs her up, takes her to the warlock, and she is either forced to work for said warlock, or a ceremony is performed to transfer her powers to another witch, one whom the warlock can control."

"The blood heir dies in the process," Gigi added. "And now they know we have one in Salem."

"Does he know it's Deph?" Annette asked. "That she's a charmling? Is that why he followed us to the café?"

Roane's gaze slid past us. "I don't know yet. I'm not convinced he followed us. He may have simply been scoping out the area when we showed up."

"And you felt him?" I asked.

"Yes. I sensed the dark magic. I've never felt power like that before. It's like yours, only dark."

"How long has he been here?"

"The wolves sensed a presence in town a few days ago, so my gut tells me he's just fishing. Otherwise, he would've been sniffing around the house. But now... there's simply no way to tell what he knows, which is why I need to get back out there."

"But what drew him here in the first place?"

"I don't know," he said, his voice little more than a growl. Whether his frustration stemmed from the hunter or me was hard to tell.

Gigi put a hand on his arm, her own mind seeming to swim in worry and doubt if her expression was any indication. "Roane, when Defiance first regained her powers a few months ago, she was vulnerable for an entire day. Could they have felt the surge then? Before she learned to camouflage her magics with the protection spell?"

"That would be my guess. Otherwise, why show up now? But I need to hunt him down to find out for sure."

"And I ask again," I asked again. "To do what? To what end?"

He turned around as much as the seat would allow. "Are you concerned for him? For a thing who would just as soon kill you as look at you? Once they're made, they're no more human than a demon is."

Admittedly, I was more concerned for Roane. "You can't know that."

"Wait, demons are real?" Annette swept the area around us with a wary gaze.

"I can, actually. You must understand, Defiance. They're controlled by the warlocks who created them. They have no say. No qualms. No morals or reservations about doing the right thing." He leaned closer. "They aren't like us."

"So, how often does a blood heir inherit powers? How many heirs are there?"

"There's no way of knowing," Gigi said. "In fact, it was assumed for many years the original bloodline had died out. That is, until you were born, Defiance." Her face softened at the memory. "Before you, there hadn't been a true blood heir in decades. And even if there were blood heirs walking around out there, the witch holding the power would have to die for the magics to be transferred to one of them. The warlocks won't allow that power to escape. Each time an aging charmling grows weak, the warlock enlists a younger, stronger witch to take her place. So the magics are never set free to seek out a rightful heir, so to speak."

"Naturally, the older witch dies in the process," I said, trying not to let my revulsion for the process show.

"Yes. That's how it's been done over and over for centuries."

"So, if the charmling dies before the power has been transferred to another witch—"

"Presumably, a blood heir will inherit it. If there are any left."

I sat back in thought. "Is that what happened with me? A charmling just happened to die at the same time I was born?"

She lifted a frail shoulder. "It would seem so."

"You do realize the odds of that are astronomical."

"I do. And I've pondered that very subject often over the years. It could be that someone knew you were a blood heir and somehow managed to kill a charmling when you were born."

"Who could possibly know that?"

She held up a finger. "That's not the hardest part."

"What is?"

"Killing a charmling," Roane said.

"Like I've told you, dear, charmlings are very well protected, most often by very dark magics. For one to die of natural causes, much less be killed, speaks volumes to the power of the being who did it."

"Okay, then who has that kind of power?"

Her gaze flitted to Roane.

"Oh, come on, Gigi. We've come this far."

"It's just... Roane and I have discussed that very thing. The way we see it, there's only one person it could've been. One person with the power and the knowledge to pull something like that off."

Annette and I both held our breaths and leaned closer.

Gigi hesitated, then said softly, "Your father."

I straightened in surprise. "My... my father? But you don't know who he was?"

She shook her head. "I'm not even sure your mother knew, truth be told, and I'm guessing he wanted it that way."

"Why?"

"Maybe he had plans for you? Maybe he's a warlock and wanted you for himself? The fact that you were born into a long line of witches could not have been a coincidence. Only a legacy witch would know what you were. What to do with you. How to protect you. We think whoever your father was, he chose your mother on purpose, knowing her family connections."

"But why not come for me when I was born? My own mother almost killed me to get the powers I possess. Why let that happen?"

"She would've been weaker," Roane said. "We're just guessing, but your mother would've been weaker than you. Easier to control than you would've been."

Gigi nodded. "He's right. A legacy witch may be able to possess your powers, but she will never be as strong as a blood heir. Maybe he wanted her to take them so he could then take control of her. We just don't know, Defiance."

"Can you unlock the doors now?" Roane asked. "Percy is an added layer of protection for all of you, and I need to find the hunter."

I dismissed the spell with a twitch of my fingers and the doors unlocked.

Roane climbed out, then went around to help Gigi.

Annette hesitated, scanned the area one more time, then lunged out her door and hightailed it toward Percy's front entrance.

We followed at a slower pace. "So, hunters are real, but chasing rogue charmlings can hardly be a full-time job. What else do they do?"

"Anything the warlock wants them to do," Gigi said.

"Wet work mostly," Roane added, putting it more bluntly. "They're trained assassins first and foremost. But they're also good at collections. You don't ever want to be indebted to a warlock."

"Wait." I stopped. "Could he have caused the explosion?"

Roane shook his head. "No. I checked. I kept losing his scent at Bridge and Webb, but he was nowhere near the house. Even so, he would never try to kill a charmling."

"Okay, but what about those around her? Those, say, protecting her?"

They exchanged glances again, and Gigi nodded. "That he would do."

"Wait a minute," I said, narrowing my field of vision to focus solely on my grandmother. "You told me when I first came here that hunters had been dispatched the day I was born. That they would kill me in a heartbeat."

She arched a graceful brow and brushed at her sleeve. "Did I?"

"Gigi. Why would you tell me that?"

"Two reasons. I was trying to incentivize you. To help you get up the protection spell. It's like a shield."

"I know what it's like. And two?"

"Because they *would* kill you in a heartbeat, just not out of the blue like that. They would never risk all that power slipping away. They would first take you to their warlock so he could perform the ceremony to transfer it. Then they would kill you. It's a process."

That sucked. Though I knew she was exaggerating. The

ceremony would kill me regardless. The hunter wouldn't have to. "There's something we haven't considered. What if he's not here for me? You said it yourself, charmlings have tried to escape their warlocks, right? Maybe one escaped and came here to Salem."

"That would be a horse-sized coincidence pill to swallow."

"But it's possible he's after another charmling? Or not after a charmling at all, right?"

Roane helped Gigi with her coat.

"I suppose," she said. "If a charmling escapes her warlock and, in turn, her protective coven, other hunters would swoop in and try to grab her for their warlocks unless she's powerful enough to disperse her magical fingerprints, as it were. It has happened, but they are always found. Sadly, charmlings are both the most powerful and most vulnerable witches in the preternatural world."

"No offense, Gigi, but your world is messed up. And warlocks suck."

"Yes, they do. Not as much as vampires, but—"

"Wait, vampires are real, too?" Annette asked.

Gigi chuckled. "Only metaphorically."

We headed for the kitchen as Roane checked out the house to make sure no one had entered while we were gone. "Are warlocks always male?" I asked Gigi.

"Not at all. Your great-great-aunt Petunia was a warlock. Clearly, she was the black sheep of the family."

"Clearly."

She stopped and faced me. "And there are some warlocks who are kind at heart or who use their extreme gifts benevolently. To become a warlock, however, one must master the black arts. That usually denotes a dark heart."

"Do you know any warlocks?"

She bowed her head and continued toward the kitchen. "I've... I've known one or two."

"Can I meet them?"

"No."

"Can I meet them if I wear a disguise?"

"No."

Annette stayed close behind us. So close, in fact, she ran into me. Twice.

"It's all good," Roane said, walking back to us after his inspection.

"Excellent." Gigi padded past him. She touched his arm, and he bent down to let her kiss him on the cheek. "I'll be downstairs doing some research."

"Let me know if you need anything."

She nodded and disappeared around a corner as Roane continued toward us. The light from the kitchen silhouetted his form. His wide shoulders. His long arms. His tapered waist. He walked like a predator. Like the wolf that he was. He noticed my noticing and stopped directly in front of me. "You can make coffee if you need to. I checked it out."

"No arsenic?"

One corner of his mouth rose, creating a tantalizing dimple under the scruff. "No arsenic."

"Thank the Goddess." I shoved past him to get to the kitchen, brushing my entire body against his as though we were in a narrow passageway. "Sorry," I said, faking awkwardness. The fact that one could drive a semi through the short hall under the balcony that led to the kitchen occurred to neither of us as I continued to pass. And slide. And rub.

He lowered his head and watched as my breasts brushed along his chest. Then he lifted a hand to my hip.

Pulled me closer. Brushed his mouth over my jaw. "I'll let you know if I catch his scent again."

"You never answered me."

"You never answered me, either," he countered.

"What will you do?"

"If I catch him?"

"Yes."

He pressed into me, and heat pooled between my legs. "That'll be up to him."

"I'm serious, Roane. From what I understand, they're very powerful."

"He was created by a warlock," he said, resting his mouth at my ear. "I was created by a charmling. I promise you I am more so."

"You can't know that. Just be careful."

"I'd be more prone to caution if I had a fiancée to come back to."

I stifled a chuckle. No need to encourage him.

We turned when we heard breathing close by. Annette stood there. "So," she said, the tremor in her voice belying her nonchalant demeanor, "ballpark figure, how many demons are roaming the earth as we speak?"

He grinned and squeezed past us since we'd sandwiched him in. "I'll keep you updated."

"Please." When he closed the front door, I turned to Annette. "Real coffee." Decaf didn't quite have the same effect.

"Right?" she said with a snort, staying right on my heels.

"Oh, no, you don't." I pointed upstairs. "Nap. The coven is not due for another couple of hours, so nap. For real, Annette. You haven't had any real sleep in, like, two days."

She sat at the table and pouted. "I'm having dreams.

Very surreal dreams."

"Really?" I made quick work of measuring out the coffee grounds and turning on the pot. It started gurgling immediately, aka, my theme song. I sat across from her, her bow-shaped mouth almost pouty. "What kind of dreams?"

She blinked at me. "Why? What did you hear?"

"That you're having surreal dreams. Wait." I leaned closer. "Are they sexy-time dreams?"

She snorted. "No."

"Dude, you are honestly the worst liar."

"Okay, they're very... explicit."

I lifted my hand for a high-five. "You go, girl."

"Deph, this is serious. They're about..." She gritted her teeth and gestured toward the cabinets.

I frowned in confusion.

She lifted a shoulder and leaned to her other side.

I looked to the side and saw nothing but the island and a blown-up oven.

She rolled her eyes and fingerspelled something. Goddess only knew what. And it took, like, a year. We'd tried to learn sign language in middle school. We managed a vocabulary of about twenty-five words, and most of them were dirty.

"Annette," I said, showing my palms.

"Oh my God." She took out her phone and texted some-one. Now was hardly the time.

Then my phone dinged. I grabbed it and read: *Percival!!!*

My stunned gasp echoed off the walls for a solid minute. "Annette! You're having dirty dreams about my grandfather?"

"Shhh," she shushed, looking around in paranoia. "He'll hear you."

"What the hell?"

"I'm not doing it on purpose, Defiance."

I couldn't seem to unhinge my jaw. I just gaped at her. When I finally found my voice again, I whispered, "So, like, you're having sex with a plant?"

"What? No! I mean, kind of. Sometimes he's a guy. You know what? Forget it. I'm just not sleeping well. And now there are malevolent spirits in the attic and demons all around us and a hunter trying to kill us. I liked it more when I was oblivious."

That made me sad. Not terribly. Not lost-puppy sad. "But you love this stuff."

"Yeah, when it's happening to someone else."

"True. So, like, for real?" I wiggled my brows and gestured toward, well, Percy.

"Stop."

"Is it... I mean, do you...?"

"Stop. I should never have told you."

I giggled and got up to pour myself a cup of coffee. "It doesn't even matter. You need to get some rest."

She draped her body over the table. Normally, Annette could sleep through a hurricane. Maybe that was the problem. Maybe Percy was more than a hurricane. Maybe he was a tsunami. Yeah, baby. A Percy tsunami.

"I'm going to do some research. Try to find out who our mystery man from the café was."

"Oh, great, thanks. I have a couple of things to do, too."

"Really?" she asked. "Like what?"

"Things. Go. First, nap. Then research."

She let out a long sigh and went upstairs. I waited an appropriate amount of time, grabbed a flashlight, and hurried up to the mezzanine. I had a revenant being to confront.

NINE

I like it when people call me "ma'am."
I just wish they wouldn't follow it up with
"you're making a scene."
—Meme

I sought out the entrance to the secret passageways for two reasons. One, because I wanted to check on the thing in the attic. *Bead-uh.* The revenant being I'd trapped there when I was a kid, according to Gigi. Why would I do that? And why did I wake up there this morning?

Two, I wanted to check out the caves beneath the house. I'd recently found out the secret passageways that led to the mysterious attic, the passageways that Percy could not go into, also led to an even more mysterious cave beneath the house. The passages were lined with shiplap from actual ships. Ships that had soaked in the ocean for years. The salt kept out all manner of ilk, the spectral kind anyway, but I worried the salt and brine could throw off someone with a really good sense of smell. Someone like a wolf shifter.

And the caves were accessible from the outside. If someone knew about them, they could feasibly enter the house through the passageways undetected. But I didn't know where all of the first-floor entrances were. The second floor had one in each room. Mine was off my bathroom. But I got lost in the passages easily, so I'd never discovered the ones on the first floor. Mostly because the passages were such a maze, and I rarely even knew what floor I was on. No time like the present, however.

The caves were the only explanation as to how someone could get past both Roane and Percy. There were caveats to my theory, of course. Roane also had a wicked sense of hearing, for one. He would've been able to hear someone coming in unless they did it while he was out patrolling with his wolf pack at night.

And how could someone actually get into the kitchen without Percy knowing and without Roane picking up the scent?

I decided to eat the big frog first, as they say. To face my biggest fear. The being in the attic. Whatever or whoever Bead-uh was, it was bad enough that I'd apparently summoned a witch from the past to cast a spell on the house just to lock it up. Percy did not originally have gables, and now he had six with a room in each one.

I eased the panel on the mezzanine aside, but before ducking inside, I noticed a handful of vines sliding toward me. He didn't like me going into the passageways. A place into which he could not follow. He could not protect. I held out my hand, and a vine curled into my palm and around my fingers, the embrace warm and loving. "It's okay, Percy. I'm just checking out a couple of things. I won't be long."

He shrank back. I was a little surprised. The last time I'd gone into the passageways, he'd done everything in his power to stop me. Of course, at that time, I was being stalked by a Puritan jerkface.

I eased into the passageways and closed the panel. I was more familiar with this area. I found the stairs going to the attic and started climbing them, feeling a little like Alice in Wonderland. The stairs made no sense. They went up and down and then up again, over rooms and around closets until I could finally go no farther.

I stepped onto the landing and turned in a circle. A high, pointed ceiling topped the cone-shaped room. And it had no windows. I turned to the farthest door on the right of the stairs and started toward it. Boards creaked beneath my feet as I eased closer, waiting for the knock or a loud bang like the first time I'd tried to get into the room.

Sweat beaded on my upper lip as I raised a shaky hand and drew a spell on the door. Light, bright and hot, burst from the lines and seeped into the room. I pressed my hand to the wood and reached out with my magics. I felt exactly what I'd felt before. A vast nothingness. A perpetual darkness. An endless void. Whatever the room beyond the door held, it was not confined to the salt-laden walls.

The last time I'd done this, the thing inside attacked me. Attacked my energy. Scratched and clawed at it, and I couldn't pry my hand off the door. Then it rushed me. Trying to break through. That was about the time I practically fell down the stairs, I ran so fast.

I waited, but nothing happened, so I sent my magics out farther. There had to be something there. Something other than the being I'd locked inside. But there was nothing. I felt only a cold, dark void. And I'd locked a creature inside of that for over forty years. What would that kind of isolation do to an intelligent being? Then again, what did the creature do to force me to conjure a prison just to lock it away?

Whatever the case, I couldn't find the being either. It was either messing with me or pouting in a corner somewhere. If I could find any corners in the void, I'd search there, but there simply were none.

I dropped my hand and stood back. "Look," I said, standing my ground, "you and I are going to have to get along if you want me to figure all of this out. I don't know why I put you in there. I don't remember. But if you keep messing with me, we'll get nowhere fast."

Still nothing. I examined the antique doorknob. It had a skeleton keyhole underneath. I wanted to peer inside, but I'd seen far too many horror movies to do something that inane. Instead, I reached down and tested the knob.

After Roane had tried everything to get the doors open over the years—locksmiths, sledgehammers, blowtorches—the fact that the knob turned and the latch released stunned me. I froze. My eyes wide, my pulse galloping at a breakneck speed, I stood glued to the spot. Fear swallowed me whole. If the creature tried banging on the door now, tried to break through it, would it succeed in escaping? Or would the salt in the attic keep it locked inside the room?

If it did escape, would it kill me? Could it? It irked me that I had no memory of why I'd locked it in there in the first place. No clue as to what it was or what it was capable of.

I stood motionless. I couldn't move or breathe or think. My thoughts ricocheted through my mind, conjuring all kinds of horrible fates for me and everyone else in the house. Struggling to get a freaking grip, my lids drifted shut, and I slowly, painstakingly released the knob. The latch clicked back into place just as the creature slammed into the door from the other side. A thunderous boom shook the walls around me, and just like before, I stumbled back and fell on my ass.

Another boom exploded around me, and this time I could've sworn I heard wood splintering. I looked at the door to make sure it hadn't cracked, but it seemed as solid as ever. A third crash had me scrambling for the stairs and, just like before, I half ran, half fell down them.

When I got to the second-floor passageway, I almost ran to my room before remembering my second goal: to look for evidence of someone coming and going via the passages from the cave. And I needed to find out where the first-floor secret entrances were. If it would be possible for someone, even a mundane, to enter the house without Roane or Percy knowing about it.

After descending one million steps, give or take, I stopped to catch my breath, then found the door to the cave again. I opened it, and the musty scent of salt and brine hit me first. I stepped down onto the rock floor. Water pooled here and there, and the sound of the ocean wafted toward me. As did the cool breeze, but no way was I going back for my coat. Far too many stairs, and the trip up was about a thousand times harder than the trip down.

I looked to my right. The barest hint of light emanated from that direction. I'd made the trip to the entrance of the cave when I had to escape Percy one night. Hidden by vegetation, the opening sat not ten feet from the water. It had a locked metal gate to prevent trespassers, but the hinges had been cut at some point, and the gate sat askew. Anyone could've entered. Because it had been night when I found it, I couldn't tell how recent it had been cut. Not that I could in the light of day either, but it was worth a shot.

Thankfully, I'd donned hiking boots and a sweatshirt that read *In a world full of princesses, be a witch* before embarking on my venture. The sweatshirt was hot in the attic, but I was terribly grateful for the protection against the elements down here.

I followed the standing water, steering clear of any small openings, and kept to the main Batcave until I came to the round gate. The few times I had to brace a hand against a wall for balance, the moisture seeping from the walls caused little rivulets to run up my arm. Like before, the metal grate was covered in bushes and vines, hidden from the outside world, but it did seem like the vegetation had been cleared on one side at some point. Just enough to wrench the gate open.

The portal wasn't tall enough to stand upright when going through it, perhaps more of a drain than an access point, but the gate was old and rusted. I turned on my flashlight and leaned in to inspect the hinges. If only I knew what I was doing. What I was looking for. The only way... I stopped. The metal had been cut by something very sharp or very hot, and while the hinges were covered in rust, the metal where the cut had been made was not. A bit of vegetation had regrown over the cut hinges, and they were dirty, but the metal that had been cut through had no rust.

I fished out my phone and focused to take a picture when a male voice asked, "What are you doing?"

I jumped and knocked my phone against the grating. It flew out of my hands, only to be caught a microsecond before it hit the water. I pressed a hand over my heart and turned toward the intruder. "Damn it, Roane."

He wore an unrepentant grin that weakened my knees as he examined my most prized possession. Which, surprisingly, was not my sanity. "You're taking pictures of this because?"

"I'm trying to see how long ago this metal was cut."

"Ah." He stepped close to take a look, close enough for me to breathe in the sandalwood soap he used.

I tried to back up. To give him room. But there was nowhere to go.

"No rust along the cut lines. Looks like it's been cut sometime in the last few months."

"Exactly." I leaned closer and ran my fingers over the jagged metal. "Maybe, like, six, six and a half months ago?"

He straightened then lifted up the bottom of my sweatshirt and pushed the phone into my pocket. "You think whoever poisoned your grandmother gained access to the house through the caves and the passageways."

"Yes, I do. And if that's the case, it could've been anyone. Witch. Warlock. Hunter. Mundane. I need to check out the secret openings on the first floor. Do you know where they come out? Which rooms?"

"I don't. I've only ever gone to the attic and a couple other rooms on the second floor."

"Like mine," I said, remembering the first time I caught him working under the sink in my bathroom. The shelves had been pushed aside. That was my first discovery of the secret passages. And they'd used them to keep an eye on me when I'd been in a state of suspended animation for six months. It was the only way they could get close to me, as Percy would let no one enter.

"Like yours," he agreed, stepping closer.

"Are you picking anything up?"

"Besides you?"

A titillating pleasure raced over my skin. "I meant, an intruder of some kind. Someone who could've snuck in and spiked the flour with nitroglycerine, perhaps?"

"Ah." He looked around. "No, I'm not. If someone did come this way, they didn't do it recently."

"You can tell that even with the salt?"

"It's more difficult, of course, but not impossible." He knelt down for a better view through the grating. "The ground hasn't been disturbed either. No one has come through here for a while."

Disappointment washed over me. I really thought I was onto something. "Then how, Roane? How is someone getting inside?"

He rose to his full height of *towering with a side of sensual*. "I'm not convinced your grandmother's death has anything to do with the more recent events."

"The chief is doubting it, too. But why?"

"The person who poisoned Ruthie did it slowly over time before giving her a lethal dose. It was subtle and unmitigated cowardice. Not the actions of someone who would try to blow up the house or poison an entire group of people."

I lifted a shoulder. "I guess."

"And their motives were different."

I crossed my arms over my chest, the chill getting to me. "How so?"

"Think about it. Think about the possible motives. Let's say whoever poisoned her did it to draw you out. Why do that and then try to kill you before getting to your powers? If it is a hunter doing a warlock's bidding, they would never kill you first. They'd abduct you and take you somewhere safe to perform the ceremony."

"Okay. Good point."

"So what are the other motives? To become the doyenne? There are any number of people in line for that."

"Right. And Serinda is next. She doesn't even want the position."

"They'd potentially have to kill several people to get the crown, but why not just start a new coven? Why kill to become the leader of hers? There are no financial incentives. Nothing to gain besides the notoriety."

"Okay, so not a witch."

"And revenge is a no-go. Ruthie hadn't made anyone angry. She hadn't been getting any threatening calls or letters."

"True. That leaves the house."

"And the money," he corrected, lifting his T-shirt over his head. "The oldest motive in the book."

"What are you doing?" I asked, trying to focus on the conversation while ogling him. There was something magical about a shirtless man in a kilt. Especially one covered in tattoos with messy hair and days-old scruff.

He stepped over to me and tugged at my sweatshirt. "Off."

I looked around. "Here?"

A single dimple appeared as he repeated, "Off."

Eyeing him warily, I lifted the sweatshirt over my head. He took it and handed me his tee.

"I think you're getting the better end of the deal here."

When he only gestured for me to put on his tee, I pulled it over my head, thankful I'd worn a pretty bra. He lifted the sweatshirt over my head and helped me put my arms in. After tugging it down over my hips, he asked, "Better?"

The warmth of his T-shirt embraced me. I hugged it to me. "Aren't you cold?"

Please say no. Please say no. Please say no.

"No."

Score!

"Where's your coat?" he asked.

"I didn't think about it until I got to the Batcave, and I was not about to take all those stairs back up any more than I had to."

He chuckled, a rich, deep sound so intoxicating I got a buzz just hearing it.

"So... um... where were we?"

"The money."

"Right. Yes. But she left it all to me."

"Which leads us back to the fact that there were a handful of people who knew about you. You were named in the will, after all."

"And even if they didn't, she lived frugally. Very few people knew she even had money. Which leads us back to the house. And here we go again, chasing our tails."

"Is that a wolf reference?"

"No," I said, trying not to smile.

"Good, because the only tail I want to chase is yours."

"Yeah?" I asked, suddenly winded. "Well, in case you're wondering, you're the only person I want chasing my tail."

He turned and looked out the gate again. "Good."

I hugged his shirt tighter. "Maybe whoever did it had no clue I existed and thought they'd be able to get the house when she died, but why? I mean, Percy is amazing and I'd kill for him, but why would anyone else?"

His mouth hardened as he did a strangely alluring version of the deadpan. "I can't imagine who would want a house full of mystical energy."

My shoulder sagged. "So, you *do* think it was a witch?"

"I do think it's a possibility we can't ignore."

"But you also think that the person who killed her and the person trying to kill us now are two different people."

"Again, I think it's possible."

I turned and waded through a puddle so he wouldn't see the frustration welling in my eyes. "We're going in circles. Not getting anywhere. Speaking of which, when did you get back?" Did he hear the creature almost knock the house down?

"A few minutes ago."

"How did you know I was down here?"

"You're about as quiet as a church moose."

I snorted. "Thanks? So, then, did you hear the bangs?"

He tilted his head. "Apparently not. What bangs?"

"The creature in the attic. It's a long story. So, the hunter?"

His jaw muscle jumped in frustration. "I lost him. I keep losing him. He's using magics to cover his trail. He has to be, and I'm worried I'm only leading him closer and closer to the thing he wants most."

"What do you mean?"

"I think he was just scoping out the town. Maybe he knew there was a charmling in town, but not who you were or where to find you. The more I track him, the more he can zero in on not only my location, but yours as well."

"I didn't think of that."

"Now he'll be like a dog with a bone. I should have just left it alone. Either way, I need to pull back while I figure out my next move. But first, I need to weld the hinges back and put new locks on this. And just in case, I'll put a sensor on it to alert me if anyone opens it."

"Good idea. I could've taken care of the hinges, but it's iron. I can't do anything with iron."

"I know." He took my hand and started back toward the

passage, his wide shoulders almost brushing both sides of the Batcave at times when it narrowed. "Why do you think I ordered a set of iron handcuffs?"

I almost stumbled with his confession and couldn't decide if he was serious or not. We took the stairs up past the basement level and stopped off for him to get another shirt. Damn it. I'd been wondering where the panels on that level opened up to, and now I knew. One opened up to his apartment and one to Gigi's. I waited just inside his apartment. The panel opened up to his bedroom, and that realization sent my mind reeling with possibilities.

He opened his closet, and it occurred to me I was still wearing his shirt. "Oh my God, you can have yours back." I lifted my sweatshirt over my head and then his tee. "I wasn't thinking."

A wicked grin stole across his face. He crossed his arms over his chest and leaned against the doorframe of his closet, enjoying the show.

I was doing something quite similar. His biceps thickened when he crossed his arms. His shoulders flexed. His pecs bunched. I cleared my throat, then walked over to hand him the shirt. Just as he was about to take it, I pulled it back. "Maybe I should wash it first."

He grabbed it out of my hands like I'd offended him. "Don't you dare." He pulled it on. "Your scent is... soothing."

I ducked my head to hide a smile and pulled on the sweatshirt. "So, all this time, you've never gone to the cave?"

"Nope. The stairs didn't go down that far."

I looked at him in surprise. Gigi had told me the exact same thing. The secret passageway stairs ended at the basement. Until I went down them. She'd suggested that I'd somehow made them appear, but the stairs had to have been there. They were just like the rest of the passageway. Were they hidden? If so, how? And why? Gigi had lived in the house her entire life. It would take some serious magics to block them.

But maybe the culprit didn't need to block the stairs. Maybe he only needed to block Gigi's memory of the stairs. To hide his way in and out of Percy.

The first scenario put a serious dent in my theory about how someone got inside the house six months ago and poisoned Gigi. The second supported it.

I needed to know everything about witchcraft, black magic, and everything in between ASAP. Mostly, was it possible for someone to alter another person's memory? A witch's? Apparently, I'd altered the minds of every mundane in Salem when I'd called upon an ancient Mesopotamian charmling to help me imprison Bead-uh, the creature in the attic. But only mundane. Gigi and Serinda both eluded the memory shift. Clearly, to alter the mind of a powerful witch was another level of magic.

"Ready?" Roane asked, waiting patiently.

I snapped back to the present. "Yes."

We went up the stairs to the first floor, and once again I had to hold my breath to keep from huffing and puffing. I needed to get in a couple more cardio sessions a week. Which would bring me up to two.

The staircases were narrow and claustrophobic, but the passages afforded us a little more elbow room as we sought out the access points. The maze of corridors was straight out of a horror movie. Or a gothic romance. Depending on one's mood. Watching Roane lead the way, I was leaning toward romance.

The first door we found opened a built-in bookcase in the drawing room. "This is all very Sherlockian," I said, both impressed and horrified. "Do you realize anyone could watch us at any time and we wouldn't know?"

"I'd know."

"Well, those of us without super hearing, then."

He winked at me and closed the case. We found the next secret panel quickly. It opened into the great room via an access panel that slid to the side.

"I get so turned around," I said, trying to get my bearings. "I thought we were near the back of the house."

"We're getting warmer."

We made our way through the rest of the passage and eventually came to a dead end. "No," I said, turning a full circle. "There has to be more. Only two doors on this entire floor?"

"Look." Roane pointed to a section of the horizontal shiplap that sat between two vertical boards about three feet apart.

We walked back to it. "Is this another one?" The other access panels were a solid piece of wood. Easy to spot. If this was one, it blended in well.

He tested it. "I can't tell." He pushed again, and it creaked open, but not into a room. Into yet another passageway only a few feet in length.

The shiplap in this section seemed much older. Spiderwebs hung down like curtains, and one section had been braced with a two-by-four, creating a diagonal barrier.

We ducked under it to get the last panel.

I swatted a spiderweb out of my face. "This whole secret passageway thing just veered into horror-movie territory."

Roane tossed a grin over his shoulder, his olive eyes

shimmering in the beam of my flashlight. He tested the panel and tried to slide it to the side. It didn't budge. Then he pushed. Still nothing.

As he tried to get the panel open, something washed over me. Like a rubber band snapping into place. It was just a feeling, but I instantly thought of Joaquin Ferebee from the café. His odd behavior. He was livid when I'd questioned him, but when he brushed past me, when my skin made contact with his, I felt a sadness. A bottomless well of despair. It had been weighing on me all afternoon, but it vanished. In its place was something even darker. Something even more desperate.

He'd made a decision. About what, I couldn't say, but I got the feeling it was not a positive thing.

I shook out of the thought and shined my flashlight on the panel, trying to help Roane find a latch of some kind. The wooden panel was marred, like something had tried to pry it open with a crowbar.

"Roane," I said, astonished.

"I see it." He said the words through gritted teeth. "Those marks aren't that old. This has to be how they gained access."

My pulse sped up. "We shouldn't touch it. There could be prints."

He lifted off his T-shirt again and used it while he tried to wrench open the door.

I dropped the light and saw quarter-circle scrapes along the wood floor. "Wait. It looks like it opens into the passage." If it did, it would be the only one like that we'd found. All the other doors opened into the rooms, not out of them.

He nodded and felt for a latch along the frame, careful not to actually rub the frame. He stilled when we heard a soft click, gestured me to his other side, and pulled.

An entire column of shelves in the pantry swung open into the passageway. The pantry where Gigi kept her soup mix.

TEN

My gasp echoed around us. "Roane, that's it!" I pressed a hand to my mouth. "Percy can't come into the passageways. And the intruder didn't have to enter the house to poison her. The shelves open into the passage. Into the salt barrier."

"How the fuck did I not know this was here?" He jerked his shirt back on so hard, a seam ripped along his rib cage.

"Roane, this isn't your fault."

"The fuck it isn't."

I took out my phone. "We have to call the chief. Get a forensics team in here."

"What will he say? Nobody knows she was poisoned."

I hadn't thought of that. Then I realized I didn't have to. "The chief is a master at coming up with excuses for all of the goings-on in this town. He'll come up with something." I looked up as the phone rang. "Percy! Are you here?"

The floor hummed beneath our feet, and vines slid across the ceiling into the pantry.

"Did you know this was here?"

It seemed to take him a moment, then the vines rushed en masse over the other shelves and around the barrier, as though exploring. Learning.

"I'm going to take that as a no." My call went straight to voicemail. "Chief, get over to the house. We found something. And bring a crime scene tech."

"Look at this passageway," Roane said, taking in our surroundings.

I hung up. "Exactly. The other passages seem newer. Better maintained."

"Yes. And this offshoot was the only part of the passage that was blocked off by another panel."

"Is that significant?"

"I don't know. It was purposely concealed, though. No doubt."

"Then how did the intruder know about it? How did the intruder know about any of this?"

Percy shrank back, and sixty seconds later, Gigi came running up the stairs from her apartment.

Her stunned gaze would suggest she didn't know about that particular panel either. "Good Goddess," she said, inching into the pantry. "Where did that come from?"

I stepped through and gave her room to inspect the area. "Gigi, you've lived here your entire life. You never knew this was here?"

She shook her head. "I did not."

Roane stepped out of the pantry and into the kitchen as well, even though there was plenty of room. The storeroom was the same size as the laundry room that sat next to it.

"And look." I pointed to the shelves. "They open into the passageway. None of the others do that."

She leaned into the passage, careful not to touch anything.

"I called the chief to bring a crime scene tech. There could be prints."

She nodded and looked around in a daze. "I had no idea this was here."

"No way," Annette said, rushing into the kitchen. She'd showered, her hair now in a single bun on top of her head, and gotten some rest if her puffy eyes were any indication. Percy must've roused her as well. She poked her head into the pantry. "This is crazy."

"Are the passageways in the floorplans? You mentioned once you'd seen the original plans from when the house was built in the 1800s."

"No. The measurements on the plans had to be adjusted to accommodate them."

"You mean falsified?" Roane asked.

"Yes. It was all very clandestine, but can you blame my family?"

"What do you mean?" I asked.

"I mean, I come from a long line of witches. Actual witches. Not those poor souls who were killed in the witch trials."

"And your family needed a way to hide in case history repeated itself and they came for them."

"Precisely. So you can see why the plans that were registered with the county, as primitive as they are, were a little less than forthcoming."

Annette studied the entry. "What's the point of secret passageways if they aren't a secret?"

"Well, someone knew about them," I said, waving the chief back to us.

He took one look, and his years of perfecting his legendary poker face, to which every law enforcement officer aspires, were all for naught. He couldn't have concealed his surprise if I'd paid him to. Which, why would I?

"You found it." He stepped into the pantry.

"This has to be how they did it, right?"

"Yes. I would say so. Everyone out."

He shooed us all out of the pantry and called in a tech to process the area, telling her there was a break-in and leaving it at that. The tech, a pretty brunette who was searching for a dog she'd lost a year earlier and a boyfriend she'd lost just before that, came in to dust for fingerprints.

"Gigi, does this change anything?" I stood beside her, her gaze a thousand miles away. "Can you think of anyone who would've known about that particular access point?"

She walked to the great room and stood at the window, looking out at the dreary day, her hands clasped behind her back. I followed her, motioning for everyone else to give me a minute alone with her.

"I just don't know, Defiance."

"It's okay, Gigi. We're getting closer."

She nodded, and her chin quivered.

I draped an arm around her shoulders. "Gigi, what is it?" I couldn't imagine how finding that door would upset her. If anything, it got us closer to our goal.

"You can't imagine what it's like knowing someone murdered you. Someone hated you enough to take your life."

"No." I filled my lungs. "I can't imagine that, but I don't think they hated you, Gigi. I think they wanted something. Something you had."

"The fact that my life meant so little to them is almost worse than the hate. Indifference. A complete and utter lack of care or concern that I was a person. I had a life."

Her despair washed over me. Made me more determined than ever to find who did this to her. "Why don't you get some rest? The coven will be here in a little while."

She nodded, and the chief came in to escort her to her apartment.

Roane and Annette joined me at the window. What many would see as a depressive day, I saw as a work of art. The bouts of nourishing rain. The sunless sky. The soft light that seemed to reflect my own dreams back onto me. The grayness filled my soul in a way that nothing else could.

I turned to them, renewed and refocused. "I have an errand to run before the coven arrives."

Roane scoffed in astonishment. "Do you, now?"

"Yes."

He crossed his arms over his chest. "With a hunter running around?"

I crossed my arms back. "Roane, you said it yourself. You have no idea if he was even after me."

Annette crossed her arms too, but just watched our conversation intently.

"And we're supposed to use that as an excuse to gamble with your life?" he asked.

I pursed my lips, then turned to Annette. "I need to know more about the man at the café. Can you find out where he's staying?"

"Joaquin Ferebee? On it. Wait, why?" she asked,

suddenly intrigued. "Did something happen to him since this morning?"

"No, and I'd like to keep it that way. I felt something a few minutes ago. A... release. Like he's made a decision that goes against the universe's plan for him."

"Okay. I'm on it." She hurried up the stairs to her laptop, and I refocused on the wolf beside me.

"And you can be my chauffeur. Unless you have someplace to be?"

"Other than attached to your hip?"

I grinned. That would work.

Twenty minutes later, we were sitting in the waiting room at Richter, Richter, and Richter Law, Real Estate, and Wedding Offices. The purple waiting room of Richter, Richter, and Richter Law, Real Estate, and Wedding Offices. I hadn't seen Mrs. Richter in all her purple glory since the day she'd nervously insisted I sign the papers to accept a house named Percival. A house that had been bequeathed to me by a total stranger. That stranger turned out to be my grandmother, of course, and Percival the wonderful, warm house I lived in now, but Mrs. Richter had been scared to death of him. Poor guy.

I'd also previously met her assistant, Tad, the sandy-haired one who kept chancing furtive glances Roane's way. I could hardly blame him. I often did the same thing.

Roane sat with his legs outstretched, his elbows on the armrests, and his hands clasped in front of his mouth as he scanned the waiting room with a look of mild horror on his face. As much as I loved purple, I could see where it would be a bit overwhelming to the unprepared.

He looked out the window to the parking lot. "I take it that's her car?"

I followed his gaze to a purple crossover. "Yep."

Mrs. Richter stepped out of her office with a young woman in tow. "Don't worry, Cynthia. I'll call the DA now and get the exact charges. But remember, they have to prove your aunt was trying to kill your uncle with that frozen chicken to convict her. They have to prove intent, and that won't happen."

"Even though she screamed at him she was going to kill him with a frozen chicken when she attacked?"

Mrs. Richter winced. "Let's see what the DA has to say, shall we?"

The woman nodded, shook her hand, and headed out, stumbling only slightly when she spotted the large Adonis sitting in the waiting area.

Tad cleared his throat, loudly, to clue Mrs. Richter in to the fact that she'd just broken client confidentiality by saying all of that in front of us.

The woman's startled gaze landed on Roane. Then me. Then back to Roane, where it lingered a long moment before returning to me. "Ms. Dayne," she said, and I was surprised she remembered me. I'd only met her the one time, and that was over six months ago. She still wore head-to-toe purple, a sharp business suit with lilac heels to match.

I stood. "I'm surprised you remember me."

"How could I forget those remarkable blue eyes?"

Ah, yes. She'd loved my eyes.

"Please, come in." She waved us into her office, then sat behind her desk. "What can I do for you?"

"I'm here about the house."

Though her poker face was perfectly respectable, the soft gasp gave her away. "Percival?"

"Don't worry, I'm keeping him."

She relaxed and fell back against her chair. "I'm so glad to hear that. He... he's not my biggest fan."

While I wanted nothing more than to ask what exactly had led her to such a conclusion—I'd never known Percy to be outright mean to anyone—I had more pressing business to attend to. "Did anyone inquire about him after Ruthie passed away?"

"Inquire?"

"Yes. Like has anyone come in asking about the house? Maybe someone who wanted to purchase him or just find out the ownership status?"

Her brows slid together. "I'm not following."

Roane and I glanced at each other, then I reiterated, "Is anyone interested in Percy? Is there anyone that you know of who wants to purchase him?"

She glanced down, shaking her blond bob slightly, then looked up and blinded us with a huge, welcoming smile. "Ms. Dayne. It's so good to see you. What can I do for you?"

Admittedly, I was thrown. After a quick glance at Roane, who was clearly just as confused, I tilted my head and said, "Percival? The house?"

Fear flashed behind her eyes before she caught herself. "You... you don't want to keep him?"

I spoke slowly, now worried more about her sanity than my own. And that was saying a lot. "No. I mean yes. I want to keep him."

She released a breath she'd been holding and sank back against her chair. Again. "I'm so glad to hear that. He... he's not my biggest fan."

"Mrs. Richter, are you okay?"

"I am now. I was worried. So, what about Percival?"

I knew the odds of what I was about to do, but I had to risk it. "I was wondering if anyone inquired about him after Ruthie passed away."

"Or before," Roane said, and he was right. If the person

who poisoned her wanted Percival, they may very well have been inquiring weeks in advance. Or even months.

"True," I said, returning to Mrs. Richter.

"I don't understand."

Giving it one more go, I said hesitantly, "Has anyone talked to you about Percival? About who gets him now that Ruthie is gone? Or even before she passed. Who would get him if anything should happen to her?"

"Percival?"

"Ruthie's house. The one she left me?"

She rubbed her forehead, then looked back at us. "I'm Beth. Beth Richter. How can I help you?"

We were going backward. It was like she was forgetting more every time she tried to answer our questions.

"I'm Defiance. Defiance Dayne? I was asking about—"

Without taking his gaze off her, Roane covered my hand with one of his own, cautioning me. He was right. If I kept going, her entire memory could be wiped out. I guess that answered my question about the culprit having magics.

"We're getting married," Roane said, and Beth and I both gasped in unison.

"Congratulations!" She jumped up and shook both of our hands in turn while I glared at my *fiancé*. "Do you have a date in mind yet?"

"No!" I said quickly, and Roane chuckled. "No, we still have to think on it."

"Well, don't think too long. October weddings are lovely."

"October?" I asked, my voice an octave higher than usual. "Since there are only a couple weeks left, I was thinking more along the lines of something in, say, a few years?"

Beth laughed and looked at Roane. "A little nervous, is she?"

"A little," he confirmed.

"Well, you will make a gorgeous bride. And... my goodness, your eyes are stunning." She leaned closer. "I don't think I've ever seen that shade of blue before."

Those were pretty much the same words she said to me when we first met. "Thank you. We just wanted to make sure you're free to take on another wedding."

"Of course." She sat back behind her desk. "I have to keep my schedule fairly open for court dates and open houses, but planning weddings is my favorite thing to do."

"Excellent. We'll come up with a few dates and get back to you?"

"I look forward to it... Defiance, was it?"

"Yes. Defiance Dayne, and this is Roane Wildes."

"It's so nice to meet you both."

We stood to leave. "And can I just say, you have to be the busiest woman I've ever met."

"Pfft." She waved a dismissive hand. "I have to keep busy. I have too much nervous energy. I was ADHD before it was called ADHD."

"I hear you. It was nice to meet you."

"And you. Check out my website for a few possible locations. They book up pretty fast."

"Thank you, I will." We stepped out of the office, nodded to Tad, and left the purple in our wake.

I pulled my coat closer as we walked to the truck, though the day was warming up nicely. "Roane, what just happened?"

"It's hard to say. A spell of some kind, but I've never heard of anything progressive like that."

"Exactly. The more we asked, the more her memory slipped. That's messed up."

"Agreed."

He opened the door for me and waited for me to get in before closing it and climbing into the driver's side. He'd never done that before, and I had to wonder if he felt the hunter nearby.

When he started the truck, I said to him, "I have one more errand."

"I'd rather get you back to Percy."

"It's important."

He offered me a reluctant nod, and I gave him the address of a little shop on Essex. We had to park two blocks down and weave our way through the crowds that were undeterred by the frigid weather. Witch-themed decorations peppered every doorway and kiosk on the street, and the scent of fall hung heavy in the air.

Honestly, it was like the place was created just for me. The excitement and fervor stirred something deep inside. Though, admittedly, Roane stirred something deeper. Maybe it was the way he walked, his gait predatorial. His gaze alert. His silhouette alluring. And his ass... Even in the leather kilt, the shape of his steely buttocks was decidedly and beautifully round.

As usual, he garnered a lot of attention. I was growing used to the looks. Some startled at first and then mesmerized. Some longing. Every once in a while, he'd glance over his shoulder to make sure I was still behind him, but for the most part, he scanned the area like a huntsman looking for prey.

The Witchery, a small black building with gold lettering, sat between a florist and a clothing store. We stepped inside to the tinkling chime of a bell, and a girl folding T-shirts at the register waved a hello. The owner, a woman named Love, had a fantastical mixture of items for sale, from touristy knickknacks to authentic witch-related paraphernalia.

Annette had told me about the run-in she'd had with Love, but she never told me exactly what happened. Whatever had transpired between the two happened while I was on hiatus, and it was enough to get Annette banned from the store for life.

Hopefully, Love and I were good, because I had questions. Lots and lots of questions. Though, for the time being, I'd try to keep most of them to myself.

"Let me know if I can help you with anything," the girl said. She looked more high school cheerleader than witch's apprentice, but I sensed instantly what she was searching for: her diary. The one that laid bare her perpetual pining for a boy named Jamie in great and sordid detail, replete with cut-outs and graphic illustrations. The girl had talent. The fact that it had been missing for the last week mortified her, but if she knew who took it, she'd be even more mortified.

"Thank you," I said, scanning the store for its owner.

Like the last time I'd visited, I walked in during a palm-reading session. An older woman dressed to the nine-and-a-halves was having her palm read on a small raised platform near the back of the store. It was separated from the rest of the store by a three-foot iron rail with a swing gate. So anyone could listen in on them if they tried hard enough.

At first, I found that odd, but I realized she could actually block off the area. To a degree, at least. She had accordion-style panels tucked into one corner that she could pull across the area to give the client some privacy. Maybe she used those if the client was concerned about confidentiality.

An older gentleman sat in a small waiting area up front, reading the latest issue of *The Witches Almanac*. Perhaps the woman's husband indulging his wife's whims?

Love, only a little younger than Annette and me, had long blonde hair that she'd low-lighted with black and red. The bright streaks had been a shimmering purple a few days ago, but I had to admit, I liked the fire-engine red. She looked like a young and witchy Lauren Bacall.

She sat with her back to the store, her profile barely visible. The strategic position made it almost impossible to hear what she had to say, but one quick turn of her head, and she could see the entire store from her higher vantage.

She held the woman's rapt attention with deftness and skill, but the minute we stepped inside, she turned her sharp gaze on us. The first time I saw her, I felt an instant connection. A pull, as though she were a bug zapper and I was a beetle. Maybe a June bug. Or a firefly. It was the same kind of kinship I'd felt when I first saw Annette in the ninth grade, and it fascinated me.

I turned and pretended to shop, hoping she wouldn't remember me, or who I'd been with the last time I came in, because she'd paused her session to throw Annette—and me by proxy—out of the store. Also, we'd technically shoplifted. I felt bad about that.

But she'd had as strange a reaction to me as I'd had to her. She'd seemed taken aback by me, and I would've loved to know why.

I watched her from my periphery. Her gaze lingered on first me then Roane, before the older woman dragged her attention back to the business at hand by clearing her throat. Quite loudly. The silver-haired woman seemed agitated, her rubied mouth drawn into a severe line across her face as she asked Love a series of questions. I wasn't sure who I felt sorrier for: the woman or Love.

On one hand, the woman clearly had a lot riding on Love's reading. Most psychics were little more than charlatans, and though I'd gotten the impression Love was the real deal, like my grandmother or Serinda, to place so much faith in something like the reading of one's palms seemed foolhardy.

On the other, the severe lines on the woman's face, the hard expression, made me think she wanted the reading to go a certain way, and she was not going to accept anything else.

Apparently, Love obliged. The woman gasped and sat back in her chair before her gaze traveled to the man sitting in the waiting area. Thus, my concern ricocheted to him and his well-being. The woman did not seem happy with him.

I couldn't take it anymore. I turned to Roane and whispered, "What did she say?"

He chuckled softly and returned a figurine in the shape of a zombie back to its hook. "Isn't that breaking some kind of confidentiality thing you witches have?"

"What? No. Maybe. I don't know. Is that man in danger?"

"Only because he wants to be."

"What does that mean?"

Love looked over her shoulder at us, her glare speaking volumes, so I shut my mouth and continued perusing the selection. Who knew they made cauldron-shaped coffee mugs? Her divided attention, no matter how fleeting, was enough to annoy her client, a woman clearly so entitled, she'd give a European princess a run for her money. She slapped her hand on the table, the sharp sound piercing in the small shop.

My hackles skyrocketed. I started to step over to them, to defend the talented witch, but Love didn't seem to need my assistance. Slowly and with methodical care, she turned an astonished gaze on the woman.

"I am paying you for your time. I expect your full attention."

Beyond livid, Love unfolded from her seat, took out what I could only assume was the woman's check, and tore it in half. She tossed the two halves on the table and pointed to the door, saying through gritted teeth, "Out."

The woman gasped and lunged back again, as though Love had slapped her. Then she snatched up the pieces and rose in a huff, almost upending the table. "I am filing a formal complaint with the city," she said, shouting for her husband as she stormed out.

The man folded the magazine, gestured goodbye with a nod to Love, and went after his wife, his expression part dread and part annoyance. Poor guy.

I couldn't believe what I just saw. I stepped closer to Roane and asked, "People still write checks?"

"Where's your friend?" Love asked as she stepped off the platform and headed toward us. It was a small shop, so it didn't take her long.

"Um, Love?" The girl behind the cash register stood with eyes wide. She pointed to the door the woman just stormed out of.

"It's okay, Gwen," Love said.

"No, it's just, I already ran the check through the system."

The grin that softened Love's face was priceless. "I know. She'll be back, I'm sure, but until then..." She turned her sparkling green gaze, the one that was as sharp as a scalpel, back to me. "Where's your friend?"

"Home."

She focused on Roane, her poker face slipping for barely a microsecond as she took him in, then turned back to me.

"Can you tell me what she did?" I asked, wondering what in the world my BFF could've done to warrant such animosity.

Her expression hardened. "She knows what she did."

I stepped closer. "Yeah, but that's the problem. I don't."

She eyed me for a long moment like she was trying to see into my soul. It would never work. I was certain I didn't have one. After a silence so uncomfortable, I fought the urge to scratch my arms, she asked, "What are you?"

Okay, then. "I'm just a girl, standing in front of another girl, asking the second girl what on earth the first girl's BFF did that was so bad it got the first girl's BFF banned from the second girl's shop." I, perhaps, could've worded that better.

"Fine," she said. "Don't answer. What is he?" She gestured toward Roane who was perched against the checkout counter with his arms crossed.

"He's just a man, standing in front of—"

"Is this conversation going anywhere?" She turned and headed back to her mojo area. "I have another client coming in five."

"So I have five minutes?"

"You have two." When I questioned her with a raised brow, she added, "I have to pee."

"Oh, sorry. Okay, two minutes. I'll take them."

We stepped onto the platform, and she sat down. I sank into the seat across from her.

I had an entire coven I could go to, expert advice on call twenty-four-seven, but I wanted to talk to someone outside the coven. Someone without a vested interest.

"I just have a couple of questions."

She held out her hand and said, "Palm."

"Oh." I gave her my palm, but the minute my skin touched hers, an electrical arc passed between us.

She sucked in a soft breath and eased away from me, yet kept hold of my hand with one of hers. She didn't take her wary gaze off me when she leaned over the side of the table and grabbed a small bottle.

"Okay, well, I'll get right to it," I said. I didn't have a lot of time. "Can a witch manipulate memories?"

She tipped the bottle just enough to put a drop of oil on one of her fingers as she studied me.

"Especially those of another witch?"

"Depends," she said as she drew a symbol on my palm with the oil.

"That smells really nice." I picked up the bottle, but it wasn't labeled. "Patchouli?" I asked.

She lowered her head, locked her gaze onto mine, and said... I had no idea what. The language was foreign. Something old. Maybe Latin? Or Farsi? Or Spanglish?

I leaned closer, suddenly very interested in what she saw. "Well? Are you getting anything?"

"What are you?"

I frowned in disappointment. "Are you going to tell me my future or what?"

She stumbled back, almost falling out of her chair, and repeated, "What are you?"

That time I frowned in suspicion and lifted the bottle again. "Okay, what was this supposed to do to me?"

She stepped as far away as her gated mojo area would

allow. "It's... it's a truth serum. You should have been compelled to tell me the truth."

I crossed my arms. "Well, that's not nice."

"How did you... Why didn't that work?"

"Probably because... Wait. Why?" I asked, suddenly worried. "Does it usually? Is there something wrong with me?"

"Yes and yes." Her gaze darted around as though she were looking for an escape.

Did this have anything to do with the fact that I was a charmling? I could hardly ask her that. She could team up with a warlock and try to steal my powers.

I held up my palms in surrender and eased to my feet. "Look. We've clearly gotten off on the wrong foot."

"I saw your hunter, warlock," she said, her voice little more than a hiss. "You stay the fuck away from me."

Sensing his nearness, I looked over my shoulder to see Roane had come onto the platform and stood behind me.

She grabbed a small crystal off a shelf, held it in her open palm, and waved her other hand over it, chanting something in that same language. The crystal started to glow a beautiful turquoise about the same time Roane doubled over, crashing to the ground as he held his head in pain.

ELEVEN

You know you drink too much coffee if:
You go to AA meetings for the free java.
—Meme

"Roane!" I fell to the ground beside him as he tensed in agony. "What's wrong?"

"The sound," he said, his voice strained as he groaned, the pain becoming too much.

I glared at Love and stood.

She redoubled her efforts, putting her entire body into it, her chanting monotone but the words coming faster and faster. The crystal glowed even brighter, and Roane fell to his side and curled into a fetal position.

"Give me that," I said, snatching the crystal out of her hand. It stung when I grabbed it. Not horribly so, but I threw it to the side nonetheless, worried it would explode or turn into a sea monster, considering the last few days of my life.

The tension in Roane's body eased, and he rolled onto his knees, but he still held his head.

I gaped at her. "What the hell, Love?"

She gaped back for an entirely different reason. "You're not a witch or a warlock."

"Why did you do that?"

"What are you?" she yelled, fear glistening in her eyes.

I bent to help Roane onto the chair I'd vacated, his large body weakened by whatever she'd done, and knelt in front of him. His handsome face was still lined with pain, but he was breathing. "What did you do to him?"

"He's a shifter," she said. "What kind? A fox? A wolf?"

"A fuck you," he said from between clenched teeth, but talking seemed to hurt his head even worse.

"Great." I glared at her. "Now he's grumpy."

But I remembered something. I'd taken away his pain before. The pain of a thousand crushed bones. Or a hundred. Either way, I sought out the spell and drew it over him with two fingers. The thick lines seeped with the blinding glow of my magics, and I pushed them onto him.

He slumped closer, draping his arms over my shoulders as the pain leeched out of him, and he relaxed completely.

I looked over to scold our newest acquaintance again, but she lay prostrate on the ground, her knees folded under her. She was whispering something I couldn't understand.

This entire situation had spiraled out of control so fast it made me seasick. We needed to leave her be. Let her recoup. But before I could help Roane to his feet, he bolted out of the chair, moving faster than my eyes could track. He was in front of me one second and behind me the next. He wrapped a hand around Love's throat and had her braced against the wall before I could say *who's your daddy*. A low, guttural growl rumbled out of his chest.

"Roane!" Jumping up, I hurried over to them and latched on to his arm. "Roane, let her go this instant!"

She was still mumbling, and I finally recognized one of the words: Sarru.

My heart sank. "No way. Not you, too."

"Please, forgive me." She pleaded, her face flushed, her cheeks wet, her voice strained. But she did have a massive hand constricting her larynx. And her airflow.

I yanked again. "Roane, seriously."

"I didn't know, Sarru. Please—"

"—stop." I pulled Roane off her at last, grabbed a rag that smelled like lemon-scented furniture polish off a shelf, and dabbed at her cheeks. "Sweetheart, stop. What is going on?"

She dodged my ministrations and fell to the ground, going all prostrate and worshippy again. "Please, forgive me."

Oh, for the love of... "Okay. You're forgiven. Now stop it." I helped her off the ground, and we sat on our knees, gazing into each other's eyes. Or we would have been if she would look at me, but she kept her gaze downcast.

A few customers came into the shop and began browsing, but the cashier was gone. We'd frightened her off.

"Be with you in a minute," I said happily, then I looked at Roane. "Can you see to the customers while we talk?"

He glared at the audacity.

"That would be a no," I told Love.

She covered her face with both of her hands.

I gave her a moment to gather herself and spotted the can of furniture polish. It was the multi-surface kind, so I polished my nails while I waited.

The group that came in hovered nearby, clearly killing time, waiting their turns to have their palms read by a real

Salem witch. Love did have a business to run, and we'd taken up far too much of her day. And we almost killed her, so there was that.

"We'll go," I said when she continued to sob into her hands. "But can I come back later?"

She sniffed and lowered her hands just enough to show her emerald irises, her lids swollen around them. "Please don't go, Sarru."

"Defiance." I held out my hand. "Defiance Dayne."

She took it and bowed her head over our clasped hands. "It's such an honor. I've never met a real charmling."

"You know what I am?"

"Of course. No one but a charmling draws spells on the air like that. I've never seen anything like it. And"—she looked at Roane—"I thought you were a shifter."

"He is a shifter."

She blinked, confused. "He's not your warlock?"

"He wishes," I said with a snort. "Why would you think that?"

"Because I saw a hunter in town."

"Where?" Roane asked, his tone brusque.

"On the street. Like he was waiting for something. Or someone. Does he belong to your warlock?"

"No, hon." I helped her onto a chair. "He may belong to a warlock, but I do not."

The surprise in her expression said it all. She stared a really long time. Long enough for me to conjure elevator music to entertain myself. "How is that possible?"

Now was certainly not the time to get into it. I sat across from her and leaned closer. "Look, I'm new to the whole charmling thing. I've only just gotten my powers back, so—"

"Back?"

"Yes. They were... dormant. For, like, forty years. Give or take. It's a long story."

"How is that possible?" she repeated.

"You'd have to ask my grandmother. But just to be clear, you don't know why the hunter is in town?"

An idea seemed to take shape. She took hold of my hand. "He must be here for you, Sarru." Her gaze shot to Roane. "You must protect her."

"No, no. It's okay. I have a coven. Kind of. I've only met a few so far, but I'm meeting the rest this afternoon."

She shook her head. "That's not enough. You need a warlock to protect you."

"No. It's amazing how I need a warlock to protect me when they are the very reason I need protection in the first place."

She sank back into her chair. "You're right, Sarru."

"Defiance."

"I apologize. But you haven't been under a warlock's protection, how have you kept your powers for so long?"

"Again, you'd have to ask my grandmother."

Then another thought hit her, if the stunned expression she leveled on me meant anything. "But that would mean you've had your powers since you were a kid. I don't understand."

"I was born with them, apparently."

"You're... you're a blood heir."

"Yes."

She sank onto the floor and tried to do the prone thing again.

"Oh, no, you don't," I said, physically stopping her from sinking to the ground. Once I had her ass planted back in the chair, I had to ask, "How did you even know? How did you know I was... different?"

"Your energy. I've always been able to see auras, and yours is... Well, it's unlike anything I've ever seen."

"How can you see them?" I was a charmling, and even I couldn't see people's auras.

"I'm a blood witch. My mother is from a long line of witches, but she says I'm much more powerful than she ever was."

I may not have known much about witches in general, but to say Love was a powerful witch was an understatement. Anyone who could bring Roane to his knees deserved more than a modicum of respect.

"My mother believes I inherited my power from my father, though she doesn't know who he is."

Strange coincidence. My mother didn't know who my father was either. And the disturbing culture of misogyny seeps even into the witch community, a community that was traditionally a balance between the masculine and the feminine. I could see why the original witches created the charmlings. To protect their sisters, both witch and human, from the masculine regime. If they could see us now.

"I'm sorry, Sarru—"

"Defiance."

"—you had a question."

"Yes. Of course. You have customers. You need to get back to work."

"That's not it. You must get back to your coven. You must be protected."

That whole line of thinking was getting old, but I didn't tell her that. "All right. I promise to go home right after this where I'm protected by a powerful witch, a haunted house, a wolf shifter, and a feisty best friend who may or may not be a crow when I get home." Hopefully she'd been practicing. "Can a witch use some kind of spell to manipulate memories?"

"Of course. Even a low-level blood witch can do something like that. But it takes a much more powerful witch to do it for very long."

"What do you mean?"

"It doesn't stick. It's more like a sideshow trick. The memory may be altered, but only for a short time or only while the witch is nearby. But a more powerful witch..." She thought about it. "I mean, it's not like in the movies. Even blood witches can't control you."

After seeing what she just did to Roane, I wasn't sure I believed her.

"They can't make you do something against your will. Not without a little help. But they can manipulate your memories."

"Manipulate how?"

"Subtract. Add. Edit. That being said, the more precise the manipulation, the more precise the skill needed. It's like surgery. It takes years of practice with a scalpel to do such a thing, and it veers quite far into the black arts."

I chewed on a nail in thought and tasted furniture polish. "Can you think of anyone in the area with that skill set?"

She shook her head. "I'm sorry, I have no idea. But I haven't lived here long."

Though I hated my next question, it had to be voiced. "I'm sorry to even ask this, Love, but what about you? You're clearly skilled. Could you manipulate someone's memories? Perhaps another witch's?"

She dropped her gaze as though ashamed. "I would never lie to you, Sarru."

"Defiance."

"I have... dabbled. But, no. I've never tried to do what you're asking."

"You've dabbled in black magic?"

"Yes. Briefly. It was a long time ago. A teen rebellion thing."

I felt a grin tighten one corner of my mouth. "You said not without a little help. What kind of help?"

"The usual. Herbs. Flowers. Anything that pertains to memory. And sometimes..." She looked around her shop and pointed. "See that hourglass?"

I followed her line of sight to a high shelf on a far wall. A gorgeous hourglass sat inside a carved black frame adorned with engraved silver, the sand on the bottom a deep red like the iron-rich molecules of a dying star. "It's beautiful."

"It's old. It's also a relic from my black-magic days. Something like that could be used to manipulate the temporal aspects of memories."

"You mean, like, when something happened?"

"Exactly. Someone could be made to believe they'd eaten at a certain restaurant on a Tuesday instead of a Monday."

"That doesn't sound worth the effort."

"You'd be surprised. There are any number of applications for something like that. Witness tampering, for one. Again, it would take a skilled hand. Otherwise, the target's memories could be wiped completely. My mother would know more. I could ask her if you'd like."

"Please." I took out my phone and handed it to her. "Can you put in your number? I'll get back with you."

"Of course," she said.

"So all black magic is bad?"

She shook her head. "No magics are inherently bad.

Even black magics can be used for good, but because they go against a witch's philosophy, against the natural order of things, the harmonious nature we seek with the world around us, it's called black magic or dark magic. But it's what you do with the magics that counts. I would never use them to harm anyone."

I believed her, though I did have to ask my next incriminating question. Gigi had been poisoned going on seven months prior, thus... "How long have you lived in Salem?"

One of the patrons coughed impatiently, hoping to hurry us along. I'd half expected an officer to show up with the way the cashier ran out of the shop, but so far, nothing.

"A little over six months ago," she began, "I felt a really strong pull to move here. Just out of the blue. My mom suggested I listen, but it took me about three months to find a shop and get it open. Not to mention a place to live I could afford."

"Well, I'm glad you did."

A soft pink blossomed over her cheeks. "Thank you."

"I'm not," Roane said, rubbing his temple.

I tossed him a quick scowl, even though I almost had a meltdown myself when he was being hurt. "You don't count," I teased. "I just have one more question, Love."

"Anything, Sarru."

"Defiance." I leaned closer. "Why did you take your cashier's diary?"

She stilled, as though my words had solidified everything she'd already suspected, but I thought I did that when I admitted to being a charmling.

"I didn't. I found who did and stole it back. He... it would've hurt her."

Pride filled the vast cavity in my chest where my heart

should've been. Sadly, I'd given it away to the man standing beside me. "Good for you, Love."

"Elle," she said, brightening. "My friends call me Elle. Love is more like a stage name."

"Elle. Are you ever going to give the diary back?"

One corner of her mouth crinkled into a mischievous grin. "Yes. But I'm going to make her sweat first. She left it out in the open." When she realized what her words had implied, she jumped to correct herself, taking my hands into her own. "Not that her carelessness excuses the boy's actions. Not in the least. But Gwen does need to learn to be more careful, especially considering what she wrote."

"You read it?"

"Oh, Goddess, no. Absolutely not, but it's been hard. The things she told me..."

And now I liked Love—Elle—even more. That she would respect her cashier's privacy that much meant a great deal.

"Wait," she said, snapping back to me. "That makes you the finder."

"The finder?"

"Of lost things."

"How did you know?"

"There are three charmlings: the finder, the healer, and the seer."

I leaned closer, intrigued. "For real? I had no idea." And I hadn't. The fact that each charmling had a different area of expertise made the whole thing even more delicious. "My grandmother was a finder as well, though not a charmling. Not a blood heir. I just figured I got that part from her side."

"Are you sure it's not the other way around?"

"In what way?"

"Perhaps your grandmother's magics were influenced

by yours instead of vice versa. Was she a finder before you came along?"

I sat back. "I think so, but—"

Another cough wafted toward us from the peanut gallery.

"Okay, we need to go."

Love bowed her head. "Thank you for coming, Sarru." Then she cast a sideways glance at Roane. "Sorry about your dog."

I slammed my eyes shut when Roane emitted a low growl. "Now, now. Let's play nice."

She led us to the door, but before we left, I turned and said, "Oh, wait, just one more question."

"You'll have to ask her, Sarru," she said, fighting a giggle.

Damn it. So close.

TWELVE

Once upon a time,
there was a girl who really loved coffee.
It was me.
The end.
—True story

"How's your head?" I asked Roane when we walked out of Elle's shop and into the crisp air. The sun hung low, adding ribbons of orange to the already moody sky.

"Better now. But everything sounds like it's underwater."

I stopped short and gave him my full attention. "Your hearing is messed up?"

"Very much so. And there is a ringing."

"Crap." I looked back, wondering if I should go talk to her. "Surely it's not permanent."

He bit down. "It'd better not be."

"Roane, you can't kill her. She's a person."

"She's powerful. And at some point in her life, I'd say she was one step away from becoming a warlock."

"Seriously?" I asked, suddenly wary. "What makes you say that?"

He lifted a shoulder. "Even blood-born witches have to use spells to conjure that kind of power. They have to use something as a conduit."

"She did. The crystal."

"But there was no spell. It just worked for her."

"By spell, you mean something like eyes of newt and bat wings."

"Yes."

"She was reciting something."

"No. It would take way more preparation for a regular witch. Even someone like your grandmother."

"Damn. Are eyes of newt a real thing?"

A grin broke free from its restraint. "Yes, Ms. Dayne. Newts have eyes."

"Right. How do so many witches know about warlocks and hunters and charmlings when I've never even heard of such things? Well, okay, warlocks, but not about the hunters that they create or charmlings or the original witches."

"The vast majority don't. I think your coven knows so much because both Serinda and your grandmother are blood born. They come from a long line of witches, and the lore has been passed down from generation to generation."

We grabbed coffees and had barely pulled into the drive when Annette ran out, her face a shimmering frenzy of anticipation. She followed us as Roane drove around the side of the house to park in the back, his usual parking spot. I watched in the side mirror as she ran after us, waving her laptop.

"You know you could've let me out in front," I said through a fit of giggles.

He was laughing, too. "Yeah, but this is more fun."

When he went as far as he possibly could without crashing into the back fence, I opened my door. Before I could get out, however, she yelled, "Pirate booty!"

I stifled another giggle and asked, "Whose booty?"

"Pirate." She skidded to a halt, breathless with anticipation. "Think about it. Those caves were used by pirates for smuggling."

"We think," I corrected, handing her a coffee.

"They want the house because of the caves." She put her arms on my shoulders and shook, sloshing coffee out of the sippy hole on the lid. "Deph, don't you get it. There's pirate treasure in them there caves."

I shook coffee off my hand and started for the back door. "I have considered the caves. That's clearly how they got in and out. The caves are easily accessible from the outside. They're hidden from view. But how would anyone even know about them?"

The self-satisfied smirk she wore suggested she'd already thought of that. "Maps."

We stepped into the mudroom and took off our jackets before heading for the kitchen. "You found maps with the caves drawn on them?"

She lifted a shoulder. "In a way." She turned to my beau. "Strip, wolf boy."

"Boy?"

"You know, now might not be a good time, Nette."

"Why?"

"We had a run-in with Elle."

"Who's Elle?"

"You know her as Liliana Lovett?"

Annette's eyes rounded to perfect saucers. Saucers of betrayal. "You spoke to Love?"

"I did."

"Behind my back?"

"She would hardly let me into her store if you were there." I sat at the kitchen table. "And her friends, like Roane and me, call her Elle."

"We are not friends," Roane said.

"They are, he just doesn't know it yet."

Annette sat in shock. "Why?"

"Because she's nice, and I think they'll get along famously."

"No, why would you go see her? She's cray-cray."

"Please. She's very nice. And she's a blood witch."

"But... wait, really? Damn it." She sank into the chair beside me and banged a fist lightly on the table. "I should've known. She's too good at predictions to be a mundane. Almost as good as I am."

I rubbed my brow. "You and Elle are just going to have to learn to get along."

"You're just saying that because you don't know what I did."

I started to ask her about that when Samuel joined us. He climbed into a chair and propped his head on his folded hands, his little blond head barely able to reach the tabletop.

"Hey, mister man," I said, taking another sip. "Where's your friend?"

He pointed outside, a place he apparently could not go without some help. A salt barrier kept the riffraff out, but they could get in or out if attached to a host. So I'd been told. Which was apparently how he got in. He'd followed Annette and me home.

Samuel went back to pouting. His only friend had

escaped. The three-year-old released a forlorn sigh then vanished.

Annette had been gazing at him with ardent adoration, but she gasped softly when he disappeared. "I didn't know they could do that."

"I'm still learning about the departed, too. So, you mentioned a map?"

"Oh, yes." She perked up and looked at Roane again. "Do it, mister man. I need you naked."

He arched a scythe-shaped brow but lifted his shirt over his head.

If I'd known it would be that easy, I would've had him do that hours ago. I resisted the urge to rub my hands together in anticipation as the shirt slid away and was replaced with the hills and valleys of a nigh-perfect physique, almost every inch covered in ink.

Annette sprang to her feet to study him, but I sat there marveling at the work. It was gorgeous. Detailed. A giant black-and-gray skull covered most of his torso. She twirled a finger to get him to turn around, and he obeyed. An old map of Salem covered his back with a symbol overlayed in the middle. The symbol for the spell I'd used to change the wolf into the boy. He'd somehow remembered it.

She ran her fingers over his back, following a section in the middle that literally shouted *X marks the spot*. It was faint. Lighter than the other lines. "Exactly what I thought."

"What?" I stood to join her, wanting in on the action.

She pushed her glasses farther up her nose and pointed. "Here."

"What am I looking at?"

"Unless I'm mistaken, the caves."

"Why would the caves be on a topographical map of old Salem?"

"Right?" She leaned around him. "Where did you get this map?"

"It's a copy I found at the library when I was a kid. They sell them everywhere."

"No, they don't." She opened her laptop and pulled up a sepia-toned image. "Here's the map they sell all over. Notice anything?"

Roane and I both leaned in to look closer.

"Wait, you're right." I turned him around again and followed the lines of the early streets of Salem, interrupted only by the spell. "They have all the streets and the landmarks, but none of this other stuff is on there. And look." I ran my fingers along the lines that spiderwebbed out from the initial cave system. "They branch out in all directions."

Gigi came up the stairs and stopped. "What are you girls doing to poor Roane?"

"Nothing you haven't wanted to do, Gigi."

"Who says I haven't?"

Annette snorted, and Roane tossed her a flirtatious grin.

I laughed before reality sank in. Then I stabbed Annette with an accusatory stare. "How did you know?"

"Know what?"

"That the map on Roane's back was different from the maps they sell in town? Did you put a camera in his shower again?"

She choked on her coffee and smiled at Roane. "She's kidding."

"Only a little."

"My point is, someone could've realized this map had caves and come looking for the booty."

"There's booty?" Gigi asked, making a fresh pot of coffee.

"I'm sure of it." Annette set her jaw.

"Anyone could've seen that map," I said, reminiscing on the fact that anyone could've seen that map.

"Pretty much. But at least we have our motive."

"I'm not sure the hope of finding pirate booty is motive enough to kill someone. They would have to know for certain the treasure was there to risk such a move. Therefore, they would've already found it. Therefore, they would've had no reason to kill Gigi."

"Are you going to rain cats and dogs on my parade all day? We need to get down there just in case. Find it before they do. After all, you're the finder of lost things."

"Okay, let's say you're right and they haven't found it yet. Don't you think they would've been looking for it this whole time?"

She backhanded my arm. "That's just it. Not with super wolf here. And as long as Gigi was alive and Roane was working for her with his super-wolf hearing... You see the problem."

"So, not only did they know about the caves, they knew about Roane being a wolf shifter with super hearing and they killed Gigi to get rid of Roane so they could search for a pirate treasure?"

"Bingo."

"All right. I will concede that it is a possibility. Though a slim one."

She did a little dance in her seat. Either that or she had to pee. "Yay me. Wait, you never answered me. Why did you go see Love?"

"I had a few questions. She had a few answers. Now I get to call her Elle."

"What kind of questions?"

"The kind that end in a question mark."

"Did she... tell you what happened?" she hedged.

"Yep. She told me everything." I glared at her. "I'm so ashamed, Annette. That you of all people would do such a thing."

She sagged in her chair. "She didn't tell you a damned thing."

"No, but she thought about it. I could tell."

"She really didn't," Roane said.

Gigi giggled, and I suddenly remembered my bestie was having sexy times with my grandmother's ex. In her dreams, yes, but still... How would Gigi take that? Would she care? She'd been dating the chief for over forty years. I could only imagine what they did in the house my grandfather haunted.

Hoping my grandfather wasn't a voyeur, I beamed at Gigi. Perhaps a little too conspicuously.

She narrowed her lids to razor-sharp slits. "What?"

"What?"

"You're looking at me funny."

"No funnier than usual. Roane and I met a very powerful witch named Elle. She's blood born. Comes from a long line, apparently. I think you should invite her into the coven."

"Really?" she asked, pouring herself a cup of coffee. She held it out to Roane.

He breathed in the aroma and gave her a thumbs-up.

"I'll bring it up to the cove." She sat beside me, and we all watched Roane put his shirt back on.

A sadness thickened the air. "Oh," I said, bouncing back, "what about Joaquin Ferebee? What did you find out?"

Annette dropped her gaze, suddenly very interested in her coffee lid. "Right, um, I'm still waiting on my contact to get back with me."

"And what contact would that be?"

"The one I'm waiting on to get back with me."

"Annette, what did you find out?"

She caved. So easy. "It's just, there's nothing you can do to help him, Deph. I'm not sure why you're having such a strong feeling to jump to his aid. It's too late."

"Annette."

She gave in with a sigh. "His son went missing a year ago."

I refocused on her. "His son?"

"Yes. A year ago tomorrow, to be exact."

A hefty dose of adrenaline shot through my body. "I knew I felt a sense of urgency. Why didn't you tell me sooner? We have to find him."

She put a hand on my arm. "Defiance, they found the boy's backpack in an abandoned warehouse a month after he went missing. It was covered in blood. A lot of blood."

"But they didn't find his body?"

"No, but... Deph, the odds of him being alive are astronomical. I didn't want you to have to go through that."

"Through what?" I asked, more confused now than ever.

She exhaled, reluctant to even talk about it. "What if you find Mr. Ferebee? What if you read him? What if you see what he's searching for?"

I shrugged, my patience wearing thin.

"His son."

I tilted my head.

"A child," she added. "A child who was killed almost a year ago."

"You just said they didn't find a body. You can't know that."

"But what if? Do you really want to see something like that? Something you can never unsee?"

I glanced at Roane. "I've already seen it once. Don't handle me, Annette."

"It's just, you've been through so much."

"If there is even the slightest chance that boy is alive—"

"There's not," she said, her tone matter-of-fact.

"What do you mean?"

She dropped her gaze to study her cup. "I mean, I talked to the detective in Chicago in charge of the investigation. Based on the amount of blood they found at the scene, there is simply no way the boy survived."

I sank back, a familiar weight pressing into my chest. "They're certain he's gone?"

"Yes. At least, the detective sounded certain. The case is still open, of course. They wouldn't close it this soon without a body."

"Did he have any insights? Any suspects?"

"Not that he could divulge, but he did say that before they found the backpack, Mr. Ferebee had suspected his wife of abducting him. They'd gone through a bitter divorce, and he'd gotten custody of the boy. The detective hinted that the wife had a history of substance abuse. That's how Mr. Ferebee got custody."

I nodded. "What was his name? The boy's?"

"Milo." She clicked a few buttons on her phone and turned it toward me to show me the face of a gorgeous boy no more than three with curly black hair, huge brown eyes, and a nuclear smile.

I took the phone for a closer look, and my heart sank. "He's beautiful."

"He is."

"He looks like his dad."

Gigi leaned over for a look.

I angled the phone so she could see the screen better. "If he's really gone, then what I felt at the café, that urgency, must be for Mr. Ferebee. Not what he's searching for. Right?"

"Perhaps," Gigi said. She touched the screen as though she could touch Milo's face.

"I'm not sure what's going on, but we have to find him."

Annette acquiesced with a nod. "I have feelers out. I should know where he's staying soon."

When Annette turned away, I remembered one pertinent detail. How could I forget her missing brother who was also never found? "Austin."

She turned back to me. "What about him?"

"I didn't even think. I'm sorry, Annette."

"No. I'm good. This has nothing to do with him."

But it had to hit close to home. I decided not to push it and handed her phone back. "Keep me updated."

Someone knocked on the front door.

"Serinda," Roane said.

"Oh, right." Gigi rose to put her cup in the sink before answering the door. "The coven is coming over."

"How could you possibly know that's Serinda?" I asked him.

"She needs new brake pads."

I laughed softly. "So your hearing is back?"

"It's getting there," he said with a charming tilt of his head. He was leaning against the island, his booted feet crossed at the ankles.

"You know, I'm going to need another look at that map."

He pushed off the island and bent over me until his mouth was at my ear. He drew in a breath and started to say something but stopped.

I leaned back to look at him.

He drew his brows together and breathed in again, this time standing. As Gigi passed, he stopped her with an arm and sniffed deeply. Then he looked at Annette. She was scrolling through her phone, about to take another sip, when he lunged for her cup and jerked it out of her hand.

"Hey," she said, and tried to steal it back.

He lifted it to his nose before ripping off the lid and sniffing more deeply. His gaze traveled back to Annette, his expression a mixture of disbelief and dread.

Serinda knocked softly again. Percy must've let her in, because she called out, "Is anyone home?"

"Roane, what is it?" Gigi asked.

"Yeah, Roane," Annette said, slowly rising to her feet. "What is it?"

He tilted the cup and let Gigi take a whiff, holding it away and warning her with a soft "Careful."

I stood for a whiff, too. He barely let me close enough to smell anything, but Gigi nodded, and said, "Almonds."

I tried again. "No, hazelnut. Her favorite."

Roane stood staring at Annette like she'd grown another head.

I glanced over my shoulder to make sure she hadn't.

"You drank half the cup," he said, astonished.

"Yeah. It's my cup. What was I supposed to do with it? Sing it a lullaby?" When he only stared, she exploded into a full-blown meltdown. "Oh my God. What? Am I going to die?" She backed away, panting as the blood drained from her face. "I'm going to die, aren't I? Call 9-1-1! Call 9-1-1!" She grabbed her chest and fell back against the door.

I hurried to her. "Annette!" I looked at Roane. "What did she drink?"

He blinked as though he couldn't believe it and said softly, "Cyanide."

Serinda walked into the kitchen. "Is everything okay back here?"

"Nannette drank cyanide," Gigi said, and I was a bit taken aback by her aplomb.

Realization dawned for my bestie. She turned an accusatory glare on me. "Defiance Dayne. You brought me this coffee."

"What? I didn't put cyanide in your coffee, *Nannette*. Why would I put cyanide in your coffee?"

"Something's not right," Roane said, sniffing again.

"Yeah, no one is calling 9-1-1!" she shrieked. "What the hell?"

I jumped for my cell and tapped the phone icon.

"I can't breathe," she said, clutching her throat. She sank to the ground and went limp, her gaze sliding past me, presumably as her life passed before her eyes.

It was all very dramatic. So dramatic, in fact, that I was beginning to wonder about Roane's statement. I turned back to him. "What do you mean something's not right?"

"This cup isn't just laced with cyanide. It's pure hydrogen cyanide. If this room were any hotter, it would turn into a gas and we'd all be killed."

Gigi and Serinda locked arms and eased away from him.

"But there wasn't even a trace of cyanide when we got it. I would've smelled it in the truck."

I woke up my phone and hit the internet. "Okay, Annette, are you nauseous? Dizzy? Having convulsions or slipping into a coma?"

"No," she said, so weak she could barely speak. "But it

shouldn't be long now." She patted the air blindly before finding my face. "Defiance? Is that you?"

I slapped her hand away and looked at Gigi. "What is going on?"

Sadly, Gigi was no help. She stood in a stupor, shaking her head slightly.

"Annette," I said, slapping her hand away again, "if you were dying from cyanide poisoning, you'd be foaming at the mouth or having seizures."

"Really?"

"Really. If nothing else, you'd be in a tremendous amount of pain."

She frowned at me. "Who says I'm not?"

A knock sounded at the door. The coven members were beginning to show up.

Roane took out a bucket from underneath the sink and began filling it with water.

"Gigi, for real, what is going on?"

"I don't know, Defiance." She exchanged a suspicious look with Serinda.

"Wait," Annette said, sitting up. "Am I dying or not?"

"Gigi?" I asked. "Roane?"

Again, they just looked at each other, but Gigi's expression turned thoughtful.

Frustrated, I walked to over to Roane. "Are you sure your sniffer isn't on the fritz?"

"My sniffer?" he asked, totally offended. Once the bucket was full, he took the cup and poured the contents of Annette's cup into it.

"Will that neutralize it?"

"It'll dilute it enough to where I can pour it down the sink. Dilution is the solution of pollution."

"Ah. Handy. But how did it get there? Annette could've been killed."

"Or worse," Annette said, brushing herself off as she stood.

I wasn't sure what would be worse, but okay.

"Who is doing this?" She glanced at each one of us. "Who wants me dead?" When another knock sounded, this one louder, she gave up with a saucy humph and went to the door.

"Should I even ask what's going on?" Serinda said.

Gigi took her aside to fill her in on all the near poisonings while I went to the door. For the rest of the afternoon, Serinda looked at Annette with that same curious suspicion Gigi had been throwing her way. Even as the coven filed in, sometimes three at a time, Serinda's gaze rarely wavered off Annette.

Did they think she had something to do with the poisonings? She didn't. I would swear under oath to that, but who did? Someone seemed to want us all dead, and perhaps that was the key to finding the motive.

Again, I had to ask: What would the person doing this have to gain by our deaths? If many experts were to be believed, there were only three things that drove murder: greed, lust, and power. Even if no one wanted Gigi's seat in the coven, it still could've been power related. If a dark witch figured out Gigi's granddaughter was a charmling, that would be more than enough motive to kill her, to ferret me out of the woodworks, but the odds of that were slim enough as to be almost nonexistent. Even I hadn't known the truth, and I was the charmling.

The true motive almost had to be greed, though I couldn't discount lust entirely. Was someone obsessed with Gigi? Secretly in love with her? Didn't want anyone else to have her? Or maybe they thought there had been something between Gigi and Roane.

Still, greed was the most likely culprit. Money was the root and all. If Gigi and I both were to die, who would get her money? I made a mental note to check into that.

THIRTEEN

Sometimes I stand in the shower for ten minutes
before I remember what I'm supposed to be doing.
So, yes, your secrets are safe with me.
—True fact

I leaned over to Annette as we greeted new arrivals at the door. Since she knew them all now, she introduced me, her voice still shaky from her near-death experience, and reintroduced me to the ones I'd met at the luncheon a couple days earlier.

"It would seem the coven now believes it's okay to call me *sarru*. I wonder where they got that impression?" I looked over and stabbed Serinda with a vengeful glare.

She ignored it. It happened.

No one in particular had stood out when I'd researched the coven members that morning, but maybe meeting with them one on one would yield new information.

We met in the great room, though with twenty-two

members, there were hardly enough sitting spots. I insisted Gigi and Serinda get first dibs, then let the others find their own way. A couple brought chairs in from the dining room. Others stood. Roane hovered near the door, his gaze a thousand miles away as he leaned against the wall with one foot crossed over the other.

Many a furtive glance meandered its way toward him from both the women in the group and two of the three male members. It seemed Roane was as much of an enigma to them as I was. But Gigi got her fair share of attention as well, with her spiked black hair and thick dark lashes.

Minerva was the last to arrive. She gave us a quick update on Leo and took a spot near one of the massive front windows.

When the entire group had shown up—quite the feat considering it was the middle of a workday—I stood and cleared my throat to get their attention. "Thank you all so much for coming." The inner circle had already been briefed, so my next words would not surprise them. As for the rest... "First, I want to introduce you to Georgiana Bishop, Ruthie's twin sister."

An audible gasp filled the air as every gaze landed on the new member. Of course, the inner circle knew the truth because they knew I'd brought her out of the veil and spent six months in a mystical coma as a result, but that information was far too delicate to entrust to the newer members.

"She's left her coven and is going to be taking Ruthie's place among us." I specifically used the word *us* to let them know we were all in this together, though I had yet to go to a sabbath.

Gigi tore her gaze off of Annette and nodded to the ranks.

"And for those of you who don't know, I'm her grandniece, Defiance. Not Sarru, despite what some would have you believe."

Their heads bowed ever so slightly regardless, as did Serinda's. This was getting ridiculous.

I rubbed my forehead, ignored the hint of a grin on Roane's face, and charged ahead. "As you all know by now, Ruthie's death was not an accident. She was poisoned, and we're trying to get information that might help the authorities make an arrest. But first, I want you to know, no one here is a suspect." I waited to gauge their reactions. Not only was no one surprised, no one was nervous in the least. Even Minerva, who defined the word. But they still could've unwittingly leaked information to the wrong person.

"I'd like to talk to each of you individually, but you are under no obligation to do so."

A tiny woman in a bright-yellow headdress spoke first, her dark skin like glass, and I seriously wanted to know her skincare regimen. "It would be an honor, Sarru."

"Defiance, and thank you. But again, no one is under any obligation. I'll be in the drawing room—because who has a freaking drawing room, amirite?—and you guys can decide who gets first dibs. Whoever needs to get back to work, maybe?"

They nodded and glanced around at each other.

"I promise not to take up too much of your time."

Annette, Ruthie, and Serinda followed me. Roane trailed behind, intent on the conversations happening in the next room. It was like having a bug. He could hear everything. At least, I hoped he could.

"I'll get them something to snack on," Annette said, going for her jacket.

"No!" I said, far too loudly.

Everyone stopped and looked at us.

"I mean, you're tired. And you almost died. Like seven times. Let's let Minerva run to the store." I motioned her over.

She hopped up and hurried over, but Annette's blatant gaping blindsided me. It would suggest I'd offended her.

"Nette," I said, trying to soften the sting. "Netters," I added when she only glared. She crossed her arms over her chest, so I put my hands on her shoulders and tried to placate her. Not very hard, but... "Netterly, when you can learn to stop trying to poison everyone around you, you can go to the store, too. Until then, I think someone else should take up the mantle of provider. And no matter what comes into the house, Roane must check it out." I said the last to Minerva.

"I'm on it," she said, heading for the door with my keys.

"Are you forgetting something?" I asked her.

She turned back, her hair hanging in dark tangles over her powder-blue coat, her expression blank.

"Money?"

"Oh." She snorted. "Right."

I pointed to the purse sitting behind the front door, having no clue whose it was. Or if there was even money in it.

"Here." Annette reached into her back pocket and handed over the credit card. She gave Minerva a list, then ushered the first victim—volunteer—into the drawing room, which looked exactly like the great room, only smaller. Same black walls. Same wood floors. Same charcoal furniture. Gigi was totally goth, but like an elegant goth. Like if one were to put Leonardo da Vinci and Tim Burton in a blender.

Gigi and Serinda sat on a settee close to the fireplace

while Annette sat on the window seat, presumably to give us some privacy, and Roane hung out by the archway. I only hoped the coven members didn't feel like we were ganging up on them.

The first coven member to come in was the stunning woman with the bright-yellow headdress. I hadn't met her at the luncheon, so she wasn't in the cove.

"Sarru," she said, bowing her head as I took her hand. "I'm Shanti." She had a soft African accent that was almost as beautiful as she was.

"Defiance," I corrected and gestured for her to sit. "Before we get started, may I ask what you use on your skin? It's incredible."

She laughed. "I nourish from the inside out. Many things. Would you like a list?"

Yes. Yes, I would, but that might be a conversation for another time since I had a thousand other witches to talk to. "Maybe we can have coffee one day? Discuss it? Because, damn."

Her rich brown eyes lit up.

"The sooner the better," I added. I needed all the help I could get.

"I would be honored, Sarru."

Deprogramming the ranks might take a little longer than I'd hoped. "Thank you. To the best of your recollection, did anyone ask you about Ruthie in the days or weeks leading up to her death? No matter how small. No matter how mundane."

Her wing-shaped brows slid together in thought. "I will think on it, Sarru, but I do not recall such a conversation."

"Did you discuss her with anyone that you can think of? I'm not trying to blame you for anything, Shanti. Or any of the coven members. I just want to be certain no one out of the ordinary was poking around."

"I understand, Sarru. I believe I have only talked about her with our members. Nothing out of the ordinary. But if I think of something..."

"Please let me know. May I take your hand?"

She bowed her head and held it out to me. Oh, yeah. Much longer to deprogram than I'd hoped.

I took her hand in mine, though I hardly needed to. Shanti was an open book. A deep, complex book with a tragic early childhood, but an open book nonetheless. One with nothing to hide.

She was mostly searching for knowledge and acceptance. She did want to be a great witch, but for purely unselfish reasons. She loved nature. Its essence. Its purity. And she wanted nothing more than to be its advocate. To live in harmony with the life around her.

But lying just below that, underneath all of her hopes and dreams, was her true heart's search. Her lost object. A friend from school she'd lost contact with. I saw her clearly in Shanti's mind. In her memories. Strawberry-blond hair. Wide smile. Freckles across her nose. They'd been best friends since the third grade, then, after a falling out when they were freshmen, her family moved. She never heard from her again.

I lowered my head and searched for the woman, wondering why the family moved so abruptly. Then I got the answer. Her stepfather had been a fugitive, running from the law. Someone recognized him, so they moved in the middle of the night. She grew up in a rough house. It was no wonder she got into drugs, especially when her stepfather practically forced them on her.

Did I tell Shanti that? Would she want to know?

I frowned. I could not start off these relationships with lies. I pulled her hand to my heart and looked deeply into her eyes. "Valerie Coleman."

Shanti drew in a soft breath. "Sarru, how did you...?" As though realizing who she was talking to, she pressed her mouth together and nodded.

"I'm so sorry, Shanti."

I felt the coldness of dread as it crept up her spine.

"She passed three years ago."

The shock and emotion were almost too much for her. She crumpled, but she managed to keep it on the inside. "May I ask, Sarru, what happened?"

"She had a hard life, Shanti. It wasn't her fault."

She nodded, knowing what I could not bring myself to say. "At least I know, yes?"

"I'm so sorry."

She fought the wetness forming between her lashes and lifted her chin. "You wish to ask me more questions, yes?"

"No, we're good. Thank you so much for coming." She had no concerns about anything she'd said to anyone, so even if she did let certain things slip to the wrong person, she had no knowledge of it. It would do no good for me to pry any further.

We said our goodbyes, and after a few more interviews, none revealing anything we didn't already know, Gigi walked up. "Defiance, you're wonderful with them."

"Thank you. I'm a little concerned this is going to take much longer than I thought."

"I don't think so. We're almost halfway through. Once they open up, you seem to get anything you need, right?"

"Yes. As unethical as that may be."

"Nonsense," Serinda said. "They know what they're getting into. They're honored."

"Yes, I noticed." I gave her a pretend scowl.

She ignored me and waved in the next volunteer while Annette took notes. The girl was a machine.

My first male witch walked in. He intrigued me, and I couldn't help but wonder what lured him to witchcraft. To the coven. What would he have to gain from the alliance? Not that his reasons had to be nefarious. I'd wondered that about all of the witches thus far, but for some reason, the male ones were a little more intriguing.

His name was Theo, and he was part of the inner circle. A twenty-something with thick dark curls and shimmering eyes that made him look like he was about to cry all the time. At least, that had been my first impression of him. That did not change when he walked in. The effect was rather mesmerizing.

He was also the first one to resist my charms. Though very polite and just as humbled as the rest of the group to be there, he was not the open book I'd come to expect. He was harder to read, yet he didn't seem to have anything to hide.

And the question arose again: Could I compel someone to tell me the truth? Could I force my way into their thoughts? Into their hopes and dreams?

It would be a violation. It was almost a violation when they were open and I just walked right in like I owned the place, siphoning off memories like a thief siphons gas. But to do it against someone's will...

Then again, Ruthie was murdered. Someone was trying to poison Annette. Or blow her up. If he had any information that could narrow down our nonexistent suspect list, would it be wrong of me to mine it?

Yes. It probably would be, but I focused nonetheless. "So, you don't remember anyone asking about Ruthie before she died?"

"I do not, Sarru. But you can check." He held out his hand, and guilt slammed into me.

"Do you know what will happen if I take your hand?" I asked him.

"I do." He was the only male who didn't cast furtive glances Roane's way. "I am a blood witch, just so you know. My father has a coven in Seattle."

"Your father?" I asked, surprised.

"Yes. And, no, he's not a warlock," he added with a grin.

I leaned closer. "Am I that easy to read?"

"Not at all, Sarru. It's just most people don't know that men can simply be witches. No matter how hard the path."

"I'm sure it is." I took his hand and waited, but nothing happened.

One corner of his mouth hitched up.

"Did Gigi put you up to this?"

"Your grandmother would never do such a thing." He glanced at her over his shoulder. "Love the hair, by the way."

Gigi winked at him. She so put him up to it. Always testing me.

"Okay, fine." I rolled up my sleeves, metaphorically speaking, and went to work. After taking his hand into both of mine, I closed my eyes and searched for a spell, if there was one. Finding none, I concentrated. I'd have to do this the old-fashioned way. I lifted my lids and channeled my inner Dracula. If the dark prince could compel people, surely a powerful witch could. When nothing happened, I realized pretty quickly I needed a goal. Like I had with Gigi when I accidentally tried to compel her.

"Come on, Deph," Annette said, cheerleading from the sidelines. "You can do it."

I stopped and threw her a quick scowl.

"Sorry," she whispered, pretending she had a hangnail.

Theo offered me a challenging smirk. "You'll have to try harder than that, Sarru."

At least I knew he was purposely blocking me. Whether it was a spell or just his innate ability, I had no idea, but surely I could get past his defenses. I lowered my lids again and focused on my goal: information. I needed to search his mind. To see, first, if anyone had questioned him about Ruthie, and second, to find out what he was searching for. Could I compel him? Could I force him to tell me?

I gathered my energy like wisps of smoke and pulled them to my center. Then I raised my lids and locked on to him. He could not look away. He instantly grew slack and leaned a little closer.

"Theodore Ezra King, what are you searching for?"

The smoky wisps of energy folded into itself until it was only a pinprick of blinding light, and then it burst, and everything was there. Everything. His entire life laid out before me. His unique upbringing. Learning algebra and memorizing spells. Mixing chemical solutions and magical potions. Reading dead white guys and wizards of old.

His father was firm but kind. His mother soft-spoken but strong. I searched his memories for anything unusual, but his entire life was unusual.

He was not as much of an outcast at school as I would've thought. Taking after his father, he was nerdy yet charismatic. Adored by many. Not popular so much as just very well-liked.

But combing through his life like a voyeur was getting me nowhere. I pulled back to more recent times. To his high school graduation. His first day at the University of Washington Seattle. His first frat party. His move to Salem.

A quick glimpse of a moment with his father before he

left nettled its way to the forefront. "If you find her, son, if you meet her, you know what to do."

"I do, Father."

They embraced, then his mother took him into her arms. "Be safe, Theo."

"I promise."

"And if you do meet her—"

"I'll tell her," he said with a soft laugh.

"And whatever you do, son," his father said as Theo got into his car, "do not look her in the eyes. A charmling can steal your soul if she so chooses."

A charmling? The designation brought the world rushing back. I blinked out of the trance and turned to Gigi. "His parents know about me!"

Something akin to pride with a smidgen of guilt shone blatantly on Gigi's face. "Yes. Theo's father is an old friend, as was his father before him."

"Wait, what happened?" Annette asked.

I had to admit, I was a little disappointed. "I thought I was like this big secret."

Gigi and Serinda laughed softly. "You are," Serinda said. "But a select few knew about you."

"Exactly." Gigi gave me her patient smile, the one that was more of an intermission while I tried to catch up to the rest of the class. "Think of them as your godparents."

"Or emergency contacts," Serinda offered.

"Yes. If anything untoward were to happen to me, I needed someone very powerful to find you and keep you and your dads safe."

I looked back at Theo. "And that was your parents?"

"And me," Serinda said. "Though I'd rather be thought of as that sassy aunt with a dash of crazy who is a bit of a bad influence."

"A bit?" Gigi emitted a strangely ladylike snort.

Roane chuckled from behind a fist, pretending to cough.

I tried to stifle my grin. Not very hard, but... Theo caught my attention. He hadn't moved. "Theo?" I leaned into him. He still sat transfixed to the spot. Unmoving. Unblinking. Then his head bent back, the tendons in his neck pulled taut. "Gigi!"

He was having a seizure.

Roane rushed over and helped me catch him. He eased him onto the floor, then moved the furniture out of the way. Every muscle in the kid's body strained against an invisible force. His back arched. His eyes rolled back in his head.

"Gigi, what do we do?"

"Just give him room," Annette said. "I'll call an ambulance."

"What did I do to him?"

I stood with my hands over my mouth as the rest of the coven rushed to the open archway. What did his father tell him? Don't look into a charmling's eyes or she would steal his soul? Panic closed my throat.

"Did I steal his soul?" I looked from Gigi to Serinda. "Can I even do that? Holy fuck, where did I put it?" I looked around me. Like an idiot.

"He's coming around," Annette said. She knelt beside him and looked into the crowd. "Can one of you get me a damp cloth?"

The commotion that followed would suggest that several ran off to do her bidding. One of them came back with a damp cloth, and Annette pressed it to his forehead while the rest of us stood around twiddling our thumbs.

"Gigi, did I steal his soul?"

"What? Why would you say that?"

"His father warned him before he left Seattle."

"You know he's from Seattle?" Serinda asked.

"Wait," Gigi said, showing a palm. "You saw a conversation between Theo and his father?"

"Yes. That doesn't matter." I faced her, needing an answer sooner rather than later. "Did. I. Steal. His. Soul?"

Minerva stood close by. She put an arm around my shoulder to console me. I leaned into her.

Then Theo's voice wafted toward us, weak but clear. "I'm pretty sure I still have my soul, though I don't know how much of my mind is left."

I fell to the floor beside him. "Theo! Holy crap. What happened? Please tell me this happens often."

Roane and Annette helped him onto the sofa. "I'm not really sure," he said, holding his head. "What exactly are you hoping happens often, Sarru?"

"You had a seizure."

His gaze shot to mine. "No way."

"Way. Are you certain I didn't steal your soul?"

A shaky smile thinned his lips. "If you did, you are one hell of a thief."

"But how would you know? It's not like you can see it."

He laughed. "Sarru, if you'd stolen my soul, I would've never regained consciousness. I would've been a vegetable until you either returned it or I died."

I sat beside him. "Theo, I am so sorry."

Shanti brought him a glass of water.

He took a big gulp. "You knew my full name even before you got inside my head."

"I must've read it." I thought back to my research. "I did some recon on the coven so I'd know everyone."

"My middle name isn't listed on the site."

"Oh. Interesting. But I never saw what you're searching for."

"Because I already found it, Sarru." He lowered his head to show his respect. "You."

"Wow. You must be all kinds of disappointed."

He slid off the couch and sank onto his knees before me. "Not at all, Sarru. My father had a premonition when I was four. He saw that I would meet the charmlings. That I would help them fight their greatest enemy."

"Their?"

"Yes. He specifically said *their*."

"And we have to fight someone?"

"Oh!" Annette gave me a thumbs-up. "Good thing you took that three-week class in Tae kwon do when you were a kid."

"That has been my great search," Theo said. "The thing I wanted most. When my father told me Ruthie had died, he knew it had begun. He knew you would come out of hiding and that I would meet you. I would join your cause to defeat, well, your nemesis, for lack of a better word."

"And who would that be?"

He shook his head. "I don't know, but I think he's a warlock. One with an ancient power only few have been able to get their hands on."

"Great." Was it too late to back out of this whole thing? "How do you know he's a warlock?"

"Because it sounds cooler than my real answer, which is: I have no clue."

A bubble of laughter burst out of me, partly to feign bravery in the face of this great enemy and partly because I could do nothing else.

My life had become a blisteringly hot mess. I'd almost died already. Almost gotten Annette killed and Roane killed and Gigi killed. Again. And now everyone was looking at me like I was some sort of... deity. Like I had answers. I didn't even know the freaking questions, and I was no closer to finding Gigi's killer.

I suddenly felt like I was drowning. An overwhelming sense of dread swept over me and stung my eyes. Some leader I was. I fought the wetness between my lashes tooth and nail. The coven thought so highly of me. For them to see me melt down would be disastrous.

"Sarru," Theo said, drawing me back to the present, "you are exactly where you are supposed to be."

I pulled him back onto the sofa with me and leaned closer to him. After casting a furtive glance toward the wolf, who went back to holding up the archway, I hoped he didn't quite have all of his hearing back yet when I whispered, "I don't think I am, Theo. I think I am very much in the wrong place at the wrong time with powers that clearly belong to someone else. Someone more adept. Someone not me."

His smile held both admiration and a beguiled kind of reverence. Seriously, there was no getting through to these people. "With your permission, Sarru." He gestured at my hand.

I placed it in his. This kid in his early twenties who knew more about the witch world than I probably ever would.

He tightened his hold reassuringly. "Only a true charmling would say such a thing, Sarru. Only a blood charmling would be humble enough to doubt her abilities and yet strong enough to do anything in her power to protect the ones she loves above all else. You are everything I'd hoped for. Everything I'd dreamed of." He bowed his head. "And I am yours to command."

That was disturbing. "How are you with laundry?"

He chuckled, as did several coven members who were close enough to hear our conversation, including Shanti.

I remembered another oddity from the visions I'd had of his past. "Wait, you promised your mother you'd tell me something?"

Surprise flashed across his face, but he recovered quickly. "You saw that?"

"I'm sorry."

"No." He shook his head. "I'm honored. But what she told me makes no sense."

"She sounds like my kind of girl."

"She said, and I quote, 'Sometimes the fiercest predators and the strongest allies come in the smallest packages.'"

"Oh." I sat back in thought. "Well, okay, then." Did she mean Theo? At a good inch or two over six feet, he wasn't what I would call small.

His eyes sparkled with humor. "Just so you know, every time my mother says things like that, things that seem completely off the wall, they come true in some shape or form."

"Like Nostradamus."

He nodded. "Very much like Nostradamus. Mom is just... Well, she's Mom. Cryptic but profound."

I crossed my arms. "She sounds lovely. I'll keep her words in mind."

"Thank you, Sarru."

"No, thank you, Theo."

His expression was everything I didn't want, yet I appreciated everything it represented. How could I not? He'd moved here for me. Well, for the charmling. Same dif. But it was all so humbling. Him. His parents. The coven. Serinda. Gigi. And, lest I forget, even Annette and my dads moved 2,500 miles away from their home to be here.

I had a clan. I had a wonderful, dynamic, loving clan, part of whom worshipped me, but we could work on that.

FOURTEEN

What does not kill you
will likely try again.
—Meme

The rest of the interviews were far less eventful than Theo's, thank the Goddess. We cleaned up while Roane grabbed us tacos and enchiladas from Howling Wolf. Serinda stayed for dinner, and the chief joined us to give us the bad news: They found no prints other than ours on the poisoned jar of parmesan. Aside from that, the two partials they'd collected in the pantry that didn't belong to any of us were not in the system. We were basically back to square one.

My dads showed up with baklava and a majestic stuffed snowy owl named Virgil. They tried to convince me he would bring me luck. The sales clerk assured them as much. I was beginning to doubt I had any of the good stuff left. Maybe the owl would help.

"Of course she did," I said to them, trying not to drool over the baklava that lay in wait. If it ended up being full of something deadly like thallium or drain cleaner, I didn't care. I was getting at least one bite of that stuff. "She wanted to make a sale."

They laughed. "If it makes you feel any better, Virgil was her pet. He died at twenty-eight of old age. According to the clerk, he lived a happy, mice-filled life."

Suddenly more reverent of the creature, I asked, "Why would she sell him?"

Papi lifted a shoulder as he took a Roane-approved bite of his taco. "I don't know. She seemed rather insistent that we take him. Said she wanted him to have a second life."

"Sounds suspish to me, but thank you. He's gorgeous." I took the magnificent beast, his white feathers like snow—which was the whole point—and put him on the hutch in the dining room for the time being.

Thankfully, we had a great, poison-free dinner. The chief had a city council meeting to attend. Gigi and Serinda went downstairs to look through some old texts—apparently there was an old spell that would reveal an intruder—while Annette and I finished in the kitchen. When we finished up, she went upstairs to check with her contacts, assuring me they could find out where Joaquin Ferebee was staying.

And I once again missed my chance to seduce the enigma known as Roane Wildes. The wolves were on the scent of the hunter, and he took off after them.

After enduring a full day of idol worship, nothing I ever dreamed I'd have to try to grow accustomed to, I started for the stairs when a hand covered my mouth from behind. I squeaked as a strong arm slid around my waist and pulled me back against a rock-hard chest. The scent of pine and sandalwood filled my nostrils with a hint of something deeper. Something richer. Musk, perhaps.

Roane waylaid me in the hall between the kitchen and the great room. We lingered in the shadows, and I reveled in the feel of him while admitting to a certain amount of surprise. Despite the furtive glances from underneath his thick lashes, I'd wondered if he lost interest in me with my refusal. He'd been all business all day while I'd longed to touch him at every turn. To run my hand over his scruff. Down his stomach. Up his kilt.

I'd also wondered if he was going to hold me to his ultimatum. Marry him or else. Part of me balked at both the idea and the threat. I would not be forced into marriage. But as much as it pained me to admit, part of me was flattered that he would want to spend his life with me. He wanted some kind of guarantee. I could respect that, but we'd only just met. In the flesh anyway. If one didn't count the six months I was incommunicado, we'd literally just met a couple of weeks ago.

And yet here he was. Holding me tight. Burying his face in my hair.

"I give up," he said softly.

I wrapped one arm around his as it slid around my neck and the other fell to my side. I reached around and pulled his hips closer. He pressed into me, his interest evident, the hard outline of his cock pressing into my backside. "What exactly are you giving up on?"

"Marriage."

The disappointment that spiked in my chest and stole the air from my lungs surprised me even more than this encounter. I hadn't wanted to get married. So why the disappointment?

"That didn't take long," I said, trying to conceal my regret.

"It's not fair to try to force you into something you're not ready for. I just want you to know, I can wait."

"You can?"

He lifted my chin and angled my head so he could cover my mouth with his. The kiss was the stuff of legend. And romance novels. And, possibly, porn movies. Intense. Passionate. Desperate. He tasted like honey, the barest hint of sweetness as he dipped his tongue inside me. I sank against him, giving way to any and all things he wanted to do to me, but he broke off the kiss to look at me. His eyes glittered in the low light, his expression severe.

"How long?" I asked. "How long can you wait?"

"Until the stars burn out." He kissed me again, a fervent and all-consuming thing. But he let go just as quickly, his movements almost reluctant.

"So that's it?" I asked, breathless. I turned to face him. "You're promising not to leave? Then what? I just get to pine over you until I say yes?"

"No." He pushed me against the wall and pressed into me again, this time the evidence of his interest hard against my abdomen. "That's not what I mean." He eased my legs apart with a knee and sent a hand between them.

I'd changed into sweats before dinner. They offered little protection against his advance. The passion he stirred rose up heavy in my abdomen.

He trailed kisses across my jaw and nipped at my ear, sending tendrils of ecstasy spiraling up my spine as he pushed a hand down the front of my sweats. His fingers burrowed beneath my panties, sliding lower until his finger-tips brushed over my clit.

I grabbed his wrist, but he pushed inside me, the

promise of an orgasm tightening my muscles around his fingers.

Then he stopped. His breathing heavy, he slid his hand around to cup my ass and put the other on the wall behind me, his jaw tense.

So close.

"Roane?"

"You have company," he said through gritted teeth.

"What?" I looked toward the door. "Who?"

"Parris."

"What the fuck?" I scraped a hand over my face. "She can wait."

"No. You need to interview her. Get into her head. Maybe she's seen something and doesn't realize it. That woman doesn't miss a thing."

"You mean, do what I did to Theo?" I eased away from him. "Roane, I can't. Not ever. Especially to a mundane."

He put his head against mine, still recovering himself. "Theo was protected by powerful magics. I think that's what caused his seizure. The two magics warring with each other. One protective and one invasive. You won, naturally—"

"Naturally?"

"—but I think maybe it was an overload to his system."

"So you don't think that would happen to a mundane?"

"I don't. They have no protection. And I think you've already been doing it unwittingly."

Alarm bells rang out in my head. "When? Did I hurt someone? Did I steal their souls?" I looked around for any extra souls lying around.

The inevitable knock sounded at the door.

"Just try to find out if she's seen anyone suspicious hanging around. If what you're saying is right, someone is messing with people's memories. And that can only mean powerful magics."

"Okay, I'll try. But seriously, we have to get back to this ASAP."

He nodded. "Agreed." He pulled his hand out of my sweats and waited for me to go to the door.

As I started for the door, he said, "Just so you know, I still want a yes. I'm not swaying from that. But I can wait."

I smiled inwardly as I walked to the door. I opened it to a blast of arctic air, and a brunette with a bottle of wine in each hand beamed at me.

"Girls' night?" she asked, her voice full of hope, her grin infectious despite the red nose.

I waved her inside before she froze to death. "I'd love a girls' night."

Annette peeked over the upstairs balustrade. "Did I hear *girls' night*?"

How was that woman still awake?

Parris shimmied inside and held the wine up to her.

"I'll get the glasses!" She ran down the stairs, spry for a five-footer. But I was a little worried about her. She was coming up on probably forty-eight hours with only a couple hours sleep. If that. I'd have to check her room for coke later. I'd confiscate it, of course. Save it in case I ever needed a pick-me-up.

"Oh, hi, Roane," Parris said, skidding to a halt.

"Parris." A man of few words. Annette grabbed glasses out of the dining room, and Roane took the wine from Parris with a congenial "Allow me." More *few words*. I liked 'em. There were so many things I would allow him to do, especially after his performance in the hall.

After Roane poured us each a glass of wine, checking for arsenic and/or plastique, he gave me the A-OK. Then he was gone. I didn't know where he ran off to, but I had a feeling he didn't go far. Or maybe that was wishful thinking.

Parris, whose smile would've been prettier had she'd foregone the lip injections, sat on the sofa with me while Annette took a wingback.

After about half a bottle of wine each, the conversation veered toward the strange and bizarre things happening lately, and I made the mistake of commenting on the fact that a couple of the upstairs windows had been broken.

Annette pointed at me accusingly. "Maybe they wouldn't be if someone hadn't turned me into a bird."

I gaped at her, then laughed nervously. "She's kidding. It's a thing we do. We were in a play. And what's wrong with birds?"

"Why couldn't you turn me into something sexy like a cat? Or a cougar?"

I was not touching that. "Annette, you don't have to not be a bird to be sexy."

"What?"

"That came out wrong. Bottom line, you were the sexiest bird I've ever seen."

She dropped her head against the wing. "Really?"

"Really."

"You're not just saying that?"

"I would never."

She released a dreamy sigh and, after a rough start, we did indeed talk girl stuff. Hairdressers. The best nail techs. Spray tans. And I couldn't help but wonder if there were spells for such things. Still, Parris seemed a little obsessed. I got the feeling the woman led a lonely life, though according to her, the fact that she and her husband lived in two separate houses was her idea.

"Stretch marks," Parris said, adding to the list of malfeasance we were going to discuss with whoever was in charge once we crossed the Earthly bounds. We had grievances. And suggestions. A few tweaks here and there.

Annette shouted a hearty "Amen, sister!" seconds before she passed out cold. Whether her blackout was from her lack of sleep or the bottle of wine she singlehandedly finished off in under half an hour was debatable. But at least she was asleep. She needed the Z's. Unfortunately, there'd be hell to pay when she woke up, slumped over the arm of the chair like she was.

I made sure Parris had gotten more than her fair share of the second bottle. Once she was sufficiently buzzed, I gathered my magics, leaned closer, and locked my gaze with hers. It seemed that once I locked gazes with someone, they couldn't look away. For lack of a better phrase, they fell under my spell.

Parris's grin vanished, and she leaned closer, too.

I lowered my head and said, "Parris Stephanie Walsh Hampton—"

"How do you know my full name?" She slurred the words, and I knew it wasn't entirely the wine's fault.

"—what are you searching for?"

In an instant, her life rushed at me in force, making my head spin. She was an open book. One I didn't particularly want to read. But it did give me a new respect for her. She came from humble beginnings. She'd been bullied growing up. Glasses. A severe overbite. Prominent ears. And yet when I saw her reflection in the mirror, she was all kinds of adorable.

Sadly, her peers had not been kind. Even her third-grade teacher bullied her, and my temper flared with that knowledge. She'd never learned to love herself. Not until she married well and had some work done. But even now, she searched for only one thing: perfection. When all she needed was a love and acceptance of self.

I'd judged her so harshly, and guilt bubbled up inside me like acid on metal. I tamped it down. Now was not the time. I searched her memories for anything unusual with Percy. Any strange comings and goings. Anyone watching the house that didn't belong, but I quickly realized something. While her childhood memories were bright and crystal clear, her newer memories were less so. That made no sense. They should be more prominent. More accessible.

And then it hit me. Her memories had been tampered with. Anytime I tried to access a thought that seemed unusual to her, out of place, a shadow jumped across the silver screen of her mind like the bad editing of a B-rated horror movie, dark and blurry and suffocating. I tried harder to breach the thick curtain, but the memories slipped further and further away.

When I tried a third time, worried now about Parris's mental well-being, the shadow that had flickered in and out of her memories looked directly at me.

Me.

Not Parris.

It lifted a finger over its mouth and released a shushing hiss.

I pulled out immediately and scrambled off the couch, falling to the floor. Roane was there in an instant and helped me to my feet, but Parris had yet to move. To blink. She was in the exact same position as when I went in, and I held my breath, praying she wouldn't have a seizure.

"Roane," I whispered, wrapping both of my arms around one of his.

We waited a good sixty seconds. Then, right when Roane sat in front of her, she shouted, "Beavers! Because

Brazilians hurt like the dickens." She blinked and focused on Roane, her entire attitude changing. "Oh, hey there." She giggled and leaned closer. "Have I ever told you how much I enjoy your yard work?"

Relief flooded every cell in my body. So much so, my knees almost gave beneath me, and I sat beside Roane.

"Wow," she said, shaking her head. "That wine is much stronger than I remembered."

"Clearly." I pointed to Annette.

Roane looked at her, then glanced at me from over his shoulder. "You asked me to remind you about the thing in the morning."

"The thing?"

He gestured toward Annette, then Parris.

"Right. Crap. I forgot I have to get up super early."

"Oh, goodness." Parris checked the time on her phone. "It is late. Can I—"

"I got it," Roane said, gathering the wineglasses. He nonchalantly inhaled the vapors of what was left over as I showed Parris to the door.

"Thanks for coming over," I said, waving goodbye.

She stumbled but caught herself.

"Are you okay?"

"Wonderful." She waved goodbye.

I closed the door and hurried over.

"Was that Parris?" Gigi asked as she and Serinda walked in.

"Yeah, girls' night. Roane, what's going on?"

He sniffed Annette's glass. Then, without the slightest hesitation, he jerked her off the chair and laid her on the ground.

"What's wrong?" Gigi asked, hurrying over.

Serinda followed, her brows knitting in worry.

"Ricin," he said.

I fell to the floor beside him. "Ricin? Like the poison?"

"In the wine."

I shook my head, completely confused. "Roane, we all drank from the same bottles of wine."

"Both of them?"

"Yes. We—"

Before I could get out another word, he grabbed a fistful of my hair and tilted my head back. Then his mouth covered mine. He kissed deeply, almost desperately, then eased back and frowned at me. "I don't understand."

I clasped onto his biceps for balance. "What?"

"Georgiana," he said, using her new name despite the audience. "What is going on?"

Gigi knelt beside us and examined Annette. "Put her on the sofa, will you, love?"

He obeyed, gathering Annette into his arms and laying her on the sofa. "Her breathing is fine. Completely unobstructed. Her heart rate is normal. But she ingested ricin. From the taste and smell, copious amounts of it." He bent and kissed her too, pushing his tongue inside her mouth for just an instant. He straightened and spit into Annette's wineglass then wiped his mouth on the back of his hand. When he looked up at Gigi, he shook his head. "Ricin."

My heart skipped several beats. "I don't understand."

"I don't either. A dose the size of a grain of sand is enough to kill, and she's fine."

"Gigi?"

Gigi sank into the wingback, her expression full of astonishment.

"Did you just kiss me?" Annette asked, looking up at Roane as her eyes fluttered open like butterfly wings.

"Annette!" I draped my body over her.

"Still not a hugger."

I straightened. "Annette, are you okay?"

"I don't know." She swung her legs over and sat up. "I think your boyfriend just kissed me. How's my hair?"

I took hold of her shoulders and shook her. "Annette, you drank ricin."

"Oh, crap. No wonder I have such a hangover. Is that a new kind of wine?"

"No. Ricin? Castor beans? Deadly?" When she still didn't snap, I added, "*Breaking Bad.*"

The blood drained from her face. "I did crack?"

"No, hon. The poison Walter White used to kill people."

"Oh, crap on a cracker. Am I dying again?"

I looked at Roane who, in turn, looked at Gigi who, in turn, looked at Serinda.

Annette's gaze bounced between us like a ping-pong ball. "I'm dying again, aren't I?" She stood and started pacing. "This is getting ridiculous. I've had enough of poisons and explosions and near-death experiences. Because I have to be honest, guys, I have yet to see a light at the end of a tunnel. Either I'm going in the other direction or I have been lied to my *entire* life." She threw her arms wide to demonstrate the scope of how long she'd been lied to.

I crawled onto the sofa and noticed the glances Gigi and Serinda were tossing back and forth. "Gigi?"

Roane sat beside me as Serinda sank into the other wingback.

Then something else hit me. "Wait a minute," I said, suspicion niggling the back of my mind. I stabbed Annette with a suspicious scowl. "Roane drags you onto the floor then picks you up and puts you on the sofa, and neither of those things wake you, but his kiss does?"

She shrugged. "It was a good kiss." When I continued to give her the evil eye, she rolled her eyes. "Can we get back to my imminent death?"

She did have a point.

"Surely, she's not, Georgi," Serinda said. "How would that even be possible? I mean, there's just no way. It's too coincidental."

"Do you have another explanation, Serinda?"

Annette stopped pacing. "Can you guys please share with the rest of the class? Am I dying or not?"

Gigi stood and braced her hands on Annette's shoulders, her gaze sparkling with joy when she said to her, "You, my dear, are a charmling."

FIFTEEN

I wonder how many WTFs today will bring.
—Meme

After a solid minute of staring at Gigi like she'd just told us she was going to do magic for her talent in the Miss America pageant, Annette said, "Get the fuck out."

"Nannette," Gigi admonished. That'd teach her. But the faux glower held a visible hint of astonishment.

Roane and I exchanged glances before Nannette sank onto the coffee table in front of the two older women.

"Coincidence aside," Gigi said to Serinda, "how else do you explain the fact that she drank—*drank!*—both cyanide and ricin and lived to tell the tale?"

Annette nodded, her gaze expectant as she waited for answers.

"Not to mention, no side effects." Serinda swept a hand over Annette. "No stomachache. No headache. I've never heard of such a thing."

"Never?" Annette sagged in defeat.

"I have," Gigi said, her gaze intense and thoughtful. That got Serinda's complete attention—not to mention Annette's—so Gigi continued. "Think about it, Serinda. How did she get the poisons in the first place?"

For a moment, Serinda just frowned, then she straightened her shoulders and glanced from Annette to Gigi and back again. "She's mortiferata."

Gigi nodded in wonderment.

"The alchemist," Serinda whispered. "Could it be possible, Georgi, that we have not one, but two charmlings in Salem?"

"It's the only explanation."

A telltale wetness formed between Serinda's lashes. She bowed her head to Annette. "Sarru."

I scrambled onto the coffee table and sat beside my bestie as she stewed in stunned speechlessness. A rare state for her. "Are you saying Annette's a charmling like me?"

"She has to be," Gigi said. "It is absolutely the only explanation."

"But... but how?" Goosebumps spread like wildfire over my skin. The implications. The possibilities. "What does this mean?"

Gigi didn't answer. She went back to staring at Annette as though she were a science experiment that had produced unexpected yet astounding results.

Serinda stepped up. "It means several things all at once, Sarru. But first, Annette, has anything strange happened lately?" When Annette bounced out of her stupor and gave the lovely woman sitting across from her the very best deadpan she could muster, Serinda elaborated. "I mean, something like a rush of energy like you've never felt before."

"Yes!" I patted Annette's leg in excitement. "Like with me when I came into my powers. Have you felt anything like, oh, I don't know"—I glanced up in thought—"the burning fires of a thousand suns bursting to flames inside of you?" That was a day I'd never forget. Mostly because Roane helped me into the shower and then joined me as he tried to cool me down. A perplexing contradiction considering the company.

An audible gasp echoed around us as Annette focused on me. "I thought it was a hot flash. Wait." She bent her head in thought. "That was only a few days ago. The day you woke up. I thought I was going to be burned alive from the inside out, and then you woke up. Once I learned you'd come out of suspended animation, I just thought, you know, with how wonky your powers were, maybe you accidentally tried to set me on fire when you awakened."

"Annette! Why would I do that?"

"I don't know. It's not like anything has been normal since coming to Salem."

"Gigi, do you think Nette coming into her powers is what pulled me out of the state of suspended animation?"

"I do," Gigi said, nodding. "It makes perfect sense."

"Wow." I elbowed her. "Thanks."

"You're welcome? Look, I appreciate all of this." She started pacing again. "I really do, but I am nothing like Defiance. She's... she's extraordinary."

"Nannette," Gigi said, her tone full of reproach, despite the teasing use of her nickname.

"I have to agree. *Nannette.*"

"Okay, fine, fine, fine." She dismissed our reproaches, waving her hands wildly before sitting down again. "Let's say, for argument's sake, that I am indeed a charmling and that I can magically make poison or whatever. How? And why? I mean, why me?"

"Why indeed," Serinda said.

Roane spoke up at last. "It means a charmling died."

We all turned to look at him. He sat leaning into one corner of the sofa, his expression severe.

"A charmling has to die for another to take her place. The shift of power created a rift in the vortex, for lack of a better phrase. It's what shook you awake. But more importantly, someone almost certainly killed her for reasons other than to siphon her powers."

"He's right," Serinda said. "The power has been hoarded by the warlocks who control the charmlings for centuries. If that charmling is growing weak, another witch is chosen to siphon her powers before the actual point of death. Before the power can be set free and find its way to a blood heir."

"And that witch takes the charmling's place," Gigi added. "Thus keeping the powers under the warlock's control."

"Which leaves me wondering if the faux charmling who died for me to inherit my powers died nefariously."

"Again, I've wondered that, too, Defiance. Either way, a charmling had to have died on or around the time of your birth. We knew instantly that you were different. That you had immense power. Far more power than even the strongest blood witch would have. We knew that you were somehow a charmling and that your father was a direct descendant of the original three."

"Then how does Annette play into this? What does her coming into power mean?"

"It means, Defiance, that you two are related. Either cousins or, however unlikely, half sisters."

Annette and I turned to each other. "No way," she said, beaming at me.

"I knew the minute I saw you we were destined to be friends, but I had no idea we were related."

Annette nodded. "Think about it. We've always said we were long-lost sisters. Do you think we knew somehow? Deep down?"

"At this point, I'd say anything is possible."

"Who knows?" One corner of Annette's mouth tipped up. "We could be twins separated at birth."

"True, though we look nothing alike. And we have different mothers."

"So, fraternal."

"I don't think that's how the twin thing works."

"And I'm pretty sure my dad did not impregnate your mother."

Serinda looked at Gigi. "That could mean there is more than one descendant."

"Wouldn't there be?" I asked. "It's been centuries. There are probably dozens of them."

"No." Gigi stood and went to the bookcase I'd perused a couple of times but hadn't had the time to delve deeply into. "Remember when I told you we thought the line had died out and that when you were born, it changed everything? There's a reason we thought that."

Serinda clasped her hands in her lap. "When the warlocks figured out how to take control of a charmling's powers, they had teams of their people research the lineage all the way back to the original three. Then they hunted down and killed all of the heirs, both male and female, in the seventeenth century."

"Why?" I asked, horrified.

"To ensure there were no more blood heirs who could reclaim the power that was rightfully theirs."

"You must realize," Gigi said over her shoulder. "An actual blood heir is said to be a hundred times more powerful than, what do you call them? A faux charmling?"

I nodded.

"The heirs have the blood of the originals coursing through their veins. It's both a conduit for the power and an amplifier. A faux charmling does not have that advantage, which makes them easier to control."

"And," Serinda added, "from what we've been told, that's why they age very rapidly. They only live about five years once they take up the powers."

"No warlock alive would allow his charmling to die without having another witch waiting in the wings."

"They're often killed before their time, for that very reason. They don't want to risk that power slipping away from them in the night."

I shook my head. "This is all so barbaric."

"I agree," Gigi said, leafing through a book.

"You're missing one salient point," Roane said, his ire evident in the muscles stretched taut across his jaw. "She's a charmling. A blood heir who has come into her power, and she's been walking around unprotected for days."

Gigi spun toward us, book in hand. "Oh, Goddess."

"Do you think that's why the hunter is in town?" Roane asked her. "Maybe it has nothing to do with Defiance at all."

Gigi walked back and sat down. "It's not only possible. It's very likely."

"I'm unprotected?" Annette asked. "So that means warlocks can feel me up, right?"

"They can sense you, yes," Serinda corrected.

Annette stood and started to back away. "The hunter is here for me?"

"Quick, Gigi," I said, jumping to her aid, "teach her to do the spell like you did me."

"Right!" Annette said, pointing at me. "The protection spell. That should do it. But that spell took you days to learn."

"And you watched me. You know what to do. Right, Gigi? She just needs to draw the spell?"

"We're in new territory," she warned. "I only knew about you because I'd had three years of experience with you before I had to give you up. I knew how you drew spells on the air. But every charmling is different. Each one has her own... specialized magics, if you will. Her own brand, and—"

"And each one may do spells differently," Serinda finished, getting her point. "Have you tried any spells lately, Annette? Just normal spells?"

She shook her head. "Not since the hot flash. We've been a little busy not getting killed. If you don't know how I do spells, how am I going to camouflage my powers? How am I going to hide from the hunter?" She started to panic. Her chest heaved with each breath and the lights flickered around us.

I stood and gathered her into my arms. "It's okay."

"Still not a hugger."

"I know, but you have to calm down before you blow up the house."

My soothing words of encouragement, the ones meant to soothe and encourage, did neither. The lights started flickering even faster, and I could've sworn I smelled an acidic smoke filter into the air.

Roane stood at the ready, prepared for anything. He took a wary step closer to her, to do what, I didn't know.

That was when I felt something on the ground. I looked down to see Percy making his way up Annette's legs. He wound past her hips and up her torso, weaving over her arms.

I stepped back to give him room.

"Percy," she whispered, clasping him to her breast.

Black roses blossomed all around her, the rich fragrance filling the room and soothing Annette much better than my words had.

She held out her hand, and a vine curled into it, lacing around her fingers and wrapping around her wrist. A single rose blossomed in her palm, the bloodred undertones vibrant beneath the inky blackness of the petals. She brought it to her nose and inhaled.

Annette and Percy seemed to have grown really close while I was out. Which was fine by me because the lights stopped flickering, and we had yet to be boiled alive in acid or suffocated with a noxious gas. Win-win.

"Thank you, Percival," Annette said. He'd headed off her panic attack.

She walked to the sofa, and he shrank back. But when she sat down, he slid up the side of the sofa and kept a light hold on her hand.

"Sorry," she said. "I just don't want to be some warlock's bitch."

Roane coughed softly behind a closed fist, fooling no one.

"You could do it," Gigi said, glancing at me. She put the book on the coffee table and walked over to me. "You could do at least a temporary protection spell until Annette learns to do it herself."

She was right. "Okay, I'll try."

"No," Annette said. "Do or do not. There is no try."

I gave her a thumbs-up. "Thanks, Yoda." After filling my lungs, I closed my eyes and searched for the protection spell I'd used on myself. I'd only done it a million times before it worked, but it didn't appear. Like it was blocked somehow.

Doubling my efforts, I searched harder, trying to remember where I last saw it. Was it behind...? Nope. Was it under...? Nope. I scoured the vast landscape of my very own mystical oasis and came up empty-handed. Then I realized maybe it was a different spell altogether. The one I'd used before was a protection spell for me. This time it would be for someone else. So, instead of searching for the spell, I concentrated on what I needed.

I raced past protection spells of every sort. Apparently, there were a lot of them. The symbols were a blur, rushing past faster than I could see them, then they stopped, and I found myself standing at a precipice. Beyond it was a shimmering wall of water, and beyond that, suspended in air, were the spells meant only for my sister charmlings. They glittered as though made of gold, glistened as though made of diamonds, each symbol containing as much energy as a supernova.

And in the very center was the most important one of all: protect.

I smiled and opened my eyes to an expectant Annette, hope warring with anxiety in her smoky gray irises. I raised my hand, drew the sacred symbol. A dash here. A loop there. When the spell was complete, the lines burst to life, bleeding that same blinding light, but the spell spilled out and washed over her like a wave of glitter before blanketing her and settling over her. Tiny luminous sparks twinkled around her as the spell masked her magics from any who would dare look for them.

Annette looked on with fascination. She held out a hand as though she could catch one of the sparks.

I sat beside her. "You really are a charmling, Annette. That spell, it was special. It wouldn't have worked otherwise."

She shook her head. "It was beautiful, Defiance. Thank you."

"Unfortunately," Roane said, raining on our light parade, "I do believe the hunter saw Annette uncloaked."

"When we went to eat today," she said.

"Yes. If he did, he'll know who you are either way. And he may have even figured out Defiance's deep dark secret."

I gasped. "How do you know my deep dark secret?"

"No, honey," Annette said, patting my hand, "the one about you being a charmling."

"Oh, right. Whew." That was close.

Annette nodded.

"This is just so..." I scoffed, not sure what it was. "Crazy. I've known Annette since the ninth grade when her family moved to Phoenix. Even the fact that we went to the same high school—there are dozens—is suspect."

"And not a coincidence, if you ask me," Gigi said. "How did you end up in Phoenix?"

"My dad. He got a job offer, and we moved there from San Diego."

Serinda took out her phone. "I'm just making some notes. I think we need to look closer at your life, Annette. And, if you two are up for it, we should have some genetic tests run to see how closely you're related. We didn't think a single descendant of the original charmlings survived over the centuries until Defiance was born. And now to know there are two of you."

"Is it possible one of my parents has charmling blood and doesn't know it?"

"It's a certainty. It's the only explanation."

"Didn't anyone think to keep records of that sort of thing?" I asked.

"The feuding warlocks stole them all and destroyed them. After they hunted down the descendants, naturally."

"It was bloody and brutal," Gigi added. "A dark time in our history. Several warlocks from prominent families were trying to wrangle control of all three. They each wanted the ultimate power trio. In the end, three of them managed to get one each. The other warlocks were also killed, as were their children."

I looked at Annette. "Are we sure we want to be a part of this?"

"Do we have a choice?" She gestured toward the book. "What's in there?"

"A very broad description of the charmlings and their powers. It's all that we know about them as separate entities. I was going to have you read this, Defiance, when you were ready, if for no other reason than to get to know your sister charmlings better."

"Sister charmlings?" I stood and walked to the bookcase, pretending to peruse in order to hide my agitation. "You said it yourself, Gigi, they stole the power, killing the previous charmling in the process. And I'm supposed to want to get to know them better?"

"They are enslaved, Defiance. Little more than chattel to their warlocks. If anything, they should be pitied."

I turned to her. "You told me they're like celebrities.

They want for nothing. That to meet one was like meeting a rock star."

"Yes, and how many young rock stars over the centuries have been controlled by the business in which they work? By their managers or producers or labels? How many have been swindled and lied to and cheated only to be dropped at the first sign of declining sales?"

"Dephne," Annette said, walking up behind me. "What's wrong?"

I couldn't put it into words. My elation at having Annette become a true charmling—a true sister—took a horrible turn. It was one thing when it was only me. When I was the only target of the unscrupulous warlocks in the world. But now Annette was in their crosshairs. In just as much danger. It tilted everything I'd felt up to this moment on its head.

"We're in this together now," she said. "We'll have each other's backs."

I nodded, deciding to drop it for now. It wasn't like my brooding would change anything.

"And we have an incredible coven behind us. Once you get to know them, Deph, you'll see. And there's Roane and the chief and Percival."

"And me."

We dropped our gazes to the tiny blond gazing up at us. I knelt down to him. Samuel's cerulean irises were as clear and deep as an ocean. "Hey, handsome. Did you find Ink?"

He nodded and then released a long sigh. "Yes, but him runned away again."

"I'm sorry, buddy. Do you want to hang out with us?"

He looked around and pointed at Roane. "I want him."

"He's all yours," I said, wrangling a wicked grin that tried to escape.

"No. Ruff-ruff."

I stifled a snort. "You mean, you want him in wolf form?"

He nodded, his face brightening at the thought.

I gave Roane my best pleading face.

"No," he said, defensive. "I need in on this."

"You'll be in the house. You'll hear everything anyway. That is, if your hearing is better."

"It is." He crossed his arms and put a booted foot on the coffee table to be stubborn.

Gigi rolled up a women's magazine sitting nearby and swatted his foot.

He dropped it. "Sorry, Georgi."

"If you can hear us, what's the problem?" I asked.

"I'm not a dog."

I walked over to him and helped him to his feet. "Today you are."

"Fine." He glared at Samuel, then gave him a playful wink. "But you stay here until I've shifted, okay? The last thing I need is a kid seeing me naked."

Oh, hell. That was a good point. "We'll be right here."

He lifted his shirt over his head as he entered the hall, and we all took a moment to appreciate the finer things in life.

When he was out of sight, I sank onto the sofa and motioned Samuel closer, wishing I could put him on my lap. "Okay, what's in the book?"

"Yeah." Annette sat beside me. "What are my powers? Am I psychic? I'm psychic, aren't I?"

"Well, as you know, Defiance is a seeker. A finder of lost things. Her powers lie in her ability to see into a person's soul, to find what they are searching for, and to extract the truth."

"Yeah, yeah," Annette said, hurrying her along. "Get to the good part."

Gigi pressed her lips together, but I had a feeling it was more to hide a grin than admonish the vibrant creature beside me. "Unless I am greatly mistaken, which I'm not, you're the healer. The alchemist."

"No," Serinda said, holding up an index finger. "Not just an alchemist. A mortiferata."

"Yes," Gigi agreed.

"Now we're talking." She nodded, snapped her fingers, and pointed to herself. "Mortiferata in the house."

"You don't even know what that means," I said.

"Still sounds cool."

She had me there. "So, what *does* it mean exactly?" I asked. "Mortiferata?"

"I'm not one hundred percent certain. I've never met a true mortiferata."

"But I'm psychic, right?"

"Mmm, not exactly."

Serinda shook her head. "An alchemist's strength lies in plants and chemistry and medicinal herbs."

"Meaning?"

"You use plants to heal people. But it's my understanding that a mortiferata can manipulate any organic material on a cellular level."

"Meaning?" she repeated.

"It means you can change the chemical structure of any element into, well, anything you desire."

"That's why everything she touches turns to poison? Or an explosive compound? She unconsciously wants us all dead so it was the magical equivalent of a Freudian slip?" I teased.

"If I wanted you dead, you'd be dead."

"Says the girl who can't even do a spell."

She covered my mouth with her free hand, and Samuel laughed. He captured her attention for a moment before she went back to the matter at hand. "You're sure I'm not psychic? I really feel like I'm a psychic."

"Psycho," I said from behind her hand. "You feel like a psycho. Big difference."

She gave up and removed her hand before pushing up her turquoise glasses. "So, I'm just poisonous? That's my schtick?"

"I would hardly call it a schtick," Serinda said.

"But what good can I possibly do in the world?"

Gigi scooted forward in her chair. "You are a healer. They are revered far and wide."

"More than a seeker?"

"Hey." I scowled at her. "This is not a competition."

"I know. It's just, your power is so cool." She kicked at the carpet.

"You haven't heard the best part," Serinda said. She leaned forward and whispered, "A true mortiferata can kill with a kiss."

Based off the expression Annette's face morphed into, one would think she'd won the lottery, a Pulitzer, and a Nobel Prize all in the same week. She pressed her fists against her mouth and let out a little squeak.

"But mortiferata are healers first and foremost. They're alchemists, yes, but they are so much more."

She squeaked again. "Can we get back to the kiss? Let's say I want to kiss a guy, like a certain police officer with incredible pecs, how careful do I need to be?"

The barest hint of a wince flashed across Gigi's face before she recovered. She took a moment, then said as congenially as she could, "Very."

Annette blinked at her, letting that sink in before having a total meltdown. Well, another one. "Great." She stood and started pacing again. "Like my love life isn't fraught enough already. Let's throw *deadly kisses* into the equation. Provided I don't poison him at dinner by passing the salt. My power sucks."

"Your power doesn't..."

A low growl reverberated around us, and we watched as a massive red wolf emerged from the shadows of the hall. He stalked forward, his head lowered, his teeth bared, ready to rip into whatever got in his way.

Samuel squealed in delight, not the least bit scared. He ran through the coffee table and toward the wall to the dining room.

Roane leapt over the table between us and snapped at him, his growl so low and loud, we all jumped. Samuel reemerged from the dining room and ran toward me. I opened my arms, but Roane cut him off. He screamed and giggled as he ran for the stairs.

Roane turned toward me and growled, the sound low and guttural, his teeth exposed, his irises full of warning.

Goosebumps flared over every inch of my body as my lungs seized in my chest.

He stalked forward and, right before he ripped out my jugular, he leaned in and nuzzled my neck, his tongue sliding out for a quick taste. Then he took off after the kid again.

We heard giggles and growls and a couple of crashes. I cringed. "Maybe that wasn't my best idea."

"Posh," Gigi said. "The sweet boy deserves to have some fun. And so does Samuel," she added, then laughed at her own joke.

"Right. Because who doesn't love being chased by a snarling wolf?" Serinda asked, a little horrified.

"I've had worse days." I turned back to Annette and picked up where we left off. "Your ability does not suck."

"It kind of does. Especially if everything I touch turns to poison. What's going to keep me from poisoning myself?"

"Annette, you've been drinking poisons for days. Clearly you're immune."

"True. I guess I could be a spy, what with my immunity and all. Then again, what if it builds up in my system? What if one morning I wake up after exposing an international arms dealer who found out and put a cobra in my room, and I'm dead? What then?"

"An international drug ring would hardly put a cobra in your room. They're far more likely to bust a cap in your ass and call it a day."

"A *local* arms dealer, yes. International ones are far more elegant."

"Ah."

"Nannette," Gigi said, annoyed with our arms-dealer conversation, "I do believe you're missing the bigger picture here."

"Precisely." Serinda was totally starstruck. "You can change any substance on earth into any other. From what I understand, you can change tea into snake venom. Or gold. Or a cure for cancer."

"You had me at gold."

"Your nature is to heal, of course," Gigi warned. "If what this book says about the mortiferata charmling is true, you will feel compelled to do so. You won't be able to stop yourself."

"Oh. I guess that's cool."

"And," she said, her voice singsong, "guess who else was an alchemist."

"The Dalai Lama?" Annette asked. Gigi did tell her to guess.

"Percival."

That got her attention. "Percy? He was like me?"

Percy squeezed her hand as she stared down at him.

"Wait!" she said, her gaze snapping back to Gigi's. "Can I turn water into wine?"

Gigi nodded. "And vice versa."

She reared back, aghast. "Georgi, why would anyone want to turn wine into water? Isn't that, like, counterproductive?" She gasped as another idea hit her, and she turned to me. "We can open our own winery!"

"We could, yes, but I think the real question is, can you turn water into coffee?"

The whites of her eyes shone when her eyes rolled back into her head a little. "It's like I've died and gone to heaven."

I giggled and asked the two older women, "Can she? Because coffee makes me feel less murdery, so having a twenty-four-hour supply on tap would be amazing."

They nodded in perfect unison.

"*Yes.* You said there are others? Other mortiferata?"

Serinda pressed her lips together. "While there are a few who claim to be, I'm convinced they're all charlatans. Frauds who spout nothing but flimflam."

Was that a real word?

"There is only one true mortiferata," Gigi said, agreeing with her friend. "Because only a charmling can be protected against her own powers."

Serinda leaned closer to Gigi. "Exactly. Remember when Cicely Cromwell claimed to be mortiferata?"

Gigi snorted. "The harlot. I'd like to see her drink an entire bottle of cyanide and live to tell the tale."

"Right?"

Roane walked back in, pulling his shirt over his head. I just caught the bottom half of his abs. "He found Ink again."

Gigi tsked. "That poor cat."

"Nah, it's good for him." He stopped beside Gigi's chair and gave me a once-over. A slow one that had me warming in all the right places.

"That was some show," I said. "I thought I might lose my jugular there for a minute."

"Yeah." His gaze dropped to other, more sensitive parts of me. "I would've never gone for the jugular."

SIXTEEN

THEM: *I'll see you in hell!*
ME: *Call first. No pop-ins.*
—Meme

Annette was so wound up, I couldn't convince her to go to bed. She kept pacing and ranting, one minute in love with the bizarre turn of events, the next bemoaning it, wondering what good she could possibly do. How she could help people. In the span of three minutes and twelve seconds, she considered becoming a chemist, a brain surgeon, a CIA operative, a perfumer, a tennis pro—no idea—and an assassin.

It took a while, but I finally convinced her she'd make a horrible assassin. She just didn't have the killer instinct. Thank the Goddess, because with her new abilities, she could go to town.

In truth, I could hardly blame her agitation. It's not every day a girl finds out she's a charmling. We discussed ways that she could learn to control her abilities—for everyone's safety—and spells she needed to try to learn ASAP, but I was exhausted. At midnight, I called it a day and headed for bed.

Annette followed, unable to calm her nerves. To quieten her mind.

Thus, I spent another night alone. If one didn't count Annette, Samuel, and Ink, all sprawled across my bed in every direction but a normal one. Twenty minutes later, the one bedmate who swore she'd *never* be able to sleep, not even if we gave her an *entire* bottle of horse tranquilizers—which she was probably right about, considering her immunity to all things deadly—lay snoring beside me, and I was the one who couldn't sleep. I turned over and studied Samuel's gorgeous little face—perfect in every way—only mildly curious about the fact that he was sleeping. I had no idea the departed would need sleep.

After memorizing every line, every curve from his bow-shaped mouth and dimpled cheeks to his button nose and long lashes, I gave up on sleep. I shimmied out from under the covers at exactly *uno-cero-uno*—I checked—and headed downstairs for a nightcap. When I got to the kitchen, I heard a shower running. I turned to the basement stairs. Steam billowed up from the lower level, and the scent of sandalwood filled the air.

After a short debate between my head and my heart, my heart won. It usually did. I took the stairs and found the door to Roane's apartment open. I knocked softly, then entered.

His scent enveloped me as I made my way to his bathroom. The door to it, too, was open, so I stepped inside. Roane stood behind a glass door, water cascading over his wide shoulders, down his muscular back, lower and lower until the last remnants of soapsuds slid over his steely buttocks.

"Are you just going to watch," he asked, startling me, "or are you going to join me?" He turned, and I caught a glimpse of the heavy burden he carried between his legs a millisecond before I looked up. His olive irises studied me from underneath spiked lashes.

Unconcerned for the T-shirt I was wearing, I opened the door and stepped into the shower. He didn't move back to give me room. Instead, he reached around and closed the door, forcing me to press against it. Against him. Cool on one side. Blisteringly hot on the other.

His lips found mine and my palms found his chest. They spread over his wide shoulders and down his arms until I came to his hands. He clasped them together and leaned in for another kiss. The scruff on his face was softer than I thought it would be.

He broke off the kiss to look down at me, and I marveled once again at the color of his irises. A glistening olive green like I'd never seen before. "You are so beautiful."

I wanted to argue, but I wanted his tongue in my mouth again even more. I tiptoed and pressed into him.

He drove his fingers into my hair and lowered his head. The kiss was soft. Unhurried. Exploratory. He slid his tongue between my lips and ran it over the edges of my teeth before going deeper. Then he tilted his head and pushed his tongue all the way in just as I wrapped a hand around his erection.

He sucked in a cool breath between our mouths as I tightened my hold and stroked. I took my other hand, cupped the base, and squeezed softly.

"Fuck," he ground out, before wrapping me in his arms and holding me to him. "Wait."

But the sensation, the control, was too heady. I felt the blood rushing beneath my fingers. His cock hardening to marble. His hands curling to fists at my back. Seconds before everything went silent.

At first, only the sound of my own breathing registered. Then, somewhere in the background, a single, constant note resonated around me.

I lifted my lids to find myself standing in total darkness. The cold hit me first. I was shivering, my feet bare in a puddle of water on the floor. My T-shirt soaking wet and almost frozen. The ringing deafened me. The darkness blinded me. The cold disoriented me.

My hair hung in long, wet locks over my face and down my back. Fairly certain I looked like the girl from *The Ring*, I did a quick illumination spell with two fingers, afraid to move anything else.

A soft glow brightened the hexagon-shaped room I stood in. Like the morning before, I was back in the attic, standing in front of the same door. The door that, at least on my last visit, was unlocked.

Fear crept up my body and closed around my throat. I struggled for air as a soft scratching sound scraped the other side of the door. Despite the constant note ringing in my ears, the scratching sound came through loud and clear, sending prickles of discomfort over my skin.

I considered checking the doorknob, but with the creature so close, lying in wait just beyond the thin wood barrier, I thought better of it and turned tail instead.

I had two questions as I backed out of the room. Well, I had a thousand, but two flashed salient in my mind. One, if my sexy time with Roane was just a dream, how did I get wet? And two, why did I keep waking up in the attic? Was something drawing me there? The creature? If so, how?

Either way, I'd had about enough of his antics. Not that I could do anything about it, but maybe Gigi would know something.

After making quick work of the narrow flight of stairs, I hugged myself to generate some warmth and hurried to the secret portal to my room. The shelves had been pulled open, apparently by yours truly, and I hurried through them, ready to start the day. I turned on my shower with a shivering hand and turned on the light. Yep. Just like the girl from *The Ring*. Not a good look for me.

Making quick work of the soaking T-shirt, I wrapped a towel around myself and went into my room to find the usual suspects still sprawled across my bed. As I hurried to my closet to ferret out dry clothes for the day, I checked the time: 1:01.

I stopped and stared at the digital display. I knew for a fact I had lain there for a good half hour before going downstairs. Or had I dreamed the entire thing? If I was dreaming about lying in bed unable to go to sleep, my dreams sucked.

Then again, I had dreamed about Roane. They couldn't suck that bad.

Groaning softly, I grabbed a tee and an old pair of sweats with more holes in them than I had limbs. I hopped in the shower and noticed my hair smelled like salt. Like the salt from the caves under the house.

As usual, nothing made sense. I showered, dressed, and went downstairs, this time in search of coffee. I couldn't sleep either way, and since we now knew it had been Annette's powers transforming everything to poison and not some random killer, I felt safe to make a pot of the dark elixir and look over the book Gigi had pulled out for Annette and me.

But when I entered the kitchen, a soft glow coming

from the lights under the cabinets illuminated a gorgeous man—a man named Roane—sitting at the table reading a book, his hair wet, his chest bare.

I stopped short and took him in. He wore a pair of sweats, too. Light gray with a team emblem of some kind down one side. His feet were bare, and I felt oddly voyeuristic staring at them. I'd never had a foot fetish, but—

"Are you just going to watch, or are you going to join me?" he asked without looking up. The same words he'd used in the dream. Had it been a dream? His hair hung wet. His lashes still spiked. The fresh scent of sandalwood in the air. He lifted his cup then gestured toward the coffee pot. "It's fresh."

"It's one o'clock in the morning," I said, crossing to the pot.

"It is."

His now-familiar scent wafted around me, mingling with the roasted coffee beans, and I made a mental note to have Annette make that scent into a cologne. We'd be rich in no time.

He rose to refill his cup just as I took one down from the cabinet. He pressed into me from behind. Reached around and grabbed the carafe.

When he poured me a cup then refilled his own, I asked, "Am I dreaming again?"

He replaced the carafe. "Were you dreaming before?"

"Yes. Maybe. I don't know." I turned in his arms. "Did we almost have sex in your shower?"

He pulled back. "You dreamed that, too?"

After taking a moment to study his incredible mouth, full and sculpted and sensual, I asked, "So, it was a dream?"

One corner of that mouth rose. "A dream we could easily make come true."

He was so delicious. So astoundingly and disarmingly delicious. And there I stood in all my dowdy glory.

I turned away from him. I'd never wanted anything or anyone so bad in my life. So bad it scared me, the force behind it mountainous. I bit my lip and asked softly, "Roane, can I keep you?"

"Keep me? Like chained in a dungeon?"

One thoughtful brow rose as I considered the possibilities. Then I snorted, coming to my senses. Where would I even find a dungeon? Wait. I had one. The caves beneath the house. I just needed a few chains. A rack. A torch or two. "No," I said, shaking out of my thoughts. "Just... can I have you? Forever? Not for a day or a week or a month, but forever?"

He scraped his teeth over his bottom lip then licked it. "I thought I made my feelings on the matter clear when I asked you to marry me."

"See, that's the problem." I pushed past him, cup in hand. "Marriage means nothing anymore. It's just a stupid piece of paper that no one takes seriously."

"So my asking you to marry me was meaningless."

"No." I breathed out a frustrated sigh. "No. It wasn't meaningless. It was... I'm honored."

"You misunderstand, Ms. Dayne. I'm not accusing you of anything. I just want to understand you on this. You're saying you want me. Not just for a day or a week or a month. You want me forever."

For some inane reason, humiliation surged inside me, but there was no stopping now. "Yes. I want you forever."

"Then accept me."

"What?"

He lifted a shoulder. "You have to accept me. Marrying

me would show acceptance, but it doesn't have to go that far. You can just accept me."

"Okay, then, I..." I'd started to answer but something gave me pause. Nothing for the last several months was that easy. There was always a catch. "What does that mean, exactly? Accept you?"

"It's something I read. The book Georgi gave you." He pointed toward the book with his chin. "I've read it a couple of times. It talks about how a charmling assigns a sentry, a guardian who protects her throughout her entire life."

A warmth spread in my chest. "You want to be my bodyguard?"

"Of course."

"You're hired."

"You have to say it. And there's a spell to make it official. Then I'm yours. Forever."

I narrowed my eyes. "That sounds rather permanent."

He took a sip. "It is."

"Let me read the passage and get back to you."

"So, you lied."

"What? No. I just want to read the fine print. When you say forever..."

"I mean forever. Even into the afterlife."

"I love the sound of that. Well, not the afterlife stuff, but getting to keep you forever. It's what I want. Really. But it just seems like there's more to it than you're letting on. Like, perhaps, you'll lose your free will. Your choice in the matter."

"But it *is* my choice. It's what I want, too."

"Yeah, *now*." I threw my hands up in helplessness. "What if you change your mind? What if a year rolls around and you decide you can't stand me? Then what? You're just stuck with me?"

He lowered his head. "You would be stuck with me as well. Is that so bad?"

"Holy shit. You're not kidding." I hurried to the book I hadn't had a chance to look at yet and started flipping through the pages.

He reached around me. "I can just show—"

I held up my hand. "I've got it." I positioned the book in front of me and did a reveal spell, impatience spurring me forward. The pages fanned out, fluttering in the glow from the spell, and settled on a passage near the middle. I looked down and read. Then I read again before stepping away from it as though it had a communicable disease. "What kind of sixth-century bullshit is this?"

"Defiance, it's not that bad."

I spun toward him. "Not that bad?"

He bit down, refusing to answer.

"The word is not *accept*, Roane. A charmling does not *accept* a guardian. She *claims* one. She chooses the strongest, most capable person in the land and claims them as her guardian and then they, having exactly zero say in the matter, will defend her until their death."

"Yes," he said quietly.

"Oh, but wait! There's more!" I pointed to a particularly disturbing passage and graced him with my best accusatory glare. "This says if I die, you die." I let that sink in, then repeated, "If I die, you die. Period. If anything happens to me, it happens to you. My guardian, who is bound to me forever, even in the freaking afterlife, dies if I do."

"It's a good incentive to keep you safe," he said, lifting a shoulder in utter nonchalance.

"Roane. Did you read the entire thing?"

His face darkened as he studied me from beneath his thick lashes. "Cover to cover. Several times."

"So you know that if you die, if you meet some horrible demise at the hands of a maniacal warlock while protecting yours truly, I get to go out, dressed to the nines, no doubt, and find—no, *claim*—another guardian. Just slap a collar around his neck, pretty as you please, while you're lying in a grave somewhere."

"Is that a problem?"

"Is that a problem?" I balked. "Roane, there are no take-backs. Neither of us gets to change our minds. I almost bound you to me for life without knowing all the details. You"—I released a sharp breath as reality sank in—"you did that on purpose."

He stepped closer again. "I did. But you're forgetting something." He pointed to the last paragraph. "You, in turn, protect me."

"Yeah, well, that part's pretty sketchy. How do I protect you?"

"Some of your power is transferred to me. I can't do spells or anything, but your power protects me so I can protect you. It's like a magical prophylactic."

The scoff that came out of my mouth was filled partly with humor and partly with horror. I sobered, then turned to him. "Of course," I said. "That's what all of this is about. You're power hungry."

His gaze dropped to my mouth. "Immensely."

"You want my magics for your own nefarious schemes."

"Precisely."

"You're going to try to take over the world."

"Indubitably."

"Indubitably?" I asked, impressed.

He took two fingers and gently backed me against the table. "I ran out of adverbs. It was all I could think of." He pressed into me, the sweats leaving very little to the imagination.

No more dreams. No more interruptions. I wanted the cock.

As he sent both hands up my T-shirt, the sensation delicious on my skin, I tugged his sweats down over his hips. His erection fell against my exposed stomach, and he pressed closer. He cupped my breast and slid his thumbs over my nipples before lifting my tee over my head.

Cool air washed over skin that suddenly seemed too warm. Too tight. I worried for a moment about getting caught naked in the kitchen, but he would know if anyone were going to walk in on us. Even Samuel, since he pretty much only followed Ink.

He moved the book, then lifted me onto the table and lowered me back. The cold wood felt like ice, the shock almost painful. I drew in a soft breath at the sensation, the heat of his mouth on my rib cage a study in contrast. I buried my hands in his hair as he trailed kisses over my breasts, stopping to suck the peaks. The pressure caused waves of pleasure to course through my body. A hot blush rushed over my skin.

I wanted him closer. I wanted his cock in my hands, but I couldn't quite reach. His sucking made me squirm as the first sparks of an orgasm flickered to life in my core, and then his mouth was on mine. He slid my sweats over my hips and pushed between my legs, but I'd waited a long time for this. And I wanted more.

"Stop," I said, pushing at his shoulders.

He stopped instantly and reared back. "Are you okay? Did I hurt you?"

"Yes."

"Fuck." He pulled me to a sitting position and tugged on his sweats.

I grabbed his hands, and whispered, "Stop."

At first, he looked at me, confused. But when I finished removing my sweats and panties and stood in front of him completely naked—something I'd rarely done with my exes —Roane looked like he was on the verge of eating me alive. "Defiance," he said, moving closer, but I held up a hand.

"Uh-uh," I said, waving an index finger at him. "My turn."

His eyes glistened with desire, but I held him at bay.

"I wonder what will happen if I do this..." I drew a spell with two fingers on his chest. The light burst from the lines and sank into his skin.

He let out a sharp breath, like he'd jumped into an icy lake. His knees almost gave. He stepped back and put his hands on the island behind him to support his weight.

I stepped closer, leaned in, and whispered into his ear, "Good boy. Now stay."

A low growl rumbled from his chest, but I held my ground.

"And what will happen, if I do this?" I drew another spell a little lower. It shattered and soaked into his skin.

He threw back his head with a groan. His hands, hard and masculine, started to shake as they clutched the island. As the spell caressed and stroked and nipped.

I pushed his sweats down. His erection, massively engorged, stayed upright against his abdomen. He was on the verge of climax. I drew my fingers lower, pushed the magics down until they enveloped his cock. Fire and ice and everything nice.

"Defiance, fucking hell," he bit out.

But they were coming back onto to me. The magics. I

felt them like an electric wind on my skin. Hot and stinging and sensual, they pooled in my abdomen and beat a slow, rhythmic pulse. I sank to my knees and took his cock, first into my hand and then into my mouth.

A raw sound escaped his throat, and he grabbed a handful of my hair, to stop me or assist, I didn't know. When I took him deeper, I felt a rush of blood as his climax neared. I wanted it. I wanted him to come in my mouth, but I got my answer. He held my head to stop me.

I fought him. I slid out to the throbbing tip, circled it with my tongue, and eased back onto him. His muscles constricted again, and I drew another spell low on his abdomen. Then I grabbed his hips with both hands and pulled him all the way inside.

He couldn't have stopped what came next any more than he could've stopped the sun from rising. His orgasm came in swift, successive waves. He spilled into me, his groans echoing off the walls as he came in my mouth.

But just as I suspected, I'd connected us. With every surge of pleasure that coursed through him, I was gifted the same. His orgasm clamped onto me, sank into me, lifted me up. I parted my legs as the sweet sting that was coiled around my clit burst and washed over me. I moaned and my body convulsed with wave after undulating wave of shattering arousal.

He wrapped both arms around my head and held me to him as we both finished. The momentary lack of oxygen actually sent my orgasm spiraling again, and it took me a moment to come down.

I'd clung to his hips, an anchor to wait out the storm, while I drifted back to earth. I realized I was emitting a soft moan with each breath, but I'd never felt anything like that. I didn't know orgasms could be so sharp. So delicious. So intoxicating. Nor that they could reach such dizzying heights. When the world finally stopped spinning, I cupped him in my hands, sat back on my heels, and looked up at him.

He sank to his knees, pushed my hair back from my face, and gazed at me like I'd hung the moon. It was a feeling I could get used to. Then he brushed his full, sexy lips over mine seconds before claiming them. And we kissed. A deep, long, wet kiss that left me breathless once again.

Had I known that what we just did was only the pre-show, I would've paced myself.

SEVENTEEN

Sometimes I go hours without drinking coffee.
It's called sleeping.
—Meme

I woke up in a strange place again, only this time, I wasn't alone. Roane lay snuggled against my backside, and we were in his apartment. In his bedroom. On his bed.

I grabbed a fistful of blanket and inhaled the scent of him, giddy with elation, before I tried to ease out of his embrace.

He pulled me tighter.

Laughing softly, I turned in his arms. The early morning hues filtering in through a high, ground-level window were just enough light for me to study his features. Strong. Alluring. Devastatingly handsome.

After a moment, he caught on to the fact that I was looking at him and buried his face against my neck. "You can't leave."

"I have a lot to do."

"No."

"Yes," I said, giggling when he went for an ear.

He rolled on top of me, pushed his hips between my legs, and entered me in one smooth thrust.

My breath caught, and my body tightened around him.

His mouth at my ear, he whispered, "What about now?"

The pleasure was instantaneous. I sent my hands over the roundness of his buttocks and pulled him deeper.

He hissed in a soft breath.

"I guess I can stay a few more minutes."

"I hate to break it to you," he said as he eased out and slid back in, going deeper this time, causing all kinds of rapturous delights to swirl in my abdomen, "but this could take a while."

I grabbed a fistful of his hair, gasping with each painstaking thrust, each nip along my skin, and resigned myself to the careful ministrations of a very dedicated, very skilled lover.

An hour later, we were awakened by a hungry, battle-scarred cat who was in no mood for our snuggles. It was hardly his fault. The bottom of his bowl was most likely showing through.

The horror!

I left Roane in the shower, fed the cat, then went in search of sustenance before remembering we had none, thanks to the curly-haired vixen asleep in my bed. Thus, I changed into warmer clothes and made a breakfast run, committing grand theft auto since Minerva had the Bug. I had to jack Annette's ruby-red Dodge Charger. The one with a Hemi under the hood and 425 horsepower. The trip to Red's didn't take long.

The local favorite had just opened when I got there. I

ordered enough food for a small army, or a wolf, either way, and sat at a table to wait. I was minding my own business, updating my status for all three of my followers, when Joaquin Ferebee walked in. Enshrouded in a deep sadness, he wore the same baseball cap, but he was clean-shaven, his tan tactical jacket freshly washed. And he'd decided. He'd resigned himself to the fact that whatever he was searching for, aka his son, could never be found, so he'd made a decision.

He'd started to sit down when he spotted me. He straightened to his full height, which was a hella lot. Wide shoulders. Menacing stature. A guarded posture that screamed *do not fuck with me.*

So, naturally, that was my first inclination. "Mr. Ferebee," I said, hoping he wouldn't try to take my arm as a trophy again. I had no backup this time. His words from our first meeting came back to me. *Did you send it?*

"You *do* know who I am." His words were accusing.

"No. Well, kind of." I stood and took a wary step closer. "I just... I found out your name and looked you up. Your son..."

He took a step closer too, his more of a threat than mine had been, and I readied to run. "What about him?"

"I can try to help if you'll let me."

His lids narrowed. "How?"

"My best friend and I have a business. We help people."

A server came over, but he waved her off. "What kind of business?"

"We... we find lost things." Saying it out loud sounded ridiculous, especially when the *thing* was his son. His gorgeous son.

"So the local police, the state police, and the FBI can't help, but you and your best friend can?"

I steeled my resolve. "Yes. If you'll let me."

"How? What can you do that they didn't?"

"If you'll take my hand..." I held it out to him.

He scoffed and shook his head. "This fucking town."

When he started for the door, I panicked. "Please, Mr. Ferebee, if you'll just tell me what you're searching for."

"I thought you already knew."

"I know, but... that's just how it works. You have to tell me. To trust me."

Though he hadn't ordered anything, he pulled out his wallet and tossed a five onto the counter in front of the server he'd waved off. But something fell out of his pocket when he did. A receipt of some kind.

I ran and picked it up, then went after him, but standing across the promenade was the hunter, his hair starkly white against his black duster. I skidded to a stop, and we made eye contact for a split second. I'd hoped he wouldn't know me. Know who—or what—I was. If it had been Annette's hot flash that summoned him to the area, he shouldn't have.

Clearly, he did.

He seemed surprised at first, then pleased as his gaze roamed over me, anticipation glistening in his dark eyes like a boy on Christmas morning.

I shouldn't have come out alone. He hadn't known who I was until we made eye contact. I knew it. I'd given myself away, I just didn't know how. Or what I did to clue him in. Other than stop short and stare at him, but with his looks, that had to happen on occasion. I hurried back inside just as the server brought my food around.

"Thank you," I said, wondering how to get to Annette's Charger without being kidnapped.

When I looked again, the hunter was gone. Naturally. Probably lurking in the shadows, waiting to grab me and take me to his master. I could only pray his last name was Bater. It would give me some sense of satisfaction knowing that if this all went south.

I wasn't about to risk my life by facing a hunter alone. I took out my phone to call Roane but realized just as quickly I would be risking both of our lives if I did.

Okay. I could do this. I'd just have to take a shortcut.

Raising my hand to the server, I asked, "Do you happen to have a back door?"

On a positive note, I found out that Annette's Charger cornered like it was on well-oiled rails. I hauled ass all the way home, garnering not one, but two extra-long, extra-aggravated honks.

I slid to a halt in front of Percy and glanced around before getting out. No hunter that I could see, so I made a run for it. Just as I got to the door, I heard a male voice behind me, and I froze.

"Ms. Dayne," the male said.

I turned to the bespectacled Donald Shoemaker. "Oh goddess." I sagged against Percy's front door. "Mr. Shoemaker, what can I do for you?"

"You cannot conduct business on this premises. It's not zoned for commercial use."

I opened the door and put the food in the foyer. "Don't tell me: you have a petition."

His breath fogged on the early morning air. He snapped a set of papers against his palm and handed them to me. "Signed by everyone in the neighborhood."

I took them. "At your behest, I'm sure."

"It took some bribing, yes. Some promises I'd rather not have made, but desperate times..."

After releasing a lungful of air, I unfolded the papers,

took a quick look, then refocused on him. "Are you ever going to stop?"

"Not until you leave town."

"You got breakfast!" Annette hurried down the stairs, took one look at Mr. Shoemaker, and gave him a glower that would've melted the face off a lesser human.

Then again, with her newfound powers, she could actually be able to do that.

"Annette," I said, steering her gaze toward me, "why don't you take this into the kitchen?"

"You sure you don't need backup?"

"I'm sure," I said through gritted teeth. "What with your new condition and all."

She frowned.

I frowned back. "I'd hate for anything to explode."

"Oh! That condition." She made her fingers into two guns, pointed them at me, and clicked her tongue. "Right. I'll just..." She bent to pick up the food when I came to my senses. Just in time, I might add.

I dove toward her and blocked her path. "Sorry. I forgot. You could be contagious. I'll bring these in. You get the plates down."

"Oh, yeah." She did a snort-laugh thing. "Good point." Girl finds out she's a charmling and she snaughs about it a day later. I had to admire her gumption.

I turned back to Mr. Shoemaker. "Mr. Shoemaker... Donald... Can I call you Donald?"

"No."

"The thing is, Donald, this has to stop."

"It will. As soon as you leave town."

"Why? This isn't just about Percy. Or about my business. This is about me, and I want to know why."

"Defiance?" Gigi asked behind me.

"Gigi!" I said, surprised. I snapped and turned back to Donald. "Mr. Shoemaker, this is Georgiana, Ruthie's long-lost twin sister." I guess I could drop the long-lost part, but it did help explain a few things. Like why no one had ever met her or even heard of her.

Mr. Shoemaker looked at Gigi like she was the lost daughter of a royal family. He stepped inside and walked to her.

"Okay, then." I closed the door and watched as he gazed at her in utter shock.

"Ruthie," he said, shaking his head.

"No." I hurried around to Gigi's side. "This is Georgiana, Ruthie's long-lost—"

"How is this possible?"

"Donald." Her smile channeled the brightest parts of the sun. "I should've known you'd recognize me."

"You think changing your hair color is going to fool anyone?"

"Yes." She tucked her arms over her chest in defiance. "I do."

He put his hands over his mouth and laughed, his eyes tearing up as he leaned in for a hug.

She hugged him back.

Clearly, I'd missed something. "I thought he was the enemy?"

Gigi stood back. "He is most definitely not the enemy."

"How are you alive, Ruthie?"

"Um..." I held up a finger to correct him. "Georgi. And how did you know it was her?"

He had yet to take his eyes off her. "Georgi," he conceded.

"You'll have to ask my granddaughter. But first, come in. Let's have breakfast."

They turned and walked arm in arm to the kitchen.

"We're feeding our enemies now?" I called out to them, wrestling with the bags. "Why not just invite the neo-Nazis over? Or maybe a gang of cannibalistic bikers?"

We sat at the table, making sure Annette didn't touch anything but her own food. Which meant I had to serve her as she smirked. "I could get used to this."

"You could get your powers under control. This ain't a forever thing, shortstop."

"Darn."

"Okay," I said, sitting down with my breakfast sandwich just as Roane joined us. The fact that we'd had hot, lusty sex not two hours ago warmed me all over. As did his lingering, appreciative gaze. "What gives? Why isn't Mr. Shoemaker our most hated enemy? No offense."

"None taken."

The chief came in, kissed his fiancée on the cheek, greeted the enemy, then dug in.

Gigi picked at her food. "Let's just say Donald knows about me."

"Clearly."

"No, he knows what we are capable of."

"Oh. Like...?" I wiggled my brows, and somehow that translated for her.

"Yes. Like. Do you remember the story I told you about the missing girl and the man I had to kill to save her and Houston?"

I did. It was before I was born. A little girl had been abducted, and Gigi found her. But she was worried the angry townspeople would tip the kidnapper off and he would kill her, so she sent them in the wrong direction while she and a young officer named Houston Metcalf went to find the girl themselves. They'd managed to get the upper hand and knocked him out, but he came to and pointed a gun at the chief. Gigi acted on instinct. She pushed all of her magics into the kidnapper and snapped his neck.

"He got the upper hand," I said. "You had no choice."

"That little girl was Donald's sister."

"Oh my God," I said, stunned.

The smile he gave her held more devotion than a devout coffee addict. "I've been a fan ever since." He squeezed Gigi's hand. "But you... you did—"

"Die. Yes."

"Okay." He nodded as though trying to absorb it all. "Then, if I may ask, how are you here?"

"Let's just say my granddaughter is very powerful."

He blinked at me and shook his head. "Why am I not surprised?"

"Wait. I don't understand. You've been trying to get me out of this house—out of this town—for months."

"Yeah, sorry about that. I was worried about you. I didn't know what happened to Ruthie, but I knew it wasn't on the up-and-up."

"You knew she was killed?"

"I suspected."

"Did you suspect me as a murderer?"

"No. I'm sorry. It's just, she was the picture of health, and then, not only does she get sick, she goes downhill like a bobsledder on winter break? No. I knew something was off."

"You're apparently the only one," Roane said, still angry with himself.

Gigi tsked him, then turned back to Donald. "You were trying to protect my granddaughter."

"I thought if I could just get her out of town..."

"Why?" I pointed at him when it hit me. "You may not

know who, but you know why someone wanted her dead, don't you?"

He shook his head. "Again, I only suspected. Sure, there's the money, but I had no idea who would get that until you showed up. The only other thing I could think of was Percival." He glanced up as though to look at him.

"That's what we were thinking. We just aren't sure why. Not that Percy isn't wonderful!" I hurried to correct. A gentle hum vibrated beneath our feet. Then I remembered something. "Gigi, you guys found Mr. Shoemaker's sister before I was born. You were already a finder of lost things."

She'd taken a bite of a breakfast burrito, so it took her a moment to ask, "Yes, why?"

"Oh, just something Elle said." I sat back in my chair. "She thought maybe my powers had a reverse effect and had somehow transferred to you. So instead of me being the finder of lost things because of you, because of my family bloodline, she thought maybe I was the finder and that you got it from me."

Gigi blinked in surprise. "Defiance, she could be right." She looked at Houston. "I was, what? Mid-thirties when we found Donald's sister? You had just joined the force."

He nodded. "A fresh-faced kid who fell in love with a witch."

"A much, much older witch," she corrected.

Annette reached out for a high-five. "You go, Georgi."

Gigi caved and returned the gesture. It was officially the first high-five I'd seen my grandmother give. We were totally rubbing off on her.

"Before Pania came home pregnant with you, I'd been just a regular witch. I did do spells to find lost things, but they didn't always work. Or they took us to something close but not the real object. Then you came into the house, so to speak. I could sense your power even before you were born. I think you came into your powers while Pania was pregnant. She chalked up the heat rushing over her and the sudden light-headedness to hormones. We, naturally, had no idea you were a charmling. We would never have dreamed such a thing."

Either Mr. Shoemaker knew what a charmling was or he didn't want to pry. He sat listening, his attention rapt.

"But the strangest thing happened. I suddenly got better."

The chief stopped eating and focused on her, his gaze probably as loving as that fresh-faced officer's had been over forty years ago.

"Even on the little things, I could suddenly find items that had been lost for decades. Not like you, Defiance. I was nowhere near as talented as a charmling would be, but my spells started working. They were more accurate. And I became known as a finder of lost things." Her stunned gaze landed on me. "You did that. From the womb, no less."

"Elle was right," I said, astonished.

Gigi folded her arms. "I think I need to meet this Liliana Lovett."

"I agree."

"Wait, what?" Annette sat up, startled.

"Thank you for trying to protect me, Donald. May I call you Donald?"

He chuckled. "Yes, Ms. Dayne. You may." Then he sobered. "But you still can't hold séances here."

"Oh, really?" Annette got her handy-dandy notebook and pulled out a piece of paper. "Because this here business license says we can." She pulled it taut, snapping the paper in his face.

The grin that softened his mouth was saturated with mischief. "It was worth a shot."

When Donald and the chief started talking about fishing lures, Annette and I zoned out of that conversation and into our own.

"How are you today, Nette the Jet?"

She took a bite of a bacon and egg sandwich and thought about it as she chewed. After a moment, she nodded. "I'm good. Better, anyway. It's all so... so..."

"Surreal?" I finished for her.

"Exactly!" she said, perhaps a little too loudly. She cleared her throat and started over. "Exactly. It's like it's not real."

"Which would be the definition of surreal."

"Right. Right." Her gaze slid past me as she lost herself in thought, only to bounce back just as quickly, resilient creature that she was. "Wait, you have a séance to perform tonight."

"No. Absolutely not." I got up to clear the plates.

She followed me. "Deph!"

"Annette, we have so much going on."

"Most of the attendees are from the coven. You'll be among friends. It'll be like a trial run."

"Most?"

"Yes. We did have a few other interested parties."

"Just how many tickets did you sell?"

"Twelve. And a half. I'll be there, but I'm not sure I count."

"Did you find out where Joaquin Ferebee is staying in town?"

"I'm just waiting for a call," Annette said. "Get this. I called his work, said I found his license, and gave them my number to give to him. He should be calling any minute."

"And what happens when he opens his wallet and sees his license tucked safely inside?"

"Crap. I didn't think of that. Do you think he'll call anyway?"

I had my doubts. "I saw him this morning. I really need to find him."

"You did what?" Roane asked.

"I saw him. Joaquin Ferebee. When I went for breakfast."

He looked at Annette. "I thought you went for the food."

"Nope," she said, eyeing him suspiciously.

He straightened in his chair. "But it was your car."

"Yeah," I said, "because Minerva has mine."

"No, she brought it back last night and left with Leo, the guy we helped the other night. Your VW is parked behind Percival beside my truck."

"Oh. Well. I guess I committed grand theft auto for no reason."

"It's not GTA if you have a key, Deph. You really must learn the rules."

"You went out by yourself?" Roane asked, his voice slicing through the air. Everyone stopped talking and turned toward us.

"You told me he saw Annette. She would've been in danger. Not me."

"I told you we couldn't know for certain either way. Defiance, you're a charmling. You can't just stroll through town with a hunter on the loose."

"I was hardly strolling." When he deadpanned me, I tried to growl. I failed. "Look. It doesn't matter. He took one look at me and left."

Roane shot to his feet. "He saw you?"

"Yes."

"And you saw him?"

"Really?"

"Son of a bitch." He started to head out, but Gigi stopped him.

"What is it, honey?"

"He's back," he said, grabbing a jacket off a hook in the mudroom.

I walked over to him. "I didn't know he ever left."

"The wolves lost his scent. I thought—I'd hoped—he left town."

"Maybe it's not the same one. This one had white hair and black eyes."

"They all have white hair and black eyes."

"Oh. Right. I knew that."

"We need to keep an eye on him. And you," he said, stepping closer, "stay the fuck put."

Unfortunately, I didn't like being ordered around. I raised my chin a visible notch. "Or?"

He bit down, then leaned closer. "You said forever."

"What?"

"Last night. This morning. Whenever. You said you wanted me forever."

I slipped a hand inside his jacket and slid it along his ribs.

His muscles contracted in response.

"I do. That will never change."

"Yeah, well, I want you forever, too." He buried his face in my hair. When I wrapped an arm around his neck, his mouth found my ear, and he whispered, "Not a day. Not a week. Not a month. Forever." He nipped my earlobe, sending a wave of pleasure spiraling straight to my core, then he turned and left.

"Defiance?" Gigi's voice was soft with worry. "Is everything okay?"

"No." I sat down at the table. "Look, I get it. Warlocks, bad. Hunters, possibly worse. But Annette and I are true charmlings, Gigi. We're more powerful than any warlock. Doesn't that count for anything?"

She stirred her coffee, more out of habit than necessity since she took it black. "I have to tell you, Defiance, all warlocks I've met are ruthless, cold-hearted bastards. Other than your great-great-aunt Petunia. She was just... misguided. But I fear hunters ten times over."

"Why?"

"They have no conscience. They're robots. And they're powerful. I'm not sure they're even human anymore. And if there is one in town, you can bet your bottom dollar he's after a witch. Possibly even a charmling."

"We need intel," Annette said. "We're blind. We need to know what he's up to."

The chief shrugged. "That would be nice. So far, my men have yet to keep him in their sights."

Surprised, I said, "I didn't know you had men on him."

"They've tried, but he seems to vanish into thin air every time they get close."

"Yeah, I got his disappearing act as well."

"Can I do anything?" Mr. Shoemaker asked.

I considered being an asshole and telling him to get a petition going stat, but I liked the guy. He reminded me of the sweet uncle I never had. "Probably not," I said, drumming my fingers on the table, "but there's something I can do."

"What?" Gigi asked.

I smiled and looked up, the spell I'd need materializing in my mind's eye in glorious Technicolor.

EIGHTEEN

I live by trial and error,
but mostly error.
A shit ton of error.
—Meme

I stood at the door in the attic, an illumination spell lighting the paint-chipped shiplap around us. It was quiet now. No knocking. No scratching. Just the soft breaths of the being on the other side of the door, as though he'd been waiting for me. For this moment.

For some reason, I'd been drawn to him the last couple of days. I'd come to think of the rooms in the attic as prison cells. If so, what was he in prison for? As far as I knew, only this room was occupied. But I didn't really know about the others. I'd never gotten that far.

Perhaps my prying that first visit, my peering into the universe beyond the door, woke the creature up. Or perhaps he was the only one imprisoned here, and I'd created this prison when I was little just for him. Either way, he was here for a reason, and it was high time I found out what that reason was.

I'd asked everyone to leave the house just in case. Mr. Shoemaker had to get home and the chief had to go back to work, but Gigi and Annette swore they wouldn't leave if I paid them to. I tried anyway. A thousand bucks each. It didn't work.

Thus, they both stood behind me, huddled together, their eyes wide with curiosity and fear. Served them right. I had no idea what to expect. The creature was volatile and angry, and they wanted to watch me try to bring him to heel.

I turned back to them. "Last chance. If this creature kills you both, it'll be your own fault."

They nodded and huddled closer.

"We've never been able to open the doors," Gigi said.

"Yeah, well, I apparently created the place with the help of one of my charmling ancestors. I guess if anyone can open it..."

I did mention that I'd found the door unlocked yesterday. Gigi was beside herself. And not with joy.

Swallowing hard, I took a cautious step closer and put my hand on the antique doorknob. It turned with a soft squeak and a click. "Shit," I whispered.

"Shit indeed," Gigi echoed.

I looked over my shoulder. "You guys sure?"

Their nods were not particularly enthusiastic, but they were there.

I pulled, and the door opened to an empty room with a cathedral ceiling. No vast universe. No creature. Though the darkened corners seemed pretty sketchy. And very horror-movie-ish.

Gigi and Annette came up behind me for a look.

Annette reacted first with an unimpressed "Hmm."

But when I went to step inside, both women grabbed hold of me and pulled me back.

"Are you crazy?" Annette asked as I slapped her hands away.

"Defiance," Gigi said in her grandmother voice, "I'm not sure you should go in there."

"Do you want to go?"

She lifted her elegant chin. "I'd rather eat broken glass."

"Well, then. I've read enough of the texts and journals you gave me to know how this part is done. I just need to find the little devil."

I turned back to the room, closed my eyes, and looked beyond the obvious. Beyond the façade.

There.

I found him hiding in one of the farther corners of the universe. I reached out and dragged him closer. I was surprised by him. I didn't feel hatred or anger or violence. I felt fear and the tiniest amount of reverence. It had me wondering why I'd put him here in the first place.

Bedoliel. I'd told Gigi his name was Bead-uh, but that was clearly short for his real name: Bedoliel.

I knelt down at the threshold between this world and the other—the other being one of billions beyond our physical realm—and held out my hands. The creature, no more than a swirl of black smoke, a scattered mass of energy, didn't fight. He simply accepted, his lonely, fractured mind stressed and apprehensive. I'd had no idea I would be gone so long. He'd basically been in solitary confinement for more than forty years, and the fragile state of his psyche showed it.

Once I hauled him closer, I drew the spell, then concentrated his energy in my hands, one on bottom, one on top. In the blink of an eye, I considered his form. What would best suit my needs. All forms had advantages and disadvantages. A bird could see a lot from overhead but could also be attacked by a predator. A mouse could get into tiny spaces but wouldn't be able to cover much ground. A dog could cover a lot of ground but would be too noticeable hanging out on the streets. So, at the risk of being cliché, a cat it was.

I bound the spell to his molecules, light filtering in a thousand different directions, and molded him to suit my needs. And then he was in my arms. Massive and fluffy and black. He closed his olive eyes—the same color as Roane's—and pushed his head against the underside of my chin, where he purred as though we'd been best friends for years. I lifted him up and turned toward my partners in magic.

"Okay," I said, explaining what I'd learned, "his name is Bedoliel, but that's a mouthful. So how about... Olly?" I asked him.

He purred again and raised up in my arms to smell my mouth, his paws perched on my cheeks, his whiskers tickling my lips.

"He's like a real cat," Annette said, going in to pet him. Olly let her, though he didn't seem to enjoy it, and he swatted at her when she got too close to his ears.

"He is, isn't he?" That fact surprised no one more than me. How did he know what a cat would do? How it would act? Its behaviors and mannerisms? It was fascinating.

Gigi came in to pet him as well. He seemed to enjoy her touch, then I remembered I'd created her out of a mouse. I could only hope that wouldn't become an issue. She rubbed his ears, and he purred louder.

"Really?" Annette asked, totally offended.

"I've never seen anything like this." Gigi cupped his

fluffy head and went in for a *kunik*, rubbing her nose against his. He ate it up.

"I thought familiars were common in the witch world?" I asked, running my hand over his black coat. He was long-haired, but not a real cat. Surely he wouldn't shed.

"They are. Animals that have been trained with magics. Not creatures created from the pure energy of an unknown being."

"See?" I said, bouncing him in my arms. "You're special. Now, find the hunter."

He rose up again, put a paw on my mouth, and locked his gaze with mine. In that moment, I saw myself through his eyes. My hair needed a good brushing. Otherwise, I wasn't any worse for wear. But it was the colors that blew me away. Colors I'd never seen before. Shades of blue I never dreamed existed as he dove into my psyche through the varying hues of my irises.

After he searched my mind like I'd searched his, he found the hunter. He purred again, jumped out of my arms, and took off down the stairs.

"Can he get out?" Annette asked.

"I have a feeling he can. And now," I said, quite proud of myself, "we have a spy."

There was just one little problem. One wrench in my plan prickling the back of my neck. I was wrong. The attic wasn't a prison. It was a safe house. And I'd just sent the creature out into the world I'd been protecting him from.

AFTER TEXTING ROANE A DOZEN TIMES, I could wait no longer. Annette was trying to get a location on Joaquin Ferebee and preparing for the séance at the same time. We were apparently having it in the dining room, and when I left, she was trying to convince Percy to do something *viny* to impress the masses.

At least she hadn't tried to poison us all today. Baby steps.

But I wanted to go to the county clerk's office. Or the property assessor's. Or a tax assessor. Some kind of assessor. Anyone who could answer a few questions for me. I would just have to risk it, no matter what Roane said. I couldn't stay cooped up all day when I had a murder to solve.

Besides, I had a bodyguard. Olly and I had a psychic connection, for lack of a better term. I could see everything he saw when I wanted to. And he could pop into my mind when he needed to, like when he wanted to chase a mouse instead of look for the hunter and I had to tell him no. I found it amazing that he'd taken on all the characteristics of the form I'd chosen for him.

I entered his mind and watched as he scanned the promenade where I'd last seen the hunter. Nothing, so I called him back to escort me to the clerk's office. While he scouted ahead, I drove to city hall. I would catch glimpses of the city through his eyes. People's feet as they walked. Bushes and fences and other animals who didn't quite know what to make of Olly. He did have to dodge a little girl dead set on bringing a cat home, but he was fast. Like lightning when he sprinted. A black blur racing across the road.

And he didn't get winded. He didn't tire. He was pure energy, but even energies had to be replenished. I wondered what fuel he would need to sustain himself, praying it wasn't mice.

I parked and walked up Washington to Salem City Hall, a beautiful Greek Revival cinder block. Olly stood guard as I went inside. So far so good. No hunter. While I could've just called, I needed a little more info than what they might be willing to give over the phone and knew the best way to get it would be to go in person.

After roaming the bright halls, I found the property assessor's office and spotted a brunette not much older than me behind a dark-wood reception desk.

Her heels clicked as she walked over. "How can I help you?"

"Hi. I have a strange question about my grandmother's property. So, she died recently—"

"I'm sorry."

"Thank you. And, well, the executor of her estate found me. My grandmother had left me everything in her will, but I was wondering, what if she hadn't?"

"I'm sorry?"

"Well, if my grandmother hadn't made a will and no one knew I even existed—I was adopted when I was three—and she had no descendants, what would happen to the property?"

"If she had passed away intestate, meaning with no will, and she had no spouse or descendants, then intestacy law most often ensures the property be distributed to the closest living relatives. That would be based on what is called the Table of Consanguinity."

I opened the Notes app on my phone and jotted a few things down, mostly because she was using words I'd never heard before in my life. "And if there are none? No living relatives?"

"But there are," she said, indicating me with a sweep of her hand.

"Right, but—"

"I guess if you didn't exist, and the state couldn't find a

single living relative, then the property could escheat back to the state."

"Got it. *Essheet.*" The app did not like that word so, clearly, I spelled it wrong. "Do people come in here to ask about properties? Like who owns what?"

"All the time. Mostly developers. Why do you ask?"

"So you have a record of who has inquired about which property?"

"Not as a general rule. Most of them are just fishing to see if a property is owned by an individual or a company."

"But you're here most days, right?"

Her brows slid together. "I am."

"Could you tell me if anyone has inquired about my grandmother's house in the last few months?"

"I'm not sure I can just—"

"I know. It's asking a lot"—I looked at the nameplate on the reception counter—"Beverly, but it's very important. You can call Houston Metcalf if that would help. The chief of police? We've only recently realized my grandmother died under suspicious circumstances."

"Oh, goodness. Well, all I can do is try, but we get a lot of people in here."

"No, I get it. It's 33 Chestnut? My grandmother was Ruthie Goode."

"Oh, yes. The Goode house."

"Yes."

She drew in a dreamy breath. "That place is lovely. It's so hauntingly beautiful."

"Thank you." I knew I liked Beverly. "I couldn't agree more."

"But as to whether anyone has inquired... let me think." She tapped a pen on the counter. "Wait, I do believe there was a man in here a few months ago."

My hopes soared.

She went to her desk and started rifling through her message book. "I had a number. I was supposed to look something up for him, I just can't remember what."

So someone was in. If she could just remember who or what he looked like. I waited in anticipation as she flipped through page after page. "Right, here it is." She came back with the book and pointed to the message.

I leaned over it and squinted. Really hard. The tear-away sheet was blank, the line she pointed to empty. "I don't understand."

"Oh, hello," she said, shaking her head. "Didn't see you there. What can I help you with?"

Was she kidding me? This again? I sighed the sigh of a devastating defeat. So close yet so far. One thing was certainly made clear: the murderer had been after Percy. No doubt in my mind.

"I just had a question."

"I'll do my best."

I tapped on my notes. "How do you spell consanguinity?"

After some confusion, Beverly resigned herself to the fact that I was at the property assessor's office to learn how to spell a word I would likely never use again.

In the meantime, Olly found the hunter. The image filled my vision as he peered through a set of white blinds into a hotel room as the hunter got dressed. He shrugged into a white button-down, ran his fingers through wet shoulder-length hair that was almost as white as the shirt, and then lifted a black duster off the bed.

My pulse went into overdrive as I made a hasty escape. When the hunter opened the door, I told Olly to hide and follow him from a safe distance, though I had no idea what a safe distance from a hunter would be.

The hunter walked to the Ugly Mug Diner, a local favorite.

I fired off a text to Roane, realizing he must be in wolf form not to have answered me. Either that or he really was mad about breakfast. Surely not. No one could stay mad long when breakfast burritos were involved. He was probably tracking the hunter as well, but in wolf form, how much could he do in the city in broad daylight?

Olly heard the squeak of a mouse, his hearing possibly as good as Roane's, and I had to insist he ignore his baser instincts and focus on the task at hand. Honestly, he wasn't even a real cat. How did he even have baser instincts?

I considered what I knew thus far as I hurried to the Bug, which wasn't much. The hunter's bed had been mussed, so they did sleep. He walked into a restaurant, so they did eat. I knew more about hunters now than I had a few minutes ago, but my database was still fairly worthless.

No time like the present to find out more, however. Where was a wolf when I needed one? I texted Roane one more time with my plan so he couldn't get mad at me for not informing him beforehand, then I drove to the café.

I sat in the Bug as Olly watched him eat. He got all kinds of strange looks from the other customers. This coming from a town that had at least three vampires running around at any given moment. Some people were simply curious, some were full of disdain, and a few were downright wanton.

The hunter didn't seem to notice any of them. He paid for his meal and got up. A nervous energy rushed along my nerves.

I couldn't wait for Roane. Olly stayed on his heels,

quickly jumping out of sight if the hunter happened to turn around, but I needed a plan, and quick, because he was coming straight at me. He slowed his step and glanced to the side, as though checking his six through his periphery. His gait was casual, but his steps were purposeful. He turned a corner, and when Olly caught up, he was gone. Again.

Damn it.

I blinked out of Olly's mind, hurried out of the Bug, and went around a shop that sold T-shirts to hopefully cut him off. Roane was going to confront him, but he seemed to be having a hard time getting a face-to-face. My chances were even slimmer, but I had to try. I quickly told Olly my plan, based on the fact that the hunter almost certainly realized my familiar was following him, and waited.

Sure enough, when Olly turned a corner, the hunter was ready for him. He waited until Olly passed by a court-yard with an iron-and-brick fence, and then he jumped down off the fence to corner him in the blocked-in area.

Startled, Olly caught the tail end of the jump and started to dart off, but the hunter threw something on him. Dust of some kind. Powder. And Olly couldn't move.

I took off, trying to get to my familiar before the hunter did something.

He knelt in front of Olly, tilted his head, and tried to look inside his mind. Olly couldn't even blink, so the hunter had free rein as he tried to peer inside.

"Who sent you?" he asked, his voice deeper than I would've suspected.

I found the courtyard at last and skidded to a halt behind the hunter. He stood and whirled around, and I knew I had to do something fast. I just didn't know what.

I had no idea if it was Olly in my head or Gigi in my

head or my magics taking over, but I brought up my hand and drew a spell just as the hunter threw the same powder at me.

My spell first blocked the powder, then bound the hunter.

His handsome face blanched with surprise. He blinked at me and tried to move but couldn't. My spell had bound him to the spot.

Yes!

Now what? Blood rushed in my ears. What did one do with a hunter who would just as soon kill me as look at me? And I had to ask again, where was a wolf when I needed one?

The hunter calmed, as though accepting his fate. "I'm impressed."

I swallowed hard, lifted my chin, and demanded, "Release my familiar." The confused expression on his face had me wondering what I said wrong. "Now."

He could move his head. He turned it just enough to look at Olly, who still stood frozen before fixing his gaze back on me. "That's not a familiar."

"He is, too. How do you know?"

Honestly, the looks he was giving me made me question my own sanity. "You're a charmling."

"And?"

"Do you even know what that is?"

"Look, just release him, okay?"

He gave me a once-over, as though trying to figure me out. "It'll wear off. But as a charmling, you would know that."

"Right." I nodded. "And I did. I knew it. I was just testing you." Gawd, I was such a good liar. I checked my phone, panic beginning to take hold. If the powder wore off, would my spell? Was it only a matter of time?

Olly shook his head, already coming out of it. He released a loud mew of aggravation as he tried to walk and tipped over. Poor little guy.

"Almost there, buddy." Words of encouragement could only help. I checked my phone again. A lot could happen in two seconds. Nothing, so I refocused on the hunter. "Why are you here? In Salem?" When he didn't answer, I moved in and locked gazes with him. His eyes didn't waver, so dark they looked like the ocean at night, deep and dark with mysteries galore. "What are you searching for?"

The hunter narrowed his lids. "You can't compel me, witch. Who are you?"

"My name is... Tiffany."

"No, it's not. Your power is old—"

"Old?"

"—but you know nothing about it."

"How old?"

"The power my employer felt—the one that was taken— was different."

"Is that what you call him? Your employer?"

"You're a seeker. The charmling who was killed was a healer. Her power escaped and found a descendant. A blood heir."

"Is that supposed to mean something to me?"

"It means you're not the one I was sent after."

Sharp pinpricks of anxiety rushed up my spine. He really had been after Annette. "And yet here I am."

He smiled. "Oh, we'll take you both, Sarru."

"Mm, that doesn't work for me."

"You misunderstand." He cocked his head to one side like we were having a polite conversation and he hadn't just threatened to kidnap me and my best friend. "My employer can protect you. He has the last of your sister charmlings under his protection."

"Is that what he calls it? His *protection?*"

"For the first time in centuries, the powers of two charmlings have found their way back to actual blood heirs. This is unprecedented. And my employer simply wants to help."

"Yeah, I'll bet he does. So, this faux charmling... where is she?"

"Safe. In hiding. With two charmlings murdered now, one can't be too careful."

"Two?" I asked, alarmed.

"You didn't know?"

I crossed my arms over my chest and waited.

"The first charmling was killed over forty-five years ago, murdered in her sleep. Her power escaped, but it was quickly cloaked before any of the founding warlocks could locate it."

"And what exactly did these *founding warlocks* find?"

"We'd wondered for decades if it returned to a blood heir," he said, ignoring my question. "I guess now we know."

"And the second one?"

"Murdered a few days ago the same way the first charmling had been killed decades earlier."

"No doubt a charmling who stole the power from its rightful heir."

He shrugged, not denying it. "No doubt. But you must understand, we didn't know there were any rightful heirs left."

"Either way, she was no sister of mine."

"Be that as it may, my employer is... concerned. Charmlings are impossibly strong, but they're even stronger together. You could combine your powers. Find who killed your sister charmlings."

"So you want me to follow you into the spider's web?"

"It's actually a rather modest house in Poughkeepsie, but yes. It would be a mutually beneficial arrangement."

"Funny how the scales of such arrangements always tip in favor of the one with the penis."

"I tracked the power here," he continued, "but couldn't stay locked on. It was sporadic. The energy. Coming in and out like a faint radio signal. Intermittent and random."

Yep. Definitely Annette.

Olly struggled to sit up, then began licking his paws.

"Olly, come here." He hobbled over to me, one leg still stiff, and I picked him up.

The hunter frowned. "I wouldn't touch that if I were you."

"Hey. Do I dis your familiar?"

He lifted a shoulder, giving up.

I heard running and turned toward the gate to the courtyard, worried this was all a setup and I was about to be ambushed. Roane cornered the building and stopped as he took in the scene, breathless and astonished.

I held up a hand. "Before you get mad, hear me out."

Roane blinked between me and the hunter, then took a wary step toward me. "You... you captured him?"

"Yes, but in my defense, he was about to petrify me with cocaine."

Roane gaped at me for, like, an hour, then said, "You are such a badass."

"Wait, really?" I laughed and waved a dismissive hand. "Stop."

He stepped closer and looked me over. "Are you okay?"

I stepped closer too, close enough to feel the heat radiating off his body. "Yes." I couldn't stop taking in the lines of his perfect face. The sensual shape of his mouth. The—

"Please, just kill me."

We turned toward the hunter, but Roane seemed to notice the gigantic black cat in my arms for the first time. He looked down at him.

Olly put a paw on his cheek and went in to smell his mouth.

"What is that?" he asked, keeping his lips as closed as possible.

"Olly. The creature formerly known as Bead-uh. My familiar."

"That's not a familiar."

"Why does everyone keep saying that?"

"I've been completely honest with you," the hunter said. "Mind releasing me now?"

"Why? So you can go back to your master—"

"Employer."

"—and tell him about me and Annette."

He lowered his head. "Is that her name?"

Shit.

"My employer is willing to risk his life to protect you both. Something bad is coming. The charmlings can only stop it if they work together. He offers you his services."

"Yeah, well, he's going to have to service someone else. That came out wrong, but you can tell him no and thank you."

"Then I am going to take advantage of the fact that you know very little about your powers."

"Oh? And how are you going to do that?"

A malevolent grin stole across his face a microsecond before he shifted. Shifted! Clothes and all! He shifted into a white hawk right in front of us. My binds fell away, dissipating on the air, and he catapulted into the sky with one giant push of his powerful wings. Another push got him over the building while I looked on with my jaw unhinged.

"He's a shifter?" I screeched. "No one told me hunters were shifters!"

"I didn't know either. Let's get out of here. Who knows what other tricks he has up his sleeves?"

"Or feathers."

Roane took my arm and ushered me out of the court-yard, keeping an eye on the skies above us.

"That explains why you kept losing his scent."

"Yes, it does."

"You know, he just didn't seem that horrible to me."

"Remind me to tell you about the massacre of '74."

NINETEEN

Trauma?
Oh, you mean the reason I'm fucking hilarious.
—T-shirt

"And then he shifted!" Naturally, I had to tell everyone what happened the second we got home. I started with Annette and Gigi because they were the only ones in the kitchen when I rushed in, practically bursting at the seams, adrenaline shooting through my nervous system like I'd been hooked up to a drip.

"So," Annette said, leaning close, "was he like another shifter we all know and love?"

"In what way?"

She smiled and then spoke without moving her lips, like that would prevent Roane from hearing her. "Was he hot?"

Unsure of where the wolf had run off to, I looked at my bestie and nodded, just in case he really was listening. Then

I whistled softly and fanned my face. Right as Roane walked in.

"I heard that." He put down a bag of groceries. "You do realize he's an emotionless assassin who—"

"I know!" I stopped him with a hand. "Who would just as soon kill me as look at me. I got it. But that was so cool how he just launched into the air, almost before he'd completely shifted. And he did this hawk screech thing."

"He didn't screech."

"I think he screeched."

"You screeched."

"Either way, it was crazy. I sent Olly after him again, but I don't have high hopes. He keeps getting distracted. I think he's hungry."

Gigi put down her coffee and the book she was reading to spear me with one of her grandmotherly glowers.

"I'm not sure I like the tone of your glare, missy," I said, teasing her.

"Defiance—"

"I know." I held up my hand again. "I get it. We have to kill the hunter."

All three gazes landed on me.

"He came here for you," I said to Annette. "He didn't even know I existed. His warlock is apparently worried about his faux charmling and wants us to team up with her."

"A team? Really?" Annette asked. "How exciting. We could be called the Charmers. Or the Hexers. Or the Witchettes."

"So your big plan is to kill him?" Roane asked.

"'Parently, but I have to find him first." Killing in self-defense was one thing, but could I really take a life *just in case*? Probably not. I liked to think I could, though. Pretend I was a hardened killer with mad skills. That I'd be okay if I were ever sent to prison. Sadly, I'd be somebody's bitch before the first sun set through the bars in the big house. Just one more incentive not to go to prison.

"Not yet, missy," Annette said. "We have a séance to get ready for. It starts at sunset."

"Annette." I tapped my phone to bring up the time. "That's in less than three hours. There's a hunter out there, and I need to find Joaquin Ferebee. Did your ruse work?"

"The one where I pretended to twist my ankle so that the stupid-hot bagboy at Crosby's would help me to my car?"

"No." I blinked at her. "Annette." I blinked again. "The one where Joaquin Ferebee was going to call you to get his license back."

"Oh, right. No. You nailed it. He probably just checked his wallet."

"I guess I'm just going to have to go door to door at all the hotels in town. How many can there be?"

"I checked. There are over fifty in Salem alone. Only five of those would tell me if they had a guest under the name Ferebee, and that took some smooth talking. You could do a location spell."

"True. I have this." I pulled out the receipt Mr. Ferebee had dropped that morning. The one that was getting warmer in my pocket and now emitting a soft glow. That was the universe's way of lighting a fire under my ass.

"Perfect," Annette said just as someone knocked on the front door. "Can this wait, though? The caterers are here. They want to see the space before they bring the food." She hurried toward the door.

"Caterers? What the hell?"

"Would you rather I cook for our guests?" she yelled over her shoulder.

She had a point. I called out to her as she opened the door. "Annette, no one expects to be fed at a séance."

"Now you tell me!"

AFTER THREE FAILED attempts at locating Joaquin Ferebee—I used to be so good at this sort of thing—and a good bit of convincing, I talked Roane into accompanying me to the police station. I was going to do everything in my power to see if the chief could ping the guy's phone. I had no idea what laws were involved with such a thing, but hopefully he could help.

The locator spell seemed to work one minute, and then it would just stop. Like he would vanish. Maybe he was a shifter, too. Doubtful, but something was blocking me.

We sat in the chief's office, trying to convince him to ping Mr. Ferebee's phone.

"Why don't you just call him, Daffodil?" The chief had gotten the man's cell number for me and the make and model of his vehicle while he looked into his case, but apparently there were laws when it came to pinging. Something about civil rights violations.

"How can we be violating his civil rights if we're trying to help him?"

The chief deadpanned me.

"I've tried calling. It went straight to voicemail. If you just pinged his phone, I could hunt him down and talk to him face-to-face."

"You mean stalk him and then use magics on him."

"Yes. The universe wants me to help him, and I'm going to do it, damn it. If you'll ping his phone."

"I can't ping his phone without a warrant. And I can't

get a warrant without proving exigent circumstances."

"But these are exigent circumstances. They are totally exigent." I leaned over to Roane. "What does exigent mean?"

"It means pressing or demanding," the chief said.

"Exactly! The universe is pressing and demanding that I help this guy. I have no idea why, but you've seen enough of our world to know it's important."

"I have." He drew in a deep breath. "Look, I know a friendly judge. I'll talk to her."

"Thank you!" I jumped up and rounded his file-laden desk to hug him.

He chuckled and patted the arm I was nigh choking him to death with. "Don't get your hopes up, Daff. I'm going to have to give her a very good reason. I'll make something up. In the meantime, why isn't your location spell working?"

"It must be on the fritz. Either that or he's just driving around town, back and forth, for no reason."

"Almost as if he's searching for something?" Roane asked.

"Yeah. Wait, you don't think he's still searching for his son, do you?"

"I hope not," the chief said. "I spoke to the same detective Annette did. There is just no way that kid survived. There was way too much blood at the scene."

My chest tightened at the thought. "And they're certain it was his son, Milo's?"

He nodded. "And all of this happened in Chicago. Why would he be searching here?"

"That's a good question. Someone sent him something. I don't know what. He asked if I'd sent it, and it really upset him. Do you know what it could've been?"

"I have no idea. Just be careful. If he doesn't want your

help... You can't save everyone, Daff."

"I know, but that doesn't mean I can't try. Let me know on the ping thing?"

"Roger that."

Roane and I ended up driving around town in search of both Mr. Ferebee and the hunter. The hunter's hotel room was empty but, thanks to a tiny reveal spell, the desk clerk told us he'd checked in under the name Hunter Arawn, which, according to Roane, was the name of the Welsh god of hunting. So, we were back to square one.

I'd sent Olly in search of the hunter as well, but I was beginning to reconsider and have him search for Mr. Ferebee's truck: a dark-gray Dodge Ram with Illinois plates.

When we got back to Percy, the front door swung open before we even got to it.

"Deph!" Annette ran up and clutched onto my arm. "Oh my God, I was worried you wouldn't show."

I heard voices coming from the dining room, and the edges of my vision blurred. "Annette, please tell me this isn't really happening."

"It's totally happening. Snap out of it. You have to do magic, and you'll need your wits about you." She dragged me closer to the sounds but stopped and gave me a once-over. "What are you wearing? You're supposed to be dressed like a medium."

"I am a medium. I just like loose-fitting clothes better."

"Here." She ran to a closet and brought out a dressing gown of old. Like really old. A burgundy velvet thing that hung like curtains to the floor. She wrestled it over to me as Gigi came out.

She'd clearly spiffed up for the event. Her black hair fairly glistened, and she wore a long dark dress that made her look part 1920s flapper and part awards-show thespian.

"Gigi! Oh, thank the Goddess. You can do this, right? You used to do séances?"

"I did. For fun with friends."

"Then you know what to do and... Oh my God, did you actually wear this?" I asked, holding up the thick dressing gown.

Annette shoved the thing over my shoulders as Roane and Gigi looked on.

Gigi stared in horror. "I have never seen that before. Are those my curtains?"

"I found it at the Salvation Army. I think it belonged to a sultan."

I shrugged out of it and turned to her. "I am not wearing that ridiculous thing."

"Fine. At least wear the headdress." She held up a hot-pink terrycloth headwrap. The same hot-pink terrycloth headwrap that I used to put up my hair after a shower.

"Gigi, you have to save me."

"It wasn't real," she said. "I'm not a seer. I could just find lost things. Like you. So, you know, do that."

Serinda peeked around the corner. The gang was all here.

Humiliation surged inside me. "Did you guys actually buy tickets?"

"Hell yes, we did," Serinda said. "Now get in here. We demand to be entertained."

I rolled my eyes and let Annette literally push me into the dining room. Eleven people sat around a table and all but two of them were from my grandmother's coven. All but two of them bowed their heads when I entered.

"I don't know how to do this," I whispered to Annette.

"You know what they say."

I turned to her and asked from between clenched teeth,

"No, Annette, what do they say?"

"Fake it 'til you make it." She patted the chair at the head of the table, her excitement infectious.

The scent of barbeque wafted toward me, and my stomach growled. "I'm going to kill you, but the food smells divine." They'd set up the buffet on the sidebar. The very aromatic food, so that wouldn't be distracting at all.

"Sarru," Theo said when I looked at him, his face full of exhilaration. These poor people had been swindled, and they didn't even know it. This was going to be sad.

"Theo. Shanti." I addressed several of the coven members and then looked at the two guests I hadn't met yet. "And you are?"

"Oh, no," Annette said, shoving me into the chair. "You have to figure that out all by yourself. They paid good money for all of this."

Great. I looked around as Roane went to the sidebar and started making himself a plate. Annette glared at his back. The mirror in front of him proved he didn't care. In fact, I'd say he was on the verge of laughing.

They were all so expectant, so excited, that I caved like a spelunker. "Look, I'm not a psychic or a medium or whatever I'm supposed to be. I'll just do what I can."

Gigi nodded as though that was exactly the right thing to say.

I started with the person on my left: Shanti. I held out my hand to her.

Shanti shook her head. "You've already read most of us yesterday, Sarru. Please feel free to skip us."

"You paid good money for this."

"To be in your presence. I expect nothing more."

I leaned closer to her. "Will you be my best friend? Mine has gone crazy."

"And she is also sarru," Shanti said, squeezing her hands to her chest. "We are so honored."

All of the coven members bowed to her as well.

I guess word had gotten out. Annette looked at me and shrugged in helplessness, not sure how to take their reverence either.

"Okay, then, if the gentleman in the back would kindly take a seat."

Roane turned to me, his grin the stuff of fantasies, and sat at a small bistro in the corner.

"I guess, maybe we should—"

A female voice interrupted. "Oh, I'm sorry."

We all turned to see a young woman standing under the archway. She wore a thick gray sweater that was two sizes too big, and patches of auburn hair hung over her face. The rest was loosely secured in a hairclip, and her eyes were red and swollen. Haggard was the first word that came to mind.

"I'm so sorry to bother you," she said. "I knocked and the door just opened. I'm sorry."

She started to rush away.

"Wait," I said standing.

She turned back to us. "It's just, I tried to get into the séance, but it filled up immediately and I... I lost my daughter yesterday."

The news stole my breath. I pulled out my chair and gestured for her to sit.

"I'm so sorry," she repeated, her voice cracking.

I knelt in front of her. "What do you mean you lost your daughter? Is she missing?"

She pressed her lips together as the wetness gathering between her lashes spilled over them. "I miscarried. I was five months pregnant, and I just wanted to know if she was okay."

Her agony pressed into my chest. I fought for air as I explained. "I am so sorry, hon, but this isn't really what I do." I gestured toward the room. The table. The ridiculous situation I was in.

"Can you try? Please. Can you search?" Her chin quivered. She was barely hanging on.

I had to at least try. I could see the departed on this plane, but to cross into the veil and look for one in the veil was another matter altogether.

Still... I lowered my head and searched for a spell, if there was one. They rushed past me. Spell after spell until... There. Hiding in a dark corner. It sat unassuming and innocuous, like a wallflower at a Regency ball, obscured by brighter, more eager spells. The finder of lost souls. I brought it forth and drew it on the air. Light burst from the lines and sprang to life before me, leaching out and blinding me for a moment. I touched her arm and searched.

Souls are not an age. They may take the form of the human age of their chalice, but that was a residual effect from the seer's perspective, the human's memories, not the soul itself. They are eternal. They are hourglasses that never run out of sand.

"Samantha," I said, finding her at last. She would have had red hair like her mother, only curlier. Hazel eyes like her father, only greener.

A child of about four in the veil, she turned and waved at me, then ran off to play with a little boy named Eric. Red hair. Hazel eyes. Her little brother who was not due on Earth for another year. And then she'd have to wait ninety-seven years more for him to come play with her in the sandbox again.

"Defiance?"

I heard Gigi's voice from a distance, but I needed to

know. I turned to the girl's grandfather. "You'll keep her safe?"

"Always," he promised.

"Defiance," Roane said, and I lifted my lids.

He knelt in front of me, his expression worried. "Where were you?"

"I was... past the veil." I looked at Gigi then the woman. Margie. I had a feeling her name was Margie. "I found her."

She clutched at her sweater, her eyes filled with hope.

"She's there with her grandfather and her little brother."

Margie frowned and shook her head. "I don't understand. She doesn't..." And then my words sank in. She covered her mouth with both hands. "I'm going to have a son?"

I felt a slow smile tug at the corners of my mouth, and her emotion wrenched a single sob from her throat. "Thank you." She leaned over and pulled me into her arms. "Thank you so much."

We stood, and I only realized my cheeks were wet when cool air washed over them.

"You said my daughter's name. Samantha. Do you happen to know what my son's name will be?"

"Are you sure you want to know?"

She nodded. "More than anything."

"Eric."

She inhaled softly. "That was my father's name."

I nodded. "He's so happy he can watch over Samantha until you get there."

She gathered herself and then backed out of the room. "I'm so sorry again, but thank you, Ms. Dayne. Thank you so much."

I turned to the room. Each face looked at me with awe.

Even Annette. Gigi and Serinda were more proud than awestruck, but I'd take it.

"So," I said, clapping my hands together. "We're going to have to do this pretty quickly, because this piece of paper is burning a hole in my pocket. Literally." After a drawn-out silence that defined awkward, I sat back down and made a suggestion. "Maybe we should hold hands?"

They all complied. Each member took the hands of their neighbors and waited. Just like I did. I waited. For a sign. For inspiration. For the ground to open up and swallow me whole. This was going to bomb so bad. Especially because the burning in my pocket kept stealing my concentration.

"Hold on," I said to Shanti. Taking my hand back, I dug the receipt out of my jeans and put it on the table. It glowed. It wanted to tell me more.

Annette's eyes rounded to saucers, and I remembered the last time this happened, she couldn't see the glow. But that was just a few days ago. She'd come into her powers already. Perhaps she'd just needed time to adjust. Her body needed time to adapt. Or maybe the explosion knocked something loose in her psyche. She'd only started seeing into the veil after that.

But the glow was calling to me. Mr. Ferebee was in trouble.

"Okay, this isn't working. I'm sorry. Can we reschedule?"

"Sarru," Theo said, "you've already made contact with one soul. You have done exactly what a séance is designed to do."

"True, but I know everyone would like me to try to contact their loved ones."

"You do what you have to do, Sarru," Shanti said. "Me thinks there are greater games afoot."

"Thank you. Thank you so much," I said as I stood and started to back out of the room. "But eat. Drink. Be merry. We will reschedule." I looked at Annette. "I need to know where he is."

"Joaquin Ferebee?"

"Yes."

"I tried everything. I can't find him."

I could hardly blame her. I couldn't find him either. I looked up, confronting the universe as a whole. "Look, you want me to find him so bad, you show me where he is."

The receipt grew brighter on the table, but that was about it.

"Fine." I scooped it up. "I'll call the chief. Maybe he had some luck with the ping thing."

Annette hurried around to join me. "The ping thing?"

But as I turned, the receipt got hotter. I turned back, then around again. "It is literally playing the Hot and Cold game with me."

"Let's go," Roane said, grabbing his jacket off a hook in the hall.

"Save me some barbeque," I said to Gigi and started out, but a second before I hurried away, I caught the gaze of one of the guests. The unguarded gaze.

I whirled back around and locked on to her.

She jumped, startled by my sudden attention. She was a member of the coven. I'd spoken to her the day before. Johanna, perhaps? Midthirties. Dirty blonde hair. A hard jawline that made her look more masculine than she liked. She tried to glance away, to avert her gaze.

I. Did. Not. Let. Her.

I continued to stare, going deeper and deeper, astonished at what she was searching for: vengeance. She was using dark magics to torture a man she had been stalking for years. A man who, from what I could tell, only wanted her to leave him alone. She was ruining his life on every level— financially, psychologically, medically—all because he'd rejected her.

Oh, hell no.

How I missed all this the day before was beyond me. She was good, though. With black magic. She'd come prepared tonight to continue to thwart my attempts to see beyond her shield, but my hasty exit had set her mind at ease. She'd dropped her guard. She'd practically invited me in.

What she was doing to that man was unacceptable, and anger burst out of me in one volatile wave. The only thing standing between us was the table, so I removed it. I splintered it into a million pieces. They fanned out like the fragments of an exploding supernova, then froze in midair.

Everyone reared back as the pieces hovered in the air around them. Not touching. Just suspended temporarily so I could confront the woman sitting across from me.

I walked through the pieces, twirling several as I brushed past, and stood over her. She was blood born, but her mother, a dark witch kicked out of every coven she'd ever joined, was a vindictive bitch. She grew up with hatred seething in her heart. That didn't, however, excuse her behavior.

Easing closer, I searched harder. She was more than capable of screwing with someone's memory, but she had nothing to do with Gigi's death. While I could see that, she'd had nefarious plans for a couple of the coven members, including Shanti. Her jealousy of the woman bordered on psychotic.

"What should I do with someone like you?"

I heard Gigi behind me. "What is it, Defiance?"

"Black magic."

An audible gasp echoed around me.

"Vengeance. Resentment. Vehemence. And pretty much all seven of the deadly sins."

"Johanna?" Serinda said in disbelief. She had them all fooled.

I knew once the coven found out about the black magic, she'd be cast out, but I needed to make sure things were set right for her target, a contractor named Phillip. "Do you know how quickly I can strip your mind and leave you a drooling vegetable?"

She raised her chin, utterly remorseless when she forced out the words, "I'm sorry."

"No, you're not. But I am." She would not stop. It was inside her. Buried deep in the marrow of her being. What did one do with someone like this indeed? If one is a charmling, she protects her sisters.

"You're right," Johanna said. Though her reverence for me was real, the toxicity inside her, the seething hatred, would fester inside her soul until the end of time if left unchecked. "It's the black magics. They changed me."

"No, they didn't. They nourished the wolf you fed." I drew a spell on the air just as she lunged at me. Roane jerked me back as it ripped her soul to shreds. Stripped her of her magics. Relieved her of any talent, blood born or otherwise, completely. It didn't mean she couldn't still hurt people. She would just have to do it the old-fashioned way, and that required a lot more work.

The force of the spell knocked her breath away. She sank back into the chair, stunned.

"Get help," I said to her. "Then come back to see me."

We walked back through the table shards. I grabbed my jacket and snapped my fingers to release them. By the time I looked back, the table was reformed, sturdy as ever.

Roane stopped, looked at the table, then grabbed his jacket and headed toward the door.

"You coming?" I asked Annette.

She rehinged her jaw and nodded, scooping up her jacket on the way.

"You think I was too harsh on her?" I asked Roane as we hurried to his truck.

"What? No. Hell no. I promise you, Scrinda will be harsher. It's just, the table thing. That was new."

"Right? How'd I even do that?" I looked at Annette. "I was always so bad at puzzles and then *poof!* It's back together."

Roane opened the doors for us. "Yes. That's what I'm most impressed with. Your puzzle prowess."

"You're being sarcastic."

"Nooo," he said, climbing into the driver's seat. He pulled onto the street while Annette called the chief.

"He's made a decision," I said to them. "Mr. Ferebee. I just can't figure out what that means. What kind of decision and why the universe is so against it."

"Not the universe," Roane said as I gave him a general direction to drive in based on what the receipt had indicated. "You. Your magics are tied to your morals. Your sense of justice. So whatever he's decided, it goes against what you would want for him."

Annette lowered her phone. "He pinged Mr. Ferebee's phone. He's at a park. I think I know what he decided. What he has planned."

"What?" I asked.

"I think he's going to kill someone."

TWENTY

Be the reason someone smiles today.
Or the reason they drink.
Whatever works.
—Meme

"The chief is meeting us there," Annette said as Roane sped toward Salem Woods.

I clutched onto my seatbelt when he took a turn particularly fast. "Why do you think he's going to kill someone?"

"According to the chief, he bought a gun."

My heart sank in my chest, finally understanding. "He's not going to kill anyone but himself."

"How do you know?" Roane asked.

"The sadness I felt in him. The frustration. It's too much."

We found the dark-gray Dodge almost immediately. He'd parked near a hiking trail, facing a thickly wooded area, his silhouette placing him in the driver's seat. When our headlights flashed across his windows, the light glinted off something metal in Mr. Ferebee's hand. At that exact moment, the receipt burned my hand. I dropped it and jumped out of Roane's truck before he'd come to a full stop.

"Defiance!"

I heard him call out to me as I ran to the truck, but I had to stop Mr. Ferebee. That was all I could think. I was about ten feet away from his door when a massive wolf jumped into my path and lunged at me, forcing me back. Even in the darkness, his fur almost shimmered as he stalked toward me, a deep growl rolling out of his chest, moonlight glinting off his bared teeth.

I fell and tried to scramble back, but he kept coming until he was standing over me, looking down. He put one massive paw on my chest and pushed me to the ground, then leaned closer, his teeth barely an inch from my face. The low rumble that came out of his chest sent goose bumps spiraling over my skin.

Before I could say anything, he turned and launched himself onto the hood of Mr. Ferebee's truck with one thrust of his powerful hind legs.

I could see the man's profile. He reared back when Roane lowered his head and watched him through the windshield, his growl the stuff of nightmares. He barked and lunged at the glass like he was going to break through.

Though the man was protected, he looked terrified, and Roane's ploy worked. He dropped the gun and held up both of his hands as though to protect himself.

I eased closer to the truck, and Roane growled a warning. Ignoring him, I knocked softly on Mr. Ferebee's window.

The look on his face when he finally wrenched his gaze

off the wolf defined astonished. Dumbfounded might have been a better word for it.

I did the signal for him to roll down his window, and he gaped at me.

"Mr. Ferebee, please."

He shook his head.

Roane snarled and lunged again.

"Roane, you're not helping."

Giving in, he licked his chops and lowered himself onto his stomach. His body stretched the entire length of the hood. I didn't even want to think about what it would cost to fix the scratches in it. I decided to think positive and believe they could be buffed out.

I did the signal again.

Mr. Ferebee finally cracked the window.

"You don't want to do this, Mr. Ferebee."

His warm eyes were swollen with emotion, his dark skin splotchy. He had several days' worth of scruff, and his clothes were rumpled. None of that detracted from how handsome he was. What did detract was the fact that he had given up.

The chief pulled into the lot, his lights reflecting off the trees around us. He came with backup. A second patrol car pulled in behind Mr. Ferebee, blocking him in.

Mr. Ferebee reached for the gun on the seat beside him, and Roane went into attack mode again. His snarls ferocious as he snapped and growled at Mr. Ferebee through the windshield, he gave the man a warning bark, so loud I almost jumped out of my skin.

Annette was standing by Roane's truck, taking it all in. She crept forward.

The chief bolted out of his cruiser, and I held up a hand

to stop him. "Mr. Ferebee, please unlock your door so the chief can get the gun. For everyone's safety."

He lowered his head, and fresh tears formed rivulets down his face. After a moment where I wondered if he would still go for the gun, if he would still take his own life, he gave in and hit the unlock button.

I opened Mr. Ferebee's door as the chief opened the passenger-side door and grabbed the gun.

"No more choices," I said to the grieving man. "The universe wanted me here, Mr. Ferebee. In this moment. It wanted me to stop you from doing what you were about to do."

"Is that his name?"

"Whose?"

He looked up. "The wolf's. Is his name the Universe?"

A soft laugh escaped me. "No. His name is mud after tonight's performance." I looked around the windshield. He'd planted himself on the hood again and panted happily. "Bad wolf."

He released an annoyed whimper then decided to lick his paws, unconcerned with my scolding.

Officer Flynn—or Officer Pecs, either way—made his way around the front of the truck, eyeing the wolf warily, his hand on his gun.

"Just stay close to me," Annette said to him, stepping to his side as though to protect the officer twice her size, "and you'll be safe."

"Officer Flynn," the chief said, "it's all good. The wolf's with me."

"Right, Chief." He was not the least bit convinced.

I put a hand on Mr. Ferebee's arm to get his attention. "Mr. Ferebee, please trust me. I don't know why I'm here.

To stop this, yes, but it's more than that. Please, please, please trust me."

He had a toy truck on his dash, a gray Dodge Ram just like the one he was in. He finally looked at me, his dark eyes glistening with still more tears. "I don't understand. How did you know?"

"I don't really understand it all either, but I think we both will if you'll just let me in."

"How? How do I do that?"

"I don't really know that either. Some people I can just see into, and others seem to have the ability to block me. Usually with witchcraft of some kind, but..."

He shook his head.

"You think I don't know how you feel, but I do. I was the ultimate skeptic a few months ago, but then I was... blessed with this gift. Or cursed. Either way."

"So you have this gift and I'm blocking you?"

"Yes."

"I don't know how I'm doing it or how to undo it, so where does that leave us?"

"I think it has to do with trust. Why are you here in Salem? Are you still looking for your son?"

Surprise registered on his face.

"Oh, that wasn't witchcraft. That was old-fashioned research."

He nodded. "I got a letter. Another one."

I leaned back against his open door as Roane, apparently bored with licking his paws, jumped off the hood and trotted off into the darkness.

Annette patted the officer's biceps. "You should probably still stay near me. In case he comes back."

Officer Flynn shot her a dubious scowl.

"A letter? Is that what you thought I sent?"

"Yes. Sorry about your arm."

"It's okay. I have a spare. The letter?"

He drew in a deep breath to steady himself. "My son went missing a year ago. He... Evidence showed up a month later. The detectives told me he was probably dead." He fought a soft sob. The sob won.

Annette walked up to stand beside me, and the chief stood at the open passenger-side door, keeping a guarded eye on the man.

"We spoke to the detective in charge of the case in Chicago," Annette said. "He told us about the backpack and the... about your son."

Another tear escaped the man's lashes. He nodded. "Since then, I've gotten five letters. I take that back. I've received dozens of letters from people trying to help. Swearing they've seen Milo at this gas station or that park. But there have been five letters from the same person telling me he's found my son. But he can't get involved. No cops. If I show up to whatever location he sends me to, he'll meet me there with Milo." He broke down again.

"But he was never there," I said.

He raked a hand over his face and shook his head.

"And this time he sent you here to Salem?"

"Yes," he said, his voice strained.

"Did you tell the detective?" I asked, knowing the answer. Surely the detective would've said something when the chief talked to him.

"Not this time. At first, I only gave the cops the notes after I'd already gone to the place and came back empty-handed. I was afraid they would scare him off. But with the fourth note, I gave it to them beforehand. I showed up to the meet. A marketplace in Bangor, Maine. There were a couple of cops undercover. More waiting in the wings. I don't know how, but the guy figured it out. The next note said if I do that again, he would kill Milo and leave his body for me to find instead." Another sob racked the poor man's body.

"Why Maine?"

"I don't know. The first note sent me to a McDonald's at Union Station in DC. Another to a sushi grill in Kalamazoo. And so on."

"He's sending you all over the country," Annette said, confused. "Why would anyone do that?"

I pointed at her. "That's the key." Roane walked up then, fully clothed, and I remembered my manners. "I'm sorry, Mr. Ferebee, I'm Defiance. This is Annette, Roane, and that is Chief Metcalf."

"And Officer Flynn," Annette added, wiggling her fingers at him.

"Please, call me Joaquin. What do you mean, that's the key?"

"It's someone you know. Someone who's messing with you in the cruelest way possible. Someone with a vendetta."

He frowned and looked down in thought. "I don't get along with everyone I meet, but I can't imagine who would be that cruel."

Roane ran a hand over his scruff in thought. "When your son went missing, you were in the middle of a divorce."

"Yes. She was just as devastated as I was."

"Exactly," I said. "Does she, perhaps, blame you?"

"Yes. Yes, she does. And she has every right to. I had him for the weekend. We were at a park near my apartment when he... he just vanished. But I just can't see her—"

"Where is she now?"

He rubbed his forehead and thought about it. "Last I heard, she was living with her parents outside of Chicago, working in a dentist's office. She hasn't spoken a word to me since they found Milo's backpack."

"I'm sorry, Joaquin." Hopefully, the man was learning to trust me a little more. "Do you have the letters?"

"Just this last one. The police have the others."

He took it off of his console. He'd been reading it.

The chief closed the door and came around to read the letter with us.

"*Last chance,*" I said, reading aloud. "*Woods Park. Salem, Massachusetts. You know the date and time. Don't be late.*" I looked back at him. "You know the date and time?"

"Yes." His voice cracked, and he had to stop. "Milo's birthday was a few days ago."

"And the time?"

"He was born at three in the morning." He looked away. "I sat here all night. All the next day. The police finally ran me off, but I've been back every night since."

"That's very specific," I said, suspicion niggling in the back of my mind. I took the letter firmly in hand. "Joaquin, do you think you can trust me for the next ten minutes? That's all I ask."

"To do what?"

"To see inside your soul, for lack of a better phrase."

"Because I'm blocking you," he said matter-of-factly.

"Because you're blocking me."

"Look, I'm grateful for what you're trying to do, but I just don't believe in that shit. I'm sorry. And even if I did, I have no idea how to block you, much less how to unblock you."

I held out my hand. "How about you let me worry about that?"

He released a resigned breath, took my hand, and looked into my eyes. "What do I have to do?"

I lowered my head and captured his gaze. "You're doing it." He sat completely still, unable to move as I scoured his thoughts. I dove deeper and, when the time was just right, I asked him, "What are you searching for?"

"My son," he whispered.

I found him in his memories. The gorgeous little thing. Then I drew a quick spell with the hand holding the letter and sent out my magics. The seekers. The finders of lost things.

One corner of my mouth slid up when I found the object he wanted most. The boy with huge round eyes and a movie-star smile. He turned five while he was away and, while he loved his mother and his grandparents, he missed his father terribly. And the boy knew his name wasn't really Michael. It was Milo. His dad called him Milo, and he would keep the name safe in his heart forever no matter what his mother said.

The author of the letters got brazen, sending Joaquin here. I looked back at him. He was blurry, and I realized a wetness had gathered between my lashes. The man was about to get the surprise of his life. I released him and stepped back before looking at Officer Pecs. "Chief, can you have Officer Flynn put Joaquin in the back of his cruiser, please?"

The chief gave me a brief, quizzical brow, then nodded. "Officer Flynn."

The officer, while confused, stepped forward to comply.

"Wait," Joaquin said, his ire skyrocketing. He glared at me.

"Joaquin, I thought you said you'd trust me for the next ten minutes?"

His brows slid together. "And you have me arrested?"

"Not at all." I beamed at him. "Not at all."

AN HOUR LATER, we were staked out at a yellow Cape-style home in Swampscott. The chief had coordinated with local PD. Five police cruisers sat waiting for the word to move in.

It helped that the chief of police of Salem had requested the backup. Otherwise, we'd have to explain to the Swampscott chief of police how we knew what we knew. That Milo Ferebee was alive and well and living with his mother and grandparents in the affluent town. It would seem Joaquin's in-laws had the means and the motive to set up a fake abduction, all because Joaquin wanted to divorce their princess.

I sat in the back of the cruiser with Joaquin as the police waited for the go-ahead.

"Is this for real?" he asked, his voice pleading.

"It is. Milo is alive. We just have to keep him that way." Not that I believed the boy to be in any real danger, but in a confrontation like this, one just never knew.

He could hardly take his eyes off the scene and held his breath every time someone came on the radio. Which was a lot.

Officer Flynn parked the car, then joined the chief and the other officers at the mobile command post as they waited for the tac team to infiltrate. Dressed head to toe in tactical gear, the team set up position to go in as quickly as possible to minimize the chance of a hostage situation.

"I can't believe she would do this. That she hated me so much."

"Hon, anyone who does something this depraved, when they're not doing it to protect their child, is more than a little unstable."

He scoffed. "It runs in the family. Her mother is just... She was a flea in Diane's ear, constantly criticizing everything I did."

"I'm sorry, Joaquin."

He finally looked at me, shook his head, and asked, "How?" It seemed to be the only word he could come up with to ask the million questions running through his mind. How did I do it? How did I know? How did I find his son?

I smiled, but before I could answer, a hushed voice came over the radio. "Preparing to breach."

Another voice came on. "You're a go."

Even from our position, we could hear the breaking of the door and the yelling for everyone to get down. Joaquin doubled over and covered his head with his arms, unable to hold back the emotion any longer. His fear and hope and exhilaration charged the air around us with electricity.

Then our doors opened. The chief helped me out as Roane and Annette ran up. Officer Flynn opened the door for Joaquin and pointed, and I saw a grin on the officer's face for the first time.

"I think you might know this young man."

Joaquin started to step out.

"Oh, wait!" I'd almost forgotten. I reached in my bag and took out the toy truck Joaquin had on his dash. An exact replica of his Dodge Ram, right down to the color and chrome running boards. Milo's favorite toy. "You might need this."

He took it but was in such a state of shock, he stepped out of the SUV in a daze as a female police officer carried a five-year-old wrapped in a blanket toward us. They were instantly surrounded by a medical team, but she charged forward.

The boy was in shock as well as he looked around at all

the police and emergency responders who had swarmed the place. Joaquin hurried toward the officer, but his son seemed less than impressed with him. He turned away shyly but kept his gaze on his father as though unable to place him.

"Milo," Joaquin said, stopping short. He scraped a hand down his face in disbelief, then held out the truck. "Do you remember this?"

Milo finally turned toward him, his little brows drawn in confusion. "Daddy?"

Joaquin sobbed and took him into his arms. "It's me, buddy." He fell to the ground with him, holding on for dear life.

I wrapped my arms around Roane as we looked on.

Annette, ever the non-hugger, patted my shoulder. "You did good."

"*We* did good."

We watched as they brought three people out of the house in handcuffs: an older couple and Joaquin's ex, Diane. I only needed one thing from her.

"Chief, can I have a minute with her?"

He nodded and escorted Roane, Annette, and I past the onlookers—who had already started to gather—and under the police tape. "Officer," he said to the patrolman putting Diane into the back of a cruiser. "Can we have a minute?"

"Of course, sir."

I thought about not talking to her at all. Not asking her why. Was that really something I needed to know? I could tell from Joaquin's thoughts and memories what an incredible dad he was. And husband. He had given their marriage his all, but it was never quite enough for her, and neither of them were happy.

But there was one question burning in my brain. I

needed the answer, not only for Joaquin, but for the detectives on the case as well.

I walked up to her. She was a pretty brunette with creamy skin and, well, she looked completely normal. No one would've suspected she'd abducted her own child. In fact, no one did.

"I just need to know one thing," I said to her.

She kept her jaw wired shut, not realizing she didn't need to speak. I read her instantly, and she was so much like Johanna, the coven member I'd just stripped of her magics, it was unreal. Vengeful. Malicious. Only Diane didn't have magics. Nothing I could take from her, except maybe one thing, but I would get to that in a minute.

I stepped closer and lowered my head. "The blood."

I saw it instantly. Her father was a doctor, and they'd hatched the plan together. After the initial abduction, he'd taken Milo's blood a little at a time. It took him over a month to accumulate enough blood to fake the crime scene. Then, when the time came, her mother took his backpack to the warehouse, spread the blood around, and called in a tip from a burner saying she found the body of a young boy. Just as they'd hoped, the police believed the killer came back for the body to hide the evidence. The blood, combined with the phone call, was enough to convince them Milo had been killed. They didn't stop searching so much as divert their efforts to more pressing cases.

The letters to Joaquin were simply Diane's way of rubbing her victory in Joaquin's face. She wanted him to suffer. To pay. Her actions were so juvenile, so merciless and cruel, it was hard not to drain the life from her body right then and there, and I realized just how dangerous my magics could be. One split second, one wrong decision, and lives could be changed forever.

At least I knew Diane would do well in prison. And she would have her mom, so there was that. But there was one thing I could take from her that she would miss.

I stepped closer until I was about a foot away from her and said, "Guess what they don't have in prison?"

She looked me up and down, cool as a refrigerated cucumber.

I let my mouth slide into a wicked grin and said, "Wine."

Her eyes rounded for a fraction of an instant, as though just realizing the one thing she practically lived for would be in short supply for the foreseeable future.

"*Bam*, beotch," Annette said from behind me. "You'll have to drown your sorrows in toilet wine from now on. Yum."

"Annette," I said, admonishing her as the officer put Diane in the cruiser. "Wineaholism is a disease."

"Whatev. Good luck with the DTs. I hear they're a bitch." The officer closed the door, and Diane turned away from us. "I wouldn't turn water into wine for you if you were the last wineaholic on Earth," she continued. That'd show her.

Houston pinched the bridge of his nose. I could hardly blame him.

We walked back to Joaquin. He sat in the back of an ambulance with Milo.

He turned to me as the first responder took Milo's vitals. "If I had done it, if I had gone through with it..."

"I know. That's all in the past now." I gazed at Milo, adoring every curve of his face. Every curl on his head. Every spark of love when he looked at his father. Children were a special kind of magic all on their own. "And your future is looking really bright."

"Are you ever going to tell me how you did that?"

I laughed softly, and whispered, "Smoke and mirrors."

———

THE CLOCK STARTED CHIMING JUST as we walked in the door and continued until it had reached the midnight hour. Gigi had waited up with Serinda, so we filled them in before heading to bed. The chief stayed at the scene but promised to stop in to see Gigi before going home. Honestly, the two were affianced. Why he didn't just move in was beyond me.

Vowing to wait up for Roane, who'd gone to check on the wolves, I took a quick shower, mostly to get warm, then looked in on Olly. He hadn't reported back, so I figured he hadn't found the hunter again. I was right. When I peered through his eyes, he was stalking... a cow. My first thought was, *Good luck with that, buddy.* Then I reconsidered. He wasn't a real cat. Could he really eat a cow?

Alarmed, I popped into his head again. *Step away from the livestock,* I ordered. *Don't even think about eating that cow, mister man.*

He stopped mid-stalk and let out a mew of disappointment before darting back toward town. Little shit.

I curled up under the covers and fought the heaviness of my lids. The heaviness won. My eyes drifted shut, and the edges of a dream had just wafted over me when I heard a scream.

Feminine.

Shrill.

Blood-curdling.

I bolted upright, scrambled out of bed, and ran to the

window. Another scream splintered the air, and I zeroed in on Parris's house.

Though her lights were on, I couldn't see anything, even through the sheer curtains.

I jammed my legs into a pair of sweats and pulled an ancient sweatshirt over my head that announced my blood type to the world—dark roast—before grabbing my sneakers and running to Annette's room.

"Annette?" I said into the darkness, but she was snoring softly. No way was I waking her.

I went back and scooped up my phone then hurried down the stairs. After almost tumbling headfirst—twice—while attempting to run and put on my shoes at the same time, I sat on the steps to tie them like a normal person. I considered checking to see if Roane had made it back, but he would've heard the scream before I did. He could already be over there.

A third scream pierced the air, this one weaker. More pitiable, as though the woman was pleading with someone. It spurred me out the door and around our respective fences. I sprinted up Parris's walkway and under the columned balcony to find her front door open.

"Parris?" I eased inside.

A bright-yellow light illuminated her foyer. The layout was very similar to Percy's in that it had two matching staircases on either side that led to a second-floor landing. Only Parris's house was all shiny marble and gold filigree with a massive chandelier hanging down from the third-floor ceiling.

I took another step inside. "Parris? Are you okay?" After an initial sweep of the immediate area, I took out my phone to dial 911. I found no evidence of a struggle, but somebody had screamed for a reason, and Parris's door had been wide open. Anyone could've gotten inside.

A male voice came over the phone. "Nine-one-one, what's your emergency?"

"Hi, I heard screams coming from the house next door, and I can't find the owner."

"Are you inside the house now?"

"Yes. I'm going to check upstairs."

"Do you think that's a good idea?"

I stopped with my foot on the bottom step. It was an odd question coming from dispatch. "Should I wait for a patrol car?"

"You could," he said, "but you'll be waiting a long time."

Dread raced up my spine. I looked around, trying to find any sign of Parris. "How did you intercept this call?"

"Are you sure that's the most important question at this juncture?"

The field of vision narrowed. "What happened to Parris?"

"That's for me to know and you to find out."

I hung up and pressed Roane's number while backing toward the door.

After two rings, the same male voice came on the line. "Nine-one-one, why did you hang up on me?"

The air grew thick around me as I backed toward the front door. Walking through it was like walking through Jell-O. My eyes began to lose focus. I recognized the skips in time as I glanced at a cream-colored vase. It was there one minute and gone the next, only to reappear with the next blink of my eyes. The sensation was startlingly familiar.

I'd experienced this same kind of erratic imagery when I was in a state of suspended animation for six months, as though my synapses had malfunctioned. As though they were damaged, firing sporadically, and showing me things in the wrong order.

Back when the darkness tried to get in.

Percy held it at bay, but the parts that did seep into my psyche messed with my equilibrium. My sense of space and time, like a video that skipped and bounced, then played things either too fast or too slow.

I backed into the closed front door. The same front door I hadn't closed. I turned the doorknob only to find it locked.

"You'll never find her if you leave now," the man said.

I couldn't help but wonder if I was asleep. If any of this was real. The world tilted to the side, and I gripped the doorknob harder. "Where is she?"

"I'll give you three guesses."

He was clearly having fun. That did not bode well. I launched myself off the door and headed for the stairs again, just trying to stay upright until I could get to the balustrade. I clutched onto the handrail and took an unsteady step up.

"I wouldn't go that way."

I struggled to keep the phone at my ear and hold onto the balustrade. "She's not upstairs?" I asked just as the railing vanished and my support dropped away. I fell to the side only to slam my ribs into the rail when it reappeared. The impact knocked my breath away.

"One down, two to go." His voice wasn't deep, and it sounded strangely familiar. I racked my brain trying to place it, but the stairs turned upside down and swallowed me before I could manage it.

TWENTY-ONE

Underestimate me.
That'll be fun.
—T-shirt

"You are horrible at the guessing game."

My lids fluttered open to a dark figure silhouetted against a thousand-watt bulb. At least it seemed like a thousand-watt bulb, but when he moved aside, only a single candle glowed behind him. I blinked against the brightness, then felt the ropes cinched tight around my wrists, cutting off my circulation. My hands were tied behind my back, but something was wrapped over them. A cloth of some kind. Wet and acidic against my skin. Another rope circling my waist kept me semi upright in a chair, and my ankles were strapped together. "I think my luck is changing," I said, my voice groggy and hoarse.

"Yeah?"

"It's getting even worse. I didn't think that was possible."

"We make our own luck. Clearly, you suck at it."

I blinked up, trying to place the voice, then I saw a brunette fussing over a table of disturbing instruments off to the side. "Parris. You're okay."

She turned like a runway model and beamed at me. "I am. Sorry about the screams. I took an acting class once. That's where I learned to project. Did you know there are dozens of types of screams? You can fill a scream with every kind of emotion imaginable. But it does take a trained professional to get the nuance right, so don't try it at home, kids. Who knew that ridiculous class would come in handy one day?"

The man—Harris—knelt in front of me. Harris! I'd only spoken to him a couple of times, and he was the most normal mundane I'd ever met. Well, other than the fact that he lived two houses down from his wife. "I want to know why my magics aren't working on you."

The world tilted again and I forced it to recenter like the pointer on a GPS. "I'd say it's working just fine."

"Nah. This is easy. A simple time-displacement spell. You're basically living in two different moments in time, each a second apart from each other. It messes with the equilibrium. I've been trying for months to get inside your head." He poked my forehead. "I finally had to lure you into the house to get them to work. A house I've been infusing with magics for weeks, just so I could penetrate that thick skull of yours." He poked again. Asshat. "Parris said you did some kind of spell."

"She did." She walked up behind him. "I've never seen anything like it."

"You told me." His voice was edged with impatience. "So, you're a witch like your grandmother was?"

"'Parently." I worked at the restraints, my efforts having the exact opposite effect. The more I yanked, the tighter they got. "What are you?"

He snorted, stood, and walked over to the table that held the candle.

I could hardly see beyond the glow of the flame. The light was pulsing, strobelike, but my eyes were beginning to adjust. We were in a cavernous, cold room with fantastic acoustics. A basement, perhaps?

"You're clearly a novice if you don't know by now."

Holy shit. "Are you a warlock?"

"Bingo. You know more than I thought. Did you learn from your grandmother?"

"Did you *kill* my grandmother?"

"You first."

I fought a wave of dizziness as time slipped beneath me again, and said, "I feel like my question trumps yours."

He let out an annoyed sigh as he heated water in a pan over a hotplate. Witchcraft in the twenty-first century, ladies and gentlemen.

"Is the hunter yours?" I asked.

He stilled and looked over at me, his image distorting, then skipping ahead a fraction of a second. "There's a hunter in town?"

I'd take that as a no. "There is."

He put down the spoon he'd been stirring with while Parris straightened the instruments on the tray like a nurse gleefully preparing for surgery.

I ignored the fear that hardened like cement in my chest and tugged at my restraints again. Then it hit me. I suddenly understood the wraps on my hands. I couldn't do a spell. Something was stopping me.

"Why is he here?" he asked. He'd seemed so nice. Harris Hampton. Maybe even a little whipped. My ability to read men had just reached an all-time low.

I was never going to trust my gut instincts again. "I don't know why he's here. He said something about a rogue warlock practicing magic irresponsibly."

"Irresponsibly?" He laughed. "That's practically a requirement of the profession. You'll have to do better than that."

I couldn't help but wonder what went wrong. Maybe something in his childhood. Not that I particularly cared, but it was something to think about. "Shouldn't you have a cauldron for that?"

"Why?" he asked, stirring the pot with what looked like a ceremonial dagger. "I'm just making tea."

"I'm more of a coffee girl."

"Oh, you'll like this one."

Somehow, I doubted that. "It was you controlling that purple lady's memories." What was her name again?

"The purple lady?"

"That bitch lawyer," Parris said. "Something Richter."

"Oh, right. So easy."

"And the clerk at the property assessor's office?"

"Guilty." He knelt in front of me again. "Why is there a hunter in town?"

"I don't know if you are aware of this, but hunters don't talk a lot. Though, admittedly, that was the first one I've met."

"You met him? And you're still alive?" He seemed bizarrely impressed, and a huge piece of the puzzle fell into place. He wasn't part of the inner circle. He didn't have friends in low places like I did.

"What's wrong?" I asked, slurring my words only slightly as nausea swept over me. "Have they not let you into their secret club?"

He leaned closer, and I finally got a good look at his spray-tanned face as he whispered a heartfelt "Fuck you."

"Are the other warlocks not playing nice?" The slap echoed along the walls before I even realized I'd been hit. Again, great acoustics.

In all honesty, the slap hardly registered. My world kept teetering this way and that, so a slap actually helped me refocus, if only for a few seconds. I fought to get the cloth off my hands. It was wet, the liquid abrasive against my skin. Like acid. Or holy water.

I snorted at my own joke, wondering if there was something out there that would hamper my ability to do spells. I'd have to hit the books when all of this was over. Dive deep into the world of witchcraft and magic. I'd known I was out of my depth from day one, but this drove it home like a Lamborghini on glass. "Why did you kill my grandmother?" I didn't ask Harris. He was a dick. And he'd slapped my face. So, I asked Parris.

She straightened, thrilled to be in the spotlight again. "For Percival."

I knew it. I knew they wanted Percy. But... "You killed my grandmother to get her house?"

"C'mon," Harris said. "The woman was eighty if she was a day. She'd lived a good, long life."

"And she just... would... not... die," Parris added, throwing her arms out in helplessness.

"Are you wearing a nurse's uniform?"

"We tried to be nice," she continued, unfazed. "We tried to buy Percy from her, but she wouldn't sell."

"That house has been in her family for generations," I said, taken aback by their callousness.

"Whatever," Parris said.

I shook my head. It was the wrong thing to do. I slumped in the chair as the world turned upside down.

"For fuck's sake." Harris came over and shoved me upright.

"She never told me you tried to buy it."

"Because I erased her memory every time. Believe you me, it wasn't easy. Ruthie was a powerful witch. More powerful than most."

"So... so you killed her instead?"

"Hand me that," he said to Parris, pointing to a rope.

Parris picked it up and handed it to him. He wrapped it around my shoulders, anchoring me to the chair.

"Why would you do that? If you can control minds, why not just get Ruthie to sign it over to you?"

"I can't control minds," he said, tightening the rope painfully. It cut into my skin, but at least I could stay vertical. Kind of. "I can manipulate memories, which are in the past. Big difference."

"Big," Parris added.

"Huge."

"Wait," she said, her brows sliding together. "Have you ever screwed with my memories?"

"What? No, baby."

I rolled my eyes. The world tilted again, but it was worth it. "He has, Parris. I felt it when I delved into your memories."

She jammed her fists onto her hips. "You tried to read me?"

"Yes. I'm sorry. I was just trying to find out what happened to my grandmother, and I wondered if you'd seen anyone staking out the house or trying to break in."

"I feel strangely violated."

"No way," I said, sarcasm dripping from each syllable, and I wondered if she was even capable of seeing the irony in that statement. "We figured out how you poisoned her but, again, why? Why do you want Percy so bad, and how is killing me going to get him for you?"

They exchanged glances and laughed.

"We aren't going to kill you," Parris said.

"We're going to do what I've been trying to do since you got here. We're going to drive you insane."

"With black magics?" I asked, my fear palpable. I knew very little about them, but they seemed really bad in the grand scheme of things.

"No," Harris said. "I've already tried that. Either you're blocking me or someone else is. I'm going to have to do this the old-fashioned way."

"With tea?" I asked.

"My own concoction. One drop on your tongue and you'll be a drooling vegetable in no time. As long as it doesn't enter your bloodstream. Then we'll have to see to that *long-lost sister*." He took the dagger out of the liquid. "The tiniest slit with this and she'll be six feet under in no time. You guys just keep coming out of the woodwork."

"Why?" I asked. "Why do you want Percy so bad? You have two houses on this block already." When they didn't answer, I added, "Just tell me. What can it hurt? I'm going to be a drooling vegetable anyway."

"She's right," Parris said. "Anything we tell her would only make her sound more insane."

"True."

Parris turned to me, excited about their plan. "If you must know, we have several houses in the area. We just rent the others out. But Percy is the one we really want. He's at the epicenter."

"Of?"

"The pentagram."

"What are you..." The world spun again, but it hit me. "The caves. The caves form a pentagram." I'd seen it on Roane's map, but we were so focused on pirate booty, we didn't look closely enough. In my defense, I did tell him I'd wanted to study that map further.

Parris clapped. "Exactly. It's over a mile wide, and Percy is dead center. He's a conduit. A cradle of mystical energy. He is literally humming with power. The longer someone with blood-born magics lives in it, the more powerful they grow." She hugged herself. "He'll take Harris's magics to the next level. But seriously, how long does it take to make tea?"

He glared at her.

If I could just get my hands free. Hard as I tried, I could not do a spell. The world tipped with each attempt, and whatever he'd wrapped around my hands was preventing me from drawing one on the air.

Just as I worked the fingers of my left hand out of the cloth, I caught a glimpse of something in the shadows. Maybe it was the way the light moved in this strange new reality. It glinted off two round objects like coins hovering in the air, and I realized Roane was easing down the stairs to the basement, taking one step, stopping, then taking another, hunkered in pure stealth mode.

"Don't you dare," I whispered to him, but he either didn't hear me—impossible—or didn't care—most likely. I had no idea what these two were capable of. Besides murder.

The magics were getting to him, too. He shook his head, as though trying to clear it, and took another step.

I tore my gaze off him so I wouldn't reveal his presence, but it was too late. Parris had followed my line of sight and spotted him. "You are the worst warlock ever. How could you not know we'd been infiltrated?"

A low rumble rolled out of Roane's chest.

"Get out," I whispered to him. "Harris is more powerful than I could've imagined. Get out."

He snarled at me, then snapped at Parris as she moved to stand beside her husband. "Do something," she said, clutching at his sleeve, and I realized for the first time he wore a robe of some kind. Something ceremonial.

"Are you wearing a dress?" I asked him. Anything to get his attention off Roane. "Not that there's anything wrong with a man wearing a dress."

"Shut up!"

Roane whimpered and fell against the wall, shaking his head again. He was losing his balance as well. His hold on time.

"Roane, go. Please."

I realized, probably too late, that I had another ally. I called to Olly, but I couldn't see him. Couldn't see through his eyes. So I tried harder. Concentrated through the fog. "Bedoliel," I whispered. His vision emerged at last. He was already hurrying in my direction. Not to help me, but because he was chasing a pack of dogs that had tried to get the better of him. And from what I could tell by the street signs around him, the little shit was in Boston. What the hell?

Come here, I said to him.

He changed directions and darted toward me at the speed of light.

Roane made it down the stairs, his growl a snarling, vicious thing, and positioned himself between me and the crazies. But he kept losing his balance, his massive body swaying to the side, so he stayed in a hunkered position, ready to leap if he needed to.

"Do something," Parris said, her voice no more than a hiss.

So he did. He shoved his wife toward Roane, sacrificing her for the greater good. Well, *his* greater good. While Roane's attention was on the woman flailing on top of him and screaming like a banshee, I couldn't help but wonder if she'd learned that one in her acting class as well. It gave Harris the precious seconds he needed to grab the knife and corner the table.

Roane's teeth were locked onto Parris's calf when Harris drove the knife between his ribs. I cried out, but the injury seemed to barely register. Roane turned and attacked so fast, his movements were little more than a blur. He clamped onto Harris's throat and had him on the ground in less than two seconds, the snarling and growling enough to weaken even the staunchest of men.

Harris tried to scream as he fought, but the pressure on his throat prevented it. In a matter of seconds, the only sound coming from him was a sickening gurgle.

I was so focused on the attack, I missed the fact that Parris had found a shovel. She walked up and drove it down in one, sharp thrust between Roane's shoulder blades.

I watched in shock as the rusty metal sank into Roane's fur. As thick crimson blood seeped out along the edges. Then his cry registered. A desperate, heart-wrenching thing. Half whimper and half howl.

Bile crept up the back of my throat, and the edges of my vision darkened. "Roane." I tried to get to him, but the fucking world would not stop spinning long enough.

He sank to the ground with a soft cry.

Parris pulled out the shovel. After tossing it aside, she held out a hand to her husband.

Anger exploded within me, then I remembered what Roane had told me. *I protect you. You protect me.* I could protect him. Some of my power would be transferred when I claimed him as my sentry. When I enslaved him to me, yes, but still the lesser of two evils.

He may grow to resent me, but his breaths were already shallow. I had no time to lose. "I claim you," I said, and he turned his head toward me. "Roane Atticus Wildes, I claim you."

I felt a small fraction of my power leach out. Watched it waft over him like gold dust on the air. But would it be enough? Was I too late?

He went limp, and my heart stopped beating as I waited for a breath. For a flick of his ear. For any sign of life.

"What was that?" Parris asked, struggling to get her husband to his feet. She had a nasty bite on her leg. The imprints where Roane's massive teeth had been were now filled with blood that oozed down her leg and into her patent leather Mary Janes.

But Harris's entire torso was covered in blood. How was he even alive? He found a towel and held it to his throat with one hand, choking and coughing. "What?" he asked. Determined to finish what he started, he stumbled to the table and began pouring the tea into a plastic bottle. They were going to force it down my throat.

"That gold. Just then." She pointed, unconcerned with

the fact that her husband was bleeding to death. Maybe as a warlock, his magics were keeping him alive.

Harris released an impatient sigh then coughed again, the sound wheezing and wet. When he spoke, his voice was strained. "Hand me the lid, but don't get any of this on you. It can work even through the skin, and that's all I need. More crazy from the cheap seats." The towel was soaked through now and I could hardly believe he was still standing.

Roane used his front paws to inch toward me. I watched through thick tears as he dragged his back legs, leaving a trail of blood in his wake.

"Roane, baby, stop." I could barely speak past the lump in my throat. "It's okay."

He looked up at me, his olive irises feverishly bright. In a last herculean effort, he lunged toward me and sank his teeth into my thigh.

I gasped as his jaws clamped down. When his teeth broke the skin, pain shuttered through me. And then I felt it. His essence. His lifeforce. The transfer of power as he staked his claim, marking me as his own.

"The crazy has already started," Parris said, clapping her hands again. "Good to know that stuff works."

Roane's lifeforce washed over me like a silk veil. Our powers combined, the sensation both heady and sobering, seconds before he collapsed.

I lay my head back, riding out the rush, then looked at my captors through new eyes. "I have to be honest with you."

They both stopped what they were doing and gave me their full attention.

"I'm not what you think I am." I'd freed the fingers on my right hand as well and did a simple spell to release the binds on my hands. They fell to the ground along with the cloth covering them, but neither of my captors noticed.

I was worried Parris would see the light from the spell, especially in the dark room, but she just stared at me. Waiting. They both did. I brought my hands around, drew another spell in plain sight, and released the rest of my bindings. My only thought was to finish this and get Roane to safety.

"How... how did you do that?" Harris asked, coughing up a spittle of blood.

Parris stepped away from him, inching toward the stairs.

The world was still thick and lopsided, so I found a stabilizing spell. Having no idea if it would work, I drew it on the air.

Parris gasped as it burst to life and the magics Harris had used to keep me off balance dissipated.

He backed away, wary of me. "What are you?"

"I'm a charmling."

"I... I don't know what that is."

That threw me. I figured as a warlock, surely he would know what a charmling was.

"That's too bad." I drew the spell that would strip him of his magics and pushed it onto him. Nothing happened. I drew it again. And again. Still nothing.

He didn't react at all. It was almost as if he couldn't see the spells, but any being with magics could see them. Then I realized the problem. He had no magics. None whatsoever. There was simply nothing to strip away.

I eyed him, suspicion narrowing my lids, until a loud thud echoed in the room. He fell forward, narrowly missing the table, and landed face-first on the cement floor.

My gaze traveled to the brunette bent over him, holding the shovel.

Her chest heaving, she watched him a moment to make sure he didn't move, then straightened and turned toward me. "That man was an idiot."

"You... you killed him."

"Duh. He was an idiot."

"He didn't have any magics."

She frowned at me. "How do you know that?"

"I told you, I'm a charmling."

"What the hell is a charmling?"

"If he didn't have any magics—"

"I know, right? Then who's the warlock?" She planted the shovel on the ground beside her, hitched an arm over the handle, and said proudly, "You're looking at her."

That was unexpected. "You're a warlock?"

"I am. Well, I'm studying to be one. None of that watered-down witch bullshit for me. All of that nature crap. Harmony and enlightenment and good deeds. My mother was a witch. Barely had enough magics to grow a watermelon, but she kept at it. Year after year. Making predictions that never came true. Creating concoctions that never worked quite right." Parris lowered her head and gazed at me from underneath her lashes. "I want more."

"I can see that." Now that I had my balance again, I eased down to Roane. He lay in a pool of blood. "Parris, I have to get him to a hospital."

"You mean a vet?" she asked with a snort. "What do you think is going to happen here? Who do you think set all this up? I'd been planning to get Percy from Ruthie for years, and then you show up out of the blue."

"*You* killed my grandmother."

"Of course I did."

My insides seethed, the acids in my stomach churning.

"My husband had the wherewithal of a banana. He

could barely tie his own shoelaces, but he was hung like a horse. And he made the perfect decoy. Who would suspect little ol' me of being a warlock?"

"But he thought he was."

"He did." She tapped her temple to prove how smart she was. "It's all in memory manipulation. That guy was so gullible."

I couldn't help but notice how she was easing closer and closer to the table.

"Why the charade?"

"For moments like this. If anything were to happen, I could claim he was batshit. He threatened me. He forced me to do it. Blah blah blah." She looked me up and down. "But you knew he didn't have any magics. How?"

"I told you, I'm a charmling."

"Yeah, I don't know what that is."

"Then you really should have done your homework, tried to learn more about the profession you're trying to infiltrate before attempting a coup like this."

"Are you going to explain it to me or not? And what are you doing on the air? What is that light?"

"Those are my spells. Charmling spells. We're very powerful."

"More powerful than a warlock?" she asked, her voice filled with doubt.

"Much." And I proved it when she went for the tea.

She scooped up the bottle and flung the tea at me. Thank the Goddess magics are lightning fast. They stopped it. Suspended it in midair.

I'd drawn a spell before I even thought about it, my movements automatic.

Parris dropped the bottle and stumbled back.

I studied the droplets as they floated in midair, but

another whimper from Roane brought the direness of the situation hurtling back to me. I pushed the liquid-filled spell toward her. It splashed on her face and neck and arms. She screamed like I'd burned her with acid. Then again, maybe I had. Had Harris lied to me? Was he really making an acid of some sort?

"Get it off!" she screamed, swiping at the wetness. She whirled this way and that like she was on fire. "Get if off me! Get it off me!"

Mercury was like that. Depending on the strength, even a drop on the skin could kill a person. But the liquid in the bottle hadn't been silver, so I hardly saw the point to her theatrics.

I went to grab a towel off the table, but Parris was twirling so much, she lost her balance. She collided with a metal cabinet and then tried to run up the stairs. At least, I thought that was her goal. She missed them and ran face-first into a wall.

"Parris, holy crap, stop." I held up my hands in surrender and tried to give her the towel.

Her skin almost glowed, her face bright red and puffy. What the hell had been in that pan?

At that point, I was just trying to protect Roane. To keep her from trampling the poor guy. "Parris, you're going to kill yourself. Stop."

"Get it off me!" she cried again. She bounced off yet another wall, the scene horrific yet strangely comical, then ran for the stairs again. Only she ran under them instead and hit her head—hard—on the underside. Her feet went out from under her, and she landed unconscious on her back.

I eased up to her, afraid to touch her. Her blistered skin was peeling. "What the hell were you going to give me?"

Realizing she was out cold, I knelt down to Roane, the knees of my sweats absorbing his blood. "Okay, mister," I said, running my hand down his body, "you're going to have to get up now. We have things to do."

The pool of blood he lay in was still growing. I looked up as I heard something padding down the stairs. Olly burst onto the scene and looked around, taking in what looked like the scene from a horror movie. He was so black, he absorbed all the light around him, so when I spoke to him, it was hard to tell if he was actually looking at me.

"Olly, go get Annette."

He obeyed instantly, tearing back up the stairs as I stood and searched around for my phone. I found it on the table. They'd turned it off, presumably so the police couldn't track it if they caught wind of my... abduction? Did this count as an abduction?

I turned it on and scrolled through my contacts. "Chief?" I said when a groggy man answered.

"Defiance? Where are you?"

"I don't know, really. I think I'm in Parris's basement."

"Parris? Parris Hampton?"

"Yes, can you please come over?"

I heard rustling like he was scrambling out of bed. "I'm next door, hon. I'll be right over. Is Parris okay?"

"Mentally or physically?"

He stopped and asked, "Either."

"Oh, well, neither one is doing great right now. And I think Harris is dead."

"Do I dare ask?"

"I didn't kill him. You know, if that helps."

TWENTY-TWO

If every day is a gift,
then today was socks.
—Meme

"I can't heal him," I said, a waterfall cascading down my face.

Gigi put a hand on my shoulder as I leaned over Roane. I didn't dare touch him. He lay unconscious, the thick red fur over his rib cage hardly moving.

"I claimed him. It was supposed to protect him, but it didn't, and now I can't heal him."

"That's not what you do, sweetheart," Gigi said.

Olly had roused Annette, and she followed them over. She was barefoot and wearing a robe over her usual boxer shorts and tee. I was indeed in Parris's basement, a room that seemed much less cavernous with the lights on, and Annette stood shivering.

"You're wrong. I healed Mrs. Touma." I'd helped a

woman with Alzheimer's a few months ago when I'd first reclaimed my powers. I'd saved her from a fall that would've killed her. In the process, her Alzheimer's disappeared.

"No, sweetheart. I think you just took away her pain. And to do that, maybe her synapses were stitched back together. Made whole again. Like a few nights ago, when you took Roane's pain away."

The ghost of Puritans past had attacked me for being a witch. He'd knocked into me like a wrecking ball, crushing every bone in my chest and then some. I'd drawn a spell, not realizing what it would do. It transferred my injuries onto Roane. Every broken bone. Every torn ligament. I was horrified.

He knew, though. He knew exactly what it would do, and he did it anyway.

"I think you took away his pain and stitched him back together enough to let his own rapid healing do the rest. And you've done the same here. You've stitched him back together enough to take away the pain, but his spine has been severed." She said the last with a sob. "He's not feeling pain."

"But... he can heal from this, right?"

Her entire visage sagged. "I don't know, Defiance."

"There has to be something we can do." I looked at Annette. "You're the healer. You have to heal him."

She stumbled back and almost tripped on Parris's arm.

The chief had checked both Parris and Harris. They were dead. Even Parris, and I didn't know if it was because of the tea or her hitting her head. "What happened to her face?" he asked, horrified.

I didn't dare look.

"Deph," Annette said, "I can't. I don't know how. I

haven't done a single spell using my charmling powers. What if all I can do is make poison and blow things up?"

I grabbed her hand and pulled her to me. "Annette, you have to try. Please."

She knelt down to him, tears filling the space between her lashes. "Defiance," she whispered just as a tear escaped, "what if I fail?"

And then I knew. I could feel the power coursing through her veins. I brightened and gazed at my best friend. "You have no idea."

She frowned. "What do you mean?"

"Annette, I can feel your power as easily as I can feel my own. The moment you *wanted* to do a spell, I felt a spark inside you. Like the ignition on the engine of something wonderful."

"I kind of did, too." She nodded. Gathering herself, she breathed in through her nose and out through her mouth. "Right. I can do this. I just... what? Do I draw spells like you do?"

We clutched onto each other, our fingers lacing together. "I don't know. I haven't read the book yet."

"Me neither. I was so tired. I thought I'd have more time."

"I'm sorry. They lured me over here, and I fell for it hook, line, and sinker."

"Please. I would have too, if I didn't sleep like the dead." She did the Lamaze thing again. "I can do this."

Now that we'd claimed each other, I could feel Roane on a visceral level. His pulse weakened with every heartbeat, and panic crept up to cinch around my throat. "Close your eyes."

"Okay." She obeyed. "Now what?"

"I just kind of search my mind for the spell I want. For the symbol."

"All right, then. Searching now." Her breathing slowed, and she lowered her head.

"Are you getting anything?"

"There are so many."

I inhaled sharply. "You're seeing the spells?"

"How do you keep track of them all?"

"Concentrate on what you want to accomplish."

"There you are," she said, as though from a trance. She raised her left hand into the air, her being a lefty, but then she dropped it to the cement floor beneath us.

I wanted to say something, but I had to trust she knew what she was doing.

She dipped her fingers in Roane's blood and drew a spell with it on the cement. One I didn't know. Then she flattened her palm over it and waited.

Still holding her free hand in both of mine, I chewed on my lower lip and squeezed, chanting *please* over and over in my mind.

A light broke through from between her fingers. Neon green and almost as blinding as mine, it shot into the air. Gigi and I reared back and watched in awe as a plant rose from the ground. Not just a plant. An entire tree. It pushed through the cement and buckled parts of it around its thick trunk, rising and rising until it hit the ceiling. Limbs branched out, slid across the ceiling, and canopied the entire room. Long thin leaves grew on the stems from the branches, and a pungent odor filled the room.

We all took a step back and gaped at it. The chief dropped his cell phone.

Annette patted the trunk and smiled up at it. "There you are." She stood and reached up, but the branches were too high. That didn't stop her. She coaxed a branch down to her with a finger. It bent to her will, as though glad to do it, and she stripped a couple of stems of their leaves. After gathering them in her hands, she explained, "This is a neem tree from India."

"That tree is from India?" I asked, stunned.

"Yes. That's why it took so long to get here."

"Oh... of course." We stood back and let her work.

She cupped the leaves in her hands and closed her eyes. The green light shot out from between her fingers again, and when she opened her hands, they were filled with a dark, glowing oil. She bent down and rubbed it into Roane's wounds.

Then she looked up at me. "It's like riding a bike. Your body just naturally knows how to balance. It just knows what to do."

I knelt beside her, my chin trembling as I ran my fingers over Roane's fur. "That was the coolest thing I've ever seen."

"Please. Have you even seen yourself do a spell?" she asked.

"Annette." I gaped at her. "You grew a tree. In a basement."

"True." She huffed on her fingernails and polished them on her shirt.

"It smells really bad, but it's still a tree." I threw my arms around her. "Thank you. He's already breathing better."

She hugged me back. I should've known the minute she did it something was up.

"You just got that stinky oil all in my hair, didn't you?"

"It's your own fault."

I laughed and hugged her again.

"I'm so proud of you, Nannette," Gigi said.

We both chuckled but stopped instantly when we heard creaking on the stairs. Mr. Shoemaker stood halfway up them, all the blood drained from his face.

"Guys?" We looked over at the chief. He stood with his mouth agape, much like Mr. Shoemaker. "Where are the bodies?"

Annette and I shot to our feet and scanned the room. Gigi did the same. All four of us just stood there looking around like a bunch of pigeons searching for French fries. Then our gazes landed in unison on the object Mr. Shoemaker was staring at. The fluffy black cat sitting on the table licking its paw.

My hands flew over my mouth. I asked from behind them, "Olly, did you eat the Hamptons?"

He didn't answer, of course, because he was a cat. Instead, he looked me right in the face, reached out his newly groomed paw, and pushed a jar off the table. It crashed onto the cement and shattered just as Olly darted for the stairs. His belly looked a little bigger, but not two-humans bigger.

I hurried to the stairs and called out to him. "Bad kitty! Don't come crying to me when those heels get stuck in your intestines!" Honestly, of all the things that'd happened in the last few days, this was probably the most... unexpected. I cringed when I took in Mr. Shoemaker's pallor. He must've seen Olly eat at least one of the Hamptons. "Hi, Mr. Shoemaker."

He didn't move.

The chief just stood there too, probably trying to figure out how he was going to explain it all.

"Chief?" I said, coaxing him back to us. "Can you help with Roane?"

He snapped back to the present. "Of course, Daffodil." He looked up at our new guest. "Donald, I—"

"Go," Mr. Shoemaker said, descending the stairs and giving him a solid pat on the shoulder. "I've got this. No one will know anything untoward happened down here by the time I'm finished."

The chief held out his hand. "Thank you."

Mr. Shoemaker took it. "Of course. Someone will report them missing in a few days, and I'm guessing that's not such a bad thing?" He looked at me when he asked it.

"No," I said, suddenly sad. I looked back at Gigi. "At least now we know."

She nodded. Mr. Shoemaker helped her up the stairs as the chief lifted a giant red wolf into his arms.

I held Roane's head, marveling at the fact that we do indeed make our own luck.

THE CRESTING SUN ribboned pinks and oranges across the sky as I lay spooning with a sleeping wolf. He had yet to shift. I smoothed my hand over his fur and breathed him in. He was somehow both the wolf and the man. Pine and musk and sandalwood. His chest rose and fell softly. Though he was completely healed, I took great care not to put any pressure on his spine.

I'd been sleeping off and on, unable to believe the events of the last few days. The last few months. What a crazy turn my life had taken. And Annette's! She was like a stick of dynamite. Powerful. Compelling. And a little scary.

My lids drifted shut yet again as I smoothed my hand down Roane's back. His fur gathered between my fingers, and then it didn't. Skin slid beneath my palms, and my eyes flew open.

He'd shifted, but his breathing was still deep and even. He'd shifted in his sleep. And I'd missed it. I sought out the wound on his back. All that remained was a faint curve like an upside-down crescent, the scar barely visible among the ink.

I ran my fingertips over it and frowned. I leaned back and looked at the tattoo as a whole. The white scar line changed the symbol he'd remembered from his childhood. What had been the spell for transformation, from when I'd brought Roane out of the veil using the life force of a wolf cub, was now the spell for possession. That one line changed the meaning of the entire spell. I'd claimed him, and the tattoo reflected that.

"Lower," Roane said, his voice deep and groggy.

I laughed and slid my hand down the thick muscles on his back, brushing over the scar where the knife wound had been. "Is this low enough?"

"No. Lower."

My fingers traced the tattoos on his lower back, then I flattened my palm and explored the shape of his buttocks. "How about this?"

"You're getting warmer."

A bubble of laughter escaped me, and I snuggled against him, carefully drawing him closer, burying my face in his hair. How did it always smell freshly washed? "I think we need to give it some time."

"No."

"Yes."

With a heavy sigh, he rolled onto his back and pulled me onto his chest. His arms encircling me, he kissed the top of my head. "I'm sorry."

"For arguing about sex when you clearly need to rest?"

"Hell no. I'll argue about sex until the stars burn out. I'm sorry I couldn't protect you."

I propped up on an elbow. "Roane, you did. Your essence... somehow it made me stronger."

"You protected me, too."

"When I claimed you?"

He nodded.

"How? I did nothing. The spell did nothing."

He leaned back to look at me. "The tea. Or whatever that was. I felt it seeping into me. Poisoning my mind."

I cupped his scruffy cheek. "I'm sorry."

"It stung like hell, and I could feel it penetrating my bloodstream. It made me sick and dizzy and confused, like it was scrambling my brains."

"You mean that's really what it was supposed to do?"

"Yes. But your spell, I don't know, it somehow neutralized it. I can't explain it, but I felt a warmth spread, and then I was okay. I don't know how, but I could think clearly again."

"It's okay. You don't have to explain. I can't explain half of what my magics do." I put my head on his chest. His wide manly chest that I'd wanted to use as a pillow since the first time I saw him. "But they didn't heal you." Before he could protest, I asked, "What the hell was that stuff anyway?"

"I don't want to know."

"I bet Annette could tell us."

"She's pretty amazing."

I rose up. "Do you remember what she did? How she healed you?"

"I remember a tree."

I chuckled. "Yep."

"And a warmth on my back."

"Yep again."

"You'll have to tell me everything, but I think we should have sex first."

After a soft snort, I shook my head. "You need a little more time. Your spine was severed, Roane."

"Okay. We can give it a few more minutes."

I inched up and kissed him.

He buried his fingers in my hair and pulled me closer, deepening the kiss. He rolled on top of me, kissed his way down my stomach, and came to the bite on the inside of my thigh. "Sorry about this."

"I'm going to have an amazing scar."

"Mark."

"Ah, right. You marked me."

He bent and kissed each puncture wound before making his way to the cleft between my legs.

I sucked in a sharp breath as his tongue feathered across my clit. But I needed to ask the wolf something before we got too carried away. I buried my hands in his hair.

He looked up at me from over the horizon of my girl parts.

I gazed into his olive irises, and asked, "Will you marry me?"

A lopsided grin emerged from beneath the scruff. "Why, Ms. Dayne, I thought you'd never ask."

TWO HOURS LATER, I went down to make us some coffee. Roane's wound had indeed healed. There was nothing stopping that man from performing his bedroom duties. Or his shower duties. Or his dresser-top duties.

"Hey, guys," I said to Gigi and the chief. They were

talking quietly, their heads bowed close to one another in soft conversation. I saw the rustling of vines and looked up. "Good morning, Percy." A rose bloomed overhead.

Gigi glanced over at me. "Hello, Defiance. How's Roane?"

"Good. Much better." I poured two cups and walked back to them. "How are you? And why is Virgil on the table?"

"Virgil?" the chief asked.

I pointed with my chin. "The owl." Someone had moved the stuffed snowy owl my dads had bought me to the table.

"Oh, yes," Gigi said. "That was a reminder to tell you to call them. They're very upset."

"Why?" I asked, alarmed.

"You're not answering your phone."

"Crap. I forgot to charge it. I'll call them."

"And Minerva texted. Leo is much better but she thinks she should stay with him, just in case."

"Oh, good. Has she been with him this entire time?" I'd kind of forgotten about her.

"Apparently. I think she's in love."

"That's adorable. Hey, is everything okay with you?"

"Of course, sweetheart. Why?"

I sat across from her. "It's just, I'm sorry again about trying to see into your thoughts the other night. That was wrong of me. But I do feel like you're purposely hiding something from me. Like something is bothering you but you don't want to tell me."

She lowered her head and stirred her coffee. It was her classic deference maneuver. "I was just telling Houston. I thought it was the fact that someone had killed me."

"What was?"

"I don't know how to explain it. I feel like something has been left undone. And I thought it was my murder. But now we know, and I still feel this way. In my stomach."

I reached over and took her hand. "I'm sorry, Gigi. What can I do?"

She quit stirring and rubbed her head. "I don't even know how to ask. I don't know if it's possible."

"Gigi, what is it?" But she'd looked up at me, and I caught her gaze. I didn't mean to. It was just suddenly there, out in the open for all the world to see. Or me. Probably me. "You want my mother's forgiveness."

She inhaled softly and then acquiesced with a nod. "I think so."

"Her forgiveness for what?"

She pursed her mouth and thought a long moment. After a while, she said softly, "For you."

"Me?"

"Defiance, when you were born, you became my everything. My world. My universe. I think... I think your mother grew jealous of you. Of your powers. I think I drove her to do what she did."

"Gigi, no." I shook my head. "That was her. You can't take that on."

"No, I know. I understand that. But maybe someday, when you're feeling up to it, you could try to... contact her?" She cringed when the words left her mouth. "I can't believe I'm even saying this. You know what? Forget it. I shouldn't have said anything." She stood to rinse out her cup.

I followed her. "Gigi, I would love to try. If I've learned anything in the last few days—in the last few hours—it's that we must try. We may fail, but we must do our best."

She turned away so I wouldn't see the wetness in her

eyes. "Not now. Just, you know, when you're feeling in the mood."

I laughed. I couldn't help it. Just how did one get *in the mood* to contact the dead? "There's no time like the present." I was feeling good. Really, really good thanks to Roane's special brand of therapy. "What could it hurt?"

Her mouth formed a pretty O. "Well, okay. Do you want to sit down?"

But I was already there. I felt a soft breeze rustle over my skin like a summer wind, and I thought about what Parris had said about Percy. A conduit. A cradle of mystical energy. Was that how I slipped so easily into the veil? So effortlessly? I dove into the blue depths of Gigi's irises, slid past her, and sought out my mother.

Before I could find her, however, something else caught my attention. Ink darted past my periphery, breaking my concentration just as Samuel appeared, chasing after him. I looked to my right, and the snowy owl was there in the same spot. Only it was really him. His soul. His essence. He spread his massive wings and shrieked.

Samuel stopped and gazed up at me as though unable to understand how I'd infiltrated his world. "Deph," he said, raising his arms for me to lift him like he'd done many times before.

So I did. As energy swirled around me, I bent down and lifted him up at the precise moment the owl flew straight at us. It startled me, and I rocketed back to the physical plane.

Where I stood.

With a three-year-old.

In my arms.

ANNETTE

Some days, it's like trying to nail Jell-O to a wall.
—True story

I'd just gotten out of the shower when I heard a godawful shriek coming from downstairs. I shrugged into my robe, blew a kiss to the picture of Percy I had on my nightstand—the man, not the plant—and hurried downstairs. "Did a velociraptor just die? Because stranger things have happened in this house."

Before anyone could answer, Defiance caught my attention. Or, more to the point, what she was holding caught my attention. I gaped at the blond-haired, blue-eyed angel in her arms. Gigi gaped at Defiance. The chief gaped at them all. But Samuel laughed and threw his arms around Deph's neck. Then he looked around and asked her, "Cat?"

Her jaw fell to the floor. To bring someone out of the veil, she had to use the life force of a living creature. Did she use Ink to bring Samuel out? And if so, how was she going to tell Roane?

That was a conversation I did not want to be a part of. I wanted to watch it, of course, but from a safe distance.

I walked up to them, pinched Samuel's cheek, and looked at my BFF. "I guess you have a kid now. This week just gets weirder and weirder. Oh! Coffee."

Read more about the adventures of Annette Osmund in *Moonlight and Magic: Betwixt & Between Book Four.*

THANK YOU!

Thank you for reading **BEGUILED: A PARA-NORMAL WOMEN'S FICTION NOVEL (BETWIXT & BETWEEN BOOK 3)**. We hope you enjoyed it! If you liked this book – or any of Darynda's other releases – please consider rating the book at the online retailer of your choice. Your ratings and reviews help other readers find new favorites, and of course there is no better or more appreciated support for an author than word of mouth recommendations from happy readers. Thanks again for your interest in Darynda's books!

Darynda Jones
www.daryndajones.com

Never miss a new book
from Darynda Jones!

Sign up for Darynda's newsletter!

Be the first to get notified of new releases and be eligible for special subscribers-only exclusive content and giveaways. Sign up today!

Also from DARYNDA JONES

PARANORMAL

BEWTIXT & BETWEEN
Betwixt
Bewitched
Beguiled
Moonlight and Magic
Midnight and Magic
Masquerade and Magic
Love Spells
Love Charms
Love Potions
Samuel

CHARLEY DAVIDSON SERIES
First Grave on the Right
For I have Sinned: A Charley Short Story
Second Grave on the Left
Third Grave Dead Ahead
Fourth Grave Beneath my Feet
Fifth Grave Past the Light
Sixth Grave on the Edge
Seventh Grave and No Body
Eight Grave After Dark
Brighter than the Sun: A Reyes Novella
The Dirt on Ninth Grave

The Curse of Tenth Grave
Eleventh Grave in Moonlight
The Trouble with Twelfth Grave
Summoned to Thirteenth Grave
The Graveyard Shift: A Charley Novella
The Gravedigger's Son

THE NEVERNEATH

A Lovely Drop
The Monster
Dust Devils: A Short Story of The NeverNeath

MYSTERY

SUNSHINE VICRAM SERIES

A Bad Day for Sunshine
A Good Day for Chardonnay
A Hard Day for a Hangover

YOUNG ADULT

DARKLIGHT SERIES

Death and the Girl Next Door
Death, Doom, and Detention
Death and the Girl he Loves

SHORT STORIES

Nancy: Dark Screams Volume Three
Sentry: Heroes of Phenomena: audiomachine
Apprentice
More Short Stories!

ABOUT THE AUTHOR

New York Times and *USA Today* Bestselling Author Darynda Jones has won numerous awards for her work, including a prestigious RITA®, a Golden Heart®, and a Daphne du Maurier, and her books have been translated into 17 languages. As a born storyteller, she grew up spinning tales of dashing damsels and heroes in distress for any unfortunate soul who happened by. Darynda lives in the Land of Enchantment, also known as New Mexico, with her husband and two beautiful sons, the Mighty, Mighty Jones Boys.

Connect with Darynda online:

www.DaryndaJones.com
    Facebook
    Instagram
    Goodreads
    Twitter

Made in the USA
Columbia, SC
08 January 2022

53862147R00221